The Rising Sea

A Novel from the NUMA® Files

CLIVE CUSSLER
and GRAHAM BROWN

PENGUIN BOOKS

PENGUIN BOOKS

UK | USA | Canada | Ireland | Australia
India | New Zealand | South Africa

Penguin Books is part of the Penguin Random House group of companies
whose addresses can be found at global.penguinrandomhouse.com

Penguin
Random House
UK

First published in the United States by G. P. Putnam's Sons 2018
First published in Great Britain by Michael Joseph 2018
Published in Penguin Books 2019

001

Set in 11/12.98 pt Garamond MT Std
Typeset by Jouve (UK), Milton Keynes
Printed and bound in Great Britain by Clays Ltd, Elcograf S.p.A.

A CIP catalogue record for this book is available from the British Library

ISBN: 978-0-241-50783-4

www.greenpenguin.co.uk

MIX
Paper from
responsible sources
FSC® C018179

Penguin Random House is committed to a
sustainable future for our business, our readers
and our planet. This book is made from Forest
Stewardship Council® certified paper.

Cast of Characters

JAPAN (HISTORICAL)

Yoshiro Shimezu – Samurai warrior, engaged in rebellion against the Shogun.

Kasimoto – Shogun, feudal lord controlling much of central Japan.

Goro Masamune – Japan's greatest swordsmith, crafted the Honjo Masamune, considered the finest Japanese sword ever created.

Sengo Muramasa – Alleged to be Masamune's apprentice, second-greatest swordsmith of historical era, crafted the Crimson Blade.

CHINA

Wen Li – Powerful, shadowy figure in the Chinese government and Communist Party, shrewd strategist also known as the Lao-shi or *learned Master*.

Walter Han – Half Japanese, half Chinese, wealthy industrialist, sometimes proxy for Wen Li.

Mr Gao – Han's chief engineer, robotics and computer expert.

General Zhang – Important member of the Chinese secret service, head of the Ministry for State Security.

NATIONAL UNDERWATER AND MARINE AGENCY

Rudi Gunn – Assistant Director of NUMA, graduate of the Naval Academy.

James Sandecker – Former head of NUMA, now the Vice President of the United States.

Kurt Austin – Head of NUMA's Special Projects division, world-class diver and salvage expert, once worked for the CIA.

Joe Zavala – Kurt's right-hand man, expert in design and construction of engines and vehicles, also an accomplished helicopter pilot and amateur boxer.

Paul Trout – NUMA's lead geologist, also tallest member of the Special Projects team at six foot eight, married to Gamay.

Gamay Trout – Marine biologist, married to Paul, Gamay is a fitness aficionado, an accomplished diver.

Priya Kashmir – Multidisciplinary expert, was supposed to join a NUMA field team before a car accident left her unable to walk, assigned to the Rising Seas Project.

Robert Henley – NUMA geologist, assigned to the Rising Seas Project in Paul's absence.

JAPAN (MODERN-DAY)

Kenzo Fujihara – Reclusive scientist, and former geologist, now leader of an antitechnologist sect, developed method for detecting Z-waves.

Akiko – Sergeant at arms for Kenzo, formerly connected to the underworld, acts as his protector.

Ogata – Member of Kenzo's antitechnology sect.

Superintendent Nagano – High-ranking member of the Japanese Federal Police, assigned to the Fujihara case, expert on the Yakuza and organized crime.

Ushi-Oni – Former Yakuza assassin, now a rogue force, also known as the Demon, distant relative and sometime associate of Walter Han.

Hideki Kashimora – Yakuza underboss in charge of the Sento, an illegal gambling establishment and fight club on the outskirts of Tokyo.

Blood and Steel

The thunder of charging horses gave way to the clang of swords as two armies met on a field in the highlands of Japan.

From the saddle of his horse, Yoshiro Shimezu fought with a combination of power and grace. He whirled and slashed, maneuvering his steed with precision, all without *hakusha*, or spurs. The samurai did not use them.

Clad in brightly painted armor, Yoshiro sported wide shoulder boards, heavy gauntlets and a helmet adorned with stag horns. He wielded a gleaming *katana* that caught every bit of the light as it cut through the air.

With a flick of the wrist, he disarmed his nearest adversary. A backhanded cut followed, snapping another opponent's sword in two. As that soldier fled, a third foe lunged at Yoshiro with a pike. The tip struck his ribs, but his scaled armor that lay in pleats prevented mortal damage. Yoshiro wheeled around and killed the man with a downward hack.

Free for a second, he turned his horse in a tight pirouette. The horse, dressed in armor to match Yoshiro's, reared up, kicking with its front legs and then leaping forward.

Its iron-clad hooves smashed a pair of attackers in the

1

face, sending them bloodied and battered to the ground. It came down on a third man, crushing him, but enemy soldiers were now massing on all sides.

Yoshiro turned one way and back again. He'd taken the field against the Shogun, who arrived with overwhelming numbers. The battle had gone predictably and Yoshiro was facing the end.

Determined to take as many foes with him as possible, Yoshiro charged the closest group, but they pulled back in a defensive formation, raising shields and long pikes. He turned and galloped toward another formation of troops, but they, too, held their ground, cowering behind a forest of spears.

Perhaps they meant to capture him. Perhaps the Shogun would demand he commit seppuku *in front of the court. Such an end Yoshiro would not accept.*

He urged his horse one way and then the other. But with each move, the foot soldiers drew back. Yoshiro pulled up. He had no wish to see his steed uselessly killed. It was a beautiful animal and his only advantage.

'Fight me!' he demanded, turning from quarter to quarter. 'Fight me if you have any honor!'

A primal grunt caught his attention. A spear was hurled his way. With superb reflexes, Yoshiro parried the incoming missile, slicing through the wooden shaft with his sword, both deflecting and dividing it. The weapon fell harmlessly in two pieces.

'Do not attack!' a voice shouted from behind the mass of troops. 'His head belongs to me.'

The soldiers straightened at the sound of the command

and one section of the circle opened, allowing the rider to enter.

Yoshiro recognized the silk draping of the horse, the golden breastplates of the armor and the winged helmet. The Shogun had come to fight at last.

'Kasimoto!' Yoshiro called out. 'I did not think you'd have the courage to cross swords with me in person.'

'I would not allow any other to vanquish a traitor,' Kasimoto said, drawing a sword of his own, a *katana* like Yoshiro's, though it was a darker weapon with a thicker blade. 'You swore allegiance to me as feudal lord. You are in rebellion.'

'And you swore to protect the people, not murder them and steal their land.'

'My authority is absolute,' the Shogun bellowed. 'Over them and over you. I cannot steal what is already mine. But if you beg for it, I will be merciful.'

The Shogun whistled and a small group of prisoners were brought out. Children. Two boys and two girls. They were forced to kneel while servants of the Shogun stood behind them with daggers.

'I have more than a thousand captives,' the Shogun said. 'And with your rabble defeated, nothing stands between me and the village. If you surrender now and take your own life, I will kill only half the prisoners and leave the village standing. But if you fight me, I will slaughter them to the last man, woman or child and I'll burn the village to ash.'

Yoshiro had known it would come to this. But he also knew that many in the Shogun's ranks had grown weary

3

of the brutality, expecting it to land on them sooner or later. That gave him one flicker of hope. If he could kill the Shogun here and now, wiser minds might prevail. At long last, there might be peace.

Yoshiro considered his chances. The Shogun was a cunning warrior, strong and possessing great expertise, but he and his horse were unmarked by blood, sweat or soil. It had been a long time since the Shogun fought for his life.

'What answer do you give?'

Yoshiro kicked his horse in the side and charged, raising his gleaming sword above his head.

The Shogun reacted slowly but deflected the attack at the last moment and urged his animal forward, passing Yoshiro on the left.

The warriors swapped sides, turned and charged once again. This time, the armored animals collided at the center of the circle. Both horses buckled from the impact. Their riders were thrown to the ground.

Yoshiro sprang up first, attacking with a deadly thrust.

Kasimoto parried the assault and jumped to the side, but Yoshiro spun and slashed downward.

With each clash of the swords, sparks flew from the blades. The Shogun regained his form and an uppercut from him tore Yoshiro's helmet off, opening a gash on his cheek. A return strike from Yoshiro took off one of Kasimoto's shoulder boards.

Angered and in pain, the Shogun came on furiously, slashing, feinting and hacking, using a deadly combination.

Yoshiro reeled from the attack, nearly losing his balance.

4

The Shogun went for his throat with a cut that should have separated head from body, but with a desperate flick of the hands, Yoshiro deflected the strike with the flat side of his sword.

The impact should have broken his weapon into useless pieces, but Yoshiro's blade took the blow, flexed and deflected the strike away from him.

In a counterattack, Yoshiro unleashed a powerful crosscut that found Kasimoto's midsection. The edge of the blade was so sharp and the strike so fierce that it gashed through the painted steel plate and the hardened leather, drawing blood from the Shogun's ribs.

A gasp came from the soldiers gathered around. Kasimoto stumbled back, clutching his side. He gazed at Yoshiro in astonishment. 'Your blade remains in one piece while my armor is carved like wet cloth. There can only be one reason for that. The rumors are true, you hold the weapon of the great swordmaker. The Masamune.'

Yoshiro held the gleaming sword proudly. 'This weapon was handed down to me from my father and from his father before him. It's the finest blade of all the Master's works. And it shall bring an end to your vile life.'

The Shogun pulled off his helmet in order to breathe and see better. 'A powerful weapon indeed,' he said. 'One I shall treasure when I pull it from your dead hand – but my sword is the greater of the two. It is the blade that thirsts for blood.'

Yoshiro recognized the *katana* in the Shogun's hands. It was the work of Japan's other great swordsmith: Muramasa, protégé to the famed Master.

It was said the two swordmakers had lived in a state of bitter contention and that the Muramasa had infused his weapons with the jealousy, hatred and darkness he felt for the one who had taught him. They had become weapons of conquest, destruction and death, where the works of Masamune were used to uphold the righteous and to bring peace.

Legends to be sure, but there was always some truth to them.

'Trust in that dark sword and it will bring you to ruin,' Yoshiro warned.

'Not until it brings me your head.'

The two warriors circled each other, wounded and catching their breath, each of them preparing for the final clash. Yoshiro was limping and Kasimoto bleeding. One would soon fall.

Yoshiro would have to act decisively. If he missed his mark, Kasimoto would kill him. If he struck a wounding blow, the Shogun would retreat out of fear and order his men to swarm over Yoshiro. If that were to occur, even the magnificent weapon he wielded would be unable to save him.

He needed a lightning strike. One that would kill the Shogun instantly.

Limping more noticeably, Yoshiro came to a halt. He assumed the classic samurai stance, one leg back, one leg forward, both hands on the sword, which was kept near the back hip.

'You look tired,' the Shogun said.

'Test me.'

The Shogun responded with a defensive stance of his own. He would not take the bait.

Yoshiro had to act. He lunged forward with surprising speed, the flaps of his layered armor spreading like wings as he charged.

In close, he thrust the *katana* at the Shogun's neck, but Kasimoto blocked the attack with an armored gauntlet and brought his own blade downward.

It sliced into Yoshiro's arm. The pain was excruciating but Yoshiro ignored it. He spun in a full circle and launched into a new assault.

The Shogun staggered backward under the weight of the attack. He was pushed to the right and then back to the left and then over to the right again. His legs shook. His breath came in gasps.

Overpowered by the attack, he tumbled, by chance landing beside one of the young prisoners. As Yoshiro began a lethal stroke, the Shogun pulled the child in front of him.

Yoshiro was already in the process of striking, but the sword caught neither the Shogun's head nor the child's. It continued down, glancing off the Shogun's ankle and plunging its tip into the soft trampled earth.

Yoshiro pulled, but the blade stuck in the ground for just a second. That was long enough for Kasimoto. He threw the child aside and swung for Yoshiro with both hands on the hilt of his weapon.

His blade sliced through Yoshiro's neck and took his life instantly. The samurai's headless body fell in a heap. But the dying was not over.

Kasimoto's forward lunge had brought him up from a crouch. As he stepped down, his ankle buckled where it had been smashed by Yoshiro's final blow. He stumbled forward, reaching out toward the ground to break his fall, and he turned the point of his own sword back toward himself.

It pierced his chest where Yoshiro had cut the armor away, puncturing his heart, skewering him and holding him off the ground.

Kasimoto's mouth opened as if to scream, but no sound came forth. He lay there, propped up by his own weapon, his blood running down the length of its curved blade.

The battle ended this way, as did the war.

The Shogun's men were tired, weary and now leaderless. They were many weeks from home. Instead of pressing on and burning the village, they gathered up their dead and left, taking with them both the gleaming sword of the Masamune and the blood-soaked weapon forged by Muramasa the apprentice.

Tales of the battle would grow from that day forward and soon became embellished until the claims were beyond imagination.

Yoshiro's *katana* would eventually be known as the Honjo Masamune, the ultimate creation of Japan's greatest swordsmith. It was said to be unbreakable and yet able to bend nearly in half as it swung and whipped through the air. One legend insisted it shined from within, casting enough light to blind its opponents. Others said the blade was so finely honed that when Yoshiro held it before him, it split the light into a rainbow and rendered him invisible.

The Shogun's dark sword would become only slightly less famous. It was a charcoal color to begin with and was said to have grown darker and reddish in tint after soaking in Kasimoto's blood. It came to be called the Crimson Blade. Over the centuries, its own legend would grow. Many who took possession of it came to great wealth and power. And most of them came to tragic ends as well.

Both weapons would be passed down from samurai to samurai, from feudal lord to feudal lord, becoming national treasures of the Japanese people. They would be held by the powerful families, revered by the public and prized, until they vanished without a trace in the chaotic days at the end of World War II.

The Serpent's Jaw

The gray submersible traveled slowly across an aquatic paradise. Sunlight filtered down from above. Kelp beds waved in the current. Fish of every conceivable size and shape darted about. Off in the distance, an ominous shadow loomed in the blue infinity; a huge but harmless whale shark, its mouth gaping wide as it strained the water for tiny clouds of plankton.

From the command chair in the nose of the submersible, Dr Chen marveled at the stunning array of life around him.

'We're approaching the Serpent's Jaw,' a female voice said beside him.

Chen nodded at the information and kept his eyes on the world outside. This would be his last view of natural sunlight for a month and he wanted to savor it.

The submarine continued across the kelp bed until it gave way to a band of coral and then a V-shaped canyon. At first, the canyon was no more than a fissure, but it widened as it ran off into the distance, and from above resembled an open mouth.

The Serpent's Jaw.

As they traveled out over the canyon, the seafloor dropped precipitously.

'Take us down,' Chen ordered.

The submersible's pilot manipulated the controls with utter precision and the submarine, filled mostly with supplies, nosed down and descended into the steep-walled canyon.

Five hundred feet down, they lost the light. Nine hundred feet later, they found it again. Only, this time, it was artificial in nature and coming from a habitat anchored to a sidewall of the canyon.

Chen could make out the small living space and the stack of additional modules lined up beneath it. They went all the way to the canyon floor, where a tangle of pipes and tubes could be seen snaking into the ground.

'I trust you can handle the docking,' Chen said.

'Of course. Stand by.'

For the first time, Chen turned to study the pilot. She had wide, expressive eyes, smooth skin and plum-colored lips. It was a pretty face, but her designers hadn't given her any hair and in places the mechanics of her operating machinery were on full display.

He could make out bones of titanium and polished gearing where the joints of each arm connected to her torso; tiny hydraulic pumps and servos along with bundles of wires that ran like arteries until they vanished beneath white plastic panels sculpted to look like human curves.

The body panels covered her chest, midsection and thighs. Similar panels covered her arms but gave way once again at her wrists. Her fingers were pure machinery; powerful and precise, made of stainless steel, with rubber tips to facilitate grasping.

As an engineer, Chen admired the mechanics of her form. And as a man he appreciated the attempt at human beauty. That said, he wondered why they'd given her such a pretty face, soft voice and attractive outer form without finishing the job. They'd left her stuck halfway between human and machine.

A pity, he thought.

He turned back to the view port as the submersible eased up against the docking collar, bumped it softly and locked on. With the docking confirmed and the seal in place, Chen wasted no time. He stood, grabbed his pack and unlocked the submersible's inner door. The pilot neither looked at him nor reacted. She just sat, not moving and staring straight ahead.

No, he thought, *not half human. Not quite.*

Entering the habitat, Chen passed other slow-moving machines traveling on caterpillar tracks. *Distant cousins of the submersible's pilot,* he thought. *Very distant.*

These machines were more like self-driving pallets crossbred with a small forklift. They would unload the supplies and equipment from the submersible and take them to the appropriate storerooms, all without a command from anyone at the station.

At the same time, other automatons would load the sub with the ore extracted from a deep fissure beneath the seabed.

Such a plain word for it. *Ore.* In truth, the material

was unlike anything that had ever been mined before, an alloy trickling up from deep within the Earth, stronger than titanium, a third of its weight and imbued with other unique properties not found in any existing alloy or polymer.

He and the others – and there were very few others who knew of it – called the alloy Golden Adamant, or GA for short. The submerged mining facility had been constructed in secret to excavate it.

To keep that secret, and to maximize the station's efficiency, it had been built to be almost fully automated. Only one human was stationed there at a time, directing the efforts of two hundred automated workers.

The machines came in all shapes and sizes. A few had humanoid form, like the submarine pilot; others were referred to as mermaids, since they combined human-like grasping arms and a spherical camera-filled 'head' with a propulsion pack where a human swimmer's legs would be.

Others looked like the classic ROVs of aquatic exploration, and still others resembled heavy machinery at a construction site. Most of the later models worked on the seafloor or within the deep borehole itself. All of them operating on batteries recharged by a compact nuclear reactor that had been repurposed from a Chinese attack submarine and secured in the lowest module.

On his first visit, Chen had been in absolute awe of the station. He'd spent time in every nook and cranny. His second posting had been exciting as well. But now he rarely left the upper level, the only section of the habitat truly designed for humans.

He arrived at 'the office,' his home for the next thirty days. Inside, he found the man he was due to replace. Commander Hon Yi of the People's Liberation Navy.

Hon Yi was packed and waiting, his duffel bag resting beside the door.

'I see you're ready to go.'

'You'll feel the same after another month down here with no one but machines for companions.'

'I find some of them interesting,' Chen said. 'Our submersible pilot in particular. And some of the dive robots have expressive features. I understand they're working on a full human replica to keep us company.'

Hon Yi laughed. 'If they make her too real, you'll be fighting over who should make dinner.'

Chen laughed with Hon Yi, but he wouldn't have minded a robotic companion that looked human, providing they could eliminate the eerie dead stare that happened when the machines settled into an inactive mode.

'What's our status?' he asked, getting down to business.

'I'm afraid the recovery is faltering,' Hon Yi said. 'Worse than last month. Which, as you know, was worse than the month before.'

'And the month before that,' Chen added with a grimace. 'It seems the yield is falling off a cliff.'

Hon Yi nodded. 'I know how valuable this ore is. I know what you and the engineers say it can do, but if we don't find more of it or a more efficient way to extract it, someone in the Ministry is going to be brought up on charges for spending all this money.'

Chen doubted that. The Ministry had endless money.

And in this case they were partnering with the billionaire who'd developed the robots. He doubted either group would miss their pennies, but when he looked at the numbers on the computer console, he was surprised by how little of the Golden Adamant had been processed. 'A hundred kilos? Is that all?'

'The vein is played out,' Hon Yi said. 'But don't think I'm going to tell our bosses that.'

The intercom crackled. A human-sounding voice, male this time, spoke. 'TL-1 reporting. Deep-basin injectors ready. Harmonic resonators charged. Impact range, Z minus one hundred and thirty.'

Far below the station, the robots were getting ready for the next phase of the mining operation. By the sound of it, they were targeting the deepest section of the fissure.

Chen looked at Hon Yi. 'You've gone to the depths.'

'Ground-penetrating sonar indicates the only remaining vein of ore runs straight down. If the operation is to continue, we must excavate the deep vein. The only other option is to shut down.'

Chen wasn't sure about that. There were known dangers in mining too deeply.

'Shall I give the order?' Hon Yi asked. 'Or do you prefer the honors?'

Chen held up his hands. 'By all means, make it your order.'

Hon Yi pressed the intercom button and spoke the order in the specific manner in which they'd been trained to command the robots. 'Proceed as scheduled. Overriding objective: maximize ore recovery and speed. Continue operation until ore recovery falls below one ounce per ton unless otherwise directed.'

'Confirmed,' the TL-1 replied.

A distant humming sound filled the station seconds later. It was a side effect of the mining. It was so constant when the operation was running that Chen knew he'd forget about it in a day or two, only to be reminded when the machines took a break to repair themselves, reevaluate the process or switch batteries.

'The station is yours,' Hon Yi said. He handed over the command keys and a tablet computer.

'Enjoy your ride to the surface,' Chen said. 'It was sunny when I came down.'

Hon Yi grinned at the thought of sun, grabbed his duffel bag and hastened out the door. 'See you in a month.'

Chen was left alone. He immediately looked around for something to do. Of course there were plenty of reports to read and paperwork to shuffle – they'd yet to build a robot to handle those chores – but he had plenty of time for all that and no wish to rush into the monotony.

He put the tablet computer down on the desk and walked over to the fish tank. Several types of goldfish lived in the tank: fantails, bubble eyes and one lionhead. Hon Yi had suggested they get a beta and put it in a separate tank on the shelf, since betas couldn't live with other fish. But Chen had talked him out of it; there was enough solitude going on down there as it was.

Looking through the glass, Chen noticed that the fish were darting about the tank. They always became agitated when the excavation first resumed. To calm them, Chen picked up the shaker of food and sprinkled some in. As soon as the flakes hit the water, the fish raced to the surface to eat it.

Chen couldn't help but smile at the irony. A tank within a tank. One kept fish alive in an air-dominated environment and the other kept him and Hon Yi alive in the depths of the sea. Both groups with nothing to do but stare out the window and eat. If the pattern held, he'd be ten pounds heavier when he returned to the surface.

Chen sprinkled in more food, but the fish stopped eating and went still without warning. All of them at the very same instant. Chen had never seen that before.

They drifted downward. Their fins weren't moving, their gills were flat. It was as if they'd been stunned or drugged.

He tapped on the glass. Instantly, the fish began darting around, racing from one side of the tank to the other. They seemed panicked. Several of them slammed into the glass walls like bees trying to get through a window. One went to the bottom of the tank and began burrowing in the gravel.

As Chen stared, ripples formed on the top of the tank and the gravel at the bottom began to jump and dance. The walls of the habitat began to shake as well.

He stepped back. The vibration of the mining operation was growing louder. Louder than it should have been. Louder than he'd ever heard it before. Books and pieces of decorative coral began to vibrate on the shelf. The fish tank fell and smashed down beside him.

He pressed the intercom button. 'TL-1,' he said, calling

out to the command robot. 'Cease mining operations immediately.'

TL-1 responded calmly and immediately. 'Authorization, please.'

'This is Dr Chen.'

'Command code not recognized,' the robot replied. 'Authorization required.'

Chen realized instantly that robots were listening for Hon Yi's voice. He had yet to log on the computer and replace Hon Yi's authorization with his own.

He reached for the tablet computer and tapped the screen furiously. As he typed, a deep rumbling sound became audible, like boulders grinding against one another. The pounding grew louder and closer with terrible speed until something hit the station.

Chen was thrown to the floor and then the wall. Everything tumbled end over end. A jet of water burst through a torn seam in the metal, slamming him with more force than a fire hose. It broke bones and gouged flesh and crushed him against the wall as easily as a speeding truck would have.

In seconds, the module filled with water, but Chen was dead long before he would have drowned.

Outside the habitat, the submersible had just detached from the station when the shaking began.

Hon Yi heard the rumble through the walls of the sub. He saw the destruction coming from above as huge slabs of rock fell through the glare of the work lights higher up. At the same time, clouds of sediment were exploding upward from below.

'Go,' Hon Yi said to the pilot. 'Get us out of here.'

The pilot reacted with mechanical efficiency but no true urgency.

The avalanche hit the top level of the station and sheared it from the rest of the structure, the impact sent debris raining down on the submarine.

Instead of waiting for the robot to sense the mortal danger it could never perceive, Hon Yi reached over and grabbed the controls. He tried to push the throttle to full, but the robot's grip was unbreakable.

'Relinquish command.'

The robot let go of the controls and sat back impassively. Hon Yi pushed the throttle to full and turned the valve to blow the ballast tanks. The submersible accelerated and began to rise.

'Come on,' he urged. 'Go!'

The sub pushed forward. A wave of pebbles hit the outer hull, sounding like hail. A fist-sized rock slammed against the canopy, chipping it. Larger stones hit the roof and dented the propeller housing.

Hon Yi attempted to guide the sub away from danger, but with the propeller housing bent, he couldn't get the craft to move in a straight line. It turned, even as it accelerated, and wandered right back into the danger zone.

'No!' he shouted.

A second wave of tumbling debris hit the sub square on. The canopy shattered. A boulder crushed the hull like a tin can and the avalanche of debris drove the submarine downward, slamming it to the bottom of the Serpent's Jaw.

I

Outskirts of Beijing
One Month Later

At first glance, the scene was a bucolic one, two old men sitting in a park, hunched over a game of pure strategy. But the park, with its trees and bushes and black-water pond, was actually the private yard of the second-most-powerful man in the Chinese government. The sculpted garden hid surveillance cameras, the flowering vines in the distance covered a twelve-foot wall. And the wall was lined with sensors, topped with razor wire and watched by armed guards in case anyone was foolish enough to approach too closely.

Beijing sprawled outside that wall, frantic, crowded and chaotic. Inside lay a sanctuary.

Walter Han had been a guest here many times before. Never had he remained for so long or with such little talk between himself and his mentor. With no words between them, he was forced to concentrate on the game board between them, a nineteen-by-nineteen grid partially filled with black and white stones.

They were playing the ancient game of Asia. Older than chess and infinitely more complex. Called Weiqui in China, the game was known as Igo in Japan and Baduk in Korea. Westerners simply called it Go.

Sensing an opening, Han pulled a small white stone from a cup at his side and placed it into position. Satisfied with his move, he sat back and admired the gardens. 'Whenever I come here, I'm amazed to know we're still in the city limits.'

Han was in his late forties. Taller than most Chinese men, he was also lean and wiry. Some would describe him as spindly. Born in Hong Kong to a Chinese father and a Japanese mother, he'd been given a Western name because that made it easier to do business with the European and American companies that so loved the island outpost.

At the time of Han's birth, his father was already running a small electronics company. Unlike many in Hong Kong, Han's father chose to align himself with the mainland government rather than fight a losing battle for independence. That decision paid handsome rewards. Han's family were millionaires by the time the British stood down. And in the decades since, Han and his father had built the largest conglomerate across China: ITI, or Industrial Technology, Inc.

With his father gone, Han had spent the last decade running the company on his own. Not only did he maintain close links to the government in Beijing, he expanded them. Some considered him a fifth pillar of the government. The money, power and prestige made him a force to be reckoned with. And yet, he still deferred to the man across from him.

'A place of solitude is essential. Otherwise, one cannot think beyond the noise.' The words came like poetry from Wen Li, a small man with a few locks of white hair remaining on the sides of his head. He had mottled skin and a slight droop to the right side of his face.

As a strategist, Wen had seen the Party leaders through six decades of turmoil. He'd been a soldier, a statesman and a strategist. He was rumored to have personally ordered the crushing of the Tiananmen Square protests and, in their aftermath, to have guided China onto the path of capitalism without giving up the rule of the single party.

He held several offices within the Party, but his unofficial title was more impressive. They called him Lao-shi, the word literally meant *old person of high skills*, but applied to Wen it was the equivalent of *learned Master*.

Wen made a move on the board, placing a small black stone beside one of Han's white stones. Essentially, cutting it off from the rest of Han's pieces. 'You come to me with a heavy heart,' he said. 'Is the news that bad?'

Han had been waiting for the right moment to speak. He could wait no longer. 'Unfortunately, yes. The survey of the mining site is complete. Our worst fears have been confirmed. The avalanche destroyed most of the exterior modules, filling in parts of the canyon and scattering debris across the Serpent's Jaw. The reactor was untouched, but the project cannot be rebuilt without a massive effort and expenditure.'

'How large?'

Han knew the numbers by heart. 'To excavate the debris would cost a hundred billion yuan. To reestablish the operation and rebuild the station . . . at least five hundred billion more. The time frame would be long. Especially if the need to operate in secrecy remains.'

'It does,' Wen said.

'In which case, it would be three years before the mine begins producing again.'

'Three years,' Wen said.

The old man sat back, drifting off into his own thoughts.

'At least three years,' Han repeated.

Wen came back from his reverie. 'How much ore was the mine producing at the time of the accident?'

'Less than half a ton per month. And falling.'

'Was there any hope of increasing the yield?'

'Very little.'

Wen grunted his displeasure. 'In that case, why would we spend so many billions and waste so much time digging additional holes in the seafloor? Why would we even consider it?'

Han took a breath. He'd expected to have Wen on his side. After all, the old man had been the chief proponent of the secret mining operations from the beginning. He'd understood the strategic value of the alloy right from the start.

'Because the *ore* cannot be priced in yuan or time wasted,' he explained. 'As you well know, the Golden Adamant is unlike anything the world has ever seen. A living metamaterial. Five times stronger than titanium, capable of accomplishing things no other material derived from the Earth or created in a lab can match. With it, we can build a generation of aircraft, ships and missiles that are virtually indestructible. Not to mention a thousand other uses our engineers are dreaming up. This mine – our mine – is the only place in the world this material has ever been found. You know this, of course. The cost is irrelevant. We must rebuild.'

The old man looked up menacingly and Han wondered if he'd gone too far.

'Do not lecture me on what must be done,' Wen said.

Han bowed slightly. 'I apologize, Lao-shi.'

Wen released Han from his gaze and turned his attention back to the game. 'You are partially correct,' he said, placing another black stone. 'The ore, as we so blithely call it, is the key to the future. Like bronze over copper and iron over bronze. History has always been a tale of who has the sharpest and strongest sword, the lightest and most resilient armor. The nation that controls the Golden Adamant will become unassailable. But you are incorrect to suggest we dig in the same exhausted location.'

Han cocked his head to the side. 'But there are no other deposits.'

'None that have yet been found,' Wen replied.

'With all due respect, Lao-shi, we've had people scouring the world for years. We've found no trace of this alloy anywhere. Not in Africa, South America or the Middle East. Nor throughout our own territory or on the volcanic islands in the South Pacific. Nowhere that we expected it to be. We've taken ten thousand core samples from the depths of the sea and found nothing beyond this one source.'

'All true,' Wen said. 'Nevertheless, I've developed information about another deposit that may exist, and far closer than one would think.' He pointed to the board. 'Please, make your move.'

Han looked down at the board. He found it hard to concentrate on the game with such information hanging in the balance. Still, a quick look revealed his side was in a perilous situation. His white stones were being surrounded. Any additional moves he made would only put Wen in a better position. He had to hope the old Master would make a mistake. 'Pass,' he said.

Wen nodded. 'That is your right.'

'Please, my friend. Tell me, where is this other deposit?'

Across from him, Wen hesitated, rolling the smooth stone between his fingers before putting it on the board. 'Somewhere on the island of Honshu.'

Han took a second to process the answer. 'Japan? The home island?'

'Possibly offshore,' Wen said. 'But most likely on the mainland. And if I'm correct, very near the surface.'

The words were spoken without emotion, but Han felt the wind knocked out of him. 'How do you know this? And, more importantly, how can this possibly help us? Even if we find it, we can't mine without being detected. And should we try and be discovered, all we'll have accomplished is bringing the existence of the ore to the attention of the Japanese. And that means giving it to the Americans. We'll be handing our adversary the very thing we seek to control ourselves.'

'Precisely,' Wen said. 'And for that reason we have yet to follow up on the initial information.'

'Then we're at an impasse,' Han said.

'Are we?'

Wen reached down into the cup and pulled a handful

of black stones from the container. 'Tell me,' he asked, 'what is the objective of this game?'

Han tried to hide his frustration. He'd grown used to the Lao-shi trying to impart wisdom through unique methods and recognized this as one of them, though he didn't enjoy it. 'The object of the game is to surround your opponent, deny him liberty and thus deny him life.'

'Precisely,' Wen said. 'And which nation has the greatest players?'

'China,' Han said. 'After all, we invented the game.'

'No,' Wen said, placing a black stone. 'That is ego, not wisdom.'

'If not us, then Japan.'

Wen shook his head once more, Han passed and the old man placed another black stone.

Han frowned. He was losing the game. And the argument. He passed again. 'Korea is known to have many renowned players,' he said, a tinge of desperation in his voice.

'The Americans,' Wen told him. 'They are the greatest players this game has ever known. More precision and mastery have they displayed than any nation on Earth.'

Han resisted the urge to scoff. 'Are you sure? I can't think of a single American expert.'

'Because you're looking at the wrong board,' Wen said. 'Look again and think of it as a map.'

Thoroughly confused, Han studied the board once more. He noticed a vague resemblance between the board and the world map. Not the Western maps with North America in the middle but the Asian where China took center stage.

His force of white stones in the middle was China. Black stones looping up one side and down the other might have been Europe and North America.

Before he could speak this thought, the Lao-shi continued with the lesson. 'They have armies in Europe,' he said, placing another black stone. 'They control the Atlantic, the Mediterranean and Indian oceans. They have bases in the Middle East, they station troops in territory that used to be Communist Russia. They launch aircraft and ships from islands around the Pacific.'

Wen was no longer playing the game; he was searing the lesson into Walter's mind, naming one American asset after another, placing stones to represent each one. 'Hawaii, Australia, New Zealand,' he said, as three black stones went down. 'Korea, the Philippines and Formosa – which they call Taiwan – and, of course . . . Japan.'

As the last stone went on the board, the white pieces representing China were encircled.

With the lesson complete, Wen looked up. The intensity of his gaze banished any thought of frailty. 'From their island continent, the Americans have surrounded the world. Our world.'

Han's confidence was replaced by the sting of embarrassment. 'I understand. But what can we do?'

Wen pointed to the board. 'Which stone would you remove?'

Han studied the game once more. It was the last one that mattered most. The one that had closed the circle and ensured that the white side – that China – would die. 'This one,' he said, sliding the piece off the board. 'Japan.'

'And so it must be,' the Master told him.

The enormity of Wen's suggestion hit Han at once. His heart pounded at the thought. 'You can't be considering military action?'

'Of course not,' Wen said. 'But if Japan were changed from black to white – from an American ally to a Chinese one – the board would be redrawn instantly. We would not only begin to roll back American dominance, but we'd be free to mine all the Golden Adamant known to exist in this world.'

'Can it be done?' Han asked. 'There are centuries of animosity between us. War crimes and territorial disputes.'

'A plan is already in motion,' Wen said. 'One that you are uniquely qualified to see through.'

'Because I'm half Japanese.'

'Yes,' Wen said. 'But there is another reason also: the corporations you control and the various technologies your engineers have mastered.'

Han listened to the veiled words and wondered exactly what Wen was getting at. He knew the details would only come forth once he'd committed. 'I will do my part,' he said. 'Whatever it is that you need.'

'Good,' Wen replied. 'Among other things, this task will require more machines. Automatons that can impersonate human behavior. You have been funded for years by the Ministry to study such a project. Now you must report your progress. Can you make them perfectly? They must be indistinguishable from those whom they will replicate.'

Han smiled. He always assumed the blank check had

come as part of some strategy. The Lao-shi must have been crafting this plan for years. 'We're very close.'

'Good,' Wen replied. He cleared the board and placed the stones back into their respective cups. 'My secretary will give you a package on the way out. Instructions lie within. Your first meeting will be in Nagasaki. A deal is being crafted to build a factory there and a Friendship Pavilion to celebrate the new ties. The factory will be yours. It will be your base of operations.'

Han stood, energized. 'And what if the Americans interfere?'

'They know nothing of this,' Wen insisted. 'But this is not a game for the fainthearted. At the end, one side will be denied liberty and denied life. If the Americans attempt to stop us, you will make sure they fail.'

2

Greenland
Eleven Months Later

The Navik Ice sheet was a lonely and desolate place. Tree-less, barren and flat, it was shrouded in mist and lit in a pale light. Even at high noon, the sun hung just above the horizon.

Two figures trudged across that landscape. Both of them bundled in red snowsuits that brought a shock of color to the monotone world.

'I don't understand why we're bothering to check so far north,' the smaller of the two figures called out. Wisps of blond hair stuck out from her fur-lined hood. Her accent was vaguely Nordic. 'The other readings told us what we need to know.'

The larger of the two figures pulled back his hood and removed a pair of goggles, revealing a rugged face and deep, iridescent blue eyes. Kurt Austin was in his mid-thirties, but he looked older. Crow's-feet at the corner of his eyes and wrinkles in his forehead suggested a lifetime in the elements instead of an air-conditioned office. The silver color of his hair gave him a knowing and dashing quality, while the rest of his face was covered with a month of unshaven beard. 'Because I have to be sure of the truth before I hand my government a report they won't want to believe.'

The woman pulled her hood back and raised her goggles as well. Ice-blue eyes, chapped pink lips and mid-length straw-blond hair confirmed her Nordic heritage. She pursed her lips and arched an eyebrow. 'Seven readings from seven different glaciers isn't enough proof for you?'

Her first name was Vala; her last, a long mix of consonants, umlauts and other letters that Kurt found completely unpronounceable. She was a Norwegian geologist whose assistance and knowledge had been invaluable, especially here on the top of the world.

'I wish it were only seven,' Kurt replied. 'I've been on thirty glaciers in the last six months. And my conclusion is going to require a perfect record to generate any help. That means no gaps or missing data.'

She sighed. 'So that's why we fly out in the helicopter to reach the station. And when the clouds begin to close in, we land and then we hike. Okay, fine. But what I don't understand is the obsession. The urgency. We've discovered exactly what we expected to discover. So far, everything has proven to be' – she paused, looking for the right word – 'copacetic,' she said finally, using a word he'd been uttering far too frequently of late.

'That's the problem,' Kurt said. 'Nothing should be copacetic.'

He wasn't at liberty to explain any further. And they didn't have time to talk anyway. He put the goggles back in place. 'We have to keep moving. There's a storm coming.

We need to find the station, get the data and get out of here or we're going to be building an igloo and keeping each other warm until spring.'

'I could think of worse ways to spend the winter,' she said with a grin. 'But not without food.'

He double-checked the bearing, set his feet and continued on.

The first sign of their goal was a bank of solar panels, black and glossy against the endless white field. The panels were designed by NASA for use on distant worlds at a cost of a million dollars per square foot, but the automated station required an incredible amount of power, and acres of standard solar cells would have been needed to generate what these four small panels were able to provide.

From the solar array, they followed a power line toward a suspicious-looking dome of white. It rested in a slight depression on the otherwise flat landscape.

Clearing away the windblown snow revealed metal plating with NUMA stenciled on it in block letters.

'National Underwater and Marine Agency,' Vala said. 'I'll never understand the American obsession with labeling every last piece of equipment.'

Kurt laughed. 'You never know when someone is going to come along and steal your hubcaps.'

'Up here?'

'Probably not,' he said. 'But when ten million dollars of equipment suddenly stops transmitting . . . well, the thought crossed my mind.'

Kurt scraped more snow and ice from the automated modules. They hadn't been stolen, but something had obviously gone wrong. They were tilted over at an angle when they should have been level. 'Looks like some ice slid down from the first module and sheared off the antenna. No wonder it wasn't sending any data.'

He unzipped one of the many pockets in his jacket and pulled out a handheld computer. It looked like a cell phone, but was more rugged and winterized. Using a cable, he plugged it into a data port on the central module.

'The CPU is undamaged,' he said. 'But it'll take a few minutes to download all this data.'

As he waited, Vala wandered to the front edge of the station. 'The drill is still operating.'

The station used a heat probe to drill down into the glacier until it found flowing water. Then, by measuring the depth, temperature and speed of the water, it determined the amount of glacial melting that was occurring.

They needed the information to test a new theory, one that suggested the world's glaciers had been hollowing out from the inside instead of just retreating from the southern ends.

Kurt watched as the progress bar on the computer inched toward completion. 'What's the depth on the heat probe?'

'Eleven hundred feet,' Vala said. 'And it seems –'

The ice shifted beneath them and her voice was drowned out by a loud crack. As Kurt steadied himself, the module in front of him slid to the right and tilted twenty degrees. He instinctively jumped back and checked the ground around him. On the other side of the monitoring station, Vala screamed.

Kurt ran to her, cutting around the front of the module. A large gap had opened up beneath the monitoring station. A drop of two hundred feet loomed beneath it. The only thing keeping the unit – and the Nordic scientist clinging to it – in place were the outlying anchors.

Kurt stepped forward and the snow beneath him began sliding away.

'Crevasse!' she called out.

He could see that. He pulled an ice pick from his belt and swung hard. The tungsten point bit deeply and gave him something to anchor himself with. Gripping the pick, and then the strap at the end, he stepped dangerously toward Vala, grabbed her by the hood of her snowsuit and pulled.

She leapt toward him and grabbed onto his arm, climbing over him and onto solid ground. Once there, she did what any sane person would have done: she started running away from the widening crevasse.

Kurt was inclined to follow, but he hadn't come all this way to leave the data behind. He pulled himself up, yanked the ice pick free and rushed back to the computer, which was now dangling from the data port by its cord.

The station shifted again as two of the anchors holding it in place broke loose and their tautly stretched cords snapped across the snow like whips.

Kurt ducked to avoid the flying anchors and jammed the ice pick into the ground once again. He leaned out over the crevasse and was able to touch the computer, but the padded fingers of his gloves were so puffy that it was impossible to grasp it and pull it free.

Using his teeth, Kurt pulled the glove off and tossed it

away. The bitterly cold air bit into his skin instantly. Ignoring it, he plunged his bare hand into the snow, grabbed a small amount and squeezed it until it melted.

Tossing the rest, he extended his body, laid his fingers on the glass screen of the computer and held them there. At fifteen below zero, it took only seconds for the water on his skin to freeze to the surface.

With the compact device now bonded to his hand, he reared back, yanking it free from the data port and grabbing it tightly.

The ice cracked again and Kurt hauled himself up and dove to safety as the last anchor gave way and the entire station tumbled into the gap. He lay still in the snow until the thundering echoes of the station's demise faded.

Vala came up to him and handed him the discarded glove. 'You must be completely crazy,' she said. 'Why would you risk your life like that?'

'I didn't want you to end up at the bottom of the crevasse,' he said.

'Not me,' she said, 'the computer. The data can't possibly be worth it.'

'Depends what it tells me,' he said.

Kurt turned to the computer. Working his fingers free without losing too much skin, he was able to tap on the screen and bring up the first page of data. A hundred gigabytes of information were now stored on the device, but the main screen told him all he needed to know.

'What does it say?'

'That the glacier is melting no faster than it has been for years.'

'So nothing has changed,' she said, hands on her hips. 'Just like at the other glaciers. There is no internal hollowing out and no rapid melt off. Isn't that good news?'

'You'd think,' he said. 'But it means something else has gone wrong. Drastically wrong. And at the moment, no one has any idea why.'

3

Washington, DC

The new briefing area in the West Hall of the Congressional Building was officially known as the Samuel B. Goodwin Media Room. Unofficially, those who worked there called it The Theatre. The elevated-seating arrangement had something to do with that, as did the endless political grandstanding that went on there.

On this rainy September day, the room was packed for a closed-door briefing. No cameras were present, as both the press and the public had been barred from attending.

Joe Zavala sat in the third row of the room, wondering how much arguing might occur today. There was serious science to be discussed and a diverse group of attendees here to do it.

Looking around the room, he saw four members of the National Academy of Sciences, five attendees wearing NASA badges, three more from the White House Advisory Staff. There were a total of eight from a smattering of other agencies, including NOAA, the agency charged with monitoring the world's weather, atmospheric conditions and overall environment.

Many of these groups did overlapping work, often cooperating but also competing against one another for budget dollars. That held true for Joe's organization as well: NUMA, the National Underwater and Marine Agency.

They were tasked with monitoring the world's oceans and America's lakes and rivers and waterways. They did historical work as well, finding sunken ships and other items of a bygone era. In addition – and far more often than Joe would have believed when he first joined – they got involved in international incidents. As such, NUMA had a reputation as a cowboy agency. That was good or bad, depending on how one felt about cowboys. Spending most of his childhood in New Mexico and Texas, Joe took the moniker as a badge of honor.

Joe wasn't the only member of NUMA in the building. He was here with three others from the agency. Three others and a conspicuously empty chair.

To Joe's right sat Paul Trout, a geologist specializing in deep-sea studies and the tallest member of the team at nearly six foot eight. Paul was a gentle giant who rarely had a bad word for anyone. At the moment, he had dark circles under his eyes and Joe suspected he'd been up late, studying any data he might be asked to present.

Gamay Trout, Paul's wife, sat next to him. She was hard to miss, with her wine-colored hair and a smile that revealed a slight gap between her front teeth. Gamay was a marine biologist, and though she wasn't expected to speak, she'd spent as many hours burning the midnight oil as Paul. Gamay liked to be ready for anything.

Rudi Gunn, NUMA's Assistant Director and the highest-ranking member of the organization available for the hearing, sat in the next seat. He looked none too pleased. Perhaps because of the empty chair.

'Where's Kurt?' Gamay asked, leaning across her husband and addressing Joe. 'It's not like him to be two hours late for a briefing on Capitol Hill. For that matter, where has he been for the last three months? I haven't seen him in the office at all.'

Joe knew where Kurt had been but not where he was at the moment. 'All I can tell you is . . . he's not missing much.'

With the endless droning coming from the speakers onstage, Joe was secretly envious of Kurt's absence whatever the reason.

A stern glance from Rudi put an end to the conversation and Joe focused on the member of the National Oceanic and Atmospheric board who finally seemed to be reaching his conclusion.

'. . . And after updated measurements, collated this week in our Washington office, we've calculated the sea-level rise to be eight-point-three inches over the last six months.'

Talk about burying the lede, Joe thought.

Two different murmurs ran through the room. One of disdain and one of shock.

The science crowd took that number with a collective gasp. It was worse than anyone had expected. Far, far worse.

In stark contrast, the political members in the crowd seemed unimpressed. In a city where every discussion was peppered with *billions* and *trillions*, eight-point-three inches didn't raise the pulse much.

At least not until one multiplied that number by the entire surface area of the world's oceans.

'Are you sure of these numbers?' someone asked.

'We've double-checked the data with NUMA's independent analysis,' the speaker said, gesturing toward the NUMA contingent.

Rudi stood. 'We've come up with the same figure.'

Among the elected officials present there were several from each party. Like any group, they ran the gamut of intelligence and political beliefs.

'Is this really that big a problem?' one congressman asked. 'I mean, come on, people, eight inches? I got more water in my basement from last night's rain.'

A wave of snickers came from the senators' row.

Rudi Gunn took it on himself to reply. 'Actually, Congressman, an eight-inch rise in the sea level requires an addition of twenty-one *quadrillion* gallons to the oceanic basins. To put that in perspective, we're talking about three times the amount of water contained in all the Great Lakes combined. In a matter of six months. It is a big problem. In fact, it's unprecedented.'

Hearing it put like that, the congressman sat down.

The speaker from the National Oceanic and Atmospheric board took it from there. 'Of greater concern is the rate of increase. The pace is accelerating, with half of the increase occurring in the last thirty days. At this rate, we could see a rise of several feet by the end of next year.'

'Where is the water coming from?' someone else asked in frustration.

Joe sighed. The can of worms was firmly in place and

the speaker opened the top without hesitation. 'We believe there's been a sudden acceleration in the effects of global warming.'

That did it. The true believers rose up in arms, stating various different versions of 'We warned you this would happen' and calling in unison for 'crash programs' and 'emergency measures.'

On the other side of the aisle, the global warming deniers shouted back about 'political stunts,' questioning the data and demanding an explanation as to how such a thing could happen so suddenly after years of being told it would take centuries for the ice caps to melt and the oceans to rise.

Down on the floor, the senator from Florida, who was running the hearing, did his best to rein things in, but a few bangs of his gavel were useless against the animosity. The arguing continued until a deep boom echoed through the chamber as one of the heavy doors on the upper level swung open and banged against the wall.

Voices temporarily silenced, all eyes turned toward the sound.

A man with unruly platinum hair, a tangled beard and broad shoulders stood at the top of the stairs. He wore a dark coat, wet from the rain, and studied the crowd through intense blue eyes. If he'd carried a trident, he could have passed as Poseidon, the God of the Sea.

'The iceman cometh,' Joe whispered to Paul and Gamay. 'The beard is new, though.'

'It's not global warming,' the Poseidon-like figure called out.

The senator from Florida stood. 'And who, exactly, are you?'

'Kurt Austin,' the man said. 'Head of Special Projects at NUMA.'

The senator appeared both surprised and put out at the same time. 'My apologies, Mr Austin, I didn't recognize you. On the other hand, where have you been?'

Austin walked down a few steps so everyone could see him. 'For the last six months,' he began, 'out on every glacier and ice sheet in the Northern Hemisphere.' He shed his heavy coat and placed it on a chair. 'For the last six hours, fighting traffic on I-95, after my flight from Greenland diverted to Philadelphia. Trust me when I tell you the traffic was the worst part of the trip.'

A wave of laughter made its way around the room. Only the speaker from the National Oceanic and Atmospheric board seemed not amused. 'Are you one of those who doesn't believe in global warming?'

'I take no position on global warming in general,' Austin replied. 'Whether it's really happening or not, whether it's man-made, naturally occurring or caused by aliens, is for other people to argue over. What I'm talking about is this particular rise in the sea level. And I can tell you, unequivocally, the seas are not rising due to glacial melting, fracturing ice sheets or even the incredible downpours the East Coast has been experiencing for the last few days.'

Another wave of laughter made the rounds. The irony of a hearing on sea-level rise taking place amid flash flood warnings had escaped no one.

The speaker was unmoved. 'Our models suggest that given an increase in ground temperatures –'

'Your models have been tested on a computer,' Austin replied. 'I've been out there checking and rechecking, digging under glaciers, walking on the ice sheets, taking core samples, with other members of NUMA's science teams. We've spent months comparing satellite images with direct on-site observations of glacial retreat rates, snow depths and actual runoff data in the streams below the glaciers. We've been looking everywhere for signs of unprecedented melting and we just haven't found it. I hate to burst your bubble but the glaciers and ice caps are vanishing no faster, and no slower, than they have been over the last ten years. Which means whatever is going on here, it's not related to global warming.'

'Then what is the cause?'

'I wish I knew,' Kurt said. 'But if your acceleration numbers are correct, we'd better find out in a hurry or start building large boats made of gopher wood.'

Only half the crowd got the reference to Noah's Ark, but the senator from Florida was one of them.

'Two by two isn't going to help us,' the senator said. 'My apologies for reprimanding you, Mr Austin. Your contributions have been invaluable. I ask you all to forward the data you've collected to all groups for study. We'll meet again in two weeks. But if we don't have an answer soon, this information will have to be shared with the public. I don't have to tell you what that means.'

Politics and spin doctors and public hysteria, Joe thought. All of which would make it near impossible to get anything done.

The meeting adjourned. Joe stood up and made his way to Kurt. 'Nice entrance. I suggest a fog machine and lasers to make it more dramatic next time.'

'Been in fog all day,' Kurt said. 'Seems like we all have. We need to find answers to this mystery and we need to find them fast.'

4

Kurt flicked on the lights in the NUMA conference room. Joe, Paul and Gamay filed in behind him.

'Better get the coffee going,' Kurt said. 'It's going to be a long night.'

They'd left Capitol Hill at the end of the hearing, driven across town as everyone else was leaving Washington. By six pm on a Friday, DC was a ghost town. A wet, soggy ghost town.

Joe set up the coffeemaker while Paul and Gamay put their binderfuls of notes down on the table.

'I can't believe we're back to square one,' Gamay said. 'Are you sure there's no ice melt going on? Not even in the Southern Hemisphere?'

'It's still winter in the Southern Hemisphere,' Kurt said. 'Trust me, nothing is melting in Antarctica at negative fifty degrees. And before you say it, I checked with our friends at McMurdo Station just to be sure.'

'Well, I don't see how we can work on a solution if we don't know what's causing the problem,' she replied.

'We can't,' Kurt said. 'Which is why we're going to stay

46

in this room until we come up with another possibility for the root cause.'

'Even if we find the cause, we might be unable to stop it,' Joe pointed out. 'It might also stabilize on its own.'

'Agreed,' Kurt said. 'But let's not count on that.'

With this directive, a brainstorming session began that would have made any group of thriller authors proud. One after another, various methods of drowning the planet poured forth.

'What about increased volcanic activity?' Kurt suggested. 'Water vapor is known to be a large component of any eruption.'

'Checked on that while you were in Greenland,' Paul said. 'On a worldwide basis, volcanic activity is down thirty percent over the last twelve months.'

'What about increased rainfall?' Joe suggested. 'We've had floods in the south and out west this year. And if it keeps raining here, the Potomac is going to overflow in the next few days. What if we're dealing with a similar situation worldwide, a forty days and forty nights kind of thing?'

Kurt glanced over at Joe to see if he was serious.

'What?' Joe said. 'You're the one that mentioned gopher wood.'

'I did,' Kurt said. 'But forty days of rain would not drown the world.'

'Depends how hard it rains,' Joe said with a grin.

'It's not happening worldwide,' Gamay said, taking him seriously. 'Right now, India is facing a drought and Europe is dealing with a hot, dry summer. Besides, forty days of rain can only be powered by forty days of evaporation. It's a closed system.'

Kurt intervened. 'Brother Joe knows that, he's just grasping at straws. Let's move on.'

'What if the measurements are wrong?' Gamay suggested. 'It's notoriously difficult to measure actual sea levels when accounting for tides, waves and wind. Even landmasses exert a gravitational pull on the surface of the sea.'

'Been checked, double-checked and triple-checked using different methodologies,' Kurt said. 'It's not a data error. This is happening.'

'What if the water is coming from space?' Joe suggested.

Stern glances came his way.

'I'm being serious this time. Comets are made up of dirty ice. Many scientists believe that all the water on Earth actually came from comets to begin with. It was deposited here as they bombarded the planet during the first two billion years of its formation.'

Kurt considered this a legitimate theory, but . . . 'Haven't seen any in the sky recently.'

'They don't have to be large and visible like Halley's Comet. They could be small enough to not be seen. Or they could be pieces of larger comets that came apart. I was just reading about a comet called ISON that broke up and vanished. Instead of a flare in the sky with a long tail, all NASA found were millions of tiny flakes. If our planet was slowly passing through a field of deconstructed comets, we wouldn't notice anything, but the falling ice would be caught in Earth's gravity and dragged into the sea. If there were enough of them, it would add up rather quickly.'

'I suppose it's possible,' Kurt said. 'But I think NASA might have noticed if we were passing through swarms of micro comets. And the sheer number of comets required to raise the sea level this quickly makes it unlikely.'

Joe shrugged. 'That's all I've got. Someone else take a shot.'

No one did and Kurt stood up. After three hours of brainstorming, they had little to show for the effort except bleary eyes and exasperation.

'Adjourning?' Gamay asked.

'Coffee break,' Kurt replied.

He walked to the coffeemaker in the corner of the room. 'Believe it or not, we're making progress,' he insisted. 'With every possibility we eliminate, we must be getting closer to the real answer . . . whatever that answer turns out to be.'

'Great speech,' Joe said.

'Right . . . I didn't even convince myself.'

Kurt poured himself a cup of coffee, decided against cream and sugar and then leaned against the edge of the counter. It dawned on him that Joe and Gamay had been very animated, but Paul had barely uttered a word.

That wasn't a total surprise. Paul was the most reserved member of the team, to begin with, but as Kurt sipped his coffee, he noticed Paul scribbling notes on a legal pad. Scribbling furiously.

Stepping closer, he glanced over Paul's shoulder. A long set of calculations occupied one part of the page, a paragraph of indecipherably small handwriting and the sketched image of a large bird with something in its mouth covered the rest.

'Something to add?' Kurt asked. 'Or just bored and doodling?'

Paul looked up, appearing surprised that Kurt was so close. He must have been lost in whatever he was doing.

'Maybe,' Paul said, then added, 'possibly . . . Actually, I don't know.'

Kurt reached down. 'May I?'

Paul released his hold on the pad and Kurt slid it free. In addition to the bird, Paul had sketched a jug with a curved neck that was half filled with liquid. There were calculations galore on the right side of the pad. And a name.

'Kenzo Fujihara,' Kurt said, reading aloud. 'Either you're planning a new career in animation or . . .'

Paul shook his head.

'All right,' Kurt said, handing the pad back to Paul. 'Spill it.'

Kurt felt a little guilty for forcing Paul's hand, but Paul was a perfectionist. Given the chance, he'd run a hundred test scenarios before he put forth a novel theory.

'It's just an idea,' Paul said. 'I'll start by saying I know it's crazy.'

'Can't be any worse than Joe's swarm of comets.'

'Hey!' Joe said, feigning serious injury. 'No judgment in brainstorming.'

'You're right,' Kurt said. 'So what does all this mean? Start with the bird. I'm curious.'

Paul took a deep breath. '"The Crow and the Pitcher,"' he said. 'It's one of Aesop's fables.'

With just those words, Kurt saw the brilliance in Paul's idea.

'In the fable,' Paul said, 'a thirsty crow lands beside a pitcher of water and attempts to dip its beak in it for a drink. But the neck of the jug is so narrow and the level of the water so low that the crow can't reach the water. So the crow flies away and returns with a stone in its mouth, which it drops into the jug. The stone displaces some of the water and the water level rises. Doing this over and over, the crow eventually raises the water level far enough that it can drink from the pitcher.

'The point is,' Paul continued, 'if the ice caps aren't melting and we're not passing through swarms of micro comets, then perhaps we're looking at this the wrong way. Maybe there's no additional water going into the oceans but something displacing the existing water that's already present.'

Everyone remained silent, considering the possibility.

Paul looked around the room. 'You know, like running a bath and then getting in and having it overflow.'

Kurt laughed. 'I'm pretty sure we all get the idea.'

'Everyone's so quiet, I wasn't sure,' Paul said.

'Just marveling at your brilliance, my friend. It's a fantastic bit of thinking.'

'Absolutely,' Joe insisted.

Gamay smiled. 'You keep coming up with stuff like that, I'm going to start losing arguments at home.'

'Is there any precedent for it?' Kurt asked.

'Not in the ocean,' Paul admitted, 'but it's common in smaller bodies of water. A few years back, Yellowstone

Lake was spilling onto new ground, but it wasn't from rainfall or runoff. The rise was linked to a bulge in the ground underneath it. An upwelling of magma deeper down was pushing the surface layers of rock higher. That displaced the water, causing the lake to rise and spread out even though the total volume of water was unchanged. At the time, geologists thought the volcano under Yellowstone might have been building toward an eruption. Fortunately, over the next few years the bulge subsided and the lake returned to its original confines. It's possible that a similar scenario is happening right now in some remote part of the world's oceans.'

'Rule out the impossible and whatever remains . . .' Gamay suggested.

'My thinking exactly,' Paul said.

'Surely, someone would notice a rise of that magnitude in the ocean floor.'

'Only if they were looking for it,' Paul said. 'But I can't think of any organization, including NUMA, that spends time conducting regular deepwater scans of the ocean bottom.' He gestured to a topographic map mounted on the far wall. 'The only charts that are updated with any consistency are those plotting shallow areas around harbors and the shipping lanes. Our maps of the deep are pieced together from onetime scans and widely scattered depth soundings. Everything in between is extrapolated data. But if you measured the elevation of North America by taking one reading in Orlando and another in Santa Monica, you'd conclude it was a very flat place, never taking into account the mountains in the middle.'

Joe chimed in. 'Most deepwater data is often decades old. A lot can change in a year, let alone several.'

'How much of an upheaval would it take?' Kurt asked.

'A new seamount the size of Hawaii would do the trick,' Paul said, 'even if it didn't pierce the surface.'

'New volcanoes aren't unheard of,' Gamay pointed out. 'Krakatoa blew itself off the map in 1883 and by 1930 a new volcanic peak emerged in its place: Anak Krakatoa.'

'And they grow quickly,' Paul said. 'Anak Krakatoa is a thousand feet high now. It continues to grow and widen at an astonishing rate.'

'There's also a new peak forming in the Emperor sea-mount chain off of Hawaii,' Joe said. 'They call it Lōʻihi. We did a survey of it last year. Been growing more rapidly since 1996.'

'Those are two small islands,' Kurt noted. 'And it's taken millions of years for Lōʻihi to form. I find it hard to believe something that large could come into existence in six months.'

'I agree,' Paul said. 'But rather than expecting one giant seamount, we should look for a widespread buckling of the crust somewhere along the edge of the tectonic plates. It would show up as the beginning of a new mountain range. But even if the heights were not remarkable, the length and breadth of the mountain chain would make up for it. A low-level buckling that ran along the boundary of the Pacific or Australian plates would move a great deal of water out of the way. If it ran the full length, the hills would only have to be a hundred feet high and four or five hundred feet wide. That would displace more than enough water to raise the sea level in the manner we've recorded. The higher and wider the new range is, the shorter its length would need to be.'

Kurt was intrigued but not yet sold. 'Okay, you're in the ballpark. Now close the deal. Show me some proof. If a subsurface mountain range is forming due to a buckling plate, wouldn't we see a large uptick in seismic activity?'

'I'd expect to,' Paul said.

'And?'

'We're not picking up anything unusual,' he admitted. 'Or should I say, none of the international seismic networks have reported anything. But there is someone out there claiming to have detected an uptick of tremors.'

Kurt considered the notes he'd seen. 'Kenzo Fujihara.'

Paul nodded. 'He's a Japanese scientist who insists he's detected a new type of seismic wave that no one else is monitoring. He calls them Z-waves. He says he's detected thousands of them over the last eleven months coming from somewhere in the Pacific plate boundary layer. But he refuses to publish any details explaining what these Z-waves are or how he actually detects them.'

'Have you reached out to him?'

'By telegram,' Paul said.

Kurt's eyebrows went up. 'Telegram? Did we suddenly travel back to the eighteen hundreds?'

Joe grinned. 'Tough room. Now you know how I felt.'

Gamay laughed softly, but Paul was serious.

'The sound you hear is the other shoe dropping,' he said. 'It turns out Kenzo Fujihara is the leader of an anti-technologist movement. They are of the opinion that

Japan is destroying itself through an obsession with electronics. He and his followers don't do phone calls, emails, texts or video conferencing. He published his findings in a newsprint-style manuscript, printed on a homemade printing press. One that Ben Franklin would have recognized.'

Paul continued. 'He claims the government of Japan and the technological-industrial complex of the nation are out to get him. He and his followers have been called a radical group, sect, even a cult. And he's been accused of brainwashing people and holding them against their will.'

'Not really asking to be taken seriously, is he?'

'He was once an acclaimed geologist,' Paul added. 'A rising star. And according to his paper, the Z-waves began eleven months back, increased suddenly six months ago and increased again in the last thirty days.'

The correlation escaped no one. It matched exactly with the various stages of the sea-level rise.

Kurt gazed into the coffee cup as if the answer might lie within. 'Is this our best lead?'

'Actually, it's our only lead,' Joe said.

'Good point,' Kurt replied. 'I'll have a NUMA jet waiting at the airport in two hours. Don't anyone be late. We're flying to Japan.'

5

Tokyo

Walter Han was used to a luxurious lifestyle, but he'd grown up on the streets of Hong Kong and held a certain affinity for the back alleys of the world and the inhabitants who dwelled in them.

Traveling to a bad part of Tokyo with an escort of three bodyguards, he entered the parlor of a man who now worked for him in a freelance capacity.

Greetings were exchanged, assurances given and all parties scanned for electronic devices. With their phones and shoes taken, Han was allowed to enter the back room.

There, he found the person he was looking for. Lithe, sinuous and covered with tattoos, the man was known as Ushi-Oni, or Oni for short. The name meant *demon*, and if the man had killed half the people he claimed to have killed, he'd earned the name several times over.

Oni sat cross-legged on the floor, bathed in a reddish light. He was thinner than Han recalled. His eyes wilder.

'I'm surprised to see you back here,' Oni said.

'I have another job for you.'

'To abduct more American servicemen?'

'No,' Han said, 'this one requires blood.'

Ushi-Oni did not react outwardly. 'I'm surprised,' he said calmly. 'Those who can buy and sell don't often have such a need for such violence.'

That was mostly true, Han thought to himself. But current circumstances changed that. Blood would flow in many places before his task was done. Blood and money.

'There's someone I can't buy who is about to become a very painful thorn in my side. I need to get rid of him and his servants. If you will do it for me, I will make you wealthy also.'

'I have all that I require,' Oni said.

'Then why have this meeting?' Han asked.

'You are a half brother to me.'

Han accepted the statement without equivocation. They were cousins, not brothers. And twice removed at that. 'We will be full brothers,' he promised, 'if you assist me. Brothers of a new kind. Untouchable. Renowned. You will no longer have to hide in the shadows.'

'You must truly need me to promise such things,' Oni said.

'I do.'

The Demon put his skeletal hands together as he mulled over the idea. 'You are trusted,' he said. 'But my fees must be paid without compromising my existence.'

'I'll pay in cash,' Han explained. 'Untraceable. But I will need complete elimination. No evidence.'

'That is my specialty. Give me the name.'

'Names,' Han corrected.

'Even better.'

Walter handed over a list. Five names were on it.

'Americans?'

Han nodded. 'And Kenzo Fujihara. They will be meeting soon. I want them gone. All of them.'

'Why?'

'It's not for you to ask questions,' Han said, as boldly as he dared.

'You are mistaken,' Oni said. 'Now tell me why or seek out other assistance.'

The insistence surprised Han. 'Kenzo threatens a business interest of mine,' Han said. He wasn't about to explain that the man had been publishing papers pointing directly to the failed mining effort in the East China Sea. Or that the Americans were known enemies of the Chinese state and their meeting with Fujihara was seen as an ominous development, best prevented.

'And the Americans?'

'Will interfere with me if given the chance,' Han said. 'I want them to burn. All together. Along with everything Kenzo has been working on.'

The Demon nodded and placed the list down. 'Fire leaves less evidence, but costs more. For five deaths, I require five separate fees. For arson, I require even more. In advance.'

'Half now,' Han said.

A brief silence was enough to make Han nervous. Perhaps he'd spent too long in the clean parts of the world. It took all his strength to stand firm.

'So be it,' Oni replied.

He whistled and Han's guards were allowed in. A briefcase was placed on the low table and opened. It was filled with euros. 'The rest when I know they're dead,' Han promised.

'When do you wish this to occur?' Oni asked.

'The Americans are on their way here now. They arrive in Tokyo tonight. Once they meet up with Fujihara, destroy them all.'

6

Kurt woke up aboard the NUMA jet. After lying with his eyes closed for a few extra minutes, he sat up and looked around. They were already descending toward Tokyo. 'May I never complain about the NUMA travel department again,' he said.

Joe, Paul and Gamay were in the seats around him. They were wide awake but talking softly and, from the sound of it, had been awake for most of the flight. Something Kurt knew they would regret sooner or later.

Kurt found it easy to sleep on planes. The soft wall of noise given off by the engines and the quiet, dim cabin were more effective than any sleeping pill ever devised. And after several months of living in tents and ramshackle huts out on the ice, the sleeper seat felt like a mattress fit for a king.

'Ten hours straight,' Joe said, checking his watch. 'Must be some kind of record.'

'Not even close,' Kurt said. He put a hand to his cleanly shaven face, silently amazed at the odd feeling of having smooth skin once again.

A flight attendant walked the cabin, offering hot towels scented with eucalyptus. Kurt gladly accepted and after rubbing it across his face and neck, he was wide awake.

He looked out the window at the lights of Tokyo.

Because the wind was blowing in from the sea, the plane flew a descent profile that took it across the bay and out over the city before turning back toward Haneda Airport and the artificial island it had been built on.

It was nighttime in Japan and Tokyo did not disappoint. The place was lit up like a neon maze, with the reddish spike of Tokyo Tower at the center.

They descended toward the runway, landed with a bump and taxied to the gate.

Kurt walked off the plane feeling as if it was early morning, but with the long flight and the time change, they'd lost a day crossing the international date line and it was nearly ten pm.

As they left the customs booth and made their way through baggage claim, Joe asked the question on everyone's mind. 'Any chance you've heard from your technologically challenged friend?'

'No,' Paul said. 'But I wasn't expecting to. I'll send him a telegram as soon as we check into the hotel. And if that fails, we can try the Pony Express.'

'I don't think you'll have to,' Gamay said, pointing across the terminal.

Standing near the building's automatic doors was a young woman in white slacks and a colorful silk top that had a classic geisha pattern to it. She had a backpack over her shoulders and held a sign in her hand that read AMERI-CAN PAUL.

'I'm guessing that would be you,' Gamay added.

'Not exactly the Beatles hitting New York in 'sixty-five,' Paul said, 'but I'll take it.'

'Go say hello,' Kurt suggested, taking the suitcase from Paul's hand. 'We're right behind you.'

Paul walked over to the young woman and bowed.

'You are the American geologist who wishes to meet with Master Kenzo?'

'I am,' Paul said. 'These are my colleagues.'

'My name is Akiko,' the young woman said. 'I am one of Master Kenzo's students. He will meet with you at the lakeside retreat. It is very pleasant there. Please, follow me.'

Without another word, she led them outside and on a long hike down the terminal sidewalk. Cars, shuttle buses and taxicabs jockeyed for position on the road outside the terminal, but none of them stopped for the group of five.

Paul and Gamay were up front, Kurt and Joe trailing behind.

'I hope we're not walking to this lakeside retreat,' Joe whispered.

'Could be a horse and buggy,' Kurt said, 'Amish-style.'

'That would be something,' Joe said, 'considering they're against technology . . .'

'We are not against technology,' Akiko said, picking out Joe's words from the background noise. 'Only electronic intrusion into humanity's essence. Unlike more primitive mechanical machines, electronic computing devices are not subject to human decision making. Every minute of every day, your computers, phones and other devices talk to one another, update and change their own programs, even record your whereabouts and activities. They also pass this information along to other devices, servers and programs that study your every move and respond with methods of influencing you, primarily to buy products you do not need. But we believe there are other more sinister effects occurring also.'

'Such as?'

'Here in Japan, young people have become ever more interested in their computers, video screens and virtual reality than in actual reality and human-to-human contact. People have lost the ability to connect with one another. Restaurants, bars and hotels cater to singles who wish to eat, sleep and experience the world undisturbed by others next to them. Isolation within a crowd has become the norm. Eyes on screens, earbuds blocking outside noise and conversation. We are a nation of people living separate existences and as a result our marriage and birthrates are plummeting. If this isn't changed within a generation or two, our population will fall by half. A crash unlike anything seen in modern times.'

Considering how crowded Tokyo appeared, it was hard to imagine that in thirty years it might be half empty.

She led them to a parking lot and stopped. 'Before we begin, I require you to relinquish your cell phones, iPods, iPads, cameras and computers, along with any other electronic paraphernalia you may have brought with you.'

She slid off the backpack and began collecting the various devices. One by one, Kurt, Joe, Paul and Gamay unpacked their electronics and placed them in the pack, which Kurt noticed was lined with some type of metallic foil.

When they were finished, the pack was full. Seeing the items all piled together, Kurt had to admit it was almost embarrassing how much electronic junk they traveled with these days.

'How did we ever travel without all this stuff?' Joe asked aloud.

'We carried quarters and dimes,' Kurt said, 'and there were whole walls in the airport filled with these things called phone booths.'

Joe laughed. 'You're showing your age, amigo.'

'I'm not old,' Kurt said, 'I'm a classic.'

Akiko pulled the bulky pack over her shoulder and led them across the parking lot, where the night suddenly became far more interesting.

Kurt was expecting a bland white van or perhaps a large nondescript sedan to shuttle them to the lakeside retreat, but instead they stopped beside a pair of classic Japanese cars from the sixties.

The first was a gleaming white sedan that bore a vague resemblance to the BMWs of the era. It had performance tires, a vintage spoiler and polished chrome accents. The second car was a silver 1969 Datsun 240Z. It had a long, low hood, sleek lines and side vents that looked like gills. All of which contributed to a predatory, shark-like appearance.

A low roofline and mirrors placed well forward of the windshield and out on the fenders made it look fast even sitting still.

'Beautiful machines,' Joe said.

'I rebuilt them myself,' she replied.

'Really,' Joe said. 'I also love to work on cars. Perhaps we could collaborate sometime.'

Akiko offered a brief nod, nothing more. 'These will

transport us to the lakeside,' she said, walking to the sedan. She opened the trunk and placed the packful of confiscated electronic equipment inside. Kurt noticed another metallic lining in the trunk.

'I could ride with you,' Joe offered.

Akiko slammed the trunk of the sedan and opened the door. 'American Paul will ride with me.'

Joe took that hard.

'As will his American wife,' Gamay said.

'Very well,' Akiko replied. 'You two will follow us. Try to keep up. I will be driving quickly, as we are probably under surveillance already.'

She threw a set of keys their way, which Joe grabbed out of the air. 'I'm driving,' he said with a grin.

Kurt shrugged as Joe strutted toward the classic sports car. He reached the right-hand door the same moment Joe opened the door on the left. They dropped into the bucket seats together.

From the corner of his eye, Kurt saw Joe reach forward as if to grab the steering wheel, but there was nothing there except the padded dash. The wheel was in front of Kurt – on the 'wrong' side of the car.

'No,' Joe cried, suddenly realizing his error.

'Right-hand drive in Japan,' Kurt said. 'Might want to brush up on your Japanese automotive history before you start rebuilding cars with your new friend.'

'Very funny,' Joe said. 'I must be slipping. I blame it on the jet lag.'

'Should have taken a nap. Eight or nine hours would have done you some good.'

Joe handed over the keys and Kurt started the car. The engine fired easily. The exhaust singing in perfect harmony with the reverberation from the white sedan.

Without hesitation, Akiko pulled out and drove to the exit. Kurt grabbed the gearshift, threw the car into reverse and backed out. With a quick shift, they were moving forward and out into the Tokyo night.

Kurt had spent nearly eight months in Japan in what seemed like a lifetime ago. He'd spent plenty of time on the roads in England, Australia and Barbados as well. As a result, driving on the left came easy. The only danger came when one was changing roads at sparsely used intersections. Without another vehicle to follow, it was easy for the brain to slip back into its deeply ingrained pattern and drive down the wrong side of the street.

They picked their way through heavy traffic moving slowly all the way to the edge of the city. Finally, Akiko pulled onto a highway and began to accelerate. Kurt dropped down a gear and stepped on the gas. Soon they were racing to the southwest at almost a hundred miles an hour.

'Any chance we're really under surveillance?' Joe asked.

'I haven't seen anyone,' Kurt said. 'But they are a secret group, opposed to almost everything their country holds dear.'

Kurt reached forward and began pressing the manual analog buttons on the radio. They went in, physically moving and setting the needle on the old AM/FM radio. 'When I was a kid, this radio was the height of technology.'

Joe laughed. 'Like the lady said, it's digital electronics they're against. Analog radios are okay. And this vehicle has a carburetor, a manually adjusted camshaft to open and close the valves and it was made before computer diagnostics and engine control units were even on the drawing board. It's a pure machine. It does what the driver commands it to instead of thinking for itself.'

Kurt changed lanes, punched the gas and passed an Audi and a brand-new Lexus like they were standing still. 'That it does.'

They continued on the highway for over an hour, heading out into the foothills. Well into the second hour of driving, they pulled off an exit and onto a secondary road. This stretch of blacktop twisted into the mountains and for the first time they were driving in darkness.

Kurt worked hard to keep up with Akiko on the unfamiliar road, but eventually they broke out onto a plateau and continued on a fairly straight line, heading toward a shimmering lake in the distance.

Akiko slowed down as they approached the lakefront and turned onto a dirt track.

'Not a house in sight,' Joe said. 'And certainly nothing I would call a retreat.'

'I wouldn't rule out a log cabin or tents by the water,' Kurt said, ruefully imagining another night sleeping on uneven ground.

They continued around the edge of the lake, arriving at a wooden causeway that led across a hundred feet of water to a small island.

Akiko turned her car gently onto the bridge and eased forward slowly, which seemed prudent considering the bridge was no wider than the sedan she was driving.

As she approached the island, the lights from the sedan lit up thick walls of impressive stonework and a drawbridge that was slowly being lowered into place.

'That's no island,' Joe said, 'it's a castle.'

The ancient fortress had battlements of carved and fitted stone, overhanging ramparts and a huge pagoda-style structure set back and above the walls.

'Keep your eyes peeled for dragons,' Joe said. 'This is the kind of place we're likely to find one.'

Kurt was more interested in keeping his eyes on the road. With the high beams and the driving lights on, he could see how truly narrow the wooden bridge was. It was also noticeably rickety.

'Not the sturdiest of structures,' he said. 'But if it held up the sedan, we should be fine.'

The drawbridge locked in place and the sedan rolled across it and into the castle.

'Our turn,' Joe said.

Kurt eased forward, bumping up onto the wooden planks. Not completely certain of his alignment, he reached for a button to lower the window so he could poke his head out and look down at the front tire. Instead of a switch, he found the hand crank.

Rolling down a window for the first time in years, he leaned out over the windowsill. The sidewall of the front tire was at the edge of the bridge.

'Plenty of room on this side,' Joe said.

'Plenty?'

'At least three or four inches.'

'That's reassuring.'

Kurt drove forward, teasing the car toward Joe's side. He crossed the bridge slowly, as the boards creaked and groaned beneath them. The drawbridge was slightly wider and obviously sturdier than the rest of the structure, since its underside was armored. Kurt accelerated onto it and then into the large garage area that had once housed the castle's horses.

A dozen other vehicles were parked around them, all meticulously restored machines from the fifties, sixties and seventies.

He parked in an open space next to a vintage Mini Cooper. Instead of the iconic Union Jack, it had the Rising Sun painted on the roof. 'Quite a collection,' he said. 'Dirk's going to be jealous when he reads our report.'

Dirk was Dirk Pitt, NUMA's Director. He'd been the head of Special Projects for years before ascending to the number one post in the agency. His adventures around the world were widely known. He had a strong affinity for antique and classic cars and had brought many examples back from his foreign travels, restoring and displaying them at an airplane hangar in Washington that doubled as his home.

'You might be right about that,' Joe said, 'although Dirk usually goes for cars a generation or two older than these.'

Kurt turned off the car, pulled on the hand brake and climbed out.

A young man wearing a gray robe tied at the waist with a white sash came over and took the keys. A woman in a similar outfit took the keys from Akiko. Kurt noticed both of them carried long daggers in scabbards around their waists. Along the walls, he saw all manner of ancient weapons – swords, pikes and axes – as well as suits of pleated samurai armor.

It seemed an odd style of decoration for a garage filled with gleaming period cars, but then antique weapons could be collected for pleasure and value just as cars could.

'Welcome to my castle,' a booming voice called out.

Kurt looked up. On a balcony above the garage floor, he found the source of that voice: a man wearing a fitted black robe with shoulder boards and a white and red sash at the waist. He had no dagger but a curved samurai blade. His dark hair was pulled back in a topknot and his face was thinly bearded.

'I am Kenzo Fujihara,' he said. 'I'm afraid we must search you before we allow you to enter the inner sanctum, but please rest assured, we are proud to receive you as guests.'

Another group of robed acolytes appeared to perform the search. 'Is it me,' Joe whispered, 'or have we entered Samurai Disneyland?'

Behind them, the drawbridge began to close. It slammed shut with a resounding bang, followed immediately by the grind of iron bars locking into place.

'No phone, no email, no way out,' Kurt mused. 'Can't imagine why they get accused of holding people against their will.'

7

Kenzo's Castle

Each member of the NUMA team endured a search no worse than a vigorous TSA pat-down. The only real difference was the use of a bulky device held up by two of Kenzo's followers and slowly passed up and down the front and back of each guest's body.

During his turn, Kurt felt nothing from it and saw no sign of it displaying anything in particular. But the heavy weight, thick wires and single red light on the device indicated its purpose. 'Electromagnet?'

'Correct,' Kenzo said. 'Battery-powered and manually operated. Strong enough to erase the programming and memory of any electronic device you may have concealed on, or within, your body.'

After his watch was subject to similar treatment and then handed back to him, Kurt slid it back on his wrist. 'What makes you think we're interested in recording you?'

'You work for the American government,' he said. 'A close ally of the politicians in Tokyo. And they, through various agencies, have been persecuting my followers and me for years.'

'I assure you,' Kurt said, 'that's not why we're here. In fact, why don't I let American Paul explain?'

Paul moved forward. 'We're only interested in your study of the Z-waves and the earthquakes that no one else has found.'

'As your telegram said,' Kenzo replied. 'But why? So far, my claims have been scoffed at. If the Z-waves can't be detected by modern means, they must be irrelevant to modern discussion. Is that not correct?'

'We think they might be relevant to something else,' Paul said. 'A rise in the nominal sea levels that began a year ago and recently accelerated.'

'I began detecting the Z-waves just over eleven months ago,' Kenzo said.

Gamay cut to the chase. 'And how do you do that? I mean, if you don't use technology . . .'

Kenzo stared at her. 'That's the big question, isn't it? You do realize there are other ways to detect such things beyond the use of computers. Animals, for instance, are very sensitive to earth tremors. As for machines, as far back as the first century a Chinese scholar named Zhang Heng developed a seismograph.'

Paul knew this. 'Yes,' he replied. 'An ingenious device. As I understand it, it used a large brass drum with eight sculpted lizards arranged around the sides. Each lizard had a ball loosely held in its mouth. When an earthquake shook the palace, the balls tumbled out. Whichever ball tumbled out first indicated the direction of the earthquake.'

'Precisely,' Kenzo said. 'We have a replica I will show you later. You'll see that lizards were actually Chinese dragons and the ball that tumbled out would be caught by the mouth of a bronze frog. You should not omit such details.'

'I told you we'd find dragons in here,' Joe said.

'Statues don't count,' Kurt replied, before turning to Kenzo. 'I hope we're relying on more than brass drums and large-mouthed frogs here.'

'Come with me,' Kenzo said. 'I'll show you.'

Kenzo led them across the foyer and down a hall. Kurt noticed how Akiko never left his side – not like a servant, more like a bodyguard.

They passed through a courtyard and then along a parapet that ran above the water. The lake was like glass beneath the moonlight, and a dry moat could be seen between the outer wall and the castle.

Joe tapped Kurt excitedly on the shoulder. 'What about those?' he said, pointing.

Kurt glanced down into the moat. He saw several Komodo dragons, prowling on their short, stubby legs. 'How about that. There be dragons here.'

Joe grinned. 'I'd like to see them eat.'

'Maybe later,' Kenzo said.

He led them over the moat on a small bridge and they entered a large open room. The décor was a strange mix of ancient Japanese and early industrial.

A glass atrium covered part of the ceiling and one entire wall. Copper fixtures and pipes ran along the opposite wall, disappearing behind bamboo panels. Red velvet couches occupied the center of the room, inviting them to sit by a warm fire that crackled in an old stone hearth. Cluttered all around were polished wooden tables, antique globes and strange examples of mechanical equipment replete with springs, levers and visible gears.

Some of the contraptions held weapons; others had valves and small pressure tanks attached to them, perhaps someone's idea of ancient diving equipment. Still others were beyond understanding.

In one corner stood an old hand-cranked Gatling gun.

'Reminds me of an antiques store,' Gamay said.

Kurt had to grin. He enjoyed eccentricity and this place did not disappoint. 'There's a certain flavor to it, I must admit.'

Kenzo walked to the far wall and stopped in front of a large cabinet. 'This is my detector,' he said.

He opened one of the stained-glass doors to reveal the workings, which included hundreds of thin and tightly strung wires. Glittering crystals were suspended in the wires like insects in a spider's web. Each of them a different shape and size.

'As you probably know,' Kenzo explained, 'quartz crystals vibrate when placed in an electrical field. These wires of gold are perfect electrical conductors. When the earthquakes occur, a great deal of mechanical energy is released. Some of it becomes electromagnetic. As that energy emanates outward from the Earth, it passes over the wires, which conduct the electrical charge to the crystal and create a harmonic vibration. That gives us the signal of the Z-wave. And since no one else is using such a design, no one else can detect them.'

'What's this?' Joe asked from a few yards away.

Joe was a born wanderer, curious to a fault. He'd already

stepped away from the bulky cabinet and was standing in front of a large wall map, complete with silver-leaf borders. Like everything else in the room, it was ancient-looking, in some ways, but had been marked with myriad lines that were drawn in modern red pen.

'Those are the courses each bank of Z-waves took,' Kenzo explained.

Paul accompanied Kenzo to where Joe stood. Kurt moved up beside Gamay, watching from a distance. It was clear who the skeptics in the group were.

Kenzo reached for a tarnished protractor. Using it as a pointer, he directed their attention to the long straight lines. 'Each incoming wave was measured in strength and charted. They come from individual events, which I call ghost quakes since no one sees them but us. Unfortunately, I can only plot the direction they came from, not their precise location. But they propagated along these headings.'

'Why can't you determine a location?' Gamay asked.

'It requires a second station,' Kenzo insisted. 'Like intercepting a radio signal, one receiver can give you direction, but it requires two receivers and the crossed lines they create to get a fix.'

'So why not set up a second station?'

'We have,' Kenzo insisted, 'but there have been no additional events in the week since I did so.'

Kurt whispered to Gamay, 'Sounds like running out of film just as Bigfoot stumbles into your camp.'

'Amazing how often that happens,' she said.

'What about the numbers written beside each line?' Paul asked.

'Dates and strength indicators,' Kenzo insisted.

Unlike the American system of date notation, which went month/day/year, or the European system, which put the day first, the Japanese system placed the year first, then the month, then the day.

Once Kurt had accounted for that, he was able to make sense of the map. If Kenzo was correct, the Z-waves had been doubling in frequency and intensity every ninety days.

Kenzo was explaining exactly that when a light began to flash beside the stained-glass door of his machine.

He rushed over to it as a soft tone began to emanate from inside the box. Several of the golden strings could be seen vibrating ever so slightly. A printer that looked like it was made from an old phonograph scratched out a two-dimensional shape of the waves.

'Another event,' Kenzo said excitedly. 'With the secondary group. This is our chance to find the epicenter.'

He rushed to a large desk and grabbed a nickel-plated microphone that belonged in the booth of an old radio station. Kurt could imagine Walter Winchell using it to broadcast his news program: *'Good evening, Mr and Mrs America, from border to border and coast to coast and all the ships at sea.'*

After flicking several switches, Kenzo called out to someone.

'Ogata, this is Kenzo. Confirm you are receiving.' Letting go of the talk switch, he waited and then tried again. 'Ogata, do you read? Are you picking up the event?'

Finally, an excited voice came back. 'Yes, Master Kenzo. We're picking it up now.'

'Do you have a direction?'

'Stand by. The signal is wavering.'

Kenzo looked up at his visitors. 'This is what we've been waiting for. Your arrival is fortuitous.'

Very, Kurt thought.

Ogata's voice returned over the speakers. 'We calculate this as a level-three wave,' he said. 'Bearing two-four-five degrees.'

'Stand by,' Kenzo said. He rushed back to his own machine and rotated it carefully, using a large brass lever. It turned smoothly on a pewter gimbal. 'Two-six-zero,' he said, reading off the bearing marker.

Kenzo went to the map and placed the oversized protractor against it. From their current position at the castle, he marked a straight line running 260 degrees. It slashed down the length of Japan, crossed over Nagasaki and ran out into the ocean. Satisfied with this mark, he located Ogata's position on another part of the island and then drew a line along the 245-degree bearing.

The lines crossed out in the East China Sea. The intersection was nowhere near the edge of the tectonic plate. As far as Kurt could tell, it was solidly up on the continental shelf, no more than a hundred miles from Shanghai.

Kenzo seemed just as surprised. With the mark in place, he rushed back to the large microphone. 'Are you certain of those numbers? Please reconfirm.'

Ogata came back on the line. 'Stand by for –'

He was interrupted by a stuttering noise.

'Was that –' Gamay said.

'Gunfire,' Kurt said, suddenly on alert.

'Ogata, are you reading me?' Kenzo transmitted. 'Is everything okay?'

Thick static came first and then: 'There are men coming up the hill. They're carrying –'

Additional gunfire cut him off, but the line stayed open long enough to hear shouting and then some kind of explosion.

'Ogata?' Kenzo said, clutching the microphone tightly. 'Ogata!'

His face went white, his hand began shaking. His stricken appearance told Kurt that this wasn't part of the show.

As Kenzo waited for an answer, a deep, somber bell started ringing somewhere high in the castle. The sorrowful tone echoed repeatedly.

'What's that?'

'Our alarm,' Kenzo said.

Glass shattered in the atrium behind them. Kurt spun and saw an object crashing through one of the windows and tumbling across the room toward them.

8

As the glass shattered, Kurt lunged forward, tackling Kenzo over the back of the heavy desk. From the corner of his eye he noticed Paul and Gamay diving for cover. He never saw Joe, who'd stepped in front of the bouncing projectile, caught it bare-handed like a second baseman and hurled it back in the direction it had come.

The grenade made a second hole in the glass and exploded on the far side. An incendiary device, it was powerful enough to kill anyone in close proximity but designed primarily to spread fire and jellified gasoline. It flared like the sun, shattering every window in the atrium and unleashing a rain of molten liquid and broken glass.

As the crystal tones of falling glass subsided, they heard the roar of motorboats on the lake. Almost immediately, sporadic gunshots were fired.

Kurt helped their host to a sitting position. 'Your castle is under siege, Master Kenzo.'

'Why?' Kenzo blurted out. 'By whom?'

'I was going to ask you the same thing.'

'My acolytes will defend us,' Kenzo said proudly.

The gunfire told Kurt they were going to face a stiff challenge. 'Only if they've got something better than swords and catapults to fight with.'

'What about this?' Joe said, standing by the old Gatling gun. 'Do you have ammunition for it?'

'A few boxes.'

Joe released the brake, put his shoulder into the frame and wheeled the old weapon toward the window.

'Anything else?' Kurt asked.

'We have a cannon in the tower.'

'That won't be much use against speedboats,' Kurt said. Looking around, he spied a crossbow and a flight of iron-tipped darts sitting on a shelf. 'Get Joe the ammunition,' he told Kenzo. 'And keep your head down.'

Kurt went to the wall, switched off the lights and grabbed the crossbow from the shelf. By now, Paul and Gamay had reappeared. Paul had a spear in his hand. Gamay was holding a mace. There was something wrapped around the handle, but Kurt didn't have time to ask.

'You two stay here,' he said. 'If things get out of control, make your way to the garage, but don't lower the drawbridge unless you have no other choice.'

'Where are you going?' Gamay asked.

Kurt slung the quiver of darts over his back. 'To the tower,' he said. 'Someone needs to take the high ground.'

As Kurt rushed out of the room, Kenzo arrived beside Joe with two boxes of ammunition. Taking cover as random potshots hit around them, Joe opened the boxes. He was happy to see that the shells were modern loads and not the same vintage as the gun.

'Where did you get these?'

'We had them made by an old gunsmith.'

'Let's hope he does quality work.'

Joe emptied the box of shells into the hopper, grabbed the crank and angled the gun downward.

Turning the crank with a smooth motion, he got the barrels to rotate. The shells were drawn in and a half turn later began punching holes in the night. Joe turned the weapon slowly and smoothly, not wanting to use up too much ammunition too quickly.

'Lower,' Kenzo said.

Joe tilted the weapon down and fired again, as the entire room filled with a cloud of blue smoke.

Kurt was halfway across the parapet when the first stuttering shots from the Gatling gun sounded. Glancing back, he saw gun smoke billowing out of the window. Down below, a spread of bullets stitched a line in the water and across the bow of one of the speedboats.

The driver gunned the throttle, turned the wheel and sped off into the dark. At the same time, another boat moved forward, one gunman on the bow pouring suppressing fire into the atrium while a second man readied a grenade.

With sustained cover fire hitting the building, the Gatling gun went silent. Joe had been forced undercover, but Kurt had a shot. He rose up, aimed the crossbow over the wall and pulled the trigger.

The arms of the old weapon snapped forward and the bolt flew with surprising ease, but its feathers were warped from years of sitting around. It went off course, diving and turning like a badly thrown curveball. Instead of hitting the man in the chest, it plunged through his foot.

He cried out in pain and dropped the grenade. He stretched for it and shouted, but his foot was nailed to the fiberglass. His shouts were cut off as the boat erupted in flames.

Men in one of the other boats spotted Kurt and began firing his way. He dropped down behind the thick embattlements and listened as the shells pinged off the stone behind him.

'One down, three to go.'

Joe was on the floor, taking cover, when the explosion flared outside. He crawled to the window to get a look.

The speedboats were making high-speed runs now. Strafing the castle walls and peeling back.

He manned his gun and tried to hit them, but the old weapon was too heavy and too hard to maneuver to track the boats successfully. He fired, shouldered the gun into a new position and then fired again. Just as he reached for the second box of ammunition, the last speedboat raced out of view.

'Are they moving off?' Kenzo asked.

'Not off,' Joe said. 'To the other side of the island.'

Almost immediately, the shooting began again. This time, from the far side of the castle.

'Now might be a good time to call the authorities?' Joe suggested.

'We don't have phones.'

'Use the radio.'

Kenzo ran over to the old shortwave, tested the microphone and then switched to a channel used by Japan's emergency services.

'This is Seven . . . Jay . . . Three . . . X-ray . . . X-ray . . . Zulu . . .' he began, using his officially licensed ham radio designation. 'Request emergency police assistance. Armed men are attacking us. Repeat. Armed men are attacking us . . .'

They received no response. Nothing but static.

'The antenna,' Kenzo replied, pointing toward the shattered windows. 'It's out there.'

'Keep trying,' Joe said. 'We can't hold them off forever.'

As if to prove the point, a grappling hook flew over the wall and lodged with a metallic clang.

Joe realigned the Gatling gun and waited. The hook shimmied back and forth and a man appeared at the top. He climbed over the wall and crouched as a second man arrived. Joe raised the barrels and pushed the crank forward. The handle moved half an inch and then jammed.

Back and forth didn't free it, and Joe had no idea how to clear the old gun.

Out on the wall, two more attackers appeared. 'Time to go,' Joe said. 'We're about to be flanked.'

Kurt crossed the dry moat and made it back to the main building, where he found a stairway. He rushed up three flights and came up on the third floor of the pagoda. As he stepped from the shadows, a sword flashed through the air toward his head. He ducked at the last second and the blade cut a chunk out of the wall behind him.

Surging toward the attacker and using the crossbow as a battering ram, he found himself colliding with Akiko. He tackled her to the ground.

'Mr Austin,' she said.

'Careful where you swing that thing,' he said.

'I'm sorry,' she said. 'I thought you were one of them.'

He let her up and she stepped back, holding the sword tightly.

Kurt noticed she was now wearing a vest of loose metal plates held together by laced twine. 'I see you've changed for the occasion.'

'I am the armorer,' she said. 'I must protect Kenzo.'

She went to brush past, but Kurt grabbed her arm. 'My friends are with Kenzo. They'll protect him. Take me up to the tower; we need to take the high ground. From there, we can keep their men off the walls.'

'This way.'

She turned on her heels, pulled open a door and dashed up another flight of stairs. Kurt followed, surprised by how quickly she moved in the heavy vest.

They reached the top and broke out onto a platform that covered the highest level of the tower. The small anti-personnel cannon was there, along with bags of powder and a neatly packed pyramid of iron cannonballs. As much as Kurt wanted to fire it, the cannon was too bulky to be helpful. He ignored it and stepped to the rail with the crossbow in hand.

From this height, he could see most of the castle grounds below. The situation looked grim. 'They've made it over the wall,' he said, noticing three groups of men moving about.

When one group appeared in the open, Kurt loosed a bolt at them, hitting the leader in the thigh. As the man fell, Kurt placed the crossbow on the ground to reload and Akiko stepped forward with a longbow in her hand.

She let the arrow fly and knocked a second man in a flash before adjusting her aim and firing again. Both shots hit their targets. One man fell where he stood, the other dropped his weapon and lumbered for cover as Akiko took aim once more.

The third arrow sung as she released it, but the target had ducked behind an out-jutting wall and the lethal projectile caromed harmlessly off the stone. Still, he was injured and that group of attackers would have no choice but to retreat.

'Save some of them for me,' Kurt joked.

She didn't sense the humor. 'Unfortunately, we have plenty of enemies left to fight.'

Seeming to prove the point, an assault rifle began hammering away, shells splintering the wood above them and pinging off the heavy iron bell.

Kurt and Akiko dropped to the ground and took cover in the center of the platform as additional gunfire came in from the other side.

'We're caught in a cross fire,' Kurt said, as he crawled toward the rail and risked a look. 'They've taken cover behind the wall. Might be time to break out that cannon after all.'

Before they could do more, a muffled explosion, followed by a whoosh of flames and smoke, rumbled on the far side.

'Molotov cocktail,' she said.

'Without oysters or caviar,' Kurt said, 'just uncivilized.'

Down below, tongues of auburn flame licked at the edges of the pagoda and began snaking their way up toward its crown. The ancient wood was bone dry and lacquered in oil-based paint. Dark and noxious fumes billowed upward. The fire would soon follow.

'We need to get out of here,' Kurt said.

'You said we needed to take the high ground.'

'That was before the high ground became a barbeque.'

Kurt urged her forward and the two of them ran down the stairs only to find the door stuck. Kurt put a shoulder to it but it wouldn't budge.

'There's something up against it,' Akiko said, looking through a small window at the top.

Kurt stepped back, preparing to charge forward and hit it like a battering ram. But before he could move, a salvo of bullets punctured the wooden door from the other side.

Kurt plastered himself against the stairs and avoided being hit, but Akiko took two shots to the chest and fell backward.

Kurt rushed forward, shoved the crossbow through the small window at the top of the door and aimed it downward before pulling the trigger.

A shout of pain came from the other side of the door. It was followed by breaking glass and erupting flames of another Molotov cocktail. Flickering orange light visible through the window told him the room outside was on fire, all the beautiful tapestries and old furniture.

Staying low in case another wave of bullets came through, Kurt crawled to Akiko. She lay on her side, grabbing her midsection. She wasn't bleeding and Kurt noticed a web of Kevlar beneath the ancient metal plating.

'I was wondering why you bothered to put that on,' he said. 'Apparently, not all technology is bad.'

She forced a painful grin. 'We have to get out. This won't protect us from the smoke . . .'

'Can you stand?'

'I think so,' she said, getting to her feet and then doubling over almost as quickly.

She began to cough and Kurt could feel the irritation building in his own lungs. He needed to find another way out and he needed to find it fast. He glanced back up the stairs, took a deep breath and ran into the thickening smoke.

9

'This way,' Kenzo urged. 'Quickly.'

He spoke with nervous energy as he led them through a section of the ancient castle that Joe didn't recognize. 'This isn't the way we came,' Joe said.

'Shortcut,' Kenzo insisted. 'It'll keep us hidden. If they're out there and we're in here, it will be better for us all.'

They came to a wooden door that Kenzo opened with an old-fashioned key. It swung outward and then bumped against something.

Squeezing through, they found themselves in a rotunda. A body on the ground had stopped the door from opening all the way. Kenzo crouched beside it. 'Ichiro. One of my earliest followers. He left an abusive family to come with me.'

Joe reached down and felt for a pulse, but a quick look told him it was too late. Ichiro had been riddled with bullets at close range. 'He's dead,' Joe said. 'And this means our attackers are obviously inside the castle.'

Kenzo nodded. 'The question is, how many and where?'

A trail of blood led to a far door. 'Let's not go that way,' Gamay suggested.

The shooting picked up outside. As if things were reaching a frenzy. The scent of burning wood was growing stronger. 'We can't go back the way we came,' Paul said.

A third door in the rotunda stood across from them. The other option was a flight of stairs that wound around the rotunda up toward a small door.

Kenzo stood and rushed toward the third door, grabbing the handle and pulling.

'Wait,' Joe called out.

It was too late.

Kenzo had already pulled the door open. Pent-up flames and smoke exploded from the hall beyond, bursting forward in a flash as new oxygen rushed into what had been a stagnant, air-deprived hall.

The flashover engulfed Kenzo and threw him backward at the same time. He was flung to the floor like a rag doll with his clothes on fire.

Joe ripped off his coat and lunged for Kenzo, covering him with the jacket and smothering the flames. Gamay helped him put the flames out as Paul slammed the door shut to keep the fire from pouring into the rotunda.

'His face is burned,' Gamay said. 'And his hands. I think his clothes took the worst of it.'

Kenzo moaned once or twice but said nothing.

'He hit his head pretty hard,' Joe said. 'I think he's unconscious. Let's hope he stays that way until we can get him help.'

He picked Kenzo up in a fireman's carry and pointed to the door up above. 'Up the stairs,' Joe urged. 'It's our only chance.'

'We'll be exposed,' Gamay said, gripping the mace.

'We don't have much choice. We're rats in a burning maze and Kenzo was the only one who knew the layout.'

He urged them to move. 'Make sure the ledge is clear. I'll carry Kenzo.'

Paul went up first, with Gamay right behind him. They checked the door for heat before they opened it and went through.

Joe followed with Kenzo over his shoulders. He ducked through the door, careful not to harm Kenzo in the process.

Paul and Gamay were standing on the parapet, awe-struck. The entire pagoda was ablaze. All four levels of the ornate wooden structure alive with flames.

'I hope Kurt's not still in that tower,' Gamay said.

'He's too smart for that,' Paul replied.

'Keep moving,' Joe urged. 'We need to get to the water.'

They pressed on, crossing the bridge headed for the outer wall. As they neared it, the door swung open behind them and a pair of men came running out.

'They're headed this way,' Paul said. 'If they spot us, we'll be sitting targets down on the rocks.'

'We have no other choice,' Joe said. 'Take Kenzo. Find a place to hide. I'll keep our friends occupied as long as I can.'

Paul put down the pike, leaning it against the wall, and took Kenzo from Joe. With the injured man over his shoulder, he followed Gamay, picking his way down toward the water's edge.

As they left, Joe grabbed the pike, turned around and crouched in the dark.

The pursuers were coming on fast, racing through the smoke across the bridge. They, too, were escaping the inferno, more than anything else, but they wouldn't hesitate to shoot Paul, Gamay and Kenzo if they found them. Joe wasn't about to let that happen.

He stayed hidden, waiting until they were almost on top of him before rising up. He swung the pike in a tight curve. It caught the first man in the stomach, doubling him over. In response, the second man aimed a pistol at Joe, but a return stroke of the metal pike caught the weapon and knocked it from the assailant's hand.

The gun fell onto the rocks and discharged harmlessly. But the man lunged for Joe and tackled him. They struggled and then fell over the wall. Not forward toward the lake but backward into the dry moat, where the Komodo dragons waited.

Kurt climbed down the stairs with Kenzo's antipersonnel cannon in his arms; eyes burning and half blind with tears, he almost tripped over Akiko. She was lying on the floor near the gap in the door. A chimney-type effect was bringing fresh air in, funneling it up the stairs, keeping them alive in the process.

Kurt exhaled and took a breath as he set the cannon on the floor.

Akiko crawled toward him and helped to set it up. They packed with powder and an eight-pound solid steel cannonball. Unable to find a proper linstock, or lighter, Kurt used a wadded-up piece of paper. He touched it to the fire coming down the stairwell and held it against the fuse. For a long couple of seconds, nothing happened. Then the fuse sizzled to life, the powder charge went off and the eight-pound ball thundered into the door, blasting it to splinters.

'And I thought this thing wouldn't be useful,' Kurt mused.

Shoving broken pieces of wood aside, they enlarged the gap and climbed through, crawling over a pile of furniture that had been used to block them in. 'Which way to the garage?'

'This way,' she said.

Despite her bruised ribs and the vest of armor, she moved quickly. They found seven of Kenzo's people but no sign of Kenzo or the NUMA team.

'Is anyone else here?' Akiko asked.

One of the men shook his head.

'We have to go back,' Akiko said.

For the second time, Kurt grabbed her by the arm. By now, the smoke was beginning to creep down into the garage. Some of the rafters were smoldering. 'The floor above us has to be an inferno. Joe will get them out. Trust me.'

She shook loose and turned to the others.

'Tell them to get in the cars,' Kurt said. 'We're going to drive out of here.'

Akiko gave the command in Japanese, then added, 'I'll lower the drawbridge.'

She ran to the wall, pulled one lever to the side and then down.

The drawbridge fell with surprising speed. It banged into place. The bridge beyond was already in flames.

*

Joe and the man who'd tackled him landed in the sand and separated. They got up simultaneously, forgot about their own fight and focused their attention outward, looking for the Komodo dragons.

Two of the smaller animals were coming at them from one side. A third was holding its ground far beyond, and the fourth, the largest of the group, was lumbering toward them from the other direction.

The animals were agitated and far more aggressive than any Joe had seen before. The fire, smoke and cinders probably had something to do with that.

One of the smaller ones came forward and Joe stood as tall as he could, raising his arms in a sudden motion.

The predator stopped in its tracks, dropping lower to the ground on its oddly bent legs. It moved again and Joe repeated the motion, but the animal seemed less impressed.

'Where's your gun?' Joe shouted.

The assassin looked at Joe oddly before shoving him to the ground and running for the wall.

Joe leapt to his feet, flung some of the gravel at the dragons and dashed for the pike he'd been using. He quickly grabbed it from the ground, spun and swiped the first animal in the face.

The beast hissed and backed away.

Meanwhile, Joe's assailant was running for his life. His movement had attracted the attention of the largest dragon in the moat. The ten-foot-long, three-hundred-pound monster moved with surprising speed.

The man sprinted without looking back, leapt into a

gap in the wall and scrambled upward. The Komodo dragon rushed up behind him, reared up on its back legs and thrust its head into the gap. It managed to rake its teeth along his shoulder and arm, tearing the man's shirt off and gouging some of his flesh. It came down with the back of the man's shirt in its mouth but had missed out on a meal.

The man kept climbing, his bare back displaying a colorful tattoo that covered every inch of skin.

Joe felt a begrudging respect as the man reached the top of the wall and disappeared over it. But he was now alone with four of the most lethal animals in the world.

'I'd like to see them eat,' Joe whispered, recalling his words from an hour ago. 'Why do I say these things out loud?'

The animals moved toward him. As Joe saw it, the big one was the problem. The others were small enough to ward off with the long metal spear, but the big one would probably yank it out of his hand and use it as a toothpick once it devoured him.

He tried to outflank it, but it blocked him and forced Joe to back up.

A thunderous crash startled all of them and Joe turned to see a section of the burning pagoda tumble into the moat. A shower of sparks sent the lizards back a few yards.

'Not the kind of dragons that like fire,' Joe mused.

He moved toward the flames, pulled his coat off and wrapped it around a burning length of wood. With the pike in one hand and the flaming torch in the other, he inched toward the waiting animals.

'Back,' he said, jabbing at the nearest one. 'Back.'

The dragon swatted at the stick with an outstretched claw but retreated after making contact with the flames. The other juvenile did the same. But the alpha male stood its ground.

'Now or never,' Joe told himself. He rushed directly toward the big animal, tossing the blazing section of wood at its face.

The animal shrugged off the burning stick, knocking it effortlessly to the side with its snout. The distraction was all Joe needed. Still running, he jammed the pike into the sand and pole-vaulted himself up and over the animal, launching himself forward at the top and hitting the ground at a dead run.

The beast leapt up too late to swat him out of the sky. It came back down on all fours and spun in a half circle.

Joe was already leaping onto the wall. He found the cleft and climbed hand over hand, never looking back until he reached the top.

The Komodo dragons stood below in a tight semi-circle, gazing up at him hungrily.

Joe waved a farewell and ran down toward the lake, where Paul, Gamay and Kenzo were taking cover on the rocks. There was no sign of his wounded attacker. Out on the water, the boats were speeding off into the dark.

'They're leaving,' Paul said.

'The question is, who are they and why did they do this?' Gamay asked.

'Whoever they are, they've done what they came to do,' Joe said. 'They've burned Kenzo out and destroyed his work. All the data, all the records. It's all on paper. Everything is gone.'

'Not everything,' Gamay said.

Joe turned her way. She unraveled what she'd wrapped around the shaft of the mace. It was the blue map with the silver borders. Aside from torn patches in each corner where she'd ripped it from the wall, it was no worse for wear.

The red lines were still plainly visible. 'Someone didn't want us to find out where these lines crossed,' Gamay said. 'I thought that made this information worth saving.'

'Could it really be worth killing for?' Paul asked.

'Someone obviously thought so,' Joe said, looking at Kenzo. 'How is he?'

'He's coughing blood,' Gamay replied. 'I think his lungs may have been burned. If he inhaled the fire . . .'

She didn't have to say any more; they all knew that to be a bad diagnosis. In any case, Kenzo's only hope was a hospital with a burn center.

'We could use a car,' Paul said. 'Any chance the garage hasn't burned?'

Joe looked over his shoulder, though he didn't need to. The entire pagoda was an inferno. It no longer looked like a building, just a fountain of flame. 'Not likely,' Joe said. 'But this fire should act as a beacon and bring help; it couldn't be much brighter.'

A minute later, the sound of another boat motoring through the darkness set everyone on edge.

Joe strained to see into the night. Instead of a sleek motorboat, he saw a slow, ungainly looking craft chugging their way. Its flat front bulldozed the water rather than knifing through it, while its motor sounded like an old air-cooled VW.

'The Duck,' Joe said, recognizing the amphibious car from Kenzo's collection.

Kurt was at the wheel while Akiko and several of Kenzo's people were sitting in the back.

Joe waved frantically to get Kurt's attention. The Duck wouldn't be the fastest mode of transportation, but it could drive on land as well as water. It meant there was a chance to get Kenzo help.

10

Shinjuku Prince Hotel

After spending the balance of the night at the hospital and talking with the local police, Kurt, Joe, Paul and Gamay had been taken to a hotel, where they'd managed a few hours of exhausted sleep, before talking with Rudi Gunn in Washington.

The tone of the conversation was somber until Kurt asked Rudi's permission to sneak into Chinese waters and see what they might be hiding.

'Not a chance,' Rudi Gunn replied. 'Absolutely out of the question.'

His voice came from the speakerphone sitting in the middle of the table. The sound was surprisingly clear, echoing around the hotel suite with so much volume that Rudi might as well have been there in person.

Kurt leaned back in his chair, his eyes on the triangle-shaped speaker. 'So what I'm hearing is . . . you'd like us to be careful.'

'Then you need to get your ears checked,' Rudi said. 'The location you gave us is not just deep within Chinese territorial waters. In a section they've designated a special operations zone. It's one of their naval testing grounds. They patrol the demarcation line relentlessly. Ships, aircraft, submarines. They even have a permanent line of tethered sonar buoys out there. Something like our SOSUS lines in the North Sea.'

Kurt looked around at the others. After what they'd just been through, every one of them wanted to get a look at whatever Kenzo and his analog machines had found.

Paul took the next crack at it. 'Rudi, I've gone over what I know of Kenzo's theory. Geologically speaking, there's a reasonable chance he's onto something. Considering the situation, there has to be some method of sneaking us in there.'

'That's not like you, Paul. How bad is Kurt twisting your arm?'

'Only a minor sprain,' Paul said, tongue in cheek.

'Help us and no one gets hurt,' Kurt joked.

Joe offered a thought: 'We could have a commercial vessel wander off course, break down and request our help. Maybe even stage a fire or some other urgent need. We've done it before. If we happen to be the closest vessel –'

'Then you'd already be in Chinese waters,' Rudi said. 'Look. It's simple. The Chinese don't need our help to rescue anyone that close to their own shoreline. And they're not too keen on anyone "wandering" into their waters or airspace. A few years ago, they crashed into one of our surveillance planes – and that flight was still technically in international airspace.'

Kurt sat back. 'What if we hitchhiked aboard one of the Navy's new attack subs?' Kurt said. 'I've heard they're undetectable.'

'Already asked,' Rudi replied. 'So far, the only thing

undetectable has been an official response to my request. Apparently, the Navy isn't interested in sending their newest submarine into a shallow-water sea filled with China's most sophisticated underwater listening posts. And I can't blame them.'

Kurt looked up. Had Rudi just given something away? 'You've already asked the Navy for help? What gives?'

The room went silent, and when Rudi spoke again, his voice was slightly less authoritative. 'Would you believe, I've come to trust your judgment?'

'Not in a million years.'

Rudi sighed audibly. 'Let's put it this way. Our government hasn't detected any of these Z-waves, like your new friend, but over the past two years both NUMA and the Navy have picked up subsurface reverberations coming from that very section of the East China Sea, where those Z-wave paths crossed. Putting two and two together, it raised the possibility of there being something worth investigating.'

'So Kenzo was right,' Paul said. 'There is something going on out there. What kind of noise are we picking up?'

'It's been impossible to classify,' Rudi told them. 'Possibly deep-sea drilling, but there are enough differences in the acoustic signatures to make us wonder. Some of the Navy's data has been identified as liquid movement within the continental plate itself.'

'Oil?' Joe asked.

'That's one possibility,' Rudi said. 'Both the East and South China seas are riddled with hydrocarbon deposits – and the Chinese have been very aggressive in staking their claim, especially in the South China Sea where they've drawn that infamous nine-dashed line. Except the location Kenzo identified is in the East China Sea. Far enough behind the established border that it's unquestionably under Chinese control.'

'No need to drill in secret if you're drilling on your own territory,' Gamay said.

'We looked at a subsurface drilling arrangement two years ago,' Paul said. 'The geology team liked the idea. The accounting department had a different perspective. Nearly a hundred times as costly as setting up a normal rig. Makes no sense to do something like that where you don't have to.'

'Exactly,' Rudi replied. 'Beyond that, the sonar recordings don't match with any known drilling or extraction techniques. Some of the data indicates free-flowing liquid moving extremely fast, under intense pressure, much lighter and less viscous than crude oil. Meanwhile, a second set of echoes register something far thicker and slower. It's also coming from far deeper. Down within the continental plate itself. Deeper than anyone has ever drilled.'

Paul offered an explanation. 'If it is subsurface magma, that might indicate a range of volcanic islands building out there. It could be exactly what we're looking for.'

'Except that we're back at square one since we have no way of investigating,' Joe said.

Gamay leaned forward. 'I hate to be the voice of reason, but you guys seem intent on sneaking around and doing things the manly way. Why don't we try a female perspective and a little cooperation? We could just ask the

Chinese to let us take a look. We could give them the data on the sea-level rise. Explain that there's a possibility that a new island chain is forming off their coast or that a bulge in the tectonic plate is occurring and ask them to share in our investigation. They might even appreciate it.'

One thing Kurt had always liked was the team's differing approaches to problem solving.

'Good idea,' Kurt told her, 'but not in this case. We were all viciously attacked last night and five of Kenzo's people are dead. Kenzo is in the hospital, fighting for his life. For all his quirks, the only thing his research threatened was exposing something going on in Chinese waters. So until it's proven otherwise, we have to assume the Chinese were behind the attack.'

Gamay nodded.

'They're hiding something out there,' Kurt added. 'Whatever it is, they're not going to show it to us willingly. We'll have to find another way.'

'And I'm telling you it's impossible,' Rudi said. 'I'll send you the data on the Chinese listening posts, sonar buoys and what we know about their patrol schedules and surveillance capabilities. You'll see for yourself. It's a very tight screen and there's no way to get through. The last thing we need is an international incident that ends up with any of you rotting in a Chinese jail.'

Kurt listened to every word and nodded at Joe. *Message received.*

The sound of papers shuffling came next. 'I have another meeting to attend,' Rudi added. 'I'll check back in a few hours.'

Rudi signed off and Kurt stood. The others were yawning, but he was suddenly wide awake. A knock at the door followed. Kurt answered it and found the front desk manager standing there with a message in his hand.

'What is it?'

'Summons, of sorts,' Kurt said. 'Our presence is requested at the district office of the Japanese Federal Police.'

'I'm suddenly tired,' Joe quipped. 'Think I'll take a nap instead.'

Kurt shook his head. 'Sorry, amigo, but you're the main attraction. They want to talk to you about the guy who escaped being a meal for the Komodo dragon. You're the only one that got a look at him.'

Joe stretched. 'I suppose I could recount how I fought the great beast.'

Kurt rolled his eyes as Gamay stood and yawned. 'The long flight has caught up to me.'

'Me, too,' Paul said. 'We'll rest while you talk to the police.'

'Sorry,' Kurt said. 'No rest for the weary. You need to start right now.'

'Doing what?' Gamay asked.

'Finding a way to sneak into the East China Sea.'

Paul cocked his head to the side. Gamay's eyebrows knitted together in a confused look.

'But Rudi just told us not to try that,' Gamay replied.

'I believe his exact words were "completely out of the question,"' Paul seconded.

'His lips said no but his eyes said yes,' Kurt replied.

'You couldn't see his eyes.'

'I could imagine them,' Kurt insisted. 'Why do you think he's sending over all the data on the Chinese naval patrols and the information on the sonar buoys? He wants us to find a crack in the armor and exploit it.'

Gamay folded her arms across her chest. 'That is not what I got out of that conversation.'

'There's listening and then there's understanding,' Kurt said. 'This was an open line. Anyone could be eavesdropping. Check your encrypted email link in a few minutes. If there's nothing from Rudi, feel free to nap the afternoon away. But I think you'll be working.'

Gamay and Paul rose wearily. Joe yawned again and stretched in an effort to shake off the drowsiness.

Kurt opened the door and held it for him. 'My long nap on the plane isn't appearing so crazy now, is it?'

II

The note from Superintendent Nagano requested Kurt
and Joe take an odd route to the police station. After riding two different trains, hailing a taxi and taking a short
walk, they stood outside the prefecture building.

'Not exactly the Twelfth Precinct,' Joe said.

The structure was nothing like the typical American
police station. The outer walls were painted in a rainbow
of pastel colors, while an officer in full-dress uniform and
white gloves stood at attention near the main entrance.
He held a polished wooden staff firmly in his right hand
and neither blinked nor seemed to breathe as people
walked past.

'*Ritsuban,*' Kurt said. 'Standing guard. Letting the public know that the eyes of the police are always watching.'

'That's reassuring,' Joe said.

'Apparently, not to Master Kenzo.'

They entered the building and found themselves in a
diamond-shaped room with two doors leading in and two
leading back out to the street. Expecting a duty officer,
Kurt and Joe found only screens and a computer voice
talking in Japanese.

Kurt stepped up to one of the flat-screens. It reminded

him of the arrivals and departures monitors in the airport except everything was in Japanese. 'Can't read a thing.'

Joe tapped a spot on the screen and was rewarded with the option to change languages. Two versions of English were listed. American and UK.

Joe tapped on the American flag icon.

'Welcome to the Yamana Police Station,' the computer voice said in English. 'Please state your reason for arrival.'

'We have a two o'clock meeting with Superintendent Nagano,' Kurt said.

'Please state your name and nationality while looking at the camera.'

'Kurt Austin, American.'

'Joe Zavala, American.'

Silence followed.

'Hiram would love this,' Joe whispered. 'He and Max could double-date out here.'

Hiram Yaeger was NUMA's resident computer genius. He'd designed some of the most advanced computer systems the world had ever seen. Max was his finest creation. Built on the fastest processors and operated by special programming Hiram had created himself, Max was a unique machine with true artificial intelligence, an active mind and even a sense of humor.

A pleasant chime sounded and the door to the right of them opened. 'Assistant Superintendent Nagano has confirmed your appointment. Please enter.'

Kurt and Joe walked up three steps and found themselves in a bustling room filled with men and women watching screens and tapping away at computer consoles. The design was open and modern. Stainless steel accents and pinpoint lighting had been used to great effect. Kurt saw no dirt or grime, no tattered mug books, grimy fingerprint stations or crowded holding cells. Nor did he see any criminals. Which wasn't a surprise, since Japan's crime rate was the lowest in the industrialized world. Partly because the nation was so wealthy, partly due to effective policing, but mostly because the collective Japanese sense of order remained a pervasive influence.

Aside from a few glances, the staff ignored them until a Japanese man wearing black slacks, a crisp white shirt and a thin gray tie came over to meet them.

Tall, a highly trained triathlete, the man had a wide face, with a distinct line around his mouth and a cleft in his chin. His hair was short, thick and black.

'I'm Superintendent Nagano,' the man said.

Kurt bowed slightly, but Nagano shook his hand instead. His grip was solid steel.

'It is an honor to meet both of you,' Nagano replied. 'Please, follow me.'

He led them back to a small office that was modern to a fault. At his urging, Kurt and Joe sat down.

'This is easily the finest police station I've ever been in,' Joe said.

'No, no,' Nagano replied. 'It requires much work to bring it up to standards. But we're doing the best we can.'

Joe looked around, searching for a flaw. Kurt would explain later that the Japanese sense of humility required they not take a compliment unless they had achieved perfection.

That said, Joe wasn't wrong. The building was a work of art, the interior a high-tech wonderland. Every surface was polished and gleaming; even the rack of weapons they'd passed as they neared Nagano's office had been lit like a display case at an upscale gun show.

'Your foyer was interesting,' Kurt said. 'Wouldn't it be easier to have a receptionist or a duty officer?'

'Easier, perhaps,' Nagano said, 'but a waste of manpower. As you probably know, Japan's population is shrinking. By automating the arrival phase, we avoid wasting an officer's time that can be better spent elsewhere.'

'What about the *ritsuban*?'

Nagano shrugged at the contradiction. 'That falls under the category of crime prevention,' he said, 'though many stations are looking to end the practice or replace the guard with an automated mannequin.'

'And the world will be all the poorer for it,' Kurt said.

'At least your automated receptionist spoke different languages,' Joe said, still trying to be complimentary.

'A necessity,' the superintendent replied. 'As everyone knows, most of the crime in Japan is caused by foreigners.'

Kurt noticed the slightest hint of a smile on Nagano's face. An inside joke, most likely.

Joe didn't have an answer for that. 'Anyway,' he said finally, 'it's a pleasure to be here.'

'Thank you,' Nagano replied. 'Now I must ask you to leave immediately.'

'Excuse me?' Kurt replied.

'You must leave Japan on the first flight out,' Nagano insisted. 'We will escort you and your friends to the airport.'

'Are you deporting us?' Kurt asked.

'It's for your own safety,' Nagano said. 'We've identified the men who attacked your group last night. They were once Yakuza hit men. Heavies and assassins.'

After hearing Joe's description of the man who'd been mauled by the dragon, Kurt was not surprised. He knew the Yakuza favored wild tattoos. But he posed the obvious question. 'Why would the Yakuza be interested in the research of an eccentric scientist?'

'Former Yakuza,' Nagano reiterated. 'A breakaway group.'

'In other words,' Kurt said, 'hired guns.'

Nagano nodded. 'Once, in our past there were *ronin*. That is the name for a Samurai without a lord. They lived as nomads. As warriors for hire. These men are similar. They are killers without a master, working for whom they please. They were once bonded to particular Yakuza organizations, but years ago we managed to break up many of the criminal networks. The leaders were sent to prison or killed, but the lower-level members were only scattered and left to their own devices. Now they answer to no one but themselves. In many ways, they're more dangerous now than before.'

'Any idea who they're working for?'

Nagano shook his head. 'No doubt, they were hired for a rather large fee; their number and the brazen method of attack suggest that much. But who paid them and why . . . we haven't the slightest lead.'

Kurt knew it had something to do with the East China Sea and the disturbance that Kenzo had detected there, but without more information, guessing was pointless.

'The fact of the matter is,' Nagano continued, 'you and your friends thwarted the attack. Retribution can be expected.'

'From whoever paid these *ronin*,' Joe said.

'Or from the hit men themselves,' Nagano said. 'You've embarrassed them. Shamed them. They will want to save face.'

'So much for foreigners committing all the crimes in Japan,' Kurt said.

'Sadly, yes.'

Nagano pushed a file folder toward Joe. 'You're the only person who got a close look at any of them. It would help us if you could look at these pictures.'

Joe took the file folder and opened it up. Instead of mug shots or surveillance photos, he saw colorful designs drawn on the outline of a man's back and shoulders.

'Yakuza are known for extensively inking their skin,' Nagano said. 'Certain groups use specific designs like a brand. Do you recognize any of these?'

Kurt looked over Joe's shoulder at the designs. Each tattoo was intricate and different. Some had wings and dragons, others fire and skulls. One was kaleidoscopes of color and bladed weapons.

'Not this one,' Joe said, discarding the first sheet of paper. 'Or these.'

He leafed through several additional pages and then stopped. 'This is the pattern,' he said. 'A perfect match for the guy who escaped the dragon pit. Minus a good chunk of skin now.'

Nagano took the paper. 'As I thought,' he said. 'Ushi-Oni: the Demon.'

'The Demon?' Joe asked.

'His real name is unknown,' Nagano said. 'In our mythology, the word *oni* means *demon*. An Ushi-Oni is a particular monster with the head of a bull and fearsome horns. When he first began killing for hire, this man would draw a symbol representing that particular monster using the victim's blood. Unlike most in the syndicates, he actually takes pleasure in killing. Pleasure and large sums of cash.'

'Fantastic,' Kurt said. 'Now that you know who he is, you can go round him up and we won't have to leave.'

Nagano put the drawing aside. 'I wish it were that simple. These men are whispers on the wind. Impossible to track, let alone capture. We have been chasing Ushi-Oni for years.'

'Komodo dragons are poisonous,' Joe said. 'Considering the bite this guy took, I'd say a hospital or the morgue would be his next stop.'

'The Komodo is poisonous,' Nagano agreed, 'but we spoke to an expert this morning. We've been told the lizard does not inject its venom with every bite. A slashing attack as you saw would not likely be fatal.'

'What about the Komodo dragon's reputation for bad oral hygiene?' Kurt said. 'As I recall, they have countless strains of bacteria on their teeth.'

'Yes,' Nagano said, 'and most likely Ushi-Oni is battling infection and fever. But given high doses of antibiotics, he would probably survive. Which means you and your friends remain in danger, as I explained to begin with.'

Kurt sat back. The issue had an obvious solution. One

Nagano probably had in mind or he wouldn't have asked them to come down to the station. 'The danger would be eliminated if we helped you put him away.'

Nagano did not immediately reply.

'That's why you had us take such an odd route to the station,' Kurt said. 'To make sure we weren't followed.'

The superintendent offered a slight bow. 'You're very astute. And, fortunately, you weren't. At least not by anyone but my most trusted officers.'

'So let us help you,' Kurt said.

'And how do you propose to do that?'

It was obvious to Kurt. 'As you pointed out, this was a big operation. Several boats. A least a dozen men and plenty of weapons, including incendiary grenades. A job like this would cost a small fortune. And despite the saying there's no such thing as honor among thieves, criminals don't trust criminals. Which means no one gets paid till the job is done. At least not the full price.'

Nagano's face tightened in thought, the line around his mouth deepened. 'You're suggesting we look for a payoff.'

Kurt leaned back in his chair. 'Something I'm sure you've already considered.'

'Of course we have,' Nagano said, his mind obviously running the scenario. 'But how are you able to help?'

'Move Kenzo and the other survivors to a safe house. Announce to the media that he's died from his injuries. You could mention that two or three of the Americans have also died and that the others are in critical condition. No need to give out names. The numbers will suffice.'

'And then?'

'I can't say for certain,' Kurt insisted, 'but if I was a former Yakuza hit man, nursing a Komodo dragon bite and pumping high-powered antibiotics into my arm every four hours, I'd demand the rest of my payment.'

Nagano finished the thought. 'And with the balance of payments due, the Demon will have to come out of hiding to collect.'

'Exactly,' Kurt said.

'What if they pay by check,' Joe suggested, only half joking, 'or electronically?'

'Too large a sum,' Nagano said. 'They would never risk a government clearinghouse intercepting their money and tracing it. These types of things are done in person. It will happen somewhere very public to ensure that neither side commits an act of violence. That is the way.'

Kurt finished the idea. 'If you can find out where that transfer will happen, we'd be glad to show up, point out the Demon and leave the rest to you.'

Nagano looked to Joe. He was the one who'd seen him up close.

'Absolutely,' Joe said. 'It would be a pleasure.'

Nagano weighed the offer silently. Finally, he nodded. 'Reputations for bravery precede you both. Your actions last night live up to them.'

'Not bravery,' Kurt said. 'Just doing what anyone would, given the situation.'

'You deflect a compliment well,' Nagano replied. 'How very Japanese. Nevertheless, despite your bravery, I struggle to find a reason you would deliberately put yourselves at risk this way. I hope it's more than just bravado.'

'For starters, we don't take kindly to being attacked,' Kurt began. 'There's also the possibility that our arrival triggered this. You want the Demon for your reasons. We want to know who paid him and why.'

'You mean your government wants to know.'

'That, too.'

Nagano was an old hand. He took the measure of people quickly. He understood Kurt and Joe. He felt they were cut from the same cloth as he. Tireless government servants who preferred to get things done rather than wait for the bureaucracy to grind to life.

The superintendent straightened some papers on his desk. 'Agreed,' he said. 'But I must inform you it won't be all falsehoods. Unfortunately, Kenzo Fujihara died this morning without ever regaining consciousness. His lungs were burned beyond repair.'

Kurt set his jaw. He'd been expecting that.

'Damn,' Joe whispered.

Kurt looked from Joe to Nagano. 'Can you put the rest of his people somewhere safe in case this Demon of yours decides he hasn't finished the job?'

'I already have,' Nagano said. 'There is one fly in the ointment, as you Americans like to say.'

'What's that?'

'Kenzo's man-at-arms. Or, more precisely, his woman-at-arms.'

'Akiko,' Joe said, perking up. 'I was hoping we'd see her again. Is she here?'

'That's just it,' Nagano explained. 'She's vanished. She was at Kenzo's bedside when he passed away. She seemed particularly grief-stricken, but she left before we could get a statement. That seemed suspicious, so we took her fingerprints off of the weapon she carried. And, as it turns out, Akiko has a long criminal record, several outstanding warrants and links to the Yakuza in Tokyo.'

'And she seemed like such a nice girl,' Joe said. 'Do you think she was involved?'

'We can't rule it out,' Nagano said.

'I can rule it out,' Kurt said. 'Not the way she fought for Kenzo. She took two bullets that would have killed her if she wasn't wearing a vest.'

'I can only tell you what the record shows,' Nagano explained. 'She's something of a ghost herself. She grew up orphaned. A street urchin who learned to survive by breaking the rules. Unfortunately, that type of life often leads to the criminal underworld.'

'Or to a new life for the strong.'

'Perhaps,' Nagano said, then added sternly, 'If she contacts you, I expect to be told.'

'She won't contact us,' Kurt said. 'She wouldn't have disappeared if she were going to do that. But if I'm wrong and she does reach out, you'll hear about it. You have my word.'

'Very well,' Nagano said. 'I'll put the word out to my informants. If fortune is with us, something will turn up and we'll both get what we're after.'

12

Southwest of Tokyo

The white shape flashed across the countryside in a howling blur. It entered a tunnel, moving like a gigantic snake. It came out the other side preceded by an Earth-bound thunderclap, known as a tunnel boom.

Gamay sat by a window in the eighth car of a twelve-car train. Despite the speed and noise outside, the cabin was quiet and the ride exceedingly smooth.

'I'm glad to be getting out of Tokyo,' she said. 'Especially after what Kurt told us.'

Sitting next to her, Paul craned his neck around to see if anyone was in earshot. The Tokaido Shinkansen rail line was the original bullet train route in Japan. And though it was the most heavily used high-speed rail line in the world, the premium car, in the off-hours express, had plenty of unfilled seats to offer.

'Couldn't agree more,' he replied. 'On the other hand, Rudi wasn't joking when he said getting past the Chinese patrols would be almost impossible. Look at this.'

Paul had a notebook computer open on the tray table in front of him. He'd spent half the ride studying the information Rudi sent. He turned it her way.

Gamay adjusted the angle of the screen and found

herself looking at a map of the East China Sea. Curving lines looped here and there, representing the timing and routes of Chinese naval vessels; broad swaths were marked in gray, indicating the known flight paths taken by Chinese antisubmarine aircraft, while a row of overlapping circles tinted red told them there were no breaks to exploit in the line of sonar buoys.

'They're not messing around,' she said.

'This level of security confirms that they're hiding something down there,' Paul replied. 'But trying to sneak past all of that is a wasted effort. We might as well send them an email announcing our arrival and make our own reservations at the Shanghai jail.'

'Much as I'd like to disagree with you . . .' she began.

Her voice trailed off. She wondered if there was another way. Maybe they didn't have to cross from Japan. Maybe they could come in from the south. She expanded the map and discovered additional naval patrols in that direction. The Chinese had left nothing to chance. Then she noticed something else. 'What about the shipping lane?'

'What about it?'

'Shanghai is one of the busiest ports in Asia. If we could book passage aboard a freighter . . .'

'And then jump overboard for a leisurely swim when we're halfway there?'

'Not us personally,' she replied. 'But suppose we dropped something overboard. Something with cameras, sonar and a remote hookup that could be controlled from the ship.'

Paul brightened noticeably. 'We'd have to leave it down there.'

'A small price to pay,' she replied.

'Good point,' Paul said. 'But we still have the matter of getting passage on a freighter to China at the last minute – which might raise a few eyebrows – and then sneaking a rather bulky ROV on board without anyone checking our luggage. Not to mention dropping it over the side without the crew getting suspicious.'

'Not if we're booking passage on the Osaka-to-Shanghai ferry.'

She turned the computer his way, the dashed line of the shipping route highlighted on the screen. 'If this is correct, the ferry travels within five miles of the target area.'

'That solves the first problem,' Paul said. 'What about the ROV?'

Gamay drummed her fingers. 'I'm still working on that.'

A grin crossed Paul's face. 'I think I have the answer,' Paul said. 'When does that ferry leave?'

Gamay linked up to the internet and checked the schedule. 'It's twice weekly. The next run departs at noon tomorrow.'

'I think that will give us just enough time,' Paul said.

'For what?'

'You ever hear of the *Remora*?'

'The fish?' she replied. 'Yes, I'm well aware of it.'

'Not the fish,' Paul said. 'The Joe Zavala mechanical creation inspired by the fish. One of our newest ROVs.'

Gamay shook her head. She had a hard time keeping up with Joe's unending line of aquatic machines, but, based on the name, she could imagine how this one worked. 'The *Remora*. Sounds interesting.'

'Last I heard, it was being tested in Hawaii,' Paul said. 'If they haven't boxed it up and shipped it back stateside, Rudi can send it to us on the next flight. That should give us just enough time to buy our tickets and attach our little stowaway.'

13

Hashima Island,
off the Coast of Nagasaki

The room was sterile, cold and well lit. At the center, a headless body lay on a metal table.

'Male, six feet tall,' a Chinese technician said. The technician wore a white lab coat, glasses and sported a shaved head. His name was Gao-zhin, but he went by Gao. He was Walter Han's most accomplished engineer. 'Skin tone: Caucasian,' Gao added. 'Obviously, we have no face or hair yet.'

Walter Han crouched to inspect the body. An odor of burned plastic came off the skin, which sported an oily appearance. 'You need to run the production again,' he said. 'There are imperfections. The wrong kind of imperfections.'

Gao didn't argue. He wouldn't, of course, since he worked for Han, but the look on his face suggested he wasn't happy. 'The body panels are very complex,' he insisted. 'They have to move and flex like true skin and muscle. Even with the 3-D printing process and the new polymers, it's very difficult to achieve a realistic, lifelike surface.'

'Levels of difficulty do not concern me,' Han said. 'A blind man could tell that this "skin" is artificial. The smell alone would give it away. But should one get close enough to actually touch it, he would feel that the arms, legs and torso are hairless. That the body has not a single mole, freckle or scar.'

'We hadn't thought about that,' Gao said.

'Think about it now,' Han ordered. 'Redesign the skin. Imagine it as an artist would. It should not be perfect; it should have creases where the elbow folds, occasional marks from age or damage. And, unless we're modeling someone with a rare genetic condition, the body should have follicles.'

Gao nodded, making notes. 'I understand, we will –'

'And while you're at it, do something about the scent. It smells like a tire store in here.'

Gao looked appropriately cowed. 'Yes, sir. We'll get to work immediately.'

'Good,' Han said. 'What about scalability? Can we produce different body sizes and shapes?'

'The layers of artificial skin and muscle rest on an inner frame,' Gao explained. 'Unlike the factory models, these frames can be adjusted for any height and weight combination, ranging from four feet eight inches, up to seven feet tall. Once the frame is built, we use the 3-D printing process to make the body panels. We can even use one chassis repeatedly. Bringing it in for adjustments and new body panels, changing the head and the length of the limbs and torso.'

'Excellent,' Han said. 'Get to work. I'll be back tomorrow to check on the improvements.'

Satisfied with Gao's newfound sense of urgency, Han

moved to the door, pulled it open and walked through. In one quick step, he went from the bright confines of the laboratory, with its smooth, clean walls, to a rough-cut tunnel carved from dirty stone.

The passageway was dark, lit only by a few harsh LEDs along one wall. They gave off a pure white glow, but the dingy walls were wet with condensation and they drank the light where it landed.

Han moved slowly to avoid striking his head on a low point or tripping over a spot of uneven ground. He traveled onward and upward, passing through larger man-made chambers and then stepping out into an open area filled with natural light.

He emerged from the tunnel not in the outside world but in a vast, empty warehouse. Corrugated metal walls rose up around him. Dusky light streamed in through windows high above – half of them cracked and broken, the rest covered with years of caked-on grime. A stack of old wooden pilings lay unused in one section while a rusted three-wheeled bicycle that obviously hadn't moved in years sat abandoned in another.

His arrival startled two pigeons. They launched themselves from the rafters high above, the sound of their flapping wings strangely loud in the open room. Han watched them fly around in a circle and settle onto a new perch.

According to the technicians, the birds had found their way in several days ago and had yet to find their way out. Han felt the same way about the mission he had undertaken. At each turn, it seemed more like a self-created trap.

He'd jumped at the chance to act as Wen's vanguard, but things had grown instantly more complicated.

As he made his way toward the exit, his phone buzzed. He reached into his jacket pocket and pulled the slim black device out. No number appeared on the screen, just a code word indicating it was an encrypted call from another phone on his personal network.

He pressed the green button and took the call.

'Where have you been?' a voice asked him bluntly. 'I've called you ten times this morning.'

The Demon doesn't sound quite himself, Han thought. 'My whereabouts are none of your concern. Why are you calling me?'

'To get what you owe me.'

'You know the deal,' Han said. 'First, I have to confirm that your effort was successful. Until then . . .'

'I'm sending you a link,' Ushi-Oni said. 'It will tell you what you need to know.'

The phone chirped as the link arrived. Han held the phone out to watch. It was a Japanese news report, indicating that the death toll from the blaze at the castle was now up to eleven, including three of the four Americans and the castle's owner, Kenzo. Several others were still in critical condition and not expected to survive.

On the video, the reporter was standing outside the hospital, explaining that the cause of the fire was under investigation but that there was little information to go on.

'You should pay me extra for such a job.' Ushi-Oni wheezed as he spoke and went into a short coughing fit as soon as he finished.

'Are you ill?' Han asked.

'I was injured,' Ushi-Oni said. 'But I've done my job. Now it's your turn. I want my money.'

Han wondered how badly the Demon was hurt. Perhaps the fumes had burned his lungs as well. 'You'll be paid what I promised. But I'll have to double-check this information.'

'Do whatever you have to,' Ushi-Oni said. 'But I'm not waiting. There were survivors. I need to disappear in case the truth comes out. I want that money tonight.'

'I have other things to do,' Han said.

'Don't think you can cheat me,' the Demon snapped. 'Better men than you have died trying.'

The last thing Han wanted on his hands was an angry, jaded assassin. The money itself was meaningless but the principle mattered. 'I'll pay you tonight. I may even have another job for you – if you're up to it.'

Silence for a second, then, 'Payment first. After that, we can talk.'

'Of course,' Han said. 'I'll send you a location where the money will be distributed. You'll have to dress for the occasion.'

'I'm not coming to you.'

'Neutral ground,' Han insisted. 'The Sento. Trust me, you'll see plenty of your old friends there.'

Sento was a form of the verb meaning *to fight*. But it was also the name of an illegal club and gambling palace. Casinos weren't allowed in Japan. That didn't mean they were nonexistent.

'Fine,' Ushi-Oni said. 'I'll meet you there. No tricks.'

Han wouldn't need any. The Sento was an upscale place, hidden on the outskirts of Tokyo. It was frequented by high rollers, the young rich who wanted a thrill, criminals who exuded class and the occasional politician.

It was run by one of the prominent Yakuza cartels and there would certainly be other gangsters among the crowd, but none of them would have any connection to or love lost for Ushi-Oni. Their only concern was that nothing disrupt their business and, to that end, they employed a large force of armed men and other security measures.

All who entered were searched for weapons and wires. In Han's opinion, that made it the safest place on the entire island to finish his business with the Demon.

14

Osaka Bay

Paul stared straight ahead. Clad in a black wetsuit and a full-face helmet, he gripped the frame of the *Remora* and held tight. It felt like he was riding a toboggan down a snow-covered mountain in a stiff headwind. His hands were clenched around the two metal bars that extended from the body of the machine. His feet were wedged into a space just ahead of the propulsion duct. The propeller, shrouded by a circular fairing, lay just beyond.

'Keep the speed down,' Paul said, speaking into the microphone in his helmet. 'One slip and I'll be looking for new toes.'

The signal was relayed to the surface where a repeater sent it on to Gamay, who was controlling the ROV from a boat a hundred yards off. Her reply came over the intercom with a bit of interference. 'You insisted on going down there.'

'Next time, I'll let you win that argument.'

Keeping himself close to the body of the ROV, Paul risked a glance to the side. Off in the distance, through the murky waters of Osaka Bay, he could just make out the wake of Gamay's boat: a white slash against a dark background.

Though he was only traveling at a depth of sixty feet, the surface was a dim shadow above him. Heavy ship traffic churned up sediment in the harbor, while runoff from the urban areas and industrial pollution caused algae to bloom and chased off the fish that ate it.

'I can barely see a thing,' he said. 'How far out are we?'

'Quarter mile to go,' she said. 'I'll have to start veering away from the ferry in a moment. But I'll lead you right toward the center of the hull. Let me know as soon as you catch sight of it. From that point on, I'll adjust course based on your instructions.'

'You mean, I get to tell you how to drive?' Paul asked. 'This is a first.'

'Don't get used to it,' she replied. 'Turning now. You should see the hull any minute.'

Braced against the buffeting force of the water and counting off the seconds, Paul kept his head up and eyes forward. While he saw nothing but a gray-green background, there was plenty to hear: the high-pitched electric whine of the *Remora*'s battery-powered propeller, the fading buzz of Gamay's boat as it moved farther away and a low hum that came from directly in front of him.

'I can hear the ferry's engines,' he said.

'Can you see it?'

'Not yet,' he replied. 'But it's suddenly obvious to me why dolphins developed sonar.'

'Sound works much better down there,' she replied. 'Let me know when you see something. I'm dialing back your speed.'

Paul felt the ROV slow, and though they were doing only a couple of knots to begin with, it significantly reduced the strain on his arms.

He caught sight of a shape up ahead. 'I see it,' he said. 'Looks like they're dumping bilgewater. Steer me ten degrees to the left, would you? I'd rather not go directly under that.'

The shrouded propeller deflected to the side and the tadpole-shaped ROV turned. 'Perfect,' Paul said. 'Straight ahead now for twenty seconds. Then bring me up to a depth of thirty feet and cut the throttle.'

The hull of the ferry came into focus. The ship was a twenty-year veteran of channel crossings. Its metal plating was painted red beneath the waterline, but the rust and a coating of marine growth gave it a mottled color. It drew sixteen feet of water and Paul passed beneath the outside edge with plenty of headroom above him.

'Cut the throttle,' he said.

The motor shut down right on cue and Paul and the *Remora* coasted to a stop, dead center beneath the keel of the ship.

Paul switched on a diving light. 'And now for the manual portion of our endeavor.'

With a tether from the *Remora* attached to his ankle, Paul released his grip on the ROV and swam upward toward the overhanging hull. Diving beneath a large ship was an interesting experience, one Paul hadn't had before. Reaching out to the hull felt as if he was touching the bottom of a cloud.

'Contact,' he said.

'How's it feel to have thirty thousand tons floating over your head?' Gamay asked.

'Makes me thankful for the laws of buoyancy. I'd be very upset if they were repealed in the next ten minutes.'

Moving along the hull, Paul found the spot he was looking for. A section near the bow that the engineers at NUMA insisted would have the lowest amount of dynamic pressure once the ferry began to move. 'I've found the attachment site.'

'How's it look?' Gamay asked.

'It's a full-on barnacle convention,' Paul said. 'Apparently, the Shanghai Ferry Company doesn't care to defoul their ships.'

This layer of marine life was the reason for Paul's ride on the *Remora*. The ROV was designed to connect magnetically to the bottom of any steel-hulled vessel, but it couldn't attach securely through a layer of hard-shelled barnacles. To ensure that it stayed in place until they were ready to use it, Paul would have to scrape a section of the hull clean.

To do so required a device known as a needle scaler. The electrically powered appliance was shaped like an assault rifle, complete with a shoulder stock, a vertical handgrip and a long barrel that ended in a titanium chisel. Once Paul activated the scaler, the chisel would vibrate back and forth at high speed. Paul would be the manpower behind it, pushing the blade through the barnacles, scraping them away and revealing smooth metal beneath.

'Here goes,' he said.

He switched the unit on and it shuddered to life. Making sure he had good contact, Paul pressed the blade against the hull and shoved it forward. He had to kick with his legs to keep from being pushed back, but the scaler worked like magic and the barnacles fell away one strip at a time.

Gamay began talking. 'How thick are the layers?'

'At least four inches deep,' Paul said.

'It's amazing how fast marine growth appears on a ship,' she told him. 'Did you know that newly launched vessels have a film of microbes on them within twenty-four hours of going into the water?'

'Did not know that,' Paul said. 'Trust me, these are not microbes.'

As Paul worked, Gamay launched into a soliloquy on the subject of barnacles. She spoke about the Romans using lead sheets to protect their boats from woodworms and the British putting copper on the hulls of their sailing fleet. She said something about tin being a great defense against marine growth, but, unfortunately, that was because it releases poison into the water at an alarming rate.

Paul wasn't really paying attention. He was concentrating on keeping the chisel at the proper angle and forcing it through the colony of hard-shelled organisms. He cleared a two-foot-by-two-foot patch in one spot, a smaller section ten feet behind the first and, finally, a third spot just ahead of the main one.

By the time he finished, he was getting quite good at the task.

'. . . In fact, the process of marine fouling is really quite fascinating,' Gamay finished.

'I'm sure it is,' Paul said, certain that he couldn't repeat a third of what she'd said. 'And the defouling process is surprisingly gratifying. Like using a snowblower on the sidewalk back in Maine.'

'Are you finished already?'

'All set.' He clipped the scaler to his belt. 'I'm going to maneuver the *Remora* into position. Stand by to activate magnets.'

Manually guiding the *Remora* in the still waters of the harbor was another athletic endeavor. The ROV was set to zero buoyancy, which meant it weighed nothing, but it still had enough inertia that Paul was breathing hard by the time he'd pushed, pulled and otherwise manhandled the ROV into place.

'Activate the main magnet.'

Holding the *Remora* steady, he felt a buzz, and then a solid clunk, as it pulled itself up a few inches and attached itself to the hull. The main magnet was a large circular patch on the top of the *Remora*'s head, just like the suction cup on the actual fish.

'Activate the other two,' Paul called out.

The fore and aft magnets powered up and connected, locking the ROV in place. Paul tested it by grabbing onto the rigging, placing his feet against the ship's hull and pulling with all his might. The ROV didn't budge.

Letting go, he drifted away from the hull. 'One large metal barnacle attached where the others were scraped off,' he said. 'Heading your way.'

'Fantastic,' Gamay said. 'I'm two hundred yards off the port beam. Directly across from you. Swim perpendicular to the hull and you'll find me without any problem. Better not dawdle, though, we still have a ferry to catch.'

15

Outskirts of Tokyo Metro Area

The sun had already dropped below the horizon when the gleaming Bentley Mulsanne left the highway and drove onto a narrow road that led out of Tokyo and into the countryside.

An ultra-luxe sedan, with five hundred horsepower, the Mulsanne was the latest flagship from the famed British automaker. It was large, especially by Japanese standards, with a bulky shape, softened by streamlined edges. The design conveyed a sense of speed, power and the possibility that DNA from an Abrams battle tank was hidden beneath all the luxurious touches.

Kurt and Joe sat in the back of the three-hundred-thousand-dollar car.

'My first house was smaller than this,' Kurt said, admiring the spacious cabin.

'Probably cost a lot less, too,' Joe added.

The ride was crisp, smooth and silent enough to be a sensory deprivation chamber. The cabin was appointed with cream-colored leather, offset by mahogany trim; the seats were perfectly designed to cradle the occupants. When Kurt tilted his seat back, a footrest extended from below, supporting his legs.

Joe copied him, putting his hands behind his head for good measure. 'Too bad we only travel like this when we're undercover and headed toward our probable doom.'

Superintendent Nagano had learned from an informant that a large payoff was about to take place within the confines of an illegal casino on the outskirts of Tokyo. His informant wasn't sure if the payment would go to Ushi-Oni or not, but the timing and the location were correct.

Using other contacts, he'd arranged for Kurt and Joe to enter the casino, posing as wealthy Americans. That was the easy part. The hard part would come when they tried to place a tracking device on the Demon if they saw him.

'If anyone gets suspicious, we won't make it out of there alive,' Kurt warned.

'At least we'll look good in our caskets,' Joe said.

Kurt laughed at that. Joe was dressed in a sharply cut Armani suit. It had narrow lapels, was made of silk and fit his athletic build perfectly. Beneath the crisp black jacket, he wore a maroon dress shirt. And, for added effect, he'd shaved three days of stubble into a thin Vandyke beard. It gave him a slightly devilish look.

'If you end up in the netherworld, they're going to mistake you for management.'

'All part of my plan,' Joe said, 'just in case I haven't been as good as I think I have. You, on the other hand, are going to be mistaken for the maître d'.'

Kurt smiled and took the comment without rebuttal. He was dressed in a double-breasted white dinner jacket with a silk shawl collar, a crisp white shirt and a trim bow tie. Shades of Bogart in *Casablanca*.

Unlike Joe, he was clean-shaven, though he'd let his sideburns grow down a bit and had dyed his silver hair black to make it less likely he'd be recognized. 'How far to the Sento?'

Superintendent Nagano, dressed as a chauffeur, glanced back at them from the driver's seat. 'No more than five minutes. Enough time for me to ask once again whether you want to risk this?'

'It's the only way,' Kurt said.

Joe nodded his agreement.

Nagano turned his gaze back to the road ahead. 'You understand once you're inside, I cannot assist you. For obvious reasons, the police cannot raid this establishment without causing a bloodbath.'

'I'm not expecting any violence,' Kurt said. 'If the place is run as tightly as you suggest, Ushi-Oni won't be armed.'

'He can kill without firearms or knives,' Nagano said. 'He can kill with his bare hands or with a hundred different everyday objects. Death is an art form to him. Be extremely careful that he doesn't see you place the tracking device.'

Kurt nodded. In his pocket were two coins; inside each lay a sophisticated beacon. Joe was carrying two similar coins. The plan was to slip one into the pocket of the Demon and another into the pocket of whoever paid him off, track them, once they left the building, and take them down outside the gambling palace. Whoever found themselves in closest proximity to the targets would make the attempt. Knowing that Ushi-Oni had fought Joe face-to-face already and might easily recognize him, Kurt intended to make sure he would get there first.

'We'll be careful,' Kurt said. 'Anything else we should know?'

'Only that things should go smoothly up front,' Nagano said. 'My informant has placed you on the list. They will know Joe as a boxing promoter from Las Vegas. You are listed as a hedge fund manager with ties to Joe's company. Websites, addresses and other background details have been arranged just in case anyone checks. I suspect the owners will be interested in getting you both to the tables. Reputations for betting and losing large sums have been established.'

'At least that part is accurate,' Kurt joked. He felt the billfold in his pocket. They each carried over a million yen, a little more than ten thousand dollars, but that was just for starters. Once they burned through their cash, the Sento's staff would access accounts set up in their names and give them markers for ten times that amount.

'Where are we most likely to find Ushi-Oni?' Kurt asked.

'Impossible to say. But he's the type that appreciates brutality. Look for him in the viewing stands of the combat arena.'

'Boxing isn't necessary brutality,' Joe pointed out.

'There will be only one boxing match,' Nagano said. 'Five rounds. It's just a prelude. Bloodier combat will follow. I regret that you might see someone die on the floor in there. You will have to allow it or your cover will be destroyed.'

'Fights to the death?' Kurt said.

'Not necessarily,' Nagano told them, 'but using weapons that can easily kill. Knives, swords, chains. Deadly combat, most often performed by those in the organization who have disgraced themselves. It is a chance for them to prove themselves worthy. But for those who fail . . . Let me just say, what you're about to witness isn't for the faint of heart.'

They spent the next two minutes in silence, driving the last quarter mile beside a twelve-foot fence of iron bars that sprouted from a formidable brick wall. Finally, they arrived at a massive front gate.

Armed men dressed in suits checked their credentials, searched beneath the car with mirrors and led two dogs around the outside to sniff for explosives. When the car was cleared, they were allowed to pull through.

A long driveway led up through ornate gardens. Brightly flowering shrubs, ornamental lanterns and cherry trees filled with blossoms lined the path; as they neared the building, they drove across a decorative wooden bridge that spanned a tranquil koi pond.

The traditional cues vanished as they reached the main building, which was of modern design with a façade made up of tinted glass. It rose two stories and was capped by a layer of smooth concrete. There was a definite curve to the structure and both sides vanished into hills covered in thick grass.

'Postmodern bomb shelter,' Kurt said, voicing the first thought that came to mind.

'More like an ultra-efficient building designed to take advantage of the Earth's temperature-regulating properties,' Joe said.

'You are an optimist,' Kurt said.

'What you're looking at is only the top level,' Nagano said. 'This structure is designed like a stadium, circular and with a hollow interior, but instead of rising above ground, it punches down into it.'

Kurt had seen aerial photos taken before the building was finished. Behind the hills lay a natural depression. The hills and the man-made structure enclosed it and covered it.

While it was technically a hotel, lodging was offered only on the upper level. Farther down, one could find the darker parts of the operation: gambling, prostitution and drugs. At the bottom lay the combat arena that acted as the main attraction, visible through glass walls from everywhere else in the building.

The Bentley slowed as they approached the entry door. A valet walked up to them, but Nagano waved him off and parked just beyond the entry.

'Wish us good luck,' Kurt said.

'You have the coins for that,' Nagano replied, as he opened the door.

Kurt stepped from the car, buttoned his jacket and waited for Joe. As Nagano got back in the car and drove off, they walked up the steps and into a lobby as elegant as that in any five-star hotel.

Marble floors, crystal chandeliers and modern furniture were arranged in the open space that curved around in both directions. A pianist, with a violinist accompanying him, played quietly in one section of the lobby, while tall women in daring dresses moved here and there carrying silver trays covered with champagne flutes.

'Nice place,' Kurt said. 'Can't believe you're my date this evening.'

Joe adjusted his cuffs. 'How do you think I feel?'

They were ushered through security, where their phones were confiscated and placed in small lockers. Each of them was given a key.

A body scan came next, using a wand similar to those at the airport. It beeped repeatedly at Kurt's side. He pulled out the transmitters, holding them out for the security guard to see.

The man grinned. The five-yen coin, with its distinctive yellowish tint and small hole in the center, was considered good luck all across Japan. The guard had seen these coins before; many gamblers carried them.

'For luck,' Kurt said, offering one to the guard. The man refused and the coins went back into Kurt's pocket.

Finished with the security check, Kurt made a straight line to the nearest hostess. He took a champagne glass from the tray, smiled at the woman and glanced around.

Joe met him a moment later. 'Pretty good crowd.'

'I heard the Colosseum used to pack them in, too.'

'Split up?'

Kurt nodded. 'I'll go this way,' he said, pointing. 'Let's make a few laps and check out the levels. Look for exits in case we need them. If we don't bump into each other in an hour, let's meet back here by the piano. Feel free to blow through some of that money. The faster we go into debt, the quicker we'll get front-row seats to the fight.'

Joe scanned the crowd. 'I think I'll mingle as I toss the cash around. These look like the type of women who appreciate a large expense account.'

Kurt tipped his glass to Joe and let him wander. After

a final scan of the lobby, he turned in the other direction. Kurt moved slowly, without any sign of haste, one hand holding the champagne flute, the other in his pocket, fingers on the lucky coins.

Joe wandered the ring-shaped building, studying the faces that passed while he pretended to look at the art on the walls. Though he'd given Kurt the best description he could, Joe was the only one who'd seen Ushi-Oni up close and that meant Joe was far more likely to spot the man they were looking for than Kurt.

He made a circuit of the upper level, moved to the inner wall and gazed through the floor-to-ceiling glass. Down below, at least four stories beneath him, lay the combat arena. Circular instead of square, it was partially obscured by a bank of floodlights suspended from a metal rigging secured to the walls by guide wires and a catwalk.

The lights were off at the moment and the arena was empty – as were the seats around it. For the time being, he'd have to look elsewhere for Ushi-Oni.

Kurt was on his second glass of champagne by the time he reached the casino level. He'd yet to spot anything resembling a feverish hit man nor had he spent a single yen of the money given to him by the Japanese Federal Police. It was time to change that.

He passed several high-stakes blackjack tables, looked in on a craps game, where the players were stacked three deep, and then wandered through an aisle packed with old-fashioned machines that were clanking and clunking as heavy silver balls bounced around inside them and neon flashed and flickered in pulsating frenzy.

Patrons stared at the machines as if the mysteries of the universe would be found within, taking no notice of Kurt as he examined their faces.

'Pachinko?' a voice suggested.

Kurt turned. A seductively dressed hostess was motioning toward an open machine.

'*Arigato,*' Kurt said. 'Not right now.'

He passed through the pachinko hall and took a seat at one of the pai gow poker tables. Passing over his million yen, he was given a stack of clear chips and slid most of them into place right off the bat. The cards came out with incredible speed.

'Nine,' the dealer said, looking at Kurt. A few more cards were dealt and she pushed a stack of chips next to his.

Kurt smiled, left all the chips on the table and waited for the next hand. He received another natural 9. The highest and unbeatable score. The dealer had an 8 and lost by one. The stack of chips doubled again.

Feeling he was on a hot streak – despite the plan to lose money fast – he moved his bet, placing all of it on the dealer instead. Essentially, he was betting against himself. This time, he ended up with a 4 and the dealer had 7. Technically, the dealer won, but Kurt got paid.

The huge stacks of chips were doubled again and then pushed back toward him. 'Table limit,' the dealer said. In three hands, he'd grown his stack to eight million yen.

Kurt looked at the winnings. *This would never happen if it was my own money.*

He decided to bet lower amounts until his luck changed for the worse, tipped the dealer handsomely and pushed a few chips into place. As the next set of cards came out, he felt someone slide up behind him. A hand with perfectly manicured fingernails slid softly onto his shoulder. He turned to see the attendant from the pachinko lounge. She'd followed him to the table.

'You are lucky,' she said.

Kurt grinned. He must have been doing well if the shills were already gathering. 'So far,' he replied.

He didn't shoo the woman away. Her presence would help him blend in and her beauty would draw eyes toward her instead of him. It would make looking around the room easier and less dangerous.

The next hand was a loser, something Kurt was thankful for, but he'd made a small fortune already and would have to lose a lot more before he could ask for credit.

He bet again and continued scanning the room for any sign of Ushi-Oni. At first, nothing caught his eye. Then, at a table across from him, partially blocked by the pit boss, he noticed a familiar face. He focused through the smoke, squinting just to be sure.

'You win again, sir,' the dealer said.

'Damn,' Kurt whispered, reacting not to the latest unwanted victory but to a face he hadn't expected to see. Sitting at the table across the pit was Master Kenzo's missing acolyte, Akiko.

She was dressed elegantly, heavily made up and smoking

a long, thin cigarette, while her gaze flicked from the cards in front of her to every corner of the casino floor.

Kurt could imagine several reasons she might have chosen to be here and none of them were good.

16

The Sento

Walter Han stood in a private suite on the upper level of the Sento. He gazed briefly out through the floor-to-ceiling glass. From this vantage point, he could see the lower levels of the circular building. The crowd was gathering, and even he wanted to see the combat, but business took precedence.

He turned his attention back to the guest in his suite, Ushi-Oni. The Demon didn't quite look himself. 'Are you all right, my friend? Or is this all part of your disguise.'

'Recovering from my wounds,' Oni replied. 'All the more reason for the payment to be quick.'

As Oni spoke, a twitch ran across his face. It looked like he was snarling. With the facial tics, a yellowish tint discoloring his eyes and a gloss of moisture on his skin, Oni was beginning to look like his namesake.

'You will be paid,' Han said. 'But first, I give you a choice. Payment for the job you've completed. Or ten times that amount for an easier but more important task.'

'I've had enough of your jobs,' the Demon said. 'The last easy task nearly got me killed. Now pay me so I can leave.'

'Leaving won't help you this time,' Han said.

'What are you talking about?'

'The Federal Police have your description at long last,' Han said. 'They know what you look like. And they will find you soon enough. When they do, they'll hang plenty of crimes on you, most of which you're actually guilty of.'

'You . . . You gave them my –'

'Why would I do that if I still want your help?'

'Then how?'

'You said yourself there were survivors.'

Oni's face turned a new shade. Anger and sickness mixed.

Han continued. 'If you want to live out your days in anything but wretched poverty and constant hiding, you'll need more than just a modicum of wealth. You'll need a new life, a new identity and enough money to last an eternity.'

From his pocket, Han pulled a folded sheet of paper. Holding it between two fingers, he offered it to Oni, who hesitated and then snatched it away.

Oni unfolded the paper to see an incredibly accurate drawing of his face, right down to the fishhook-shaped scar on his lip. Below the drawing was a diagram of his tattoos. It was also surprisingly accurate.

Boiling with rage, he ripped the paper into shreds and threw it back at Han in a swirl of confetti.

Han shrugged. 'I'm sure the police have duplicates.'

'It doesn't matter.'

'You know it does,' Han snapped. 'It means your time is up. Your reign as the Demon who comes in the night is over. To make matters worse, you have no friends left. No one to help you. That is the life of a *ronin* – in the end, you die alone. I'm offering a way out, if you're up to it, but it requires you to bring something to me.'

'And what might that be? Another head on a platter?'

'That you'll do for free,' Han said. 'What I need now is information about a missing sword.'

'Sword?'

'I assume you've heard of the Honjo Masamune?'

'Of course I have,' Oni said. 'It's only the most famous sword in Japan. So what? It's been missing since the end of World War Two. Either the Americans took it or –'

'Yes, the official story,' Han said. 'I know it well. At the end of the war, the American forces demanded that all weapons, including ceremonial swords, be surrendered. Many of the wealthy were angered by this and fought to keep their swords, but Iemasa Tokagawa believed working with the Americans was the only way to ensure a future for Japan. He turned his collection over; fourteen priceless swords, including the Honjo Masamune. They were delivered to a Tokyo police station, where they were later picked up by an American sergeant named Coldy Bimore. They vanished, never to be seen again. An open-and-shut case, except American records show no evidence of the swords being inventoried and no record of any soldier, sailor or airman with that name being stationed in Japan during the entire time of occupation.'

'Obviously, a lie,' Oni said.

'Of course it's a lie,' Han said. 'But whose? I have information suggesting something other than American duplicity.'

Oni narrowed his gaze.

The hook had been baited; now Han needed to reel his catch in. Oni wanted to believe. He wanted to see and touch the legendary weapon. To hold it and even wield it. And why shouldn't he want that? Every artist longed to see the works of the masters. Painters wished to see the brushstrokes of a Picasso or Van Gogh; sculptors wished to see the *David*, to touch the marble, though it was off-limits. Ushi-Oni had made a life out of weapons and cold steel. To hold the Masamune would be transcendent.

'What information?'

'Records from the Tokagawa family and a secret communiqué issued to a member of the House of Peers, where Iemasa Tokagawa served at the end of World War Two. They tell a different story.'

'Go on.'

'Iemasa Tokagawa did indeed wish to work with the American forces, but others in his family felt differently. They had forgeries made and attempted to replace the priceless swords with the cheap re-creations. Tokagawa discovered this at the last minute and a fight ensued. Several members of his family died struggling against one another. He realized that the swords were not only a point of pride for the family but a symbol around which Japanese resistance and the idea of a greater Japan might rise again. According to a letter he wrote, Tokagawa both feared and hoped for this, but he'd seen enough death during the long war and in its aftermath to tip the scales to dread. He decided the swords should be hidden somewhere so they wouldn't become a catalyst for an uprising.

He sent word to a member of the House of Peers and the swords were intercepted. Replicas were handed over in their place, but they didn't fool anyone, and so the story of the American sergeant with the odd-sounding name was fabricated.'

'What happened to the swords?' Oni asked.

'Tokagawa's letter requests that they be given to a Shinto priest and hidden in one of their sanctuaries.'

Oni looked disgusted. 'A weapon of war in the hands of a priest.'

'So it seems.'

'Which shrine? Where? There are thousands of them.'

Han took a deep breath. 'No mention of the particular shrine was ever made,' he admitted. 'But other letters from the period indicate that the Tokagawa family supported a particular shrine in the footsteps of Mount Fuji, all the way back to a time long prior to the war. A rather obscure sanctuary at that. But if you wanted to hide something priceless, to entrust a national treasure to someone other than yourself, it's only logical to assume you would give it to someone you knew and had a prior existing relationship with.'

Oni nodded, but there was an aura of distrust about him that never quite left. 'How is it no one else has uncovered this information? Treasure hunters have been looking for the Honjo Masamune since the day it went missing.'

'I have access to records they cannot see,' Han said. 'Government records. You should know that Japanese investigators speculated on this exact possibility as early as 1955, but by then Japan had become utterly dependent on America.'

He picked up a glass of champagne. 'Loans from Washington were allowing the country to rebuild. Exports to the United States were growing rapidly, creating a new class of wealthy businessmen, while American ships, planes and soldiers protected the country from the Russian Bear and the Chinese Dragon. Considering the situation, those in power decided that nothing would be allowed to damage that relationship, least of all the sudden reappearance of a sword that was linked to Japanese nationalism, the Shoguns of old and the ruling families who'd pushed Japan into war. Nor could they explain its disappearance without implicating the Tokagawa family. So they did what all good politicians do: they buried the information in bureaucratic piles of paper that would reach to the moon, making certain the leads were never investigated and the truth went dormant.'

'Are you certain of these facts?' Oni asked.

'It's not possible to be certain,' Han said. 'But if the swords are not with the monks, then they are lost forever. But, there is also the matter of the journal. Believed to belong to Masamune and his descendants. It reveals his secrets. His methods for crafting such masterworks.'

Oni seemed to accept that, but he remained on guard. 'You've never shown any interest in collecting. Why would you start now?'

'I'm not here to answer your questions,' Han said. 'But let's just say, I have a sudden interest in the independence of my mother's country. And if you do as I tell you, not only will I grant you wealth but a new life and a full pardon for your crimes.'

'Now I know you're lying,' Oni said. 'I think I'll just take what you owe me and go.'

Han shrugged. He was done with the hard sell. He pulled a small disk from his pocket. It was larger than a normal casino chip, made of brass and octagonal in shape. It weighed heavy in the hand and had a number engraved on one side and the face of a dragon on the other.

'This marker will cover the balance of payments on your existing contract,' he said. 'Take it to any table, they'll give you high-denomination chips to play with. Or if you wish, take it directly to the cage. They will pay you in American or European currency, since those bills have larger denominations and are easier to carry. If you change your mind, hold on to the marker and call me, we'll discuss the new deal when you're ready.'

Han placed the chip on the table beside the window. Oni stepped forward and picked up the golden disk. He felt its heft in his hand as he weighed the options in front of him.

He glanced at Han once and then looked out through the glass to the activity below. His feverish eyes widened. 'No,' he whispered.

'The choice is yours.'

But Oni was neither listening nor addressing the question of the new contract. He was staring at a figure on the walkway one level below. 'No, it can't be.'

He palmed the coin, turned and stormed toward the door.

Han was tempted to grab him but he knew better than to lay hands on the Demon.

Oni brushed past, grabbing a wineglass as he went, shattering the bulb against the wall and then storming out into the hall.

17

After an hour of studying the layout, Joe was heading back toward the alcove near the front entrance. The pianist had taken a break and the sounds of a violin solo were filling the room.

Finding no sign of Kurt, he accepted another glass of champagne and took a seat in one of the lounge chairs. His back was to the crowd, but he was able to see the reflection of everyone behind him in the polished side of the piano. It was the perfect way to watch the crowd without being seen.

He studied each face that passed by, looking for Kurt in the reflection. But it wasn't Kurt that he saw. Instead, he spied a man heading directly for him and carrying something in his hands.

Joe knew he'd been made. Normal instincts of fight or flight reared up within him, but he kept calm, waiting as the deranged-looking figure grew closer.

At the very last second, Joe dodged to the side and flung the contents of his champagne flute into Ushi-Oni's face. Temporarily blinded, Ushi-Oni's stabbing attempt missed Joe and plunged into the soft back of the chair. But he threw his free arm around Joe's neck, grasping him in a headlock and thrusting the sharpened stem of the wineglass toward Joe's throat.

The crowd gasped and pulled back.

Joe was at a disadvantage. He had no leverage, but his reactions were flawless. He blocked the stem with his forearm, taking a minor wound in the process and latching onto Oni's wrist. His other hand smashed the champagne glass over the assassin's head, drawing blood and a severe uptick in rage.

Oni tore his arm free of Joe's grasp and reared back for another strike. But Joe was quicker. He placed his feet on the side of the grand piano and instead of pulling away from Oni pushed toward him with a powerful shove.

The peak of the chair hit Oni in the midsection and he tumbled backward. The chair went over, but Joe sprang to his feet and swung his left foot toward Oni's face, connecting and sending a splatter of blood and saliva flying from the Demon's mouth.

Oni rolled with the kick and stood up, licking blood off his lips.

Joe looked him dead in the eye, extended a hand and motioned for Ushi-Oni to bring it on.

Oni charged, tackling Joe and landing on top of him. Joe heaved him over, reversed their positions and landed a rabbit punch to Oni's side.

The Demon once again tried for a sleeper hold, but Joe smashed an elbow into his gut and pulled free.

Mission accomplished, Joe thought. He stood but was taken to the ground by several members of the casino's security detail. They had rushed in from all directions, swarming over both Joe and the Demon.

Joe couldn't see much through all the arms and legs, but he felt the shock of a Taser and the sudden lightness that came with being lifted from the ground by several powerful hands.

He and Oni were dragged from the lobby as the onlookers stared and the violinist stood off to one side. The last thing he saw was a man asking her to play and trying to calm the patrons down. And then he was dragged into a back corridor and thrown in a room with concrete walls, a solid floor and a door made of steel.

Ushi-Oni was handled in similar fashion by men who had no idea who he was. Despite the fact that his hands were bound, he managed to knee one of them in the gut and send him sprawling to the floor. That earned him a jolt from the Taser, which left him stunned and reeling and seething with more anger than before. As he lay there, Oni imagined different ways he would torture them when he got the chance.

They searched him for weapons but found something else instead: the golden chip. Only the casino's most valued guests carried such markers.

The rough treatment ended instantly. The guards glanced at one another and then helped Ushi-Oni up off the floor and into a seat.

Before they could ask any questions, the door opened. Two men stood there. The first man was named Kashimora; he was the Yakuza underboss who ran the casino. The second was Walter Han.

18

Hideki Kashimora stood in the unadorned room, seething with anger. A broad-shouldered man in his mid-forties, Kashimora ran the club for the syndicate. He collected the money, maintained its veil of secrecy and enforced its rules mercilessly – something those foolish enough to cross him usually discovered when they wound up in cement barrels at the bottom of Tokyo Bay.

And yet while violence was second nature to Kashimora, even he felt a certain chill looking into the feverish eyes of Ushi-Oni. If half of the stories told about the Demon were true, it made him the most lethal assassin in Japan. His penchant for toying with his victims first was a kind of sickness even a Yakuza boss disapproved of. Killing was business, not pleasure. But for Ushi-Oni it was both.

'I will not tolerate disruption in my club,' Kashimora said.

'I'm sure our friend Oni had good reason,' Han replied.

'*Your* friend,' Kashimora corrected. 'Oni burned his bridges to the syndicate years ago.'

'The syndicate,' Ushi-Oni muttered. He spat blood on the floor to punctuate his disgust.

'I should put you in the ring to finish what you started,' Kashimora said.

'Do it,' Oni suggested.

Han interrupted. 'Who was that man you attacked?'

'Don't you recognize him?' Oni said. 'He's one of the men you sent me to kill.'

'What lies are these?' the casino boss asked. 'That man is a promoter from Las Vegas.'

Oni laughed. 'He's no promoter. He's an American government agent.'

'What kind of agent?' Kashimora blurted out. 'And why would he come here?'

'You have nothing to worry about,' Han assured him. 'If Oni's correct, it's not the casino they're interested in.'

'Then what?'

'Oni has been recognized; I can only suspect they came here to capture him.'

'They?' Kashimora said. 'You think there are more of them?'

'Would you walk into a fortress like this alone?'

Kashimora was furious. He ignored Oni and focused on Han. 'You bring this wild man to my place of business and you lose control of him. You let American agents follow you without even warning me to watch out for them. I ought to kill both of you.'

'Just kill the American and toss him in your koi pond,' Oni said. 'Better yet, let me do it.'

'No,' Han said. 'We have to know if he came alone.'

'That will be difficult, if not impossible, to determine,' Kashimora said. 'For obvious reasons, there are no video cameras here.'

'So torture him or beat the truth out of him,' Ushi-Oni said, rising to his feet.

Kashimora didn't like the Demon being in his establishment. The man was too prone to unnecessary violence. And far too headstrong. 'I'm tempted to expel you both,' he said. 'If the Americans came here looking for you, I can only assume they will leave once you're thrown out.'

'Carrying with them whatever information they've picked up on their journey,' Han pointed out. 'Including evidence of who comes here and what they do. Don't think that information won't find its way back to the police.'

'I'm not worried about the police,' Kashimora said proudly. 'In the meantime, I'll throw all the foreigners out.'

'I have a better idea,' Han said. 'Put the American in the ring. Make him fight for his life. Plaster his image on every screen in the establishment. If he came here on his own, you'll get nothing but a thrilling fight. But if he has comrades in the crowd, they will no doubt come to his aid and try to rescue him. Position your men accordingly and you'll be able to grab them all with one swish of the net.'

19

Kurt gathered his chips, left his winning table and circled around the room, walking up behind Akiko. 'What's a nice girl like you doing in a place like this?' he said. 'Then again, something tells me that's the wrong question.'

She froze at the sound of his voice, her back stiffening.

'Card?' the dealer asked.

Akiko did not respond.

'Would you like a card?'

'You have sixteen,' Kurt told her.

Akiko was playing blackjack. She refocused on the game and made the motion for another card instinctively. A red king gave her twenty-six and the dealer took her chips.

'Now would be a good time to walk away,' Kurt suggested. 'And I'm not just talking about the game.'

She stood and brushed past Kurt without looking him in the eye.

He followed, moving alongside her and matching her stride. 'Aren't we on speaking terms anymore?'

'You're going to interfere,' she said.

'With what?'

She glanced at him. 'How do you even know about this place?'

'A little bird told me. What about you?'

'This was my home,' she said. 'My prison.'

Kurt grabbed her by the arm and turned her. 'What are you trying to say?'

'I was owned by Kashimora,' she replied bluntly. 'It's nothing special. They own plenty of people. But I was property and I did what they told me. You can imagine what I was used for. But, as it turned out, I had a knack for fighting and when a chance came to be more than a prostitute, I took it. I taught myself everything I could. I studied the martial arts, the samurai, the way of the warrior. A chance encounter led me to Master Kenzo and, when I had the opportunity, I left here and joined him. But they found me. They came after me.'

Kurt was beginning to understand. 'You think that –'

'They found me,' she repeated. 'Because I tried to escape them, they punished my new family. Kenzo tried to save me from myself and now he's dead. So I'm going to make things right even if I have to die to do it.'

The story was something of a surprise, despite what Superintendent Nagano had told him. He wasn't altogether convinced, but there was great determination in her eyes.

'Kashimora,' he said, just to be sure. 'The man who runs this place.'

She nodded. 'They don't like to lose their property. And they don't let people take things from them. I thought I was free, but I will never be free, so I will face my enemy and embrace him in death,' she said. 'If I was you, I wouldn't be seen with me. They might kill you for what I'm about to do.'

A group of patrons came a little too close and Kurt

hustled Akiko onto the ramp that led upstairs. He was late for his meeting with Joe anyway.

'Listen to me,' he said. 'You're making a huge mistake. I spent a couple hours with the police the other day. Those men who attacked us were once part of the Yakuza, but not anymore. And they didn't attack the castle to get you back or make an example out of Kenzo. They were trying to stop him from giving us the information we came for.'

She looked at him as if she wanted to believe.

'Trust me,' he said. 'What happened was not your fault. It was our visit and what Kenzo found in the sea that caused the attack. It's connected to earthquakes and those Z-waves he found.'

She narrowed her gaze. 'These are the people I escaped from. I know their secrets. Things they don't want coming to light.'

Kurt shook his head. 'If they remembered you, they'd have killed you the moment you walked in here. I'm telling you, you can let go of the guilt on this one.'

'I don't know if I can accept that.'

'Think about it on the cab ride home,' he said. 'You're leaving.'

'Why?'

'In case they do recognize you.'

By now, they'd reached the top floor and were nearing the piano alcove. Joe was nowhere to be found, but a distinct lack of music and the sight of staff members cleaning glass off the floor and rearranging the furniture suggested a commotion had taken place. Security members with earbuds talking to several guests confirmed it.

'Keep walking,' he said, passing the alcove and the exit and continuing in the other direction.

'I thought I was leaving.'

Kurt didn't look back. 'None of us are leaving, not without finding our own way out.'

They continued down the hall and then back down one level toward the crowded casino pit. By the time they got there, screens were updating the list of fights to bet on.

Joe's image and the false name he'd been provided with were now prominently displayed in the slot marked Fight 1, the first bout of the evening.

'What do those symbols mean?' Kurt asked.

'That's for the weapons fight,' she said. 'Nunchucks, staffs, half-staffs. Seven three-minute rounds or until either combatant cannot rise. No submission.'

All thoughts of finding Ushi-Oni or whoever paid him vanished as Kurt's mind turned to a different problem. 'I'm going to need your help.'

'To do what?'

'Rescue Joe.'

20

Kurt and Akiko moved through the crowd as the lights came on in the arena.

'How soon till the fight begins?' Kurt asked.

'Twenty minutes,' she said.

All around the casino floor, bettors were gathering up their chips and making their way to the exhibition.

Kurt continued to move with the crowd; Akiko was with him but slowing down. 'Stay with me.'

'You can't go to the arena,' she said. 'That's what they want you to do.'

'I'm going,' he said. 'But not the way they expect. First, we have to get out of sight.'

A hidden door opened in the far wall and a cocktail waitress stepped through it with a tray of drinks.

'Back of the house,' Kurt said. 'Every hotel has one.'

He led Akiko toward it, pulled up beside the smooth section of the wall and waited. It wasn't long before the door swung wide and another waitress came out.

She passed them without a second glance, navigating through the crowd toward a table. By the time the door clicked shut, Kurt and Akiko had slipped inside.

They entered an unadorned service hall. A drink station lay in one direction, empty locker rooms in the other. With the sound of footsteps coming down the hall, Kurt angled toward one of the locker rooms, slipped inside and closed the door.

When the steps in the hall passed by, Kurt knew they were alone. 'You came here looking for revenge,' he said. 'What was your plan?'

She pulled a small plastic vial from a hidden pouch in her dress. Opening the top, she produced several white tablets. 'Poison,' she said. 'Slow-acting. It would give me enough time to get out before taking effect. No one would ever know who did it.'

'Mind if I borrow that?' he asked.

She placed the pills back inside and handed it over. 'Do you think that will help?'

'I'd prefer an AK-47,' he said. 'But this will be easier to smuggle, especially considering the wardrobe requirements of the night.'

'You seem very certain,' she said.

'I am,' he insisted. 'All we have to do is take our complaints to the manager. I think he'll see things our way. But to reach him, we'll need to blend in. If you'd be so kind as to put on a cocktail server's uniform, that would be a start.'

Akiko opened several lockers before finding the right uniform and then began to disrobe without a hint of modesty. Kurt turned his back to her to give her some privacy and went through several of the lockers before he found what he was looking for: another bottle of pills.

He slipped it into his pocket and turned around.

'Aren't you going to change?' she asked.

'Not just yet,' he said.

'That white jacket stands out,' she said. 'They'll spot you as soon as you walk up.'

'I'm counting on it.'

In a different locker room, down below the arena, Joe was told to dress for the fight. The pickings were slim, different types of athletic gear and martial arts robes. 'I don't suppose you have anything in suit of armor . . . say, early Middle Ages?'

The joke was wasted on his captors. They'd been ordered by Kashimora to get him ready for the fight and force him into the arena if he refused to go willingly. Other than that, they weren't to speak with him.

With little choice, Joe picked out a two-piece martial arts uniform. The loose gray top had a V-neck collar; the pants had an elastic waistband, designed for ease of movement.

Several weapons were offered for him to practice with. He picked up a set of nunchucks and whirled them around, left and right. He'd toyed with nunchucks once before, but, without professional training, they were as dangerous to the user as to the opponent. After almost hitting himself in the face, he put them down.

The noise of the crowd reached them through the closed door. It rose and fell as a voice speaking in Japanese announced the coming bout.

'It's time,' one of the guards said.

They marched him to the door and held him in place.

The door opened to a roar from the crowd and a wave of blinding light; Joe squinted as they pushed him forward and forced him to ascend a ramp.

He stepped into a circular arena with a six-foot wall around it. It reminded Joe of a bullfighters' ring except that the floor was made of wooden planking, complete with dark swaths where it had been stained with blood.

'That's encouraging,' he muttered.

'You guys should bet on me,' Joe said to the guards in his corner. 'I'm sure you'll get good odds.'

Neither of them responded, and when Joe's opponent arrived from a gap in the far wall, Joe understood why. The man was a monster. Six foot seven and muscle-bound from head to toe. Huge rounded shoulders tapered to a washboard abdomen and then widened out on a pair of tree-trunk-sized legs.

'Never mind,' Joe said. 'I wouldn't bet on me either.'

The guards behind him snickered, but Joe couldn't have been happier. He knew he wasn't alone. Someway, somehow, Kurt would try to rescue him. All he had to do was stay alive long enough for Kurt to do it. And in that situation, a big, slow bruiser of an opponent would be far easier to hold off than a quick-hitting martial artist.

Joe was pushed to the center of the ring. Weapons were offered. Joe took a staff, like the one he'd used to vault over the Komodo dragon. The Japanese version of Hercules took a pair of sticks, one in each hand.

A horn sounded and the bout began. Joe held the staff in front of him as the giant moved in without hesitation. Joe jabbed at him a few times with the point of the staff, slowing his approach.

His opponent took the first two in the ribs and shrugged them off as if they were nothing. He responded to the third jab with a vicious counterattack. Displaying incredible speed for such a big man, he brought the left-handed stick down and knocked the point of Joe's staff into the floorboards, while simultaneously lunging forward and swinging the other half-staff toward Joe's skull.

Joe ducked just in time, hearing a distinct whistling noise as the stick passed over his head. The crowd let out a collective gasp and Joe pulled back, resuming his defensive stance.

'Take it easy, big fella,' he said. 'At least give the people a show before you cave my head in.'

He might as well have been talking to a wall. The man neither smiled nor frowned. He just charged forward once again.

This time, Joe dropped to the ground, shoved the staff between his opponent's legs and levered it to the side. The big man's knees buckled from the attack and he dropped to the ground.

Instead of injuring the man, Joe's next move was to disarm the guy. He swung his staff like a nine iron, catching one of the sticks in his adversary's hand and sending it into the third row. Patrons dove out of their seats to avoid the incoming missile and Joe laughed at them.

The sideshow gave his opponent a chance to stand. Joe hoped the man realized he'd deliberately gone for his weapon instead of his head.

Before they could spar again, the horn sounded, signaling the intermission between rounds.

The big guy returned to his starting area and was briefly tended to. Joe went back to his spot, but the guards just stared at him. He grabbed a bottle of water for himself, took a small drink and rested against the wall.

For the first time, he was able to study the crowd. It was an intimate setting. Seating for maybe a thousand people. They surrounded him on steeply sloped tiers and every seat was taken.

He looked for Kurt but found no sign of him. What he did see were security guards standing at every entrance and in each aisle. There was no way Kurt could get into the arena without being caught. A fact Kurt had no doubt already discovered. It meant Joe would have to keep fighting while Kurt found another way.

The horn sounded for round 2. Joe put the water down and stepped forward. 'Make it quick,' he whispered. 'I can't dance with Godzilla forever.'

21

In a luxury suite overlooking the arena, Walter Han watched the fight from behind thick glass. It muffled the sound of the crowd and the viciousness of the blows and allowed a sense of privacy. Scanning the arena through a pair of opera glasses, he saw nothing to indicate a rescue was under way.

'Anything?' Kashimora asked.

'Not yet,' Han said.

'So much for your plan to draw him out into the open,' Kashimora said condescendingly.

Han placed the glasses down and began to pace. The arrival of the American unnerved him. Not only because he'd been told they were all dead or in the hospital but because they'd struck so close to him. He had a survivor's instincts and they told him he was in danger.

He explained what he knew to Kashimora. 'Based on the description your doorman gave, you're looking for a man named Austin. He'll be wearing a distinctive white dinner jacket. The man in the ring is his comrade. Considering what I know about these two, neither will abandon the other.'

Kashimora smirked. 'Bravado: I find it goes out the window when the stakes get this high. If Austin knows what's good for him, he's already looking for a way out of the building.'

'An effort I assume your men will prevent,' Han said.

'Of course,' Kashimora said. 'Trust me, there's no way for them to escape now.'

Han nodded. 'Then I'll depart and let you handle it.'

'You're leaving?'

Han knew it wasn't his finest moment, but he had to get out of there. If he was exposed, the entire plan would come apart. And the leaders of the Party in China would sacrifice him to save themselves. 'What purpose does my staying serve? You said it yourself: there's no way for them to escape.'

Kashimora had been trapped by his own words. 'If this goes badly for us, you will hear about it,' he threatened.

'You forget your station,' Han said. 'I deal with those much higher in the syndicate than you. My patronage is appreciated and has been for years.' He put his hand on the door, not waiting for permission. 'If the American has friends here, I expect you to find them and eliminate them. If not, get rid of the one in the ring and leave no trace of his existence.'

Kashimora bristled but did not try to prevent his leaving. 'Take the wild man with you,' he said. 'Don't ever bring him here again.'

Han opened the door and motioned to Oni. They left together.

Kashimora remained behind, stewing for the moment and frustrated. He grabbed the opera glasses off the table and scanned the arena himself. He saw nothing out of order and lowered the glasses, pointing to his empty tumbler as a cocktail waitress entered.

'Scotch.'

He sat down in an overstuffed chair as she freshened his drink and delivered it.

Without acknowledging her, he brought the glass to his mouth, tipped it back and consumed half the liquid inside. The fiery liquid burned in just the right way and Kashimora felt instantly calmer.

He put the tumbler down and turned his attention back to the fight. The second round had gone much like the first. The hulking giant attacking and the nimble American dodging and weaving.

'Maybe Han is right,' he said to himself. 'Perhaps he is waiting for rescue.'

'Then we'd better not disappoint him,' a voice said from behind them.

Kashimora whirled in his chair. The American accent was unmistakable, the white dinner jacket confirming who it was that had spoken. Kashimora noticed the man was unarmed but smiling.

'You must be Austin.'

'I am,' the man replied, taking a seat.

'How did you get in here?'

'With surprising ease,' Austin replied smugly. 'Now that most of your men are out there looking for me, the hallways are empty. And your guards at the door were easy to distract and subdue.'

'I don't need guards to protect myself,' Kashimora said, producing a snub-nosed pistol and aiming it at the American's chest.

Instead of fear or even caution, Austin merely raised his hands in a halfhearted manner as if he were surrendering.

He wore an outright grin on his face. Not the look of a defeated man. 'I wouldn't pull that trigger, if I was you.'

'You'll wish I had when you're drowning at the bottom of Tokyo Bay with your friend.'

'And you'll wish you'd listened to me,' the American replied, 'when your heart goes into an uncontrollable fibrillation and your arteries begin leaking blood out of every pore and body cavity.'

'What are you talking about?'

'Whatever happens to me happens to you,' Austin told him. 'Either we both live or we both die. It's up to you.'

'Lies and a bad attempt to bluff. That doesn't work well around here.'

Austin held up an empty plastic vial and tossed it to him. Kashimora caught it with his free hand. A bitter residue clung to the sides.

'That was filled with heparin,' Kurt said. 'A powerful blood thinner. Very similar to rat poison. You've ingested a fatal dose in that beverage of yours. Enough to kill a man three times your size – like the one trying to beat up my friend down there. The alcohol masks the taste of the drug, but I imagine you can detect a metallic and bitter flavor on your tongue at this point.'

Kashimora began running his tongue across his teeth; he detected an unpleasant essence. He knew what rat poison could do. He'd used it on others.

'You're probably feeling flushed as well,' Austin continued. 'Your heart will be racing soon, if it's not already.'

Kashimora's face felt warm. His heart was beating firmly, a little too firmly. A bead of sweat was already forming on his brow. 'You'll never get out of here alive,' he said.

Austin raised an eyebrow. 'I will if you escort me to the door. And if you're willing to do that, I'm willing to leave you at the front gate with a firm handshake and the antidote in your outstretched palm.'

'Or I could shoot you and search your body for it.' Kashimora cocked the pistol and stared down the barrel.

'Excellent idea,' Austin said. He opened his palm, revealing a handful of tablets. There were five pills all of different colors, shapes and sizes. 'It's one of these,' he said. 'But you guess wrong, you get more poison and you die even quicker.'

Kashimora could hardly believe what was occurring. In the heart of the Yakuza stronghold, with every exit sealed and fifty armed men looking for him, Austin had turned the tables against the house.

'Put the gun on the floor and slide it over here,' Austin demanded.

He shook his head. There had to be another way.

Austin glanced at his watch. 'Wait much longer and it'll be too late.'

Kashimora tried to control his fear, but it was overwhelming. His heart was pounding now; a sheen of sweat had built up on his face. He wiped his face with the sleeve of his jacket and put the gun down. He kicked it Austin's way. 'What do you want me to do? Call off the security teams?'

Austin picked up the pistol. 'They would find that awfully suspicious.'

'Then what?'

'First, I'll take your phone,' he said. 'Mine was impounded. And then you're going to help me get my friend out of the ring. And you're going to do it the old-fashioned way. By hand.'

22

The horn blew and round 4 began. Joe noticed a new tactic from his opponent. The man was no longer charging forth, trying to land a deadly blow. Instead, he was hanging back, waiting for Joe to move first. Perhaps he was tiring. Or maybe it was a new tactic born out of Joe's ability to evade him.

Joe looked his opponent in the eye. The man waved Joe forward, daring him to move closer. Joe shook his head. The big man repeated his gesture, swinging the remaining stick in the air as if to challenge him. Still, Joe held his ground and the fight turned into a stalemate.

With the combatants circling each other instead of attacking, the crowd began to whistle. Soon a chant began. Joe didn't understand the words, but he felt the intensity growing.

The ground began to move under his feet. Not side to side but vertically. The outside edge of the circular ring was rising up, the planks being lifted by a hydraulic jack. A small section in the middle remained flat, but that was it. What had been a large circular arena – with plenty of room to move about in – began transforming into a funnel that would force the warriors into close combat.

The big guy smiled at this development and walked calmly down to the center of the funnel.

Joe held his position, crouching as the angle of the floor grew steeper. He dropped lower to keep his center of gravity down, put a hand on the floor to keep himself balanced, but as the angle passed forty-five degrees, his feet began to slip.

The crowd was chanting deliriously now. Anticipating the moment Joe would fall and tumble into the arms of the giant.

Joe knew he couldn't hold on much longer. At any moment, the friction holding him in place would be overcome by the force of gravity.

Instead of remaining still and trying to hold off the inevitable, he leapt up and ran. But he didn't run straight at his opponent, he ran at an angle, cutting across the funnel and down. Picking up momentum, he was able to curve back up the opposite slope like a speeding car on a banked turn.

The big man swept at his feet, but Joe leapt over the attack and then whacked his oversized opponent in the back of the head as he passed him.

The big man fell with a heavy thud as Joe ran up the far side of the banked platform. He was about to make another high-speed attack when the bottom dropped out. Literally.

The pneumatic hiss told the story, but Joe heard it too late. Large valves had been opened and the pent-up pressure holding the floor panels up released. The floorboards fell back to their original state and Joe fell with them, slamming against the solid ground.

Stunned, he rolled over. 'That's just not fair.'

He looked up to see his opponent rushing in. The muscle-bound specimen of a man grabbed the staff and pulled it out of Joe's hand. Almost immediately, it came swinging back Joe's way with deadly force.

Joe covered up. His natural instinct as a boxer was to bring his left arm up and protect his head. The stick crashed against Joe's flexed bicep and forearm but still caught the side of his head with a glancing blow.

His legs felt like jelly. A voice in his head told him to get up and run, but it was drowned out by the ringing sound in his ears.

He tried for a crawling position, before falling to his side and then rolling over on his back. He lay that way, staring straight up. There was no ref to count him out, only the blinding glare of the lights up above. A perfect square of incandescence with an impenetrably dark section in the center.

For a second, the giant stood over Joe, blocking the light. But the horn sounded and the big man walked off rather than attempting to finish Joe.

'Chivalry isn't dead after all,' Joe said to himself.

As he lay there waiting for the feeling to return to his legs, something fell toward him from up above. At first, Joe thought it was his imagination, but it hit the deck next to him, bounced and then rolled in a curved path until it bumped against his ribs.

He turned on his side, innate curiosity driving him to see what had fallen from the rafters. Grasping it with his fingers, he plucked the object from the floor. It was a five-yen coin, with its brassy color and hole in the middle. A token of good luck.

Joe's spirits soared. He looked back up to the rafters just as the bank of overhead lights went out.

23

'Throw him the rope,' Kurt called.

He, Akiko and Kashimora were perched on the cat-walk that ran between the lights. Akiko had a long nylon cord used to secure things to the catwalk. She dropped one end over the side, allowing it to fall straight down. It hit the canvas in the dark.

'I hope he sees it,' she said. 'After that last hit, he might not be thinking clearly.'

'If there's anything harder than a diamond, it's Joe's head,' Kurt told her. 'He'll be all right.'

Kurt had seen Joe grasp the coin and look up. He knew Joe would put it together.

'Once he's up here, you give me the antidote,' Kashimora said anxiously.

'Not until we're outside,' Kurt replied.

The rope went taut. Two pulls told them Joe was ready.

'Now,' Kurt said. 'Pull him up.' The three of them began hauling on the rope. Arm over arm. With synchronized strokes that would have done a yacht crew proud, they lifted Joe off the ground, but it was a long way up to the lighting array and Joe weighed nearly two hundred pounds.

Halfway up, Kashimora stopped. He dropped to a knee, clutching at his chest. He was sweating feverishly. 'I need the antidote.'

'Get back on the rope,' Kurt shouted.

'Not unless you give me the pills.'

There wasn't much Kurt could do. Joe was a lot heavier without Kashimora hauling in tandem. If Kurt let go, Akiko would be hard-pressed to hold him all by herself. 'I'll give you the pills as soon as he's up here. Now pull.'

With Kurt frozen, Kashimora lunged at him, thrusting his hand into Kurt's pocket and fishing around for the pills. The impact almost knocked them both over the railing. The rope slipped, Joe dropped a few feet and Kurt gripped it again.

'Give me the antidote!' Kashimora screamed.

Kurt didn't bother to respond. He pushed Kashimora back against the rail, wrapped the other end of the rope around him and pushed him over. The bulky mobster was not particularly nimble, but, in desperation, he managed to hook one foot around the railing. He stopped his fall. He and Joe were now balancing each other out.

Kurt pulled out the orange tablets. 'This is what you want.'

'Please,' Kashimora said.

'One question first,' Kurt said. 'Who paid Ushi-Oni?'

'What?'

Kurt reared back as if to throw the tablets into the dark.

'Wait,' Kashimora pleaded. 'It was Han.'

'Han who?'

'Walter Han.'

'Is he Yakuza?'

'No,' Kashimora said. 'He's a Chinese businessman. Very wealthy.'

Kurt pressed, though there was little time to do so. 'Why would a businessman hire an assassin?'

'I don't know.'

Kurt let a little of the rope out.

'I swear it,' Kashimora shouted. 'Now give me the pills.'

Flashlights were probing around down below as security members tried to figure out what had gone wrong with the lights. Time for questions had run out. Kurt dropped the pills over the side. 'You'll find them in the arena,' he said, 'have a nice trip down.'

With that, he knocked Kashimora's foot from the railing. The heavy mobster, still entangled in the rope, fell, but slowly, as he was balanced out by Joe's weight. He hit the ground with a soft thud, freed himself and immediately began looking for the orange pills.

Up above, Kurt and Akiko helped Joe over the railing.

'Thanks for the lift,' Joe said. 'Did I see someone else dropping down the other side or am I hallucinating?'

'Just getting rid of some deadweight,' Kurt said.

'Deadweight and our ticket out of here,' Akiko said.

Joe stared at her and blinked. 'Akiko? That guy must have hit me harder than I thought.'

'I'll explain later,' Kurt said. 'First, we need to create a distraction. Give me that fire extinguisher.'

Akiko picked up a red-painted tank and handed it over to Kurt. It was a dry-chemical fire extinguisher. Kurt pulled out the cotter pin, compressed the handle and tossed the extinguisher over the edge. It fell in what seemed like slow motion, trailing white vapor and hitting the arena below like a bomb.

'Fire!' Akiko yelled in Japanese. 'Fire!'

The flashlights down below converged on the billowing cloud. In the dim glow, it looked like smoke. The nervous crowd erupted into chaos and people began running in every direction.

'Let's go,' Kurt said.

They moved along the catwalk and climbed through the access door in the far wall. From there, they entered a maintenance tunnel. At a Y-shaped junction, they turned right, found another door and pushed out into the night.

By now, the lights were coming on behind them. People were rushing out every door. Cars were headed for the main gate.

'I don't suppose you brought a car?' Kurt said to Akiko. 'Maybe one of those classic automobiles from Kenzo's collection?'

'No,' she said. 'But we could steal one.'

Kurt looked toward the main gate. There was too much commotion. The security guards were out and the driveway was turning to gridlock.

'Can't risk it,' Kurt said. 'They'll be looking at every car that leaves the premises. We need to exit without saying our good-byes. Follow me.'

He led them away from the structure and out into the dark of the ornamental garden.

'They may have cameras out here,' Joe said.

'No one left in the security bull pen to watch them,' Kurt replied. 'But let's get to the fence and get over it as soon as possible.'

'Then what?' Akiko asked.

'We flag down a passing car – hopefully, something high-end with plenty of headroom.'

'A Bentley would be nice,' Joe said.

Kurt smiled in the dark. 'My thoughts exactly.'

They crossed the grounds and reached the twelve-foot iron fence. Kurt pulled out the phone he'd stolen off of Kashimora. He dialed a number from memory and waited for an answer.

He started speaking the moment Nagano picked up. 'This is Kurt. We're on the west side of the property, by the fence near the access road. Can you pick us up?'

'I'm down the road,' Nagano said. 'Cars are streaming past. What happened?'

'I'll explain when you get here,' Kurt said. 'But make it quick or they'll feed us to the koi.'

Kurt heard the Bentley's engine roaring over the phone. It was a comforting sound.

With the phone back in his pocket, he reached for the bars of the wrought iron fence.

'Don't!' Joe shouted.

Kurt turned and saw Joe pointing to well-disguised wires looping in and out of the hollow crossbar. 'Electrified?'

'Looks that way,' Joe said. 'The second wire could be tied to a sensor. One way or another, if we touch the fence, they're going to know where we are.'

Kurt looked back toward the main building. He could hear dogs barking and see flashlight beams playing across the grounds. 'They're going to figure it out soon enough anyway. Can you short it out?'

Joe was looking for a weak point. 'Not the way they've set it up.'

'They're coming,' Akiko said.

So was Nagano. Far down the access road, a pair of headlights swung into the lane. Kurt could hear the big engine of the Bentley growling as it rushed toward them. He got on the phone again.

'We're trapped behind an electric fence. You're our only hope to get out. The lower part of the fence is a brick foundation. You need to knock a hole in it for us to crawl under.'

The Bentley was closing in, as were the dogs and the security guards.

'I see you,' Nagano said. 'Stand back.'

Kurt waved Joe and Akiko back from the fence as the Bentley slowed down, swung wide and then turned toward the barricade, accelerating once again.

It hit the barrier like a three-ton hammer, bending the iron bars and, more importantly, blasting a two-foot gap in the brick foundation.

A cloud of dust swirled, lit by the Bentley's high beams. The flashlights from the guards converged on them and the dogs were released. They sprinted forward in a yelping pack.

'Go!' Kurt shouted.

Nagano pulled the Bentley free. Shoving a few stray bricks aside, Joe crawled through, Akiko followed and Kurt dove through right behind her.

By the time he got to his feet, Joe and Akiko were getting into the car and the dogs were bounding down the hill.

Kurt rushed forward, pulled the front door open as the pack of dogs made it to the fence and charged underneath. He jumped inside and slammed the door behind him, closing it against a flash of canine teeth.

'Get us out of here!'

Nagano had already stepped on the gas. The Bentley spun its tires in the gravel and charged off in a cloud of dust, leaving the guards and the barking dogs far behind.

'I hope this isn't a one-way road,' Joe said.

'Not to worry,' Nagano replied. 'It comes out on a secondary highway. We should have no problems.'

Kurt sat up and looked through the tinted back window. 'Anyone following us?'

'Not that I can see,' Nagano replied, looking in the mirror.

Joe and Akiko popped up, blocking the view.

'This is most peculiar,' Nagano said. 'I remember dropping off two passengers, fully clothed. I've picked up three and one of you is wearing pajamas. Please tell me all this commotion is not because one of you kissed the wrong woman.'

'Not this time,' Joe said.

Kurt cut in. 'Superintendent, allow me to introduce Akiko. Akiko, this is Superintendent Nagano of the Japanese Federal Police. I believe he's been looking for you.'

A scowl crossed her face, but she said nothing. Nagano was quiet as well but began to laugh softly. 'It must have been quite an evening.'

'That it was,' Kurt said. 'It's not every day you win ten million yen, find a beautiful woman and rescue your best friend from certain death, only to be chased by men with guns and dogs.'

'Don't believe a word of it,' Joe said. 'That stuff happens with alarming regularity around here.'

Akiko glanced at Joe and then looked back to Kurt. Her lips curled into a smile and she laughed softly. It was the first sign of mirth Kurt had seen from her. 'Don't forget,' she added, 'we also poisoned a high-ranking Yakuza leader.'

'Terrific,' Joe said. 'That should add to our life expectancy.'

'We never actually poisoned him,' Kurt said. 'I found a bottle of caffeine pills in the locker room. People who have to be on their feet for ten hours a day tend to use those kind of stimulants. Akiko crushed up five of them and dumped them in his drink. Between the caffeine rush and the power of suggestion, he probably felt like his heart was going to blow.'

'He may still want revenge,' Nagano warned.

'Not likely,' Kurt said. 'Otherwise, he'd have to tell everyone that he helped us escape.'

Across from Kurt, Nagano nodded. 'Considering what it's going to cost me to repair this car, I hope you accomplished more than upsetting the Yakuza.'

Kurt grew serious. 'We found out who paid for the attack. A Chinese businessman named Han.'

Nagano glanced at Kurt. 'Walter Han?' As he spoke the name, the superintendent's voice was half an octave deeper than normal. 'No, no, no. Surely, you misunderstood.'

'I heard what I heard,' Kurt said. 'He paid Ushi-Oni to attack Kenzo's castle.'

'It makes no sense,' Nagano insisted.

'Why?' Joe asked. 'Who is he?'

'Han is a high-tech magnate,' Nagano said. 'An industrialist whose companies build aircraft parts and machinery. They sell advanced robotics systems to factories here and in China. He's been a powerful voice suggesting China and Japan should end centuries of suspicion and begin working together. This is a man who spends time with Prime Ministers and Presidents, not rubbing shoulders with the Yakuza.'

'Then where would one of those Yakuza bosses get the name?' Kurt asked.

'A fabrication,' Nagano said. 'He must have made it up.'

'It's a rather unusual name to pull out of thin air,' Joe said. 'Half Western, half Chinese.'

'Han has been in the news lately,' Nagano said. 'He was at a state dinner the other night. He's opening a new production facility in Nagasaki this week. He's going to be there for the signing of the new cooperation agreement between Japan and China.'

'You're suggesting Kashimora gave me this name because he saw Walter Han on TV.'

'Possibly.'

Kurt considered that and then shook his head. 'I'm not buying it. A funny thing happens in moments of extreme duress: the mind reverts to its most primitive desire – survival. And considering the predicament Kashimora was in at that moment, I'd bet his only thought was to save his skin.'

Nagano went quiet again. 'Well, if you're right, this is

very bad news,' he said finally. 'It means our investigation is at an end.'

'Why?' Joe asked.

'Han is beyond my reach,' the superintendent said. 'He has dual citizenship and friends in the highest places. Between that and his money, he enjoys a type of unofficial diplomatic immunity. For me to launch an investigation would be pointless. It would be closed down by those above me and I would be reassigned to guard duty at an abandoned station in the mountains.'

'So he's untouchable,' Kurt said.

Nagano looked pained but resolute. 'I'm afraid so.'

'What if Ushi-Oni rolled over on him?' Joe said. 'With two different members of the Yakuza implicating Han, your superiors would be afraid not to investigate.'

'Perhaps,' Nagano said, 'but that brings us back to square one: finding Ushi-Oni. We still don't know where to look. And, after this, he will vanish like the wind.'

'Not if you activate your tracking network,' Joe said, 'since he's carrying one of the coins.'

All eyes turned Joe's way.

'While Kurt was goofing around and playing cards, I was actually working.'

Kurt raised an eyebrow. 'As I recall, you were fighting for your life in the ring of doom. And I was rescuing you.'

'Ah, yes,' Joe said. 'But how do you think I ended up down there?'

'Someone must have recognized you.'

'Someone did,' Joe said. 'Ushi-Oni. As much as I hate to admit it, he got the jump on me. But once I stopped him from giving me a complimentary tracheotomy, I realized he'd given me the perfect chance to tag him. So while we wrestled, I slipped the coins into his pocket. Assuming he hasn't tossed them in a wishing well, you should have no problem following him now.'

Kurt offered a bow of respect to his friend. 'I stand corrected and duly impressed.'

'As am I,' Nagano said.

'We'll help you bring him in,' Kurt offered.

'No,' Nagano replied. 'You've done enough already. Ushi-Oni is too dangerous, I cannot have your blood on my hands as it almost was tonight. I will bring a few of my men into it. We'll track Ushi-Oni and take him as soon as possible.'

'All right,' Kurt said. 'You have your lead and we have ours. I hope you won't stop us from looking into Mr Han's activities.'

Nagano shook his head. 'Like I said, you'll find him in Nagasaki. He's scheduled to speak at the opening of his facility on the waterfront the day after tomorrow. Be careful. At the very least, he's a powerful man with friends in several nations. But if he did hire Ushi-Oni, he's more dangerous than I would have imagined.'

24

Osaka-to-Shanghai Ferry,
East China Sea

Gamay Trout picked her way through the narrow hall on the main deck of the Osaka-to-Shanghai ferry, squeezing past people, stacks of luggage and other items that lined the passageway. Because the journey was relatively short – and most of the passengers relatively poor – cabins were shared by multiple groups. Often six or eight people were in a room that would barely fit two on a standard Caribbean cruise ship.

This morning, the halls were particularly crowded as passengers who might have gone for fresh air on the upper deck remained inside, courtesy of gray skies and an icy rain.

Making it back to her cabin, she found Paul sitting at a desk that was entirely too small for him. 'How's it going?'

Paul was hunched over a chart, plotting their position. 'I've figured out where we are, but I was starting to wonder where you'd gotten to.'

'I had to navigate by memory,' she said. 'None of the signs are in English.'

She handed him a cup of hot liquid.

'Coffee?'

'Green tea,' she replied. 'It's all they had.'

Paul took the cup with a disappointed look on his face.

'It's good for you,' Gamay said.

He nodded. 'How do things look up top?'

'No one on deck,' she told him. 'Too cold and miserable to be outside.'

'That's one thing in our favor,' Paul said. 'We're only a few miles from the target zone, closer than I thought we'd be. We should probably wake up the *Remora* and make sure all systems are go.'

'I'll get to it.'

Gamay settled in and turned on her laptop while Paul opened the cabin's window. Brisk air poured in, freshening the room.

'Who needs coffee when you have salt air?' Gamay said.

'Me, for one,' Paul said. Standing beside the window, he removed a tightly wound bundle of cable from their luggage. With a twist of his hand, he attached a waterproof transmitter to the end and began feeding the cable through the open window. It slid down the side of the ship, drifting back with the wind until it eventually reached the sea.

'Transmitter is in the water,' Paul said. 'Let's hope no one looks out the window and wonders what this black wire is doing on the outside of the ship.'

'I wouldn't worry about it,' Gamay said. 'As far as I can tell, every passenger on this ship has congregated in the hall. I'm ready to transmit.'

'All clear.'

She tapped away at the keyboard and sent a signal to the *Remora*, commanding it to power up. After a short delay, she was rewarded with a signal from the ROV and the appearance of a remote command screen on her computer. It looked like a video game display, with virtual controls and dials across the bottom and a forward-looking camera view across the top. A bank of indicators on the right side of the screen displayed readings from the magnetometer and other sensors.

'All systems green,' she said. 'Disconnecting from the hull.'

At the touch of a button, the electromagnets in the *Remora*'s hull shut off and the ROV pitched down, diving to the right and away from the ferry's spinning propellers. Turbulent water could be seen on the screen until the *Remora* cleared the ship's wake.

'What's the new course?' Gamay asked.

'The target area is almost directly south of us,' Paul said, glancing at his chart. 'Set a heading of one-nine-zero.'

Gamay punched in the course, adjusted the dive angle and let the *Remora* do the rest. They were three miles from the target zone; it would take nearly twenty minutes to get there. 'Better hope the batteries are charged.'

Paul grinned. 'First thing I checked when we picked it up at the airport.'

With little to do as the submarine moved through the dark, Gamay began flicking through the instrument readings. Almost immediately, she noticed something odd.

'Check this out,' she said.

Paul leaned closer. 'What am I looking at?'

'Based on the speed setting, the *Remora* is traveling through the water at eleven knots. But its position marker is barely making seven. We're fighting a current.'

'Shouldn't be,' Paul said, looking at his charts. 'Considering our location and the time of year, the current should be in our favor, giving the *Remora* a push to the south.'

'Maybe so,' she said. 'But we've got the nautical equivalent of a four-knot headwind.'

'That might explain why we've been traveling north of the shipping lane for the last four hours instead of on the south side. Anything on the bottom profile yet?'

Gamay pressed another key. A graphic display of the seafloor beneath the *Remora* appeared. 'Flat as a pancake.'

'So much for my mountain range theory.'

'We're still a few miles from the target zone.'

Paul shook his head. 'If there was a new range growing up down there, I'd expect to see ridges and folding in the outer sedimentary layers. And we'd certainly detect a mild upslope.'

Gamay studied the readout for any sign of what Paul was describing, but she saw nothing to suggest a change in elevation. 'Let's let it play out before we go back to the drawing board.'

'Not much else we can do,' Paul said.

Gamay sat back, reaching for her cup of tea with one hand and tapping the keyboard with the other. Lazily, she cycled through a host of other readings: virtual topography, water temperatures and salinity levels. The computer organized the information into a series of displays and graphs, but the data made no sense.

'Something's wrong with the instruments,' she said, putting the teacup down.

'Why do you say that?'

'According to the temperature profile, it's getting warmer as the *Remora* goes deeper.'

Paul glanced over her shoulder. 'Have you passed through a thermocline?'

'No,' she said. 'No sudden change, just a slow, steady increase, approximately one degree for every seventy feet. That indicates a continuous mixing instead of boundary layer.'

'What about the salinity?' Paul asked.

Gamay tapped the key to bring up another sensor reading. 'Even more screwed up than the temperature profile. According to this, the salinity is decreasing as we descend.'

'That can't be right. Can you run a diagnostic on the sensor probes?'

Gamay didn't know enough about the ROV to diagnose a problem with the sensors, let alone fix it remotely. 'Maybe if Joe was here,' she said. 'All I got was a rudimentary lesson on driving the thing.'

'Bring it back up,' Paul suggested. 'Not all the way, just a hundred feet or so.'

'What good will that do?'

'If the sensors are failing, the temperature will continue to rise,' he said. 'But if they're working properly and we are actually dealing with an inverted temperature profile, the water should grow colder again.'

'Sneaky,' she said. 'I like it.'

Gamay changed the dive angle and put the ROV into

an ascent. 'Temperature dropping, salinity rising. The sensors are working correctly. Now what?'

'Resume course,' Paul said.

Satisfied but confused, Gamay adjusted the dive profile once more and sent the *Remora* back toward the deep. She had it level off at a depth of five hundred feet so they could map a wide section of the bottom before investigating up close.

'Still flat,' Gamay noted.

'Amazing,' he said. 'I've gotten shirts back from the dry cleaner that aren't that smooth.'

'So, no mountain range,' Gamay said, 'but temperature and salinity data that defy logic. Any thoughts?'

'Not at the moment,' Paul said. He glanced at the chart. 'You're nearing the epicenter of Kenzo's earth-quakes. Change course to the west.'

She made the adjustments and the readout changed. 'We're picking up something new.'

'Ridges and hills?' he said hopefully.

'Sorry, Charlie, it's a depression. It looks like a subsur-face canyon.'

The information on the chart suggested a flat plain. But as the *Remora*'s sonar bounced off the seafloor, a deep V-shaped gash was revealed. The point of the V was aimed like an arrow at Shanghai. 'Let's take a look at that chasm.'

Gamay was already changing course and directing the sub into the gap.

'Temperature continuing to rise,' she said. 'Salinity continues to drop.'

It defied all logic. Colder, saltier water was more dense than warm freshwater. It sank to the bottom of the world's oceans, sliding down into the subterranean canyons the way glaciers slid between the peaks of high mountain ranges.

At the bottom of every ocean were frigid pools and briny currents. Oceanographers considered them rivers because as they crept across the globe, they refused to mix with the rest of the sea.

As the *Remora* entered the canyon, Gamay turned on the lights. Sediment wafted by the camera like falling snow.

'One thousand feet,' she said.

'What depth is the *Remora* rated for?'

'Three thousand,' she said. 'But Joe built it, so it'll do twice that.'

From the sonar reading, they could see that the canyon was narrowing.

'Picking up the bottom,' Gamay said. 'Shall we take the full tour?'

'We paid for it,' Paul said. 'Might as well go on the ride.'

Gamay set the *Remora* onto a new course. 'I'm really fighting the current now,' she said. 'I have to keep five degrees down angle on the thrusters just to hold the depth.'

'So the current is flowing up the canyon?'

Gamay nodded. 'It's like we've entered an opposite world.'

Paul pointed to something on the sonar scan. 'What's that?'

Gamay angled toward a strange rise in the bottom of the canyon. The *Remora* had to fight like crazy to get near it, pushing and weaving like a bird flying into the wind. As it got closer, the target resolved into a cone-shaped rise. Crossing over it, the *Remora* was pushed violently to the side and then away.

Before Gamay could circle back, another cone-shaped structure appeared on the scan. And then another.

'What are they?' Gamay asked.

'I think I know,' Paul said, 'but keep going.'

Traveling down the canyon and zigzagging as it widened, they found dozens upon dozens of the protruding cones.

'I'm moving in closer to one of them,' Gamay said.

Using full power, the *Remora* crept up to the cone. The camera focused on its edge. Small amounts of sediment were blasting out of the cone, streaming toward the surface like ash from a volcano.

'It's a subsurface geyser,' Paul said. 'It's venting water.'

'Geothermal?'

'Has to be.'

'Let's get over the top,' Gamay said. 'It'll give us an idea of how much water is being ejected and allow us to get a direct sample.'

'Great idea,' Paul said.

She maneuvered the *Remora* up and over the very center of the cone. The submersible was immediately caught in the grips of the outflow. The view spun as the craft was thrust violently upward and outward, rising like a scrap of paper caught in the breeze on a hot summer day.

Gamay maneuvered the submarine away from the rising column of water and got it back under control. 'The

195

water in that plume is nearly two hundred degrees,' she said, checking the readings. 'Salinity is zero.'

Paul sat back and scratched his head. 'I've never seen anything like this.'

'Black smokers on the Mid-Atlantic Ridge,' she suggested.

'Not the same,' he said. 'They vent toxic sludge, high in sulfur and all manner of dangerous chemicals. Basically, volcanic soot. From the look of this chemical profile, you could bottle that water once it cooled down.'

'Keep it hot and we could make coffee with it,' she joked.

'Now you're talking,' he said. 'How many cones did you count before we stopped looking?'

'At least fifty,' she said.

'Let's see if there are any more.'

She redirected the *Remora* once again and it traveled down the canyon for another twenty minutes. They counted more than a hundred cones. There seemed to be no end to them.

'Picking up a source of iron,' Gamay said, checking the magnetometer. 'But we're starting to lose the signal.'

'Head toward it,' Paul said. 'We're getting close to maximum transmission range. We're going to lose the ROV any minute.'

She adjusted course once more, but the image on-screen began to glitch as pixels dropped out and the transmission became garbled. The view froze and then cleared.

'Hang in there,' Paul urged.

'Bottom coming up,' Gamay said.

The screen froze once more and then cleared just as the *Remora* crashed into the sediment pile.

'You've hit bottom,' Paul said.

Gamay was already adjusting the controls. 'No back-seat drivers, thank you.'

The impact caused a momentary blackout, but the link reset after several anxious moments. As the view resolved, the camera focused on a tangle of metallic wreckage.

'Something else was down there,' Paul said.

'It looks structural to me,' she said. Twisted steel plating and pipes were clearly visible. Whatever it had once been, it was now half buried.

Gamay adjusted the lights and then panned and zoomed the camera. The video flickered and a new sight appeared. 'That's an arm.'

It was white in appearance and stretching away from the camera. It looked like colorless, bleached flesh. But the shape was too perfect and consistent and the *Remora*'s lights reflected off its polished surface. At the end of the arm, they found a hand and mechanical fingers.

'Interesting.'

As the ROV hovered, its thrusters scoured away the loose sediment. A shoulder came into view next and then a face appeared from beneath the silt. Perfectly shaped and porcelain white, it filled the screen. It was like unearthing a statue of Athena.

'She's beautiful,' Paul said.

'She's a machine,' Gamay replied.

'Machines can be beautiful.'

Gamay nodded. That was true in many ways but oddly

disturbing in this situation. The beautiful machine seemed a little too human. It appeared to be alive even though it was not moving. The face held a sad quality. The eyes were open and looking up toward the surface as if waiting for a rescue that hadn't come.

It was the last image they recorded before the signal was lost for good.

25

Beijing

Wen Li trod carefully as he crossed Tiananmen Square. An early snow had dusted the ground. It painted the sky gray and settled in specks on the fur hats and dark green cloaks of the soldiers guarding Mao's tomb.

Wen smiled as he passed them. As the old joke went, no one knew if they were supposed to keep vandals out or the ghost of Chairman Mao trapped within.

It is the latter, of course. Mao and true communism were the past. China had transcended that era and become a capitalist dynamo. That was the present. And, in Wen's eyes, Empire was the future.

He passed the spot where Mao's tanks had famously stopped for a single protester who thought he could hold back the might of the state. Nothing marked the man's act. No one even knew who he was or if he was still alive. The moment lived only in people's memories.

At the western edge of the square, Wen reached his destination: a vast, monolithic building. He climbed a wide swath of triple-tiered steps, passed between towering marble columns and entered the Great Hall of the People.

The monstrous building was over a thousand feet in

width and six hundred feet from front to back. Its vaulted roof covered nearly two million square feet, larger by far than the American Capitol Building, the United Kingdom's Westminster Hall or even the giant Smithsonian Museum on the Mall in Washington, DC.

Inside lay several full-sized auditoriums with droll names, such as the Congressional Hall of the National People's Congress. Hundreds of offices, conference rooms and work areas were spread about. Wen's official, Party-sanctioned office lay at the southern end.

The guards stiffened at Wen Li's approach and he was hustled through the checkpoint without a word. He arrived at the end of the hall to find an old friend waiting outside his door.

'Admiral,' he said, as he entered, 'to what do I owe the pleasure?'

'I've come here with news,' the Admiral said. 'And a warning.'

Wen had broad influence within the Party, but there were those who didn't agree with his vision of China's future, those who thought the current trajectory was sufficient. They refused to see the limits put on them by American imperialism.

'A warning?' Wen replied. 'Personal or otherwise?'

'Both,' the Admiral said. 'Perhaps we should talk inside.'

Wen opened the door and the two men passed through the outer office and entered Wen's inner sanctum: a hothouse filled with hanging plants, stacks of old books and aged furniture of the most basic type.

Wen offered the Admiral a seat in an overstuffed chair,

as he saw to his plants. 'The heat is not healthy for them,' he said. 'It dries the leaves. But the cold is no better.'

'The same might be said for men like us,' the Admiral replied. 'Have you ever thought of stepping down?'

Wen put the watering can down. 'There is no retirement for us,' he said. 'We die at our posts . . . one way or another.'

'Usually after making a large mistake,' the Admiral said, laughing.

Wen shared the joke. A major misstep could bring an end to more than a career in the People's Republic. 'Are you suggesting I've made such an error?'

'There are rumors of your partnership with Walter Han,' the Admiral said. 'And then we have your operation in the East China Sea.'

'What of it?' Wen said. 'It was an experiment. Closed down last year.'

'Yes,' the Admiral said. 'And, at your request, I have spent considerable resources protecting the area. But whatever it was your people did down there, it's begun attracting attention of a most unwanted kind.'

'What are you telling me, Admiral?'

'To begin with, there are problems with the fisheries. One-point-five billion people require a great deal of food to sustain them. Our fishing fleet is the world's largest and our trawlers scour every sea on the globe, but the banks in the East China Sea have long been one of our most fertile resources. Not anymore. Catches are down every month since you began your experiments. The sea itself is turning barren. The men who run the fishing fleets are complaining . . . loudly.'

'I do not answer to fishermen,' Wen said coldly. 'At any rate, our operations took place on the seafloor. Deep-sea mining. You know this. Nothing we did could affect the aquatic ecosystem. More likely, pollution from Shanghai and its ten thousand factories are to blame, not a tiny operation my people have long since ended.'

The Admiral looked as if he'd expected this answer. 'Have you closed it down?'

'You know I have.'

'Then why did my ships detect an American submersible operating directly in your restricted zone?'

Wen caught himself before overreacting. 'I would ask you the same question, Admiral, since it's your job to see that they don't. When did this occur?'

'Early this morning,' the Admiral said. 'We picked up a coded transmission on a known American frequency. It was a short-range transmission. In addition, our sonar buoys briefly detected the presence of a vessel, though it was lost before we could locate it.'

Wen was simultaneously angered and puzzled. 'How did an American submarine penetrate your defenses?'

'This was not a naval vessel,' the Admiral said. 'The signature is consistent with a small, remotely operated submarine.'

'Which would have to be launched from a surface ship or dropped from an aircraft,' Wen said. 'So I'll ask again: how was it not prevented?'

The Admiral took the veiled accusation of malfeasance in stride. 'I assure you, comrade, no American aircraft or vessel has entered our zone of control. But an ROV *was* detected.'

Wen took a deep breath. The Admiral was a friend. He would not have come here in person only to lie. If the security forces had slipped up and allowed an American incursion, he would have hidden it, burned the reports and erased the data tapes to prevent his own embarrassment. 'You insist there were no American ships nearby?'

'None.'

The answer came to him all at once. He should have known before grilling his old friend. The vehicle was the only clue he really needed: a small submersible, operating without a support vessel in sight. It had to be the NUMA agents who'd flown to Japan for the meeting with the reclusive geologist.

Walter Han had failed to eliminate the Americans, despite his claims to the contrary. Now Wen would see to it himself.

He stood, signaling the end of the meeting. 'I appreciate your coming to me, Admiral. I assure you, there's nothing down there for the Americans to find. That said, my people will look into this breach of our territorial rights and respond accordingly.'

The Admiral stood. 'Be careful, Wen. This is not the nation it used to be. With wealth comes power and much wealth has been generated in the last twenty years. The Party is not absolute anymore. Other voices are of equal or greater volume. That is the price of economic success.'

Wen understood the warning. The moguls who'd made great fortunes and those who rode their coattails did not want anything to derail the economic train. They needn't have worried. If his plan came to fruition, not only would the train keep running but the track ahead would be clear as far as the eye could see.

It would happen, he told himself. But first, he had to eliminate the threat.

26

Paul stood on the ferry's top deck, staring at the Shanghai skyline. It was a beautiful city. A modern metropolis, with glittering buildings, high-speed trains and multilane highways. Paul looked forward to exploring it . . . if they ever got there.

'Any idea what's causing the holdup?' Gamay asked.

They were a mile from the dock, sitting idly in the harbor, as containership after containership passed them in both directions. A pilot had come on board two hours ago, but the ferry had yet to move.

'No,' Paul said. 'The engines are still running. I haven't seen any maintenance crews moving about. Maybe we just have to wait our turn. Shanghai is the busiest port in the world, you know.'

'I'm sure you're right,' she said. 'But I'm getting the sense this isn't a normal event.'

Paul had to agree. The crowded deck was rife with murmuring and hushed conversations, most prominently among the Chinese passengers who were going home. The Japanese businessmen and the foreign tourists seemed less concerned.

When a patrol boat began moving toward them, every

eye on deck focused on it. The lethal-looking vessel was painted battleship gray, armed with multiple guns and missile racks. It flew a military flag.

'Something tells me it's not the Port Authority,' Gamay said. 'What do you say we go back inside and get something to eat?'

'Great idea,' Paul said. 'I think I left something in the cabin anyway.'

Shouldering their backpacks, they moved against the general direction of the crowd and made their way inside and down the stairs. Reaching their deck, they continued down the hall.

As they neared their cabin, an announcement came over the intercom. First in Chinese, then Japanese, then English. 'All passengers return to your cabins. Have your passports and belongings ready for inspection.'

'That proves it to me,' Paul said. 'We need to hide. Or get off this ship.'

Paul unlocked the cabin door and ducked inside.

Gamay followed, shutting the door behind her. 'Not sure our cabin is the best place to lay low.'

'We're here only for the moment,' he said, moving to the window and looking down at the sea. 'We're in luck. The patrol boat docked on the other side of the ferry. Get out the transmission cable and tie it securely to something.'

'Are we swimming for it?' Gamay asked.

'Only as a last resort,' Paul said. 'Let's move quickly. We don't have a lot of time.'

*

On a lower deck, the captain of the ferry stood nervously by the main hatch. He watched as the gangway swung toward the patrol boat and locked in place. Twenty armed soldiers came across, followed by several officers and a man in civilian clothes.

The reasons for the stop had not been given and the captain knew better than to ask. He held tight to the knowledge that he'd done everything they had ordered him to do and that, as far as he knew, there was no contraband on his ship.

Behind the soldiers and their officers was the older man in civilian clothes – a rumpled suit that looked more comfortable than stylish. The man came across the gangway slowly, clutching the rail for balance. As he stepped onto the ferry, the officers and men stood at attention.

'My name is Wen Li,' the older man said to the captain. 'Do you know who I am?'

The captain grew more nervous now than before. Party officials did not visit old ferries in the harbor – not without good reason. He remained at attention as if he were a cadet on his first patrol. Sweat trickled through his hair. 'It's an honor to have you aboard, Minister. I'm at your service. What can I do for the Party today?'

Wen offered a kindly smile. 'You may relax, Captain. I require only that you keep the ship secure until my men speak with two of your passengers.'

From inside his jacket pocket, Wen produced a folded sheet of paper and handed it to the captain. On it were two names – odd-sounding names to the captain – either European or American.

The captain called for the purser. In a moment, they had the cabin number. 'I'll take you there myself,' the captain insisted.

They went up three decks and then walked aft along the main hall. Passengers stood and gawked and then moved out of the captain's way as he came toward them with the armed soldiers close behind.

A glance back told the captain only a third of the troop was following. He suspected others had been dispersed around the ship to block possible avenues of escape.

Moving quickly, the captain checked the numbers on each door, stopping one door from the cabin they were looking for. 'It's that one,' he said, pointing and stepping aside.

Wen nodded and motioned to one of the officers. The soldiers moved past them. Weapons were drawn, batons readied. One man stood back and then lunged forward. His swift kick hit the door right beside the handle. The door flew open, the flimsy lock coming apart in the effort. Two soldiers rushed in with their batons.

No combat ensued, no shouts of desperation or demands for submission. Just chatter between the soldiers. The tiny bathroom and small closet took only seconds to check.

One of the soldiers emerged. 'Cabin secure,' he said. 'They're not here.'

Wen stepped through the door and the ferry's captain followed him. He found the cabin in great disorder. Furniture had been tossed about, clothing and boots lay near two hastily discarded packs, the contents of which seemed to have been rummaged through and dumped.

A thin black cable had been tied around the bed frame. It crossed the far side of the cabin, stretching toward the window and vanishing beneath a gauzy curtain that wafted in the gentle breeze.

Wen put his hand on the cable and followed it. Pulling the curtain aside, he discovered that the inner window frame had been bent back and forced open.

The captain studied the damage. 'The windows only open eight inches.'

'Obviously, that was not enough,' Wen said.

The captain looked outside. The cable hung straight down the side of the ship, where it vanished into the dark water of the harbor. It was evident what had occurred.

'They're in the water,' Wen told the officers. 'Get the boats out to search for them. Immediately!'

'It's a mile to shore,' one of the officers replied. 'The current is strong and the water is like ice this time of year. Surely, they'll drown if they try to swim for it.'

Wen shook his head. 'These Americans are part of NUMA. They're trained divers and strong swimmers. They may have equipment: compact rebreathers or oxygen bottles. Do not underestimate them. I want police patrols along the shore and every boat you can requisition involved in the search.'

As the captain watched, the officer put a radio to his mouth and made the call. In the meantime, Wen took one more look around the cabin, made a brief search of the backpacks – and then left without another word.

The soldiers followed him out and the captain was left in the stateroom alone.

He glanced out the window again. There was no sign of anyone swimming, but the patrol boat could be heard coming around from the far side of the ferry.

American agents. Trained divers. High-ranking officials from the Party boarding his ship.

It was more excitement than he'd seen in years. For a moment, he wondered exactly what was going on, but, after thinking twice, he realized it was better if he didn't know.

27

Gamay listened to the water lapping against the side of the ship. It wasn't long before the reassuring and repetitive sound was overcome by the roar of the patrol boat. It raced around the bow of the ferry and charged along the starboard side, slowing only as it neared the cable dangling from the window of their cabin.

From high above it, Gamay grinned. 'Pretty smooth idea, dropping the cable out the window and making it look like we'd gone overboard. They think we're swimming for shore. They're searching for us now.'

The anchor chain locker was crowded, oily and mildly claustrophobic, with several hundred feet of heavy chain piled up inside it. It was no place for comfort, but it made for a terrific hiding spot.

'I'd have preferred something in the cargo hold,' Paul said, 'but those soldiers we spotted changed my mind.'

They'd narrowly avoided one gang of soldiers in the forward section of the cargo hold and, after catching sight of a second squad, made a change of plans.

Coming forward, they pried open the hatch to the locker and climbed inside. As Paul pulled the hatch shut, he made sure to prevent it from latching.

'The *pièce de résistance* was all your idea,' Paul said. 'If you hadn't mentioned it, I'd have kept my boots on.' He wiggled his toes for emphasis.

It had been Gamay's suggestion to dump their boots, backpacks and other belongings in the room, with the exception of the laptop computer, which was now wrapped in a plastic bag and tucked under Paul's shirt. 'Nobody swims with all their luggage,' she said. 'It would have been a dead giveaway. I'm just glad they took the bait.'

'Can you see what they're doing?' Paul asked.

Large piles of heavy chain surrounded them, filling up the room and exiting through an opening called a hawsehole. Gamay was able to peer through the gap between the chain and the hull to see most of the starboard side. 'They've moved toward the stern,' she said. 'They're checking under the fantail.'

A moment later, the boat disappeared around the aft end. As it did, a second boat raced out toward the ferry and then a third. 'Calling in reinforcements,' she said.

Shortly afterward, a distant boom reached them, muffled and distorted by the hull. Over the next few moments, they heard several more. Each farther off than the last. The impact reverberated through metal skin as if the two of them were sitting inside a giant drum.

'What do you think all that's about?' Gamay asked.

'Fishing expedition,' Paul said. 'Using dynamite or grenades.'

'Trying to blow us out of the water?'

Paul nodded. 'Not a bad strategy, considering how vulnerable an unprotected diver is to shock waves.'

Because of the way seawater transmitted sound and force, a grenade explosion a hundred feet off would rupture eardrums and cause concussions. Any closer and it might kill them outright.

The explosions continued sporadically for at least the next twenty minutes, and perhaps even longer, but all external sound was drowned out when the ferry's engines came back to life.

Soon the big ship began to move. 'Looks like they're finally going to dock this ferry.'

'I'd be happier if they were sending us back to Japan,' Paul said, 'even considering the accommodations. But we couldn't be that lucky. They'll dock the ship, all right. Then they'll off-load the passengers with plenty of extra eyes at customs to watch for us in the crowd.'

'And when they don't see us in the line,' Gamay began, 'or spot our bodies floating on the surface after all those makeshift depth charges?'

'They'll search the ship again,' Paul said. 'Which means we either stay here until the ferry goes back to Osaka – which could be days, or longer if they quarantine the vessel – or we find a way to get off this boat without drawing any attention to ourselves.'

'I vote for fresh air,' Gamay said. 'I know they'll probably just tie up to the pier, but I'd rather not be in here if they drop that anchor.'

'Deafening and dangerous, at the very least,' Paul said. 'We know they've searched the cargo hold already. I say we make our way back there and find a nice container to hide in.'

'Great idea,' she said. 'Lead on.'

It would take twenty minutes to work their way from the anchor chain locker to the cargo deck, where they found an unlocked cargo container filled three-quarters of the way up with sacks of rice.

They crawled in on top of the bags, moved a few of them around to present a false wall – as if the bags were stacked all the way to the roof – and waited. Breathing was no problem, as rice shipments required plentiful ventilation to prevent condensation from wetting the grains and spoiling them.

Eventually, the ferry docked and a group of stevedores came on board to begin the unloading. It took hours. At one point, the container doors were opened and then closed. Then the container was loaded onto a flatbed and driven off the ship.

When all movement had stopped, Gamay figured they had traveled about ten miles. 'We seem to have been placed into storage,' she said.

They listened for any sounds but heard none.

'Let's find out where we are,' she said.

Paul did the honors, crawling across the sacks of rice to the corner of the container where he could gaze through one of the ventilation slits. 'Warehouse,' he said. 'I can't see anything but other containers.'

'If it's all quiet out there, we should probably make our move.'

After shoving the heavy bags aside, they opened the door a crack. The warehouse was dark and looked deserted.

'All clear,' Gamay said. 'I say we make our way to the American Consulate. If we can get inside unnoticed, we can get this information back to Washington and escape with our lives.'

28

Mountain District, Japan

Superintendent Nagano followed Ushi-Oni using the tracking coin. It was an ingenious piece of electronic design, transmitting a signal on the cell phone band and sending a pulse only once every thirty seconds, which made it virtually undetectable to any person holding it.

At a long distance, the signal was relayed by the nation's vast network of cell towers, but, closer in, Nagano used a dedicated receiver to home in on the GPS coordinates being transmitted from the coin.

The signal led him out of Tokyo and onto a twisting mountain road. When the assassin stopped at a gas station to get fuel and use the restroom, Nagano snuck up to his car and placed a second transmitter under the bumper in case Oni used or lost the coin.

With two transmitters in place, Nagano dropped well back of his quarry, keeping out of sight and waiting for the opportune moment to arrest him.

To his surprise, Ushi-Oni continued higher into the mountains, heading to the foothills of Mount Fuji, before turning onto an obscure side road and finally stopping an hour later.

Nagano studied the satellite image. It displayed nothing

but a forested hillside. A yellow icon suggested a small guesthouse was hidden beneath the trees. As was a natural *onsen* – a traditional hot spring, mineral bath. In addition, a Shinto shrine lay nearby.

Nagano drove past the guesthouse, continued several miles up the road and then pulled over. When thirty minutes had passed without any movement from either of the two transmitters, he doubled back and approached the inn cautiously.

Ushi-Oni's car remained in the lot, along with twenty other vehicles. The busy state of the guesthouse didn't surprise Nagano – both the hot springs and the Shinto shrines were popular spots to visit. Some drew millions of visitors per year, though this particular shrine was smaller and all but unknown.

According to the information he was able to pull up on the computer, it was not even open to the public. All in all, he found it a strange place for Ushi-Oni to stop.

Nagano checked on the location of the original transmitter just in case Ushi-Oni had come here to switch cars. The tracking coin was signaling him from a spot inside the guesthouse.

Convinced that Ushi-Oni was there, Nagano parked in the lot and called his most trusted subordinate. 'I've tracked the Demon to a shrine in the mountains,' he explained. 'Bring two of your best men. We'll arrest him tonight.'

After being assured that reinforcements would be there soon, Nagano loosened his tie and waited.

*

Ushi-Oni stood in a small room, pressed against the wall and peering through a tiny gap between the curtain and the window frame. Seeing no movement in the parking lot or out on the street, he eased the curtain back into place and walked away from the glass.

He opened a small case, pulled out a pair of throwing knives and slipped them into slots in the loose jacket he wore. He then closed the case, checked his watch and left the room. He still had time. Plenty of time.

He made his way through the inn and out onto a narrow path that led to the *onsen*. Disrobing completely, he showered first and then lowered himself into the bubbling water of the natural hot spring. He sat with his back against the wet black rock that surrounded the bath as the steam enshrouded him and obscured anything beyond the rim of bubbling waters.

After several minutes, a shape came down the path, emerging from the fog beyond. The new arrival wore a white robe and an oddly shaped black hat known as a crow hat, or *karasu*. He was a Shinto priest.

'*Shinsoku,*' Oni said, addressing the man by a term that meant *employee of the gods*. The term was reserved for those who took care of the shrines. 'I was beginning to doubt that you would come.'

The priest was staring at Oni's colorful tattoos. 'You are the one who contacted us?'

'Yes,' Oni said.

'You have asked for the purification ritual,' the priest said, confirming.

'Who would need it more than I?' Oni said.

The priest nodded. 'It is my duty to guide you.'

'I have already bathed,' Ushi-Oni said. 'What must I do next?'

'Put on your robe and follow me. I will show you.'

Ushi-Oni climbed out of the waters, pulled on a robe and put his feet into a pair of slippers. Clutching his folded clothes in one arm, he followed the priest on a path that took them back into the woods, away from the inn and up toward the shrine.

They traveled for half a mile, walking between tall stands of bamboo, until they came to a series of vermilion-colored gates known as *torii*. Each gate had two vertical posts, painted in the traditional red-orange scheme. They were capped by a black lintel with upturned ends from which oil lanterns hung, illuminating the path in a flickering light.

Beyond the first *torii* was another and then another. Some were old and dilapidated, others were newer. Inscriptions carved into them displayed the names of the families that had paid for them in hopes of securing good fortune.

'Is it true that the Tokagawa family once supported this shrine?' Ushi-Oni asked.

'Tokagawa?' the priest said. 'No, I'm afraid that's only a myth.'

They crested a hill and the path leveled off. Passing under the final gate, they arrived at the shrine itself: a small covered structure with an altar beneath it. A water-filled trough stood off to the side and two carved stone animals guarded the approach.

Ushi-Oni stepped toward it.

'You must wash first,' the priest said.

Ushi-Oni felt the sting of being told what to do. 'I told you, I've already bathed.'

'The hands must be clean,' the priest said.

Reluctantly, Ushi-Oni placed his clothes aside and dipped his hands in the trickling water. The water was frigid, completely opposite to the hot bath he'd come from.

He pulled his hands out, shook them off and glared at the priest. 'I've brought an offering.'

'You must rinse your mouth as well,' the priest said.

Ushi-Oni ignored the request and pulled out the marker chip that Han had given him. A marker that he'd chosen not to redeem.

'What is it?' the priest asked.

'A relic of my former life.'

The priest looked him over sternly, studying him like a disapproving schoolmaster. 'Your past is a criminal one.'

And my future, Ushi-Oni thought. 'I wish to escape who I am and reinvent myself as someone new. Isn't that what you're here for?'

'So it is,' the priest said. He picked up a ladle, filled it with water and handed it to Oni. 'But you must rinse your mouth. It is required.'

Ushi-Oni had played the part long enough. He tossed the ladle down in disgust and stepped toward the old man, grabbing him by the loose vestments.

'You are possessed of an evil spirt,' the priest said.

'You have no idea,' Ushi-Oni growled. 'Now, take me to the sanctuary. I wish to view what the Tokagawa family placed in your possession.'

The priest squirmed, but his feeble strength was no match for Ushi-Oni's. 'There is nothing there to see,' the priest stammered. 'Nothing there for a criminal to steal. Just wisdom, which you reject.'

'I'll be the judge of that,' Ushi-Oni said.

The priest tried to free himself, but Ushi-Oni slammed him against the trough, stunning him. The frail man went limp and Oni pulled his garment open. Around the priest's neck hung a set of keys.

Oni grabbed and ripped them forth hard enough to snap the chain on which they hung.

The priest cried out, but Ushi-Oni covered his mouth and then snapped his neck with a swift twist of his arms.

Dropping the body to the ground, Ushi-Oni looked around him. A cool wind rustled through the bamboo, but, other than that, the forest was quiet.

Certain that he was alone, Oni took off his robe and then removed the priest's garment and pulled it over his shoulders. The robe fit snugly; Oni was much larger than the dead priest. And, try as he might, he could not place the strange hat in a manner that looked normal. He slid the strap under his chin and left it crooked.

Before leaving the shrine, he dropped the naked priest in the trough. 'Cleanse yourself, *shinsoku*.'

With the evidence of his first crime hidden, Oni tossed the brass casino marker toward the shrine, picked up his folded clothes once again and continued on the path toward the Shinto monastery up above.

*

Superintendent Nagano was glad to see the white van pull in beside him. His most trusted lieutenant and two plain-clothes officers got out.

'Is he still here?' the lieutenant asked.

Nagano pointed toward the hills. 'He's gone up to the shrine.'

The lieutenant looked suspicious. 'What would a man like Ushi-Oni want at a shrine?'

'I doubt he's after forgiveness,' Nagano said.

'And you're sure it's him?'

'I saw him twice. It's the man Zavala described,' Nagano said. 'I want to take him alive. Preferably, out in the woods where there are no civilians.'

The lieutenant nodded. He carried a pistol and what they called a shock stick, essentially a high-powered Taser on a long pole – very useful in crowd control. The two officers had Heckler & Koch submachine guns, derivatives of the famous MP5 except with a much shorter barrel, a feature that made them excellent for close-quarters combat.

Nagano pulled out his own pistol. He was tired of waiting. 'Let's go.'

They moved quickly and silently, passing the vacant *onsen* and climbing their way up the bamboo-lined path to the thicket of *torii* gates. They arrived at the shrine without incident. There they stopped, but all they found was the hotel robe hastily rolled up and stuffed under the altar.

'He was wearing this,' Nagano said. 'He must have changed back into his own clothing.'

'Look at this,' one of the men called from beside the trough.

Nagano rushed over and the two of them lifted the dead priest out of the purifying water.

'Any doubt that this is the Demon we're tracking should be gone now.'

'Are you still getting a signal?' the lieutenant asked.

Nagano checked the display on his tablet. They were not in range of any cell towers there in the mountains, but with the direct-seeking mode, he was able to locate the tracking coin. 'He's in the sanctuary.'

They rushed along the path, arriving at the entrance to the monastery building only to find the front door ajar. Candles flickered here and there. A small fire burned in a stone hearth, but there was no sign of Ushi-Oni. Or anyone else, for that matter.

'I don't like it,' the lieutenant said. 'It's too quiet.'

'Where are the priests?' one of the men asked.

Nagano couldn't answer that. Some of the smaller shrines were sparsely attended or even left alone, but the sanctuary and the candles told him this one was occupied. He clicked off the safety on his pistol. 'We can only assume the worst.'

The lieutenant nodded. 'Which way?'

Nagano checked the scanner. The red dot blinked steady and still. 'He's in the back. Let's go.'

They moved down the hall and came upon the body of another priest. He lay in a pool of blood just inside one of the doors. They found three more in the next room. Two more bodies and a pair of ransacked rooms confirmed that Ushi-Oni was on a killing spree.

Nagano paused and made a slashing motion across his

neck. All thoughts of taking Ushi-Oni alive had vanished. They would shoot him on sight. If he lived, so be it. If he didn't . . . he would be getting what he deserved.

Nagano crept forward. They were nearing the end of the hall. The flashing indicator on Nagano's screen told them Ushi-Oni was in the room on the left.

For the first time, Nagano could hear movement. He braced himself, took a deep breath and then lunged forward, kicking the door open.

He saw a figure dressed in black who was hunched over a desk. He raised his weapon and was about to fire when the figure turned. It wasn't the face of a killer but another of the elderly priests.

The man was tied to the chair with an electrical cord. On the desk in front of the prisoner, sitting on a folded white garment, was a tiny circular object with a hole in the middle. *The tracking coin.*

Realization came too late. A shout of pain from behind him confirmed it.

Nagano spun in time to see the flash of a sword decapitate his lieutenant and take the arm off of another of the men.

The third officer was already on the ground, a throwing knife sticking out of his back.

Nagano fired once but missed and the bullet buried itself uselessly in the wall. The flashing sword hit the side of the pistol before Nagano could fire again. It took off the tips of his fingers and knocked the gun across the room.

Nagano dove for the weapon, trying to grasp it with his right hand, but Ushi-Oni was faster. A kick to the ribs sent Nagano over onto his side. He wound up against the desk with the point of the ancient sword pressed up against his neck.

He froze as the Demon stared down at him. He expected to be run through at any second, but instead Ushi-Oni laughed and held him there like an insect under a pin.

'Looking for this?' Ushi-Oni said, as he picked up the tracking coin.

Nagano said nothing. He was grasping his hand to stop the bleeding and desperately thinking of a way to reach the pistol. The truth was, any movement would split the skin of his throat.

Ushi-Oni twisted the sword a fraction and blood began to trickle down Nagano's neck. 'Did you really think I wouldn't notice you following me? I saw you below me on the switchback road. I waited for you at the gas station and watched as you placed that beacon on my car. I must admit, it made me wonder how you had been tracking me in the first place. Then I found your little coin.'

As Oni spoke, he held the coin is his hand. 'Close,' he added. 'Very, very close. But it's not quite as heavy as the real thing.'

He flung it at Nagano, hitting him in the face.

'Go ahead and kill me,' Nagano said. 'It won't save you. You slaughter monks and policemen. You'll have nowhere to hide after this. Not now that your face is known.'

Instead of killing him, Ushi-Oni crouched and picked up the shock stick, testing its weight in his free hand. 'Once they see what you do,' he said, 'they'll forget all about me.'

With that, he jammed the shock stick into Nagano's chest and sent a powerful wave of electricity through him. A second wave followed and then a third. Nagano couldn't do anything but spasm with each shock and try to endure the pain.

He lasted several minutes and then his world faded mercifully to black.

29

Nagasaki

The city of Nagasaki was sandwiched between the mountains and the ocean at the western tip of Japan. With limited space to build outward, its neighborhoods rose up into the hills, where they gazed at one another across a narrow bay.

The geography gave Nagasaki a compact, old-world feel, reminiscent of San Francisco. It was a feeling enhanced by the bustling port and the high-decked suspension bridge coated in orange paint that linked the two sides together.

Kurt, Joe and Akiko arrived in the city driving another car from Kenzo's collection. A 1972 Skyline GT-R. The four-door sedan was one of the first truly collectable cars produced on the island. Still, it was bare-bones compared to the Bentley.

'One might say our vehicular status seems to be trending in the wrong direction,' Joe said from the backseat, 'but I think I prefer this to the Bentley.'

Akiko turned to Joe from the passenger seat. 'I'm glad you appreciate it,' she said. 'This is the first car I restored for Master Kenzo. It was a labor of love.'

'The lines are classic and aggressive,' Joe said. 'Just the way I like them.'

Kurt rolled his eyes and took the ramp to the bridge. 'A rental car would have been just fine. It would have included a better heater.'

Akiko shook her head. 'Rental cars are too automated. Did you know the car companies track their whereabouts using RFID tags and the signals from the satellite radio receivers? They don't need LoJack or any other dedicated system to watch you. And many newer cars are equipped with remote operating authority. They can turn off your engine from a computer terminal whenever they like.'

Kurt grinned; something about conspiracy theorists warmed his heart. 'Which they probably wouldn't do as long as Rudi keeps paying the credit card bills. Anyway, we're not trying to sneak up on anyone. Our whole plan is based on speaking with Walter Han face-to-face.'

'And just how do you intend to make that happen?' Joe asked.

'I'm going to walk right up to him and ask him for help.'

Kurt said no more. They took the Hirado Bridge, crossed Nagasaki Bay and then drove down toward a sprawling facility that lay dockside. The gleaming complex took up a hundred acres and looked more like the futuristic headquarters of an advanced civilization than a factory. Geometrically arranged concrete buildings were set up in a campus-style arrangement. A sculpture garden lay between them, complete with walking paths and gently flowing water in narrow chutes. A track for testing automated vehicles was visible behind the facility, its snaking turns offset by a long straightaway that ran along the waterfront.

'That's Han's new facility,' Kurt noted. 'Owned and

operated by his company, China-Nippon Robotics, a joint venture with a group of wealthy Japanese investors. It officially opens today. First of two big ceremonies. The Prime Minister of Japan, the Mayor of Nagasaki and several members of Parliament are on hand. Each of them will be giving a short speech, which, if you know politicians, means a long-drawn-out talk.'

'They came all the way down here for a ribbon cutting?' Joe asked.

'There's more on tap,' Kurt said. 'The cooperation agreement between China and Japan is being signed here tomorrow. Not at the factory but at a place called the Friendship Pavilion. Also built with Han's money.'

'How to win friends and influence nations,' Joe said.

'Exactly,' Kurt replied. 'But it gives us a chance to move around unnoticed. They're running this whole thing like a trade show. Both events are open to the public. That includes us.'

Kurt navigated the narrow streets, drove onto the grounds and was directed toward an underground parking garage. After parking, they left the car, found an escalator and emerged into the hum of a bustling crowd.

Lights flashed all around them, small machines moved here and there, a holographic face projected on a veil of mist greeted them. 'The future is closer than you think . . .' its recorded voice said.

Ahead of them, neon lights and pulsating music made it seem as if they were walking into a club. Artificial arms, complete with painted fingernails, stretched from a wall, offering to shake hands.

Akiko shook her head. *'Akumu,'* she whispered, using the Japanese word for *nightmare*. 'It's like the seventh ring of hell.'

Kurt noticed her demeanor. It wasn't a phobia or discomfort, just a sort of resigned disgust, like a pious man walking into Sodom and Gomorrah. 'Consider this an educational opportunity. At least you'll know what you're missing.'

'Or escaping from,' she said.

After picking up badges at the front desk, they were given headsets that could be tuned to a specific language. As they approached the various booths and displays, a recording was triggered in the headset, explaining what they were looking at.

The first booth was a generic industrial display. 'Advanced robotics will eliminate the need for man to perform many tedious tasks,' the recording told them. 'Within a decade, our robotics will replace the boredom of long-distance driving, the backbreaking labor of working in a warehouse, delivering packages or hauling away trash. Even the construction of roads will be automated by giant machines, freeing humanity from the burden.'

'And freeing them from their paychecks,' Joe said.

'Not a fan of automation?' Kurt asked.

'Not if it renders me obsolete.'

'Now you're thinking my way,' Akiko said.

They wandered to another section of the facility where a crowd had gathered. 'Here we have the service version of our latest human assistance model, the HAM 9X.'

As the light came up, they saw a female form in a

French maid's outfit. The face was soft and realistic, although quite expressionless. The eyes were bright. The lips plum-colored and supple.

'My name is Ny Nex,' the robot said, the lips moving as she spoke. A wink followed, which pleased all the men in the crowd. 'I'm here to handle your every need.'

Kurt was surprised by the human quality of the voice. It sounded neither prerecorded nor computer-generated. He moved closer and studied the machine. In a simulated kitchen, it rinsed and dried dishes and unloaded several bags of groceries, putting everything into its proper place. It then began to make a pot of freshly ground coffee, all without spilling a single grind.

'I think we've found the solution to your girlfriend drought,' Kurt said to Joe.

Akiko gave Joe a sideways look and Joe shook his head, protesting vigorously. 'I like to work on machines. I'm not interested in dating one.'

'How wonderful,' Akiko said, her voice dripping with sarcasm. 'Soon we won't need other humans for anything. We can all live on our own, surrounded by mechanical servants.'

'Not me,' Joe said. 'I prefer a human touch.'

Kurt had to laugh. He'd never seen Joe so smitten. He glanced at his watch. 'We need to get over to the ceremony if we're going to catch Han's speech.'

They moved on, passing several other interesting displays and making their way to the great hall. It was standing room only in the auditorium. Up on the dais, Walter Han was speaking not about robotics but about opportunities for Japan and China to cooperate.

'The two great powers of Asia will change the world in this coming century, but first we must change our relationship. The past must be forgotten. The mistakes of the previous century left to history so as not to derail the future.'

'Interesting subject, considering all the tension in the South China Sea and the dispute over the Senkaku Islands,' Joe noted.

Han soon touched on that. '. . . The Chinese government is now moving to end several impasses,' he said. 'A new proposal granting Japan full control over the islands in question is being prepared. No longer will we fight over trivial things, when partnership can bring both great nations so much more.'

A wave of applause went up.

'He speaks as if he holds all the power,' Akiko replied.

'Nagano said he has a quasi-diplomatic status.'

'But did you hear the word he chose? *Granting* Japan control over her own islands.' Akiko was offended. 'The arrogance drips from him.'

Kurt didn't argue. He just turned back to Han and listened. Eventually, he finished and the ribbon was cut. China-Nippon Robotics was officially open for business and the celebration began.

While the political figures vanished – hustled offstage by their security teams – Han came forward, glad-handing his way through the crowd, stopping and talking to people on the way.

'Time for me to go introduce myself,' Kurt said.

Joe stepped aside. 'We'll meet you outside in the hall. Good luck.'

The auditorium was emptying as Kurt made his way down the aisle. The longer Han was delayed, the more effort he put into leaving. He shook hands more briskly and cut every conversation short. He brushed off one man with a quick smile and a bow and then turned to go, only to find Kurt blocking his path.

'Walter Han,' Kurt said, proffering a hand. 'So glad I caught you. Excellent speech, by the way.'

Han's face was a mask that didn't reveal much, but a look of surprise had appeared for the briefest of instants. 'I'm sorry,' Han said. 'Do I know you?'

'Not personally,' Kurt said. 'My name is Austin. Kurt Austin. I'm the head of Special Projects at NUMA – the National Underwater and Marine Agency, based out of Washington, DC. You and I haven't met face-to-face, but I – or, should I say, my technical people – are big fans of your work.'

Han's demeanor went from annoyed to pleasant. 'How, exactly?'

Kurt played the part to the hilt. 'We use a growing number of robotic and automated vehicles in our deep-sea efforts. We're currently beginning an important expedition into anomalies we've discovered in the East China Sea.'

Kurt hoped to spook Han, but the mention of the East China Sea brought nothing from the man. He remained taciturn and opaque.

'China-Nippon Robotics would be honored to work with an organization as renowned as NUMA,' Han replied. 'In fact, we have several aquatic models designed for pipeline inspection and deep-sea drilling that you may find useful. Call my office on Monday. I'll put you in touch with the operations director.'

'I'm afraid Monday will be too late,' Kurt said. 'We launch tomorrow. We feel it's urgent not to waste any time.'

'Why the rush?' Han asked, his brow knitted together for effect.

'The anomalies I'm speaking of are geologic in nature,' Kurt explained, 'a series of inexplicable earthquakes. Considering the region's history with tsunamis and other tectonic disasters, we feel the investigation cannot be delayed. In other words, we need to know what's going on down there. Any chance you and I could talk later tonight?'

Han shook his head. 'Not possible. But leave your contact information with my office. If the chance to help does come up, CNR would be glad to oblige.'

He shook Kurt's hand again. 'Best of luck. Enjoy the Expo. Excuse me.'

With that, Han brushed past. He continued down the aisle, accompanied by several of his people, and pushed out into the hall.

Kurt let him go, before meeting up with Joe and Akiko.

'Well?' Joe asked. 'Has the tree been shaken?'

'It has,' Kurt said. 'Unfortunately, it turned out to be an oak. He didn't bat an eye.'

'Did you lay it on thick?'

'Any thicker and you'd need a road grader to spread it.'

'Maybe Superintendent Nagano was right,' Akiko said. 'To continue your tree metaphor, perhaps we're barking up the wrong one.'

Kurt wasn't ready to give in. 'Let's give it time to work. If he's involved, he'll respond, one way or another.'

'And if he's clean?'

'Then he'll go back to his office, laugh about the crazy American he just met and we'll be back to square one.'

30

CNR Factory

Han made it from the ceremony to his office without further interruption. He shut the door firmly and took a seat at his desk. In silence, he contemplated the interruption he'd just dealt with. Something had to be done about the interference from Austin and NUMA.

He placed his finger on a scanner built into his desktop. After reading his fingerprint, it confirmed his identity and released the locks on his desk. From the second drawer down, he pulled out a special phone and plugged it into a dedicated jack in the side of his computer.

With a few taps of the keyboard, he initiated an encryption program and then placed a call. A yellow icon appeared on-screen as the initial connection was made. The symbol turned green once the encryption codes were accepted and matched.

'Secure line,' a voice said from the other end.

'Secure line,' Han repeated. 'Connect me to the Minister.'

'Stand by.'

As he waited, Han loosened his tie, which had begun to feel constricting around his neck. That done, he poured himself a drink and took a large gulp from the glass.

The voice came over the computer speaker. 'I have the Minister, sir. Go ahead.'

The line cleared and he was connected to Wen Li at his office in Beijing. 'We have a problem,' Han said. 'We need to call off the operation.'

There was a brief moment of static before Wen Li replied. 'We have problems on several fronts,' Wen admitted, 'but it's too late for us to turn back. Things have been put in motion that cannot be stopped.'

'We're facing risk of imminent exposure,' Han said. 'Kurt Austin confronted me today regarding a geological anomaly on the bottom of the East China Sea.'

'That would not surprise me,' Wen said, 'except that you told me Austin had been eliminated.'

Han had known they were alive since the incident at the casino, but he hadn't reported that information back to Wen. 'I was led to believe they'd been killed in the fire,' he said. 'They must have falsified their deaths and continued to investigate. An amateurish ploy.'

'Which you seem to have fallen for.'

Han burned with indignation. 'Maybe you're not grasping the magnitude of what I've just said. Austin came here – to my place of business – he walked right up to me, only moments after I finished my appearance with the Japanese Prime Minister. That cannot be a coincidence. It means they've connected CNR and me to the events in the Serpent's Jaw. They intend to survey the area. It will lead to the mining site.'

'A bluff,' Wen said.

'How can you be so sure?'

'Because they've already surveyed it,' Wen explained, 'and they found nothing.'

Han was stunned. Apparently, he wasn't the only one keeping information to himself. 'How and when did this occur?'

'Yesterday,' Wen replied. 'We detected signals emanating from an ROV. Sonar was intermittent, due to the small size of the submersible, but we're almost certain that they found the original mining site.'

Han put a hand to his temple and massaged away the growing pain. 'How could this happen? I thought naval units of the PLA had that area locked down.'

Wen explained the breach with grudging admiration. 'I will admit they found a novel way around our net. A method we hadn't considered. But, in hindsight, their discovery will prove irrelevant.'

'Not if they send the information back to Washington.'

'That will never occur,' Wen promised. 'The NUMA agents are here in Shanghai. We'll soon have them in custody. They will be charged with espionage and used as bargaining chips. And, to their dismay, they will find they've thrown their lives away for nothing. Even a detailed survey with accurate sonar maps, video footage and ground-penetrating sonar will reveal very little to anyone. The real work was deep under the seafloor in the tunnels carved out by your machines, too deep for standard sonar to reveal.

'At best, the Americans will have discovered a subsurface mining operation that was destroyed by some minor geologic activity and the wreckage of an aquatic habitat, half buried in the canyon. They will have learned nothing about the nature of the operation or the Golden Adamant. And by the time they do, we'll be in control of the Japanese government, and you and your agents will be free to mine all the Golden Adamant on Hokkaido. Providing you can actually find it.'

Han was put on the defensive. 'We're very close,' he insisted. 'I will soon be in possession of the ancient swords and Masamune's journal, which tells of their forging. Those items will lead us directly to the mine from which Masamune obtained the alloy in the first place. But none of that will do any good if the NUMA agents in Shanghai or their associates here expose us.'

Wen fell quiet for a moment, like he often did when they were playing Go. Han took the moment to take another drink.

Finally, the old man spoke again. 'You say Austin came to you?'

'He asked for my help in the exploration.'

'A bold stroke,' Wen said. 'He must have been trying to shake you.'

'I assure you, he learned nothing.'

'Still, there's a great deal to be admired in the way he plays the game. And much to learn.'

'Such as?'

'Remember the first lesson of the board,' Wen told him. 'Your greatest opportunities occur when your opponent overextends himself. He becomes easy to cut off. Austin's aggressiveness makes him vulnerable. I believe we can use his arrogance against him.'

'How?'

'We have planned to move against the Japanese Prime Minister using vaguely American assets. Is that not correct?'

'We have captured two servicemen,' Han insisted. 'The American government believes they've gone AWOL.'

'Get rid of them,' Wen said. 'Their dereliction of duty will make their actions too questionable. In their place, we will use others with more impressive résumés.'

'You mean . . .'

'I do,' Wen said. 'How much better for us if a well-known American agent who once worked for the CIA was seen killing the Japanese Prime Minister as he signed a friendship agreement with China? It would infuriate the Japanese public. It would seal the realignment like nothing else.'

Han felt a wave of energy wash over him and he began to grin. 'You're correct as always, Lao-shi. I apologize for not seeing the opportunity sooner. Austin has played directly into our hands.'

31

Shanghai

The howling grind of a large engine cut off all conversation as the double-decker bus, with its top removed, accelerated along a crowded road in Shanghai.

Modern buildings passed by on either side, while sharply dressed shoppers walked the streets with bags of brand-name merchandise in their hands. Up ahead, a construction crew worked on the outside lane, slowing traffic to a crawl.

Paul Trout stood on the lower level of the bus, his arm raised high, his hand gripping a strap that hung from the ceiling. Gamay sat in the window seat next to him. After making their way out of the warehouse, they'd bought new shoes and new clothes while formulating a plan to get themselves to the Consulate unseen.

The answer came to Paul in a brochure for Shanghai Tours Ltd. Two hours later, he and Gamay boarded the brightly painted bus and began a slow jaunt around the city.

They rode in relative comfort, surrounded by other tourists, many of whom were European or American. It helped them to blend in instead of sticking out like a sore thumb.

The route took them past historic temples, palatial government structures and even a sprawling concrete building that had once housed the largest slaughterhouse in the world. It was now renovated and filled with upscale shops and restaurants, including several that offered vegan or vegetarian fare.

They stopped briefly at the Oriental Pearl Tower, the most famous landmark in Shanghai. A bundle of spheres and huge tubular supports that rose fifteen hundred feet into the sky.

'It looks like a science experiment gone awry,' someone on the bus said.

'A Buck Rogers rocket ship,' someone else suggested.

Paul and Gamay pretended to be impressed with everything they saw, but all they really cared about was the last leg of the journey, when the bus would drive through downtown Shanghai and right past the building that contained the American Consulate.

They were closing in on that block now, the traffic slowdown giving them a chance to study the surroundings. The view was less than enticing.

'So much for the Consulate,' Gamay whispered.

Paul nodded grimly. Scores of Chinese police and soldiers had been stationed around the building and at every intersection leading up to it. Barricades had been erected and Chinese officials could be seen checking the passports of anyone seeking to be let through. 'All in the name of safety, no doubt.'

The bus came to another traffic light and stopped. As it idled there, Paul noticed another couple pointing out the security teams. He leaned toward them. 'Any idea why all the soldiers are down here?'

The couple turned his way. Based on the maple leaf pins they wore, he figured they were Canadian. 'I heard something about terrorist threats on the news,' the woman said. 'It's just horrible, really. The police were at our hotel this morning and I'm told they've surrounded the Canadian and British consulates as well. We're thinking we'd rather have gone somewhere else for our vacation. But now we can't even get home or meet our friends in Beijing because they've closed the airport and the train station.'

'I hadn't heard that,' Paul admitted. 'We're due to fly out tomorrow.'

She offered a kindly smile. 'You'd better check with the airline, sonny. I was told we might be stuck here for a week.'

Paul sighed as if it were a mere delay in the travel plans. 'I guess I should,' he said. 'Might I use your phone? I'm afraid ours was stolen.'

Paul's overall impression of Canadian citizens was that they were always willing to help out. By far the most polite people he'd encountered in his travels.

'Won't do you any good,' the husband said. 'They've shut down the cell phone networks citywide.'

'And the internet as well,' the woman said. 'It's like we're living in the Stone Age.'

'Or 1993,' her husband said.

Paul had to laugh at that. The Stone Age was not that far back, apparently. 'Are the landlines still working?'

'That's what we used,' the Canadian woman said. 'Called from the hotel.'

He thanked them for the information and sat down beside Gamay. 'Guess what?'

'I heard,' she said. 'Someone's pulling out all the stops. Think all this is for us?'

'Seems that way,' he said. 'With the whole city in an electronic deep freeze, we're going to have a problem getting this information out. We can't even use an internet café like we did in Cajamarca.'

Gamay didn't answer right away. She was staring straight ahead. 'Not everything is frozen.'

She pointed to a small TV screen in the back of the seat. It was tuned to the international feed of CNN. A reporter was conducting a live broadcast, referencing the internet blackout and the terrorist danger.

'The networks are still up,' she said. 'They have their own satellites. Direct links to Washington and New York bureaus. If we could borrow one for just a minute . . .'

She didn't need to finish. Paul knew what she was getting at. 'It'll be risky, but I've never known a reporter who didn't want a world-class scoop. If we made enough big promises, we might find someone willing to help.'

'And if we could find a mobile truck,' she added, 'we wouldn't even have to set foot in a big, easy-to-surround building.'

Paul turned his eyes back to the reporter on the screen. 'That shouldn't be too hard. Recognize the location?'

'Should I?'

'We were just there two hours ago,' Paul said. 'That's the Oriental Pearl Tower in the background. Let's get off this bus and double back.'

They left the tour group at the next stop and took a cab directly to the tower. Arriving in the parking lot felt like hitting the jackpot. There were seven different networks with trucks parked outside the soaring building, all using the famous backdrop for their shots.

Paul and Gamay walked nonchalantly past the first two mobile trucks, eyeing the satellite dishes on the roofs with a type of excitement usually reserved for the arrival of a gourmet meal.

'These trucks are local networks,' Gamay said, noting the logos painted on the sides of the various vans. 'We need an American network. CNN or Fox or . . .' Her voice trailed off. They'd come to a reporter, setting up for another shot. 'INN,' she said. 'Indie Network News. This is perfect. The whole network lives for conspiracy theories.'

Paul smiled. 'Since when do you watch that stuff?'

'It's my late-night guilty pleasure,' she admitted. 'That and rocky road ice cream.'

'Explains all the empty cartons I find in the trash,' he said. 'Let's grab that reporter as soon as she finishes.'

They walked toward the reporter and her cameraman, careful to remain out of the shot. Gawking like tourists, they waited for the portable spotlight to shut off and the reporter to disconnect herself from the earpiece.

'Intercut the voice-over with the shot of those military helicopters that flew by earlier,' she told him. 'That'll make it more interesting.'

'Sure thing,' the cameraman said.

As he got busy packing up equipment, the reporter

moved toward the back of the mobile truck. Gamay intercepted her before she could climb inside. 'Ms Anderson,' she called out. 'Sorry to interrupt you, but I'm a huge fan. The documentary you did about what's really buried under the Hoover Dam was fascinating.'

Melanie Anderson flashed a smile that almost hid the annoyance she felt. 'Thanks,' she said. 'Though, I hate to tell you, I've never been to Nevada. We used B-roll for the entire thing. But I'm glad you enjoyed it. It means we did our job.' There was a happy cynicism to her voice. 'Can I sign something, or pose for a selfie?'

'A signature would be great,' Gamay said, holding out a small pad of paper and a pen. The reporter took both items, raised the pen to the ready position and then paused as if she was thinking about what to write.

Gamay had drafted a note on the pad, explaining who they were and that they needed help.

The reporter looked up. 'Is this a joke? Did the guys at the network put you up to this?'

'I promise you,' Gamay said, 'it's anything but a joke. Can we please talk inside your truck?'

The reporter held her ground for a moment and then opened the door while calling out to the cameraman. 'Charley, give me a minute, okay?'

The cameraman nodded. And Paul and Gamay followed the reporter inside.

The back of the mobile broadcast van was designed much like the interior of an ambulance except, instead of medical equipment, the bay was filled with computers and production gear.

It was cramped, but there were two small seats. The reporter took one and Gamay the other. Paul leaned against a cabinet, crouching to give himself just enough headroom.

'Let me get this straight,' the reporter said. 'You two are employees of a secret US government agency and you're being hunted by the Chinese. And this whole internet and phone blackout is to prevent you from contacting your bureau chief in Washington. Is that it?'

'Actually,' Gamay said, 'NUMA isn't a secret agency. It's very public.'

'I've never heard of it,' she said.

'We don't exactly advertise,' Paul said.

'Okay, fine,' the reporter said. 'But the Chinese government wants you stopped at all costs, bringing Shanghai to a screeching halt if necessary.'

'I know it sounds crazy,' Gamay said.

'Explains why you came to me,' Ms Anderson replied. 'Crazy is my business. Fortunately, my producers come up with enough batty ideas to run three networks at least. We don't need any help from the public.'

'This isn't a stunt or a game,' Gamay reiterated. 'We're not secret agents; we're not spies. I'm a marine biologist and Paul is a geologist. We recorded video and sonar readings in Chinese waters that indicate a man-made – most likely, Chinese-made – ecological disaster is under way. The Chinese government became aware of our actions after we arrived in Shanghai. They're looking for us and doing everything they can to keep us from getting this information back to Washington.'

'That's all well and good,' the reporter said, 'but, as I recall, the Chinese do whatever they want in their territorial waters, just like we do in ours. Why would they care if you found out about some industrial accident? What difference does it make? They could point to *Exxon Valdez* and the *Deepwater Horizon* and tell us to worry about our own yard before complaining about what's going on in theirs.'

'Normally, I'd agree with you,' Gamay said. 'But whatever they were trying to accomplish down there, they've caused a problem that's not just affecting the East China Sea, or the Chinese coastline, or even the western Pacific. It's affecting the oceans all around the planet, raising sea levels in a very rapid manner. Forget global warming and its inch or two per decade predictions, we're talking ten feet per year – and the rate is accelerating. Low-lying islands are dealing with inundation from seawater already. Certain coastal areas will begin experiencing permanent flooding within six months.'

As Gamay spoke, Melanie Anderson seemed to perk up. 'Worldwide Flooding,' she said, as if imagining a headline. 'How bad will it get?'

'We can't be certain,' Gamay said. 'Especially if the Chinese prevent an investigation. But if you have any concept of how important the oceans are to food production, weather patterns and even national stability, you'll understand that this could be the opening phase in a catastrophe of unrivaled proportions.'

'"Unrivaled proportions,"' she said. 'Not bad. You could have a future in the copy game.'

'Ms Anderson,' Gamay said.

'Call me Mel.'

'I'm telling the truth,' Gamay said. 'Think about it. They've shut off the internet, shut off the phones and surrounded every Western consulate in Shanghai with soldiers and police. They've even closed the train stations and airports. This isn't about keeping something out; it's about keeping something in. And that something is the information we have. At this point, you and your satellite dish are the only hope we have for getting this information back to America.'

Gamay was appealing to the hero. Paul took another tactic. 'It's the story of a lifetime,' he said. 'Pulitzer Prize-winning material. And, more importantly, a direct route to the big networks. You'll be hosting *20/20* next year, not reporting on Bigfoot or alien abductions. You might even get your own show.'

She laughed. 'Maybe. Assuming you two aren't a couple of lunatics.'

'We have video and sonar data,' Gamay said, taking the laptop from Paul and handing it over. 'Judge for yourself.'

32

Washington, DC

Rudi Gunn arrived at the White House after being summoned out of the blue. The lack of information as to why suggested it wasn't going to be a pleasant visit.

After a brief wait, he was ushered inside the Oval Office, where he stood respectfully until directed to sit. The President sat behind the big desk, reviewing something through a pair of antique reading glasses. Vice President Sandecker stood beside him.

James Sandecker was normally a welcome sight for Rudi, since he'd run NUMA before accepting the offer to move to the second-highest position in the American government. But Sandecker's face was stern and Rudi felt no warmth from his old boss.

The President pushed the paperwork aside, took his glasses off and looked across the desk. 'Rudi, you know how much respect I have for NUMA in general and your leadership in particular. So, it pains me to ask you this, but . . . what in the name of God are your people up to in Asia?'

'Pardon me, Mr President,' Rudi said, 'but I'm not exactly sure what you're referencing.'

'The State Department has been inundated with communiqués suggesting your Special Projects team has been wreaking havoc in Japan. They've been seen dealing with local gangsters, accused of getting involved with an anti-government cult and burning down a thousand-year-old castle. Now we're receiving intelligence out of China that all of Shanghai has gone into lockdown and a massive dragnet has been spread across the city to locate two more wayward NUMA operatives who snuck into the country like spies.'

Rudi had been expecting heat to come down sooner or later. 'They're not wayward, Mr President. They're working on the sea-level issue, following up leads which suggest China may be responsible for what we've seen globally.'

'They appear to have violated Chinese sovereignty in their efforts.'

Rudi didn't blink. 'I directed them to take whatever action was necessary in search of answers. I'll take responsibility.'

The President appeared cross.

Sandecker offered a comment. 'I told you Rudi wouldn't pass the buck.'

'Don't cover for him, Jim.'

'He doesn't need me to. He's telling it to you straight.'

The President turned to face Rudi once more. 'Do you have any idea how delicate the situation is right now? How precarious Japanese–American relations are? China has been giving them the full-court press for over a year to become part of an Asian-only trading bloc and military alliance. Things are changing fast. Nine months ago, they settled the dispute about war crimes from World War Two. Six months ago, they began treaty negotiations. Three months ago, they held joint naval exercises for the first time ever. Tomorrow, they will sign an extensive cooperation agreement. And, next week, the Japanese Parliament will vote on whether or not to remain bound by the mutual defense treaty with America.'

'I hardly see how that –'

The President cut him off. 'Any untoward actions blamed on America will just fuel the fire. The burning of the ancient temple has been played on nationalistic websites in Japan over and over for the last seventy-two hours.'

Rudi waited to make sure the President was done. 'Not much I can do about that, Mr President. The castle was not burned by our people. It was, in fact, burned in an attempt to kill the occupants and the members of my team. We believe the kill order came from China.'

'I see.'

'As for the activities in Shanghai,' Rudi added, 'my people are investigating something that could prove far more devastating than any political setback or realignment. The fact of the matter is, if this sea-level rise proceeds unchecked, switching political alliances and signing new treaties will be a bit like rearranging the deck chairs on the *Titanic*.'

The President waved him off. 'I don't want to hear about the damned sea-level rise. I've heard it from Jim too many times already. In my opinion, you're both a little crazy.'

'Yes, Mr President, perhaps we are.'

The President stared at Rudi for a long moment and then turned to Sandecker. 'You really handpicked a stubborn bunch over there at NUMA.'

Sandecker grinned. 'Damned proud of it, too.'

'We'll see what it gets us,' the President said. 'In the meantime, Rudi, perhaps you can explain this.'

Without another word, the President aimed a remote control at the far wall. With the touch of a single button, a large panel slid backward, revealing a hidden high-definition monitor.

A short video began. It displayed the murky view from an underwater camera. Along the side of the screen were various instrumental readings.

'It's our standard ROV interface,' Rudi admitted.

The video was jerky, spliced together in a hasty fashion. For three seconds, they watched swirling water clouded with sediment. The next cut was a sonar image of what appeared to be a range of cone-shaped mountains along the seafloor. A close-up of one made it obvious that water was blasting from it like a geyser. Finally, they were treated to several shots of underwater wreckage, ending with a white robotic arm and face.

'Where did you get this?' Rudi asked.

Sandecker answered. 'It was broadcast this morning by the Indie News Network without comment or explanation. They're claiming they were hacked, but, interestingly enough, the transmission was preceded by a series of numbers. String those numbers together and you get the NUMA ID codes for Paul and Gamay Trout.'

'Your lost agents in Shanghai,' the President said.

'Yes, Mr President.'

Sandecker spoke the thought already playing on Rudi's mind, 'You may have sacrificed them, Rudi. I hope it was worth it.'

'They must have thought so,' Rudi said, 'or they wouldn't have sent this out. It's up to us to figure out what it means. And to get Paul and Gamay out of there.'

'We're not going to get them out,' the President said. 'We're not even going to acknowledge their presence in the country.'

'It'll be pretty hard to deny it if they get captured,' Rudi said.

'He's got a point,' Sandecker added.

A look of frustration and anger crossed the President's face. 'You've put us in a difficult position.'

'For that, I apologize,' Rudi said. 'But it's in all of our interests to get Paul and Gamay out of there before the Chinese catch up to them.'

'Not if it means throwing gas on the fire,' the President said. 'Our best bet is to downplay the significance of this and make no moves whatsoever. If the Chinese think we don't care, they might stop caring themselves.'

'Or they might bury Paul and Gamay in unmarked graves.'

'A risk they took when they entered China.' The President shut off the flat-screen and closed the panel. 'That's all for now.'

Rudi had spent enough time in the Navy that being curtly dismissed after getting reamed out was second nature. But that didn't lessen the sting. He stood. 'Thank you, Mr President.'

'Hang on, Rudi,' Sandecker said. 'I'll walk you out.'

Rudi left the Oval Office with Sandecker at his side.

'You know I wouldn't have sent them in without good reason,' Rudi told his old mentor.

Sandecker moved with a quick stride, hands behind his back. 'I've seen the briefing on the sea-level rise. I'm aware of the urgency. The President is, too, but his hands are tied politically. Until half of Florida is underwater, no one is going to see the need for action.'

Rudi knew the game. He and Sandecker had always tried to rise above it. 'I'd be violating the trust of the American people if I sat around and waited for that to happen.'

'Yes, you would,' Sandecker said. 'So get what information you can out of this video and we'll see what we can do. With something more than murky pictures to go on, we might be able to act. At least we'd be able to bring the truth to light. Just determining that China is behind this would be a step in the right direction. But we need to know how they caused it, why and how bad it's going to get.'

'Could we sneak a submarine in there for a more detailed look?'

'Not a chance,' Sandecker said. 'The Chinese have doubled their patrols since Paul and Gamay made this recording. We'd be risking a direct military confrontation if we violate their waters again.'

'And making the political situation worse,' Rudi said. 'I understand.'

They walked in silence the rest of the way to the foyer, where Rudi stopped and spoke his mind. 'I'm not leaving them out there to die.'

Sandecker didn't blink. 'I share your concern, Rudi. I brought Paul and Gamay on board. Sent them out on their first assignments. But you have to accept reality. We may not have any choice in the matter.'

Rudi had spent a career leaning on the wisdom of James Sandecker. For the first time in his life, he found himself in utter disagreement with the Admiral. 'I'm not leaving them.'

'Then you'd better find a way to get them back here without making things worse.'

33

Nagasaki

Kurt listened to the news about Paul and Gamay calmly. Rudi Gunn was blunt as he delivered it. There was no hand-wringing or pronouncements of *mea culpa* from either of them, nonetheless both felt the weight of responsibility.

'Can you get them home?' Kurt asked.

'I'm looking for an angle to exploit now,' Rudi said. 'In the meantime, we've been analyzing the data. Even though the mounds in the video look like volcanoes, they're not. They're spewing nothing but water. No sulfur, no arsenic, no carbon, nothing that you'd expect to find from volcanic action. Only hot freshwater and minute amounts of trace elements.'

'How big are they?' Joe asked. 'It's hard to tell from the video.'

'According to the sonar data, the closest one is the size of a twenty-story building,' Rudi said. 'We're less certain of the others, but they appear similar in scale.'

'How much water are they venting?' Kurt asked. 'Enough to cause what we've seen?'

'Based on a three-dimensional study of the geyser closest to the camera and an estimate of the velocity and volume of the ejected water, we've calculated a discharge rate of nearly half a million cubic feet per minute. To put that in perspective, ten of those jets are equal to Niagara Falls on a rainy day.'

'How many are there?' Joe asked.

'We don't know,' Rudi admitted. 'In the snippet of video Paul and Gamay sent, we counted about forty, but the time index on the recording shows that they've edited the video. It was originally much longer.'

'Just giving us the highlights,' Joe said.

'Seems that way,' Rudi admitted. 'We're pulling satellite data now, but the preliminary indication is a bulge of water forming in the East China Sea and flowing outward. It's wreaking havoc with the standard currents. Under normal conditions, a large northbound current enters the area between Taiwan and Okinawa. That current has been deflected nearly due east and replaced with an outflow heading southward. The combined effect has unsettled the normal weather patterns, bringing fog to normally clear areas, storms to normally dry areas and early snow over parts of China.

'Outflows to the north are so large, we're detecting salinity and temperature changes all the way up to the Bering Strait. The Sea of Japan is being desalinized so rapidly, in another month or two it will be little more than a freshwater lake.'

'Where is all this water coming from?'

'We're trying to figure that out now,' Rudi said. 'But to come up with any real answer – not to mention any hope of stopping this or at least estimating how bad it will get – we need to know exactly what the Chinese were doing down there. Which brings me to my next question: are you making any progress?'

Kurt explained the convoluted path they'd taken to get to Walter Han and the fact that he'd been unable to shake the man with a direct face-to-face confrontation. 'We don't have anything on him other than the word of a Yakuza underling trying to keep himself alive.'

'You may have more than you think,' Rudi said. 'I'm looking through your report now. It says here that his company designs and manufactures robots.'

'That's right,' Kurt said.

'I'm sending you a still shot from the video Paul and Gamay managed to transmit.'

Kurt glanced at the computer screen and waited. The link appeared and he clicked on it. There, in black and white, was the robotic arm, shoulder and cranium that the *Remora*'s cameras had recorded.

'Look familiar?' Rudi asked.

'Very familiar,' Kurt said. 'Apparently, Joe's future wife has a twin.'

'*Had* a twin,' Rudi corrected. 'That robot is buried at the bottom of a canyon near the anomalies Paul and Gamay discovered.'

'What was it doing down there?'

'It appears they were doing some deepwater mining. There's a great deal of additional wreckage down there, including a habitat that was crushed like a tin can.'

'Any idea what they were digging for?' Joe asked.

'Afraid not. But whatever it was, it had to be valuable. Our own experience proves that underwater mining is usually fifty to a hundred times as costly as ground-based extraction. In other words, even if they found a mother lode of platinum and gold down there, they'd be better off just leaving it there. It would cost more to pull out than it would be worth owning.'

'Then it has to be something worth more than gold.'

'The geology department is looking into it,' Rudi said. 'But, right now, they're stumped. There's nothing they can come up with that would be worth the effort.'

'Something tells me the Chinese came to the same conclusion,' Joe said. 'The place looks abandoned.'

'That's true,' Rudi said. 'Nothing on the video suggests an effort to rebuild.'

Kurt sat back. Something didn't add up. He turned to Akiko. 'When did Kenzo first discover the Z-waves and the tremors?'

'Almost a year ago,' she said, confirming what Kurt already knew.

He turned his attention back to Rudi. 'You've got faster internet than we do, Rudi. Do us a favor. Look up CNR and find out when they incorporated.'

There was a brief delay before Rudi came back with the answer. 'The partnership was announced eleven months ago.'

Kurt nodded. 'And when did China suddenly reach out to Japan and start thawing out relations?'

'Also eleven months ago,' Rudi said. 'In fact, the initial contacts coincide with CNR's incorporation to the day.'

Kurt could see the outline of the answer, even if he couldn't see what was at its center. 'The Chinese wouldn't go through all this trouble to cover up an abandoned mine or to save face from an operation that went awry. They're hiding the truth because it's an ongoing operation. One that has shifted from the bottom of the sea to the islands of Japan.'

'That's a big leap,' Rudi said.

'I don't think so,' Kurt said. 'All the actors are here. Han and his robots. The Chinese diplomats. A warming trend in diplomatic relations between the two countries that's proceeding at the pace of a bullet train. All pushed by the Chinese side after seven decades of demanding apologies and reparations for Japanese aggression in World War Two.'

'What are you suggesting?' Joe asked.

'Whatever they were looking for in that underwater canyon they now believe they can find here, in Japan or in Japanese waters. Han is an extension of the Chinese state. The warming trend is a cover under which to operate. CNR is the tool to be used when they find what they're looking for.'

'Which is?'

'Impossible to know,' Kurt admitted.

'I'll give your theory to the geology team,' Rudi promised. 'Maybe they can round up a few possibilities. My primary concerns are getting Paul and Gamay back and figuring out what the Chinese stumbled onto down there and how to stop the flooding. And our only hope of achieving either goal is by putting the screws to Walter Han.'

'Understood,' Kurt said.

'I don't care if our hides get hung out to dry,' Rudi added, 'I want you to find out what he's up to, even if you have to break into that factory and abduct him with your bare hands.'

'I don't think you'll have to go to such extremes,' Akiko announced.

Kurt turned. She had his phone in hand. A text was flashing on the screen.

'A message just popped up,' she explained. 'Walter Han is inviting you to dinner.'

34

'It's a trap,' Joe said. 'You know that, right?'

'Of course it's a trap. But that's a good sign. It means we've shaken Han more than I thought. And it's worth the risk for a good look at the inside of that factory.'

'He's not going to show you anything incriminating,' Joe pointed out. 'But he might teach you a painful lesson once he has you behind closed doors.'

'That's a risk I'll have to take,' Kurt said. 'Besides, it would be rude to turn down his invitation after I pressed him for a meeting and insisted it would need to happen tonight.'

'Rude, yes. But also wise. Some might even say prudent.'

Kurt laughed. 'Since when has prudence been our strong suit?'

Joe smiled at that, but Akiko looked on with concern. 'I can't believe you two are joking like this. He'll probably try to kill you.'

Kurt shook his head. 'He can hardly invite me to his brand-new factory and then bump me off during the tour. At worst, I'd expect thinly veiled threats, some form of intimidation and perhaps undercooked food. If he likes to catch flies with honey instead of vinegar, maybe he'll try to bribe me.'

'Accidents can happen,' she insisted.

'Which is why you and Joe are staying behind.'

'Now you've really lost it,' Joe said. 'I'm not letting you walk into a trap by yourself.'

'I need someone out here to call for help if I get in trouble,' Kurt said. 'There's a spot on the hillside that overlooks the factory grounds. You won't be able to see inside, but you can watch for trouble and dial nine-one-one if I miss my curfew.'

Joe frowned. 'So I sit around while you have all the fun.'

'I should go with you,' Akiko said. 'My job was to protect Kenzo. Now I feel a duty toward you.'

Kurt smiled. 'I appreciate the offer, but I think I can handle this alone.'

'Really?' she said. 'What if they start talking in Japanese or Chinese instead of English? Wouldn't you like to know what they're saying? They may be plotting against you or whispering secrets you'd never be able to decipher. I could listen to them and watch your back at the same time.'

'The lady has a point,' Joe said.

Akiko continued her lobbying. 'I'm very good at distracting men, should you need me to. And if it comes to a fight, you know I can hold my own.'

Kurt nodded. 'Of that, I have no doubt.' He didn't expect combat, but the language barrier was undeniable. At the very least, bringing Akiko along would give Han one more thing to think about. 'You've convinced me. But we're going to need proper attire.'

After a trip to one of Nagasaki's designer shops, Kurt and Akiko were properly dressed and NUMA's bank account several thousand dollars lighter.

Kurt wore a double-breasted dinner jacket and an ivory-colored shirt with French cuffs. Akiko sat beside him in a shimmering gray dress, intricately embroidered with a beaded flower pattern. Her neckline continued off both shoulders with sleeves falling gracefully past her wrists.

'I've never owned a dress like this,' Akiko said.

'You look stunning,' Kurt noted.

'It's rather uncomfortable.'

Kurt laughed to himself. 'Something tells me comfort isn't the guiding principle.'

Leaving the Skyline GT-R behind with Joe, they traveled to the factory in a rented sedan. They pulled onto the grounds and parked beneath an overhead light seventy feet from the front door. With the crowds gone and the parking lot empty, the place felt abandoned.

Just before getting out of the car, Akiko took a thin knife made of carbon fiber from her purse. It looked like a letter opener with a serrated edge. She slid it carefully up one of the sleeves.

'I like to be prepared,' she said. 'You should carry something as well.'

Kurt held up a metallic writing utensil. 'I've always believed the pen was mightier than the sword.'

'You were misinformed,' she insisted.

'All I have to do is twist the top, and this one will transmit everything they say and do back to Joe.'

'A secret gadget from your government?'

'Actually, I picked this up from an electronics shop down the street while your dress was being altered. Two thousand yen. Less than twenty dollars, at the current exchange rate.'

Kurt twisted the top. 'We're on-site, amigo. You reading us?'

Joe's reply came through the car speakers. 'I have an unobstructed view,' he said. 'I'll keep an eye on the car while you two are inside. Try not to have too much fun without me.'

'Do our best,' Kurt said.

Kurt twisted the pen's top and the link was broken. He and Akiko got out of the car, locked it and walked toward the front door. A security guard met them and led them into the building. Han met them on the factory floor.

'I'm so glad you could find the time to meet us,' Kurt said. 'This is Akiko, NUMA's Japanese liaison officer.'

Han bowed. His eyes lingered on her for a moment and then he introduced his assistant. 'This is Mr Gao, my chief engineer.'

Gao had a shaven head that reflected the lights in the ceiling. He wore plain slacks, a white button-down shirt and bulky glasses on which Kurt saw tiny green icons flickering and vanishing. A wire led from the frame of his glasses to an earbud and then to a power pack on his belt. The glasses were obviously a wearable computer. The flickering icons part of a heads-up display that only Gao could see and interpret.

Dangling on a cord around his neck was a heavy medallion-type badge. It had several small buttons on either side, two blinking LEDs and a meshed indentation that held a microphone and speaker. In his breast pocket were several pens, a flashlight and a laser pointer. Strapped to his upper arm was another electronic device, perhaps a fitness monitor, Kurt couldn't be sure.

Akiko stared at him like he had the plague. 'He's almost an android,' she whispered.

'By the way he looked at you, he'd toss the electronics into a lake for a single kiss. Perhaps the lure of human touch is stronger than you think.'

With that said, Akiko's demeanor changed. She feigned interest in Gao with such expertise that it almost convinced Kurt.

For the moment, they all made small talk. 'Dinner is being prepared in our executive dining room,' Han said. 'Perhaps you'd like a tour of the facility first?'

'I'd enjoy that very much,' Kurt said.

With Han leading the way, they walked across an expansive factory floor. Even though it was after normal working hours, dozens of machines were busy at work. Some were free to roam the factory floor, transporting parts from one section of the facility to another. Others were busy on a production line, welding and assembling components.

'What, exactly, do you build here?' Kurt asked.

'Robotics for other factories.'

'Machines building other machines,' Kurt said. 'Automated procreation.'

'Not quite,' Han said. 'The design and production work are done by human employees. But that will be automated one day, too.'

'Human employees?' Akiko asked. 'Does that mean you consider the robots employees also?'

'It's a figure of speech,' Han insisted. 'The truth is, robots liberate humanity from the most mundane and dangerous professions. Most tasks performed by machines are ones you wouldn't want to do. Turning the same five screws and making the same ten welds a hundred times a day, every day of your life; chiseling rock from the walls of dark tunnels in dangerous subterranean mines, where temperatures border on the limits of human tolerance and fatal accidents are common. I even have machines that will take a bullet instead of requiring a brave police-man or soldier to enter the line of fire.'

'Robotic soldiers?' Kurt asked.

'Of a sort,' Han replied.

'Show me.'

He took them across the factory floor to an even larger open space that spread out below them like the floor of a massive convention hall. Walking onto a bridge that crossed the entire length of the room, they observed mock-ups and testing areas.

The vast amount of high-tech equipment was stagger-ing. There were flickering screens everywhere; machines, small and large, performing various tasks.

Stopping above one walled-in area, they looked down on the mock-up of an apartment building, sans roof. 'Begin the demonstration,' Han said.

Gao pulled the device from his armband and tapped the screen a few times. Lights came up and the situation below was illuminated. A dozen mannequins were placed here and there. Some hiding, others out in the open. A human employee stood in the middle of it. 'A standard hostage situation,' Han said. 'Eight terrorists, seven hostages.'

The front door to the building was smashed down by a small battering ram machine on tracks. It pushed its way inside, taking fire from several of the armed terrorist mannequins. Sparks flew as bullets hit the armor plating.

'Live ammo?' Kurt said.

'Of course,' Han said. 'Limited powder, at this point. We don't want ricochets killing anyone.'

'What about your employee down there?' Kurt asked. 'How do the machines know not to shoot him?'

'He's wearing an identifier around his neck,' Han said. 'It tells the robots not to shoot him. Similar tools can be used on joint human and robotic assaults. Use of robotics will reduce friendly fire deaths by ninety-five percent.'

'Impressive,' Kurt said.

Down below, other machines with weapons pushed in behind the battering ram robot. Instead of wheels, they had six legs and they clambered up and over every obstacle with ease. They rapidly targeted and silenced the first wave of terrorists and pushed deeper into the building.

'They find their targets using a combination of heat sensors, sound waves and cameras,' Han said. 'They communicate with one another as well. What one of them knows, all of them know.'

The advancing machines paused, scanned the thermal output through the walls of the next room and broke into it. A quick gunfight ended moments later.

'And, just like that,' Han said, 'the terrorists are dead and the hostages are rescued. Not one of them has been hit.'

Kurt was impressed. 'How do the machines differentiate between terrorists and hostages?'

'We call it a discriminator function,' Han said. 'A combination of facial recognition patterns conforming to the known captives, heat sensors and a weapon recognition program that allows the processor to determine which humans are holding guns and which aren't.'

'Ingenious.'

'And the ones that are damaged can be repaired or replaced. No one has to cry over a ruined machine.'

A terminal beside them printed out a battle report. Han interpreted it. 'Twenty-one shell hits on various robots. Two machines sustained minor damage. A comparable effort using human policemen or soldiers would have resulted in the death of several personnel and at least half the hostages. The facts are unassailable.'

'Unlike the terrorist stronghold,' Kurt joked.

'Warbots like these will spare soldiers the most dangerous tasks in the field,' Han said.

'Warbots?'

'A catchy name, is it not?'

'But this is a police demonstration,' Kurt pointed out.

'Yes,' Han said, 'but ultimately armies of machines will take the fight to the world's most dangerous areas. They're more rugged, more lethal and more dependable. They can fight twenty-four hours a day, seven days a week, without the need for sleep, food or medical attention. They will reduce human death and collateral damage, eliminate decades of post-combat suffering by wounded and traumatized soldiers and their families.'

'They will cause death on the other side, of course.'

'Not true,' Han said. 'Not only are robots more accurate, thus limiting collateral damage, they are more humane. A robot has no feelings. It won't take revenge on captives that might have destroyed its comrades. It won't lose its mind at the horror of war and start killing indiscriminately. A robot will not rape or torture its captives nor steal or plunder.'

Kurt nodded. He'd heard the arguments on both sides. Some were afraid that robotic soldiers would go out of control. Others pointed out that human soldiers were prone to emotion and strain and subject to losing control themselves. Like most things, no one would know the truth until it arrived.

They moved on, coming to an overlook. On the floor down below, a slew of machines were building a section of highway. One machine used a jackhammer to break up concrete. Another machine scooped it up and lifted it into a driverless truck, which, making a tight three-point turn without hitting anything, then hauled it away, disappearing through a door at the far end of the convention hall.

'While robotic armies might be decades off,' Han began, 'self-driving vehicles are right around the corner.'

'We have them already,' Kurt said.

'A few,' Han admitted. 'But the next wave goes far beyond what exists today. CNR has even developed a driverless race car. It will compete with the greatest racers in the world and outclass them with ease.'

'Remotely guided?' Kurt asked.

Han shook his head. 'The vehicle is autonomous. It

operates completely without assistance, making its own judgments and decisions.'

'Driving around city streets is fine,' Kurt said, 'but navigating a track at high speeds to the limits of a car's ability is another thing altogether. I've raced a few cars myself. Trust me, it's a far more dangerous proposition.'

Han's reply came quickly. 'I assure you, Mr Austin, despite your fervent desire to remain at the top of the food chain, robots with artificial intelligence are now becoming superior to humans in every task imaginable. They will soon fly our fighter jets, captain our ships, salvage wrecks from the bottom of the sea. And, yes, even race our cars. And they will do all things in superior fashion.'

Kurt listened politely, but he was more interested in watching Han. The reply had come so quickly and with it a slight edge. The man had been cool as ice until Kurt questioned his machines. The rapid-fire response, a slight flare of nostrils and a deepening of the crow's-feet around Han's eyes confirmed it for Kurt. He'd finally found a button to push. And he pushed it no end.

'I'm sure you'll get there someday,' he said in a condescending tone, 'but we'll both be old men before a robot can beat a human on the racetrack. Machines can do many things, but they will always lack judgment.'

Han held his tongue for a second and then grinned. 'Care to test that theory?'

'I'd love to,' Kurt said. 'What are you suggesting?'

'We have a track here on the factory grounds,' Han said. 'And in the garage we have the prototype of the robot car along with two others still fitted out for human drivers. If you're willing to test yourself against it, we could even wager on the outcome to make it interesting.'

'I'd jump at the chance,' Kurt said, 'but you're a billion-aire and I'm a humble government servant on a fixed income. We'd have to bet something other than money.'

Han grinned. 'If you win, CNR will gladly provide whatever robotic vehicles you may find useful for your expedition.'

'And if I lose?'

'Simple,' Han said. 'All you need to do is admit that the machine is better than the man.'

35

Kurt had been expecting high-end sports cars, tuned for the track, with roll cages built onto them, racing tires and anything unnecessary pulled from the frame to reduce the weight. Stepping into Han's garage, he discovered three vehicles that were far more exotic.

'These are Toyotas,' Han said, 'though you won't find them at your local dealership.'

'Something tells me I couldn't afford them if I did,' Kurt said.

'Probably not,' Han agreed. 'This car was an alternate to race at Le Mans last year. Its twin-turbocharged V-6 makes 968 horsepower, but we've tuned it back to a mere 700 for our purposes.'

'I suppose that'll be enough.'

Kurt walked toward the gleaming orange and white machine. The car itself was a work of engineering art. The front end of the car had a lethal look to it – a pointed nose connected by carbon fiber panels to two swooping fenders that curved over the top of the performance tires and then dropped down behind them like a passing wave. A teardrop-shaped cockpit rested snugly in the center. The front was a graceful curving windshield that gave a near-panoramic view forward, while the tail end held a massive wing and three vertical fins that helped stabilize the car. 'If I didn't know better, I'd swear this thing could fly.'

'Get it out of shape and it will,' Han warned.

'I'll be careful,' Kurt promised.

Thirty minutes later, Kurt had changed into racing gear and strapped himself into the driver's seat. Dressed in a flame-retardant suit with a five-point harness and a helmet pulled down tightly over his head, Kurt was ready for the battle.

The cockpit was snug, a tight fit for someone of Kurt's size. It surrounded him in billeted aluminum and a padded roll cage. Several easy-to-reach toggle switches sat on a platform to his left. The steering wheel was removable and seemed positively tiny in Kurt's hands. The twin-turbo V-6 shook the car as Kurt revved it.

While Han's assistant readied the automated race car, Kurt got used to the controls. The pedals were so close together in the footwell, he could press both with one foot if he wanted to – useful in certain maneuvers, but not something he wanted to do accidentally. The paddle shifter was easy to reach and simple to operate. He flipped a switch and the four powerful headlights lit up the track in front of him, revealing black macadam lined with alternating orange and white rumble strips.

'The robot knows the track,' Han told him. 'To make it fair, I'll give you five laps to get used to it yourself. Take the car out. Work it up to speed. Try not to put it in the wall or into Nagasaki Bay. Turn five at the far end is notoriously dangerous. It's off camber, so you'll lose adhesion there. If you hit the fence, the car will flip and you'll be lucky to survive the impact.'

Han reached inside the car and flicked two additional switches. 'This turns on the telemetry,' he said. 'And this one will activate the navigation guidance alerts.'

'Guidance?'

'Similar to your phone, although far more accurate,' Han said. 'It'll tell you which turns are coming up and how sharp they are so you won't be surprised. Like having a navigator sitting by your side.'

'That annoys me enough in regular traffic,' Kurt joked, 'but I suppose I could use the help.'

As Han backed away, one of the mechanics lowered the carbon fiber door and offered a thumbs-up. Kurt eased the car out onto the track and spent the first two laps getting used to the layout, the navigator and the instant and precise feedback that came through the steering wheel.

By the third lap, he took the back straight at over a hundred miles per hour, racing along the waterfront as the city lights glistened on Nagasaki Bay. He slowed considerably for turn five and yet as the track tilted to the right while turning to the left, the car still felt as if it was going to fly off the track and into the bay. He ran each of the next two laps at slightly higher speeds and then pulled into the pits, ready to begin the race.

He stopped thirty feet from where Han's people were readying a yellow and blue version of the car Kurt was in. The paint was different and the CNR logo was plastered all over it, but aside from a few additional antennas, the cars were identical.

Kurt popped the door open. Despite the cool night temperatures, it was already sweltering in the cockpit. He pulled his helmet off for some air.

Akiko came up to him. 'Are you trying to be my hero?'

'Your hero?'

'Defending the cause of humanity in its epic battle against technology.'

Kurt had to laugh. 'I'd say yes, but, in all honesty, I'm just trying to get our host off balance. Keep an eye on him while I'm out there.'

She leaned in and gave him a kiss. 'For luck.'

The robot car roared to life and, once it was up and running, Han walked back over to Kurt. 'Are you ready?'

'As I'll ever be.'

'Good,' Han said. 'We'll have to keep it short. There's a storm coming in and we don't want either vehicle out on the track if it starts raining.'

Kurt nodded.

'Enjoy your ride,' Han said. 'First car across the finish line wins.'

Kurt pulled on his helmet, tightened the strap and nodded. The doors were closed and the cars lined up in a staggered formation, with Kurt thirty feet ahead.

Staging lights on a pole at the side of the track went from red to amber, then amber . . . amber . . . and finally green.

Kurt raced out of the pit quickly and worked the car rapidly through its paces. The staggered start allowed the two cars to get out of the pits without colliding at the narrow end of the lane. Moving faster than he had on the other laps, the first turn arrived quickly.

'Right seventy,' the navigation system announced.

Hitting the brakes hard, Kurt felt the rubber grab and his whole body slam against the straps of the racing harness. He worked the steering wheel in a constant state of adjustment, skirted the orange and white border of the track and slammed the throttle down as he left the turn.

The car jumped forward so deftly that Kurt was thrown back in his seat in a way he'd last felt when being launched off an aircraft carrier as a passenger in an F/A-18 Hornet.

'Chicane left,' the navigator told him.

Heavy on the brakes and another sudden decrease in speed followed. Kurt worked the steering wheel hard to the left, then back to the right. This was the slowest portion of the track, followed by a short straight and another turn.

'Left forty.'

This turn was easy to navigate and Kurt held his speed all the way through, though the car was sliding a bit before the end.

'Right thirty.'

Kurt had considered the navigator to be a distraction during the practice laps, but now, pushing the car and his own reflexes to their limits, he found it incredibly helpful. It gave him cues at exactly the right time and directed his eyes toward the apex of the turn, freeing up his mind to process everything else that was going on.

He left turn four, hammered the accelerator and cycled up through the gears quickly. The back straight was a long stretch, uphill at first until it passed under a vacant observation bridge, where it went downgrade in a straight line toward turn five.

'Left seventy, off camber.'

Kurt hit the brakes hard, felt the blood rushing to the front of his face and swung wide before cutting across the turn. Just like every other lap, he felt the car drifting, pulled toward the fence and the waiting bay by the invisible force of gravity. Since the car went where the eyes focused, he kept his eyes glued to the inner part of the turn.

The rest of the lap went smoothly and Kurt raced through the start/finish line with a nine-second lead on the robot car.

'One down, four laps to go,' Kurt said.

From the elevated viewing stand in the pit area, Han watched his ten-million-dollar robot car chase Kurt around the track. To his chagrin, the second lap was even worse than the first. By the time they crossed the line, Kurt was ahead by more than ten seconds.

He glanced at Gao. 'There must be something wrong with the car,' he said. 'How is Austin beating it?'

'There's nothing wrong with it,' Gao replied. 'Austin had five laps to warm up his tires. Our car is racing on cold rubber. It has less grip in the turns and the computer is keeping the speed down. By lap three, we'll be equal footing. We'll catch him by lap four and pass him on the front straight. By the end of the race, our car will be twenty seconds ahead of him. It won't even be close.'

'You'd better be right,' Han said. 'I don't like being embarrassed. Take the safety protocols off just to be sure.'

Gao looked at his boss questioningly and then did as he was told. With the flick of a switch, the automated car was instructed to ignore its safe operating parameters and win at all costs.

36

From the cockpit of Kurt's car, the third lap seemed to go much like the first two. But by the start of the fourth lap, he could see that the robot car was gaining on him. The glare of its headlights had become constant in his mirrors. Four diamond-white pinpricks announcing that the hunter was closing in on its prey.

The brilliant white lamps did more than aggravate. They were affecting Kurt's night vision, causing his pupils to constrict and limiting his ability to see past the swath of his own headlights.

As lap four went on, the lights grew closer and Kurt's driving became less precise. He was a little wide on turns one and two and caught the rumble strip badly in the chicane.

Aggravated with himself, he stomped the gas early and hard coming out of the next turn and almost spun the car out of control. The emotionless computer following him made none of those mistakes and the gap between them dropped to four seconds.

'Right thirty,' the navigator said. Kurt iced his own emotions and got back to driving as he had been before. He cut the wheel smoothly, sped through the turn and rode the gears higher into the red this time before shifting.

The robot car continued to close the gap.

The two cars thundered down the back straight toward

the dangerous curve. The robot car's nose so close to Kurt's back wing that the lights were no longer in Kurt's eyes. It was drafting him now and getting ready to slingshot by. And there was precious little Kurt could do about it.

'Come on,' Kurt said. 'Get around me if you're going.'

'Left seventy, off camber.'

The turn was coming up fast. Kurt needed to brake. He cut to the inside of the track and hit the brakes.

The robot car did the same, but Kurt had hit the brakes earlier than the automated car had planned to. The nose of the robotic vehicle crashed into the back of Kurt's car.

Kurt was shoved forward and sent off line. His car slid for a second, but as Kurt adjusted the wheel, the tires regained their grip and the Toyota straightened with a whiplashing snap and stayed online.

With his foot to the floor, Kurt cruised around the wide horseshoe at the far end of the track and then onto the front straight once more.

The robot car had fallen back after the impact but was gaining on him again, though not as quickly as it had done the last lap. The impact had damaged its nose and affected its aerodynamics. As far as Kurt could tell, his own car was unhindered.

He raced along the front straight, roaring past the pits and then the viewing stand. He stole a glance at Han and his assistant up on the platform. 'Reckless human drivers . . . my eye.'

Up on the platform, Han was almost foaming at the mouth. 'I told you not to lose this race.'

Gao was monitoring the telemetry. 'Nothing I can do about it now. You wanted the safeties off, that's the danger.'

'Pass him, Gao.'

'The car will make another attempt on the back straight, but Austin is putting in his fastest lap yet. He's a quick study.'

'Perhaps we should stop helping him, then,' Han said.

'What are you suggesting?'

'Shut off his navigation system.'

'He'll be waiting for the announcement and drive right into the wall,' Gao said.

'He wanted to prove humans can outdrive machines. Let him prove it on his own.'

Gao took a deep breath. 'You kill him here and his government will grow suspicious.'

'Not if it's an accident.'

'Wen told you to keep him alive!' Gao argued. 'To use him as a scapegoat.'

A wave of fury erupted from Han. He grabbed Gao by the collar. 'Do as I say! Shut off the navigation.'

Released from Han's grasp, Gao looked out over the track. Austin was making his way through the chicane and toward turn four. He waited a few seconds and then switched the relay to the off position.

Kurt knew Han's car might try to take him out again, but he never considered stopping the race. He was determined to beat Han now more than ever.

He raced hard through the familiar turns on the front

side of the track, operating with a mix of patience and restrained aggression. His orange and white Toyota carved a perfect line this time and it flew up the hill at a furious pace.

'Right fort –' the navigator said, the announcement oddly clipped in the middle.

Kurt dove into the turn, let the inside wheels hit the rumble strip to help him through it and left the apex of the curve at nearly full speed. Hitting the back straight, he spun the engine to its limits, letting the tachometer wind into the red as he blazed through the night.

The orange and white strips on the side of the track flew by at a dizzying pace. The lights shimmered on Nagasaki Bay and the robot car came on from behind, tracking him down and closing in with each fraction of a second.

Kurt flashed beneath the vacant bridge and bore down on the notorious turn five. The engine screamed in a full wail behind him. His fingers were light on the steering wheel, his foot poised to switch from accelerator to brake at the first instant of the navigator's announcement.

It took only a fraction of a second for Kurt to realize it wasn't coming. His eyes spotted the skid marks from the earlier lap. His mind calculating instantly that he was going too fast and getting too close.

He slammed on the brakes. The antilock system prevented a full skid, but an eruption of blue tire smoke filled the track. The harness dug into Kurt's shoulders and he grunted as he turned the wheel, cutting it harder and keeping his foot on the brake.

His Toyota slowed rapidly but went into a drift. The tire smoke billowed like a bomb had gone off and the wall loomed.

With no other choice, Kurt let up on the brakes and hit the accelerator to get some control back. The car continued to skid but stayed on the ground. The rubber finally grabbed and the vehicle shot forward, toward the inside of the track. It raced onto the infield, nearly clipping the robot car as it flew past him, traveling headlong into the cloud of smoke.

With its sensors affected by the smoke and its safeties turned off, the automated car waited too long to begin applying its own brakes. It shot through the smoke cloud, skidded into the turn and banged the outside wall. The carbon fiber body panels on the right side splintered and flew in all directions. The wing was ripped off the back end. It went flying over the wall like a tomahawk, slicing into the water of Nagasaki Bay. The car itself careened off the wall and slid onto a gravel trap, where it stopped.

Kurt had already come to a stop on the grass of the infield. He was safe and sound and angled just about perfectly to view the last few seconds of the automated car's wipeout. He saw it come to a stop on the gravel, two of its headlights blown out, the other two pointed toward the track.

Just when it looked to Kurt like the race would be called a draw, the wheels on the robot car spun and it began grinding its way out of the gravel trap and back onto the course.

'Oh, I don't think so,' Kurt said.

He fired up his own engine, put the car into gear and

punched the gas. The start was slow and sloppy, tearing up seventy yards of turf, before he got the nose pointed in the right direction.

One look told Kurt there was no way he could catch the robot car by getting back on the track and chasing it around the long horseshoe turn, so he took a shortcut and drove straight across the infield, heading for the other side.

Angling for the finish line, he stole a glance across the track. Han's car was picking up speed but losing parts along the way. They were heading for the same spot from different directions. A collision was imminent.

Kurt kept the gas pedal down, merged onto the front straight and cut across the finish line on a diagonal angle. The robot car, or what was left of it, crossed the line half a second later.

Locking up the brakes once more, Kurt skidded to a stop. The robot car slowed with far greater control and stopped a hundred feet down the track.

Kurt threw open the door, punched the quick release on his harness and stepped from the car.

As Akiko ran up to him, he pulled off his helmet and the fireproof hood. Meanwhile, several of Han's people rushed over to the ruined prototype that had come in second.

'Are you all right?' Akiko asked.

'Never better,' he said, though he was drenched in sweat and smelled like burnt rubber.

'I can't believe you won,' she said, grabbing his hands. 'You really are mad.'

'I don't like to lose,' Kurt said. He held up a single finger. 'Humans: one. Robots: zero.'

Han and his assistant came down from the viewing platform, looking far less excited. 'You haven't won anything,' Han insisted. 'You cheated. You cut across the infield.'

'And you said first one across the finish line wins,' Kurt replied. 'I don't recall any conditions about how we were supposed to get there.'

Han pursed his lips, looking angrily at Kurt. 'This mess doesn't prove anything.'

Kurt grinned wickedly. 'I disagree. It proves robots can be beaten. And that humans aren't the only dangerous outside forces.'

Han bristled at Kurt using his own words against him, but there was nothing he could say to refute it.

A chime toned on Gao's medallion and he checked a message on the screen. 'Dinner is ready. If anyone is still interested in eating.'

Han glowered beside his assistant. He seemed to have lost his appetite. Gao looked like he wanted to be anywhere but there. Akiko tensed, her free hand inching toward the hidden knife beneath her sleeve. Only Kurt was all smiles.

'I'm famished,' he said with a grin. 'Racing works up quite an appetite.'

37

Joe was parked at a scenic overlook on the switchback road that led up into the mountains. From there, he enjoyed a commanding view of Nagasaki Harbor, the waterfront and the CNR factory that occupied a large section of it.

He set a camera with a powerful zoom lens on a tripod and carried a pair of high-powered military-grade binoculars as a backup. Watching Han's production facility in this way, he'd seen Kurt and Akiko park and enter the building. He'd even caught part of the race on the test track behind the factory. He was glad to see Kurt walk away from the crash unscathed. Most men would have had enough at that point, but Joe knew his friend too well to expect Kurt to call it a night.

With the race over and events in a lull, Joe bit into a rather tasteless sandwich he'd purchased from a vending machine. 'Just my luck,' he said to himself. 'Stranded alone on a cliff while Kurt goes to dinner with a beautiful woman and races a million-dollar sports car.'

Leaning against the fender of the Skyline GT-R, he put the sandwich down and lifted the binoculars to his eyes. Focusing them with a light touch, he scanned the area around the factory.

Aside from the race, there had been no movement whatsoever. Kurt's rental car sat, alone and undisturbed, in the parking lot. The grounds themselves remained quiet. Joe hadn't even seen a security patrol. But then China-Nippon Robotics probably used automated systems instead of humans, making slow and obvious rounds.

Joe lowered the binoculars and checked his watch. It was just past ten o'clock. Kurt had insisted he and Akiko would return by midnight no matter what. If they hadn't reappeared by then, it was up to Joe to get them help.

Thinking that was a likely possibility, Joe had put in a call to Superintendent Nagano. He'd been told the superintendent was in the field on an assignment and would be out of reach until he returned.

There was something odd in the assistant's voice. Joe wanted to chalk it up to translating the words to English but couldn't shake the feeling that it was something more.

Regardless, he was ready with Plan B: a trunkload of industrial-sized fireworks that he'd launch into the complex as he called the Nagasaki Fire Department for help.

It was a crude idea, but it would work. These were no sparklers Joe was going to set off. He had bottle rockets the size of mortar rounds. Starburst shells and spinners that he could land on the roof of the factory, where they would flare green, red and white while pumping out huge volumes of smoke. And with fumes and fire pouring from the roof of the factory, Han's personnel would be unable to turn the fire department away. Joe would rush in right alongside them.

He hoped it wouldn't come to that. But experience had taught him otherwise. 'Come on, Kurt,' he said to himself. 'This isn't the night to linger over drinks.'

Lowering the binoculars, Joe caught sight of some-thing new. A dark sedan moving down the road toward the factory.

Retraining the binoculars on the car, Joe tracked it as it passed under a streetlight and turned toward a loading zone around the side. Joe hopped up and moved to a spot where he could see the loading zone more clearly.

The sedan pulled up to the dock. A man got out and climbed up on the loading platform. He rang the buzzer and, without waiting for an answer, began to pound his fist on the back door.

An overhead light came on, illuminating the man, but all Joe could see was his back.

The door opened. A security guard appeared and words were exchanged. It seemed like a heated discussion.

The security guard went back inside and the angry fel-low waited impatiently.

'Turn around,' Joe whispered. 'What have you got to lose?'

The man stood his ground and Joe took the moment to grab the camera tripod and bring it to his new vantage point.

By the time he'd set it up and focused, the door was open again. This time, Han appeared. He walked out to the parked sedan. The trunk was opened and Han reached in to retrieve a long wooden case. He rested the case on the roof of the car and opened it.

Joe focused as finely as he could. In the case was a shimmering sword.

'Strange hour of the night to be buying collectables,' Joe whispered.

An approving nod came from Han and the case was folded shut.

Joe expected he would lose any chance to ID the driver in a moment. He edged closer to the cliff but could not change the angle enough to see the face. Then he noticed a large convex mirror, stationed on the edge of the dock. Every loading zone had one, placed there to help the drivers back in without hitting the dock.

Joe turned the camera toward the mirror, zoomed in as far as it would go and refocused. The magnification was so high that the slightest bump made the image blur, so Joe took his hands off the camera and watched the glowing screen.

The focus tightened and Joe recognized the driver: Ushi-Oni. To his surprise, Joe noticed a passenger slumped over against the window of the car as if sleeping. Recognition came to him in a flash. 'Superintendent Nagano.'

No wonder he wasn't at his office and his assistant sounded concerned. He was lying on his side, in the back of Ushi-Oni's car, with a length of white tape stretched across his mouth.

Movement began in earnest now. Other swords were displayed. Some wrapped in leather, others were in additional wooden boxes. A leather-bound book was produced. Han kept this and offered an approving nod. He waved his hand, the entry gate was drawn back and Ushi-Oni climbed back into the car and drove through.

38

Kurt was in the garage washroom, getting dressed and making himself presentable. Ten laps in the hot box of a race car had drenched him in sweat. He was back in his own clothes and splashing water on his face when his phone began to buzz.

He shook the water from his hands, dried his face with a towel and grabbed the phone. It was Joe.

'I hate to interrupt the fun,' Joe said, 'but you've got a party crasher. Ushi-Oni just pulled up to the back gate.'

Kurt didn't bother asking Joe if he was sure. He wouldn't have made the call if there was any doubt. 'So Nagano wasn't able to track him down.'

'Wish that was the case,' Joe said, 'but it looks like the hunter got taken down by the hunted. I saw Nagano in the back of the sedan. Mouth taped, hands tied.'

'Is he alive?'

'Can't tell. He wasn't moving.'

Kurt held the phone against his chin as he pulled on his dinner jacket. 'Where's the car now?'

'It pulled through the gate and parked just beyond the loading zone by the secondary building.'

'How do I get there?'

'You need to get to the southwest corner of the building you're in now.'

Kurt needed to create a distraction. He had an idea that would dovetail nicely with the tools Joe had at his disposal. 'I'm going to make a run for it. Get yourself into position. If they leave the building, you follow them. If they stay, give me two minutes and then start the fireworks.'

'I figured you might want some help,' Joe said. 'I'm setting up the launch tray now.'

'Two minutes,' Kurt repeated. 'Not a second more.'

Joe confirmed and hung up. Kurt put the phone in his pocket, straightened his cuffs and walked out of the washroom.

Akiko waited outside chatting quietly with Gao. Walter Han was nowhere in sight.

'Are we still on for dinner?'

'I'll take you to the dining room,' Gao said. 'Mr Han will join you shortly.'

Kurt nodded and took Akiko by the hand. 'Lead on.'

Gao took them across the garage toward the inner doors. Kurt spent every second scanning for the items he needed. Workbenches surrounded them. Tool chests filled with every implement known to man covered an entire wall, but Kurt was looking for the simplest of items.

Spotting what he wanted, he squeezed Akiko's hand ever so slightly.

She looked over at him.

He nodded toward Gao.

Her eyes widened.

He held up one hand. *Wait*.

They reached the inner door. Gao pulled out his key

card and held it to the sensor. The light on the door went green and the bolt disengaged with an audible click.

Before he could pass through it, Kurt clubbed him between the neck and the shoulder with a knifehand strike. The blow landed hard on Gao's suprascapular nerve, rendered the right side of his body numb and dropped him to the floor in a daze. A right cross to the jaw put him down for the count.

'He's out cold,' Kurt said, checking on him and grabbing the key card. 'Find something to tie his hands with.'

She grabbed an electrical cord and began binding Gao. 'What are we doing?' she asked. 'You know they're watching. There are cameras everywhere in here.'

'Which means we have to move fast.'

Kurt ran to one of the workbenches. Oily rags filled a garbage bin on one side. Spray cans of WD-40 stood nearby.

'Spray the WD-40 into that pile of rags and keep spraying,' he told her.

All he needed was a spark. He found it with the battery cart they'd used to start the race cars.

While she soaked the rags with the lubricant, he wheeled the cart over to the workbench, switched it on and scraped the terminals against each other. Sparks shot in all directions.

'Are you about to do what I think you're about to do?'

'They burned you and Kenzo out,' he said. 'Now we're going to return the favor.'

Stepping around her, Kurt brought the cables up and placed them in line with the mist blasting from the can. A single touch released a new wave of sparks and the spray can was transformed into a miniature flamethrower.

Akiko held the nozzle open for several seconds before releasing it. By then, the garbage bin full of cotton rags had become a burning cauldron.

Kurt shoved it beneath a workbench so that it wouldn't go out when the sprinklers came on. Akiko tossed the can of WD-40 inside for good measure.

'Let's go,' he said, rushing to the door.

'Where are we going?' she asked.

'To the southwest corner of the building,' he said. 'Joe saw a van pull up with Superintendent Nagano inside. Let's just say he didn't come here of his own volition.'

Kurt used the key card to open the door, smashed the glass of a fire panel with his elbow and pulled the alarm handle. Lights began to flash and the alarm began wailing.

'Wait,' Akiko said.

She dashed back into the garage.

'Come on,' Kurt shouted. 'We don't have time.'

She returned seconds later, dragging the unconscious body of Gao behind her.

'He would have been fine,' Kurt said. 'This place isn't going to burn up like your old castle.'

'I wasn't saving him,' she said. 'We need a doorstop if we want to cause any real trouble.'

She wedged him between the door and the wall, keeping it open and allowing the hall to fill with smoke.

'A helpful touch,' Kurt said. 'Let's go.'

They were off and running, heading down the hall to

the southwest. At the end of the hall, Kurt found a locked fire door, but Gao's key card opened it. They made it through what had to be a design room, filled with scale models and computers, and then found an elevator lobby, with doors on three sides plus the one they'd come through.

Kurt rushed to the farthest door and opened it with the key card. He saw only offices and a conference room.

He turned to see Akiko, waving him over. She'd found an emergency escape plan plastered to the wall. It showed the entire floor plan.

'Three cheers for the Japanese version of OSHA,' Kurt said.

Akiko was looking out into the room and rechecking the plan. 'It's got to be that one.'

They ran to the door on their right, opened it and found a long hall that led along the front of the building. Running through it, Kurt saw the first of many flares and phosphorus explosions raining down on the lawn outside. 'Rocket's red glare,' he said. 'Right on time.'

39

Joe had launched exactly half of his fireworks at Han's building when he called the fire department. Using the phonetic translation Akiko had worked out for him in advance, he told them the CNR factory was exploding and burning. At least that's what he hoped he was telling them. He repeated it twice and then hung up.

Grabbing the second set of launch tubes, he loaded more of the monster-sized bottle rockets and angled them to fire downward and onto the roof ahead of him instead of up into the sky. With the press of a button, he lit them off.

The launch filled the overlook with a swirling cloud of gray smoke. Through it, Joe saw red, white and purple explosions right above the building. Another shell, designed to flare in a horsetail effect, hit the roof and spread out blazing golden embers in all directions. He listened to reverberating booms and the sound of fire engines coming from the outskirts of town.

'That should do it,' Joe said to himself.

He got up, tossed the camera and the binoculars into the back of the Skyline and climbed into the driver's seat.

The sirens were growing louder by the moment; he could see the flashing lights coming down the main road a mile or two from the factory, but it was another sound that got his attention.

He turned back toward the factory and noticed lights descending toward it from Nagasaki Bay. Amid all the chaos, a helicopter was coming in for a landing.

Joe turned the key, put the Skyline in gear and spun the tires, pulling off the dirt and out onto the road. If Han's people took Nagano out of there in a helicopter, he would never be seen again.

Gao had already come around by the time Han and three members of the security team reached him. Smoke was pouring into the hall through the open door to the garage, the sprinklers were blasting at full pressure, but the fire had been hidden so well, it wasn't being doused.

'Untie him,' Han ordered one of the men. 'And get someone in there to put out that damned fire.'

'What happened?' Gao asked groggily.

'What do you think happened?' Han snapped. 'Austin and the woman jumped you and set the place on fire.'

By now, the guard had untied Gao's hands and propped him up. Gao rubbed at his wrists, then his neck. 'Maybe they realized I was taking video of them.'

Han put his hand on the medallion around Gao's neck. It was undamaged. The high-tech computer glasses he'd been wearing lay on the floor a few feet away.

'If they were upset about you recording them, they wouldn't have left all your cameras behind. This is an act of desperation. A fire to bring the authorities into the building. An incident to put a spotlight of attention on us. It won't matter; in fact, it will be more evidence to use against them later. Did you get enough video?'

Gao nodded. 'We have video, voice recordings, movement analysis. Everything we need to construct a replica.'

'Good,' Han said. 'There's a helicopter on the way in. Get back to the island and get working on them immediately.'

'"Them"? You want more than one?'

'Oni has brought us a gift: the policeman who helped Austin back in Tokyo. I want a replica of him also; it will make it that much more difficult for the authorities to cause us trouble when we make our move.'

Kurt and Akiko made it to the warehouse. The loading bay waited just beyond.

Using Gao's key card, Kurt opened the last door. A stairwell led down to the floor, where towers of wooden crates and machinery loomed like a miniature city.

Several vehicles sat at the far end.

'We're going to need a way out of this, once we get Nagano,' Kurt said. 'See if you can find the keys to one of those cars or trucks.'

'If not, I can hot-wire one,' Akiko said.

'Good,' Kurt said. 'If we have a choice, something sturdy enough to break down metal gates and brick walls would be nice.'

'I'll do my best,' Akiko said.

'I probably don't have to tell you this after what we've seen, but watch out for the automated equipment. If Han can use machines to storm an armed compound, he can turn anything with batteries and cameras into a whistle-blower or worse.'

Akiko nodded and moved off, traveling swift and

silent. Kurt went the other direction, heading for the back door. He pressed up against it and opened it a crack. He saw Ushi-Oni, bossing around a group of Han's men. He was barking orders as the men went to work emptying the sedan.

First, they removed some long wooden boxes. Then other items wrapped in leather. They placed the boxes on a cart with great care before moving back to the car and dragging out Superintendent Nagano with far less caution.

Nagano sagged to the ground as he was pulled out of the sedan, which Kurt noticed was sporting government plates.

One of the men shouted at Nagano. A second man kicked him as they tried to force him to stand on his own.

At least he was alive.

Kurt hoped some of them would leave with the treasure they had, but they stuck together. And Kurt soon saw why. A helicopter was descending toward a concrete swath just beyond where they stood.

'Five against one. Wonderful odds.' Kurt looked around for a way to even the playing field and settled on using a forklift.

Starting the electrical vehicle was easy. Driving it a little more difficult. But he didn't need to be as precise as he'd been out on the racetrack.

He backed up, pivoted and sped forward, raising the arms of the forklift like a pair of spears.

He drove around and out through an open bay door and, from there, came flying around the edge, gunning for Ushi-Oni.

The Demon saw him at the last second and dove out of the way. Two of his men weren't so lucky. The forklift slammed them like a battering ram; luckily, they weren't skewered.

Kurt immediately pulled backward and spun to the right. The three-wheeled vehicle pivoted with surprising swiftness and the raised forks took out another of Han's men, knocking him out of the way, cracking several ribs in the process.

Gunfire rang out before Kurt could do anything else. Ricochets and near misses forced him off the forklift. He dove to the ground and took cover. By the time he looked up, Han's remaining guard was dragging Nagano to the helipad.

Kurt rose up, intending to give chase, but Ushi-Oni blocked the way. Instead of a gun, Oni held a gleaming *katana* sword.

He waved the sword toward Kurt. 'To the samurai, a blade was worthless if it couldn't cut a man in half with a single swing. They tested their weapons on captives and criminals. I'm going to test this one on you.'

He stepped forward and swung at a diagonal angle. Kurt jumped behind the stationary forklift and the blade slammed against the protective cage. Looking for any kind of weapon to defend himself with, Kurt grabbed a pry bar from the side of the forklift.

'That won't help you,' Oni said. He lunged forward again, swinging for Kurt's head.

Kurt ducked and held the pry bar up at the same time. It deflected the blade just enough to save him. But the sword came back from the other direction and knocked the bar from Kurt's hand. A third swing forced Kurt to dive away once more.

He rolled and came up bleeding. His suit was slashed, his shirt was sliced and there was blood oozing from a line on the back of his arm. The tip of the blade had made so fine a cut, Kurt barely felt it.

'The next one will take your head,' Oni insisted.

Kurt didn't doubt it, but the sound of fire engines closing in and of the helicopter landing gave him hope. 'If I were you, I'd get out of here. You'll never get to spend Han's money if you're serving life in prison.'

Kurt's words brought the fury of the Demon down on him. The sword came hard once more. Kurt moved to the side, keeping the forklift between him and Oni. Oni went one way, Kurt went the other. It was an effective defense if reinforcements showed up. But Kurt needed an offense. Now.

He lunged for the controls, reaching into the cage, turning the key and spinning the small wheel. The forklift jerked to the side and spun randomly. Oni was knocked backward, but more of Han's men were closing in.

Kurt had no choice. He jumped onto the forklift and threw it into reverse, speeding away from Oni and the men as the helicopter touched down. He raced back into the warehouse, found himself surrounded but was bought freedom when Akiko came crashing through the stacks of equipment and crates in a ten-wheeled truck.

As Han's men took cover from the avalanche, Kurt climbed into the truck and Akiko backed out of the warehouse. She drove across the lot, blasted her way through the gate and turned down the access road as the fire trucks came racing up it.

'Keep going,' he said. 'Don't stop for anything, not even the police.'

As she drove, Kurt got on the phone. 'Joe, where are you? They took Nagano in the helicopter.'

'I saw that,' Joe replied. 'I'm trying to follow it and get a tail number. But I'm running out of road.'

'Where are they headed?'

'Southwest. Along the bay.'

Joe drove with skills that would have matched Kurt out on the racetrack, but he had to deal with real-world issues: other cars, potholes and pedestrians. He swerved around a slow-moving bus, lost sight of the helicopter as it went behind the trees and then found it again as the view opened up.

He came to a one-way road, ignored the rules of traffic and followed it downhill. By the way it sloped, he knew he was heading for the shoreline.

A building blocked his view. Seconds later, a small car almost hit him head-on. Horns blared and Joe drove into the gutter, where he avoided taking out a fire hydrant. He pulled back onto a two-way street as soon as he could.

'Where'd you go?' he said, craning his neck around and looking for the fleeing helicopter.

Finally, he saw it again, farther out over the water; it was definitely heading out to sea.

He found another street, sped up again and then slammed

on the brakes as his lights reflected off a sign at the end of the road. The tires screeched and the Skyline GT-R slid to a stop inches from a fifty-foot drop.

Joe got out of the car and raised the binoculars. He tracked the helicopter for another thirty seconds and then its lights went out and it vanished in the night sky.

40

Washington, DC

The Earth Studies lab filled the basement of the main NUMA building in Washington, DC. It was located down there for purely practical reasons. Being an experimental facility, it took up a lot of space and contained bulky equipment, including large tanks filled with water, sand, clay and various other soils.

Conducting tsunami studies, seismic analyses and erosion experiments meant that sections of the lab were subjected to artificial earthquakes, weather and flooding and no one wanted overflow from the latest rogue wave simulation dripping down through the ceiling above them.

As Rudi Gunn stepped from the elevator and onto the laboratory floor, he was careful to look for puddles. He found none and made his way to the geology department, where two of NUMA's best had been working through the night and into the morning. He arrived first at the desk of Robert Henley.

Henley was one of the marine geologists who worked under Paul. Thin and ghostly pale, Henley wore his blond hair long and his beard even longer. It gave him the look of an emaciated Nordic prince.

'Morning, Henley.'

'Is it?' Henley asked. 'I'd hoped it was still dark outside.'

'Sun's just coming up. I was glad to get your message when I arrived. So you and Priya have something to show me.'

'We think we know where the influx of water is coming from.'

'That's good news,' Rudi said.

Henley looked grim. 'You'd better hold off on that until you hear the details,' he said. 'I'll let Priya explain. It was her theory that we've been following.'

Henley reached over to an intercom button and pressed it. 'Rudi's here,' he said. 'Ready to tell him what we've found?'

'Be right there,' an English voice replied.

As Henley straightened some papers on his desk, Rudi caught sight of Priya Kashmir approaching.

Priya was Indian, born in Mumbai but had grown up in London. She'd spent a year at Oxford before transferring to MIT. She had dark eyes, high cheekbones and full lips. Her mahogany-colored hair was cut to shoulder length at the moment, while a tiny diamond stud rested on the right side of her nose where she'd recently had it pierced.

It would have been easy to describe her as beautiful. Easy and a disservice. While she had classic features and an alluring smile, her beauty was secondary to her intellect and perhaps third in comparison to her determination.

Priya had graduated in the top of her class at MIT while building a foundation to bring learning material to poor children in rural India. She'd been quite an athlete as well, running track and swimming competitively while finishing her Master's.

Rudi had hired her after a single interview and she'd

been several weeks from joining NUMA when a terrible car crash had damaged her spine. Five surgeries and six months of painful rehabilitation had been unable to restore her mobility – though she had regained some feeling in her toes and that gave her hope.

Given the choice to come aboard or continue her rehab, she'd taken Rudi's offer to start working and had spent most her time in Hiram Yaeger's computer lab. She'd shown a great ability to focus on things others overlooked and, for that reason, Rudi had assigned her to work with the geology team in Paul's absence.

She came around the corner, propelling herself forward in a compact wheelchair. It was a product of her own design, modeled after the athletic wheelchairs used in sporting activities and moved by her own strength instead of a battery pack.

She rolled up to Rudi and Henley, wearing a sleeveless gray top and blue jeans. Henley couldn't take his eyes off her. Something Priya did not miss. 'What are you staring at, Robert?'

'Sorry,' Henley said. 'I can't decide what I'm more envious of, your perfect tan or your muscular arms.'

Priya broke into a surprised smile. 'Nicest compliment I've heard in ages. The tan comes from Mum and Dad. The biceps are all mine. Push yourself around in one of these for a while and you'll be buff before you know it.'

'I'd never make it out of the room,' Henley said. 'My arms are like wet noodles.'

Rudi cleared his throat and got everyone's attention. 'I understand you two have found something.'

'Yes,' Priya said. 'But I'm not certain it will be welcome news.'

'I warned him,' Henley added.

'Feelings can wait,' Rudi said. 'We need answers. What have you got?'

Priya moved to a new position. 'It starts with what we haven't found. The first possibility was a subsurface aquifer that the Chinese had ruptured. It would have to be incredibly large and under massive pressure to cause the geyser field that Paul and Gamay recorded. Hard to hide such a thing. We looked at a pair of sub-bottom profiling studies done by the Japanese. The coverage area doesn't extend much into the Chinese side, but nothing in the study indicates a major pool of pressurized water beneath the continental shelf. So we went deeper.'

Henley took it from there. 'We "borrowed" some data from an oil exploration company that charted the region several years ago. Before the price of oil crashed, everyone was looking for deepwater wells. This company took it to an extreme. They were looking for hydrocarbon deposits, several miles below the seabed. The kind that can't be extracted profitably unless the price of oil is through the roof. A hundred and fifty dollars a barrel or more.'

'And?'

'No oil,' Henley said. 'Only a few small natural gas deposits on the Chinese side.'

'What about water?' Rudi asked.

'No water either, but they did find a complex series of vertical fractures running deep into the crust, well beyond the range of the survey.'

'Vertical fractures?'

'Of a type I've never seen before,' Henley admitted. 'Nothing in the geology database matches them. It's like the survey found a new type of rock. Interesting in its own right but not an ocean of freshwater.'

'That made us look even deeper,' Priya said. 'And it got me thinking about ways to study what was down there without needing to send an ROV to the bottom. We settled on looking for Kenzo's Z-waves. And we found them. Apparently, some of the more advanced seismic monitoring stations are equipped to detect them, but the computer programs they run on have been filtering the data out.'

'Why?'

'Because the pattern they produce is identical to the signal generated by a deep-earth mining system using high-intensity sound waves.'

'Mining?'

Priya nodded.

'So that's what the Chinese have been doing down there.'

'So it appears,' Priya said. 'But I'm afraid that's not the most interesting or stunning news. Once we got ahold of the raw, unfiltered data and ran it through a program that Robert designed, we were able to determine the depth and orientation of the Z-waves. What we found was incredible. The Z-waves are propagating vertically, down into the crust and back up.'

'How deep do they go?' Rudi asked.

Henley answered. 'Through the crust and the upper

309

mantle, into an area known as the transition zone. At least two hundred miles below the surface. At the bottom of the transition zone, the Z-waves are reflected back off the denser rock and bounced back up to the surface, creating a harmonic vibration on the way in and the way out. And that tremor is wreaking havoc on a particular type of mineral within the transition zone.'

'What kind of mineral?'

'Ever heard of ringwoodite?'

'Ring-wood-ite?' Rudi shook his head. 'No.'

'It's a crystalline mineral similar to olivine that forms only under intense pressure. It's found deep in the transition zone beneath the upper mantle. In 2014, geologists studying a diamond that had been brought to the surface by a volcanic eruption discovered a sample of ringwoodite trapped within it. To their surprise, the strange mineral was not alone; it was concealing a special form of water.'

Priya finished for him. 'This led to another study. One to determine how much ringwoodite was present in the mantle and how much of that contained water. The teams that worked on it used seismic activity as their ultrasound generators and measured the results over a period of months. They discovered that the entire transition zone, one hundred and fifty miles thick, is permeated with ringwoodite and most of that is trapping water. It's normally held there under the intense pressure, capped by the rock layers above. Something like carbonated water in a soda bottle. But the Chinese mining effort has fractured the rock all the way down to the transition zone, breaking the cap and releasing the pressure.'

'And thus releasing the water,' Rudi said, grasping the rest of the argument. 'Which is forcing its way up through the crust under all that pressure. That would explain the field of geysers we've seen. And it might give us a clue how to stop it or how bad it's going to get. I'm not sure why you're so glum, I don't consider this bad news at all.'

'Perhaps you should,' Henley said. 'This isn't an oil well that can be capped or even an underground lake that will spew forth for a while and then dry up. The transition zone contains a vast amount of water. An almost *unfathomable* amount – to use a nautical term.'

'I need numbers,' Rudi said. 'Just how much water are we talking about?'

'Three or four times the amount in all the world's oceans, rivers, lakes and ice caps combined. If it all came to the surface, the landmass of the Earth would be completely submerged. This would be a water-covered planet, a shimmering blue ball without a single island. Even the tip of Mount Everest, the highest point on Earth, would be submerged beneath twelve thousand feet of water.'

Rudi didn't react to the statement offhand. He knew Henley was given to predictions of destruction – all part of his Hamlet-like nature. But the man was a first-rate scientist. He didn't twist the numbers, he just tended to focus on the worst possible outcome.

Priya, on the other hand, was the eternal optimist. It was in her nature to believe things were never as bad as they looked and that nothing couldn't be overcome. Rudi turned her way. 'How likely is that to happen?'

'Highly unlikely,' Priya said with a glance toward Henley.

'But if just five percent of the water trapped inside the transition layer is forced to the surface . . . sea levels will rise by two thousand feet.'

'Two thousand feet?' Rudi said.

Priya nodded.

'And how likely is a five percent discharge from this layer of rock?'

She shrugged. 'Impossible to say. No one's ever seen this before. We don't know exactly what is happening. All we know is, it's getting worse. The rise in the sea level has accelerated in the last six months, again in the last ninety days and once again in the last five weeks. As for predictions . . . the basic math is simple. A five percent discharge is far more likely than a ten percent surge. Four percent is more likely still. Three . . . two . . . one . . . take your pick. A one percent discharge is exponentially more probable than a five percent release. But even at that level – even if just one drop in a hundred is forced out of the transition layer – the sea level will still rise four hundred feet.'

Henley chimed in with more doom and gloom. 'You'd lose every major coastal city in the world, half the landmass of South America, most of Northern Europe, large swaths of America, especially in the south and along both urban coasts. Not to mention the most densely populated swaths of Asia and India. Two billion people would be forced to relocate. But there will be nowhere to put them and nothing to feed them, even if they could find somewhere to call their own. And as if that's not bad enough –'

Rudi cut him off. He didn't need Henley launching into depressing detail about what would happen to humanity.

He needed them to find a way to stop it. 'Is there a way for us to put a halt to this upwelling?'

'We can't be sure,' Priya said. 'We'd have a much better idea of what's possible if we knew exactly what the Chinese did down there, but there is a possibility that they've released something that can't be put back in the bottle.'

Rudi studied her face. Determination was mixed with a sense of grim acknowledgment. Better than any of them, Priya knew there were forces that human effort and engineering just couldn't overcome.

'Put all the data into a report,' Rudi said. 'In fact, give me two reports. One with all the technical data and a simpler version that laypeople and politicians can understand. I'll need them both within the hour.'

'Are you going to go public with it?' Priya asked.

'No,' Rudi said. 'Something far more dangerous. I'm going to send the information to China.'

41

Nagasaki

Kurt stared at the map with great intensity, as if by force of will he could make it reveal the destination of Han's helicopter.

'The helicopter was traveling on this course,' Joe said, using the mouse to draw a line on the screen. 'It flew right over this building and out over the harbor in this direction.'

The line ran to the southwest.

'Maybe they're taking him to China,' Akiko suggested.

'Odd course to take, if they were,' Kurt said. 'Shanghai is the nearest city and most likely destination, and that's due west.'

'Too far away,' Joe said. 'That was a small helicopter. Short-range model. Shanghai is more than five hundred miles away. It couldn't reach the Chinese mainland from here. Not in one hop.'

'What about refueling?' Kurt asked.

Joe sat back. 'I didn't see anything to suggest it could refuel in midair, but that doesn't rule out landing on a ship.'

'That's what I was thinking,' Kurt said. 'Which is why I brought up the ship tracker.'

At the touch of a button, the position and direction of every ship within a hundred miles of Nagasaki Harbor appeared on the screen. The map went out a hundred miles and could be expanded farther, if needed, but the problem became apparent rather quickly.

'There must be hundreds of ships out there,' Akiko noted.

'Doesn't Han own a yacht?' Joe asked.

Kurt looked it up online. 'Three, actually.'

'Seems like a good place to start.'

Kurt typed the identification numbers of Han's yachts into the search window, requesting locations. He was given a worldwide map. 'One yacht is in Monaco, one docked in Shanghai and the third is undergoing upgrades in Italy.'

'We can rule out his yachts,' Joe said.

Kurt brought the original screen back up. Typing quickly, he set a new search in place. Eliminating all ships under five thousand tons and deleting all vessels incapable of handling a helicopter. 'That brings us down to forty-nine ships in a hundred-mile radius.'

'We can't search forty-nine ships.'

'We can rule out some of them by nationality,' Kurt said, continuing to type. 'Assuming Han wouldn't land on an American- or European-flagged vessel cuts the number to twenty-six.'

'How many of them along that course line?' Joe asked.

Kurt tapped the keyboard and brought up Joe's line once again. 'None,' he said, surprised. 'The closest ship is fourteen miles to the north and is headed *into* Nagasaki Harbor. Not out to sea.'

'The helicopter could have changed course,' Akiko said. 'After all, it did shut off its lights.'

Kurt looked at Joe. 'That seem odd to you?'

'Not if he didn't want to be watched,' Joe said. 'The only way I could track him was by the position lights. As soon as those lights went off, that bird literally vanished in the sky.'

'But how could Han or the pilot know you were following them?' Kurt said.

Joe tilted his head. 'You're right. They couldn't possibly know. So why shut off their lights at all?'

Kurt had an idea. 'How high were they?'

'Low,' Joe said. 'Less than a thousand feet.'

'Were they climbing?'

'Not that I could tell. More like they were flying straight and level.'

Kurt turned back to the map.

'You have a theory?' Joe asked.

Kurt nodded. He zoomed back in on the course line. 'I think they flew low to stay off Nagasaki radar. And they went dark not because they thought you were watching but because they didn't want anyone to watch. And the only reason to fly like that is if you were going to touch down in sight of the mainland and you didn't want anyone to see you do it.'

Kurt was looking for an island, not a ship. But there was no shortage of those either.

'Gunkanjima,' Akiko said.

Kurt and Joe turned her way.

'Battleship Island,' she explained. 'Its real name is

Hashima. It sits off the coast a few miles. The island was a coal mine. At one point, thousands of workers lived there. Miners and their families. The island became so built up, with concrete buildings and seawalls, that it resembled a fortress guarding the approach to the city. That's how it got the nickname.'

She pointed to the island on Kurt's computer screen. It was sixteen miles downrange from Han's factory, but because the peninsula ran that way, the island was only a few miles off the coast.

Kurt had heard of Hashima. It was a crumbling relic of a bygone era, often listed as one of the world's most haunting, abandoned places. 'I thought they'd turned that island into a tourist trap.'

'They did,' Akiko said. 'It was very popular until about a year ago. But then high levels of asbestos, arsenic and other poisons were discovered in the soil and the buildings. The tourists roaming through the city were stirring it up and breathing it in.'

Kurt pulled up an article on the mysterious island. 'The federal government shut it down eleven months ago, three weeks after Han and CNR broke ground on the new factory. Something tells me that's not a coincidence.'

'Coincidence is reserved for the trustworthy,' Joe said. 'Everyone else must live under a cloud of suspicion.'

Kurt double-checked the flight path, as Joe had recalled it. It went almost directly at Hashima Island, but . . . 'There are other islands along the flight path,' Kurt noted. 'Takashima and Nakanoshima.'

'Takashima is built up and populated,' Akiko told him.

'There's a museum on the island, along with small hotels and large homes.'

'Hard to land a helicopter there without disturbing the neighbors,' Joe said.

'Nakanoshima Island isn't much more than a rocky outcropping,' she added. 'There's not even a good spot to land.'

Looking over the satellite image, Kurt agreed. 'If they're out there, they landed on Battleship Island.'

'The fact that it was closed to the public shortly after Han arrived seals it for me,' Joe said. 'But why bother with an island lair at all? He's got a sprawling, well-defended factory right here.'

'Because he has something to hide,' Kurt said. 'Something he couldn't risk being discovered during a Japanese safety inspection or by intrusive foreigners like us.'

'We could contact the authorities,' Akiko said.

Kurt shook his head. 'A dead end. Han has friends in high places around here or he wouldn't have gotten the island closed in the first place. All we'd accomplish is tipping our hand. They'd hide whatever they're up to and feed Nagano to the sharks. We're the superintendent's only hope for rescue and that means we have to get ourselves onto that island and fast.'

42

Nagasaki Bay

Two hours later, Kurt, Joe and Akiko were moving across Nagasaki Bay in a thirty-foot bowrider with a powerful inboard engine. The V-shaped hull cut through the swells as they followed a heading that took them out to sea and away from the darkened island.

There had been no time to order up the usual high-tech gear from NUMA's quartermaster so Kurt had 'borrowed' the powerboat and a modicum of diving gear and other equipment from a rental outfit. All of which would be returned in one piece or paid for by a disgruntled NUMA accountant.

Akiko was at the wheel while Kurt checked the wind and Joe prepped the diving gear.

'Turn to the northwest,' Kurt said. 'Take us out a couple miles and then turn back to the island.'

Akiko turned the wheel to the right and the boat leaned into the turn. As it straightened up once again, Joe arrived from the stern.

'I'm sure you know what you're doing, amigo, but the island is thataway.' Using his thumb, he pointed over his shoulder. 'That's going to make for a long swim.'

'Observant as usual,' Kurt said, 'but having studied

satellite images and a hundred other pictures, I can tell you swimming is not the way to go here.'

He pulled out the laptop and showed Joe a high-resolution aerial photo. 'There's a forty-foot seawall encasing the entire island, complete with waves breaking against it and tricky currents sweeping past. If we didn't get battered to death against the rocks and the foundation of the wall, we'd be quickly dragged past and dumped back in the bay.'

Joe nodded. 'There's a dock here and pilings on the far end. Stairways in three different places. We could use those.'

'The dock is concrete and designed for a larger boat,' Kurt said. 'The pilings are a concrete jumble at the far point of the island. You know what the surfers say: points draw the waves. We'd be fighting the current and the breakers. As for the stairs, those are the most obvious points of access on the entire island. Unless Han is a fool, they'll be monitored and guarded.'

'So why bring all the diving gear?'

'We need a way off the island when we're finished,' Kurt said. 'If we can find Nagano and get him out before the tide changes, we'll have an easy ride into the bay.'

'I'm glad we have an exit strategy,' Joe said. 'Thinking ahead. I consider that growth. But how do we get on the island in the first place?'

'Did you wonder why I took this particular boat?'

'It has nice lines.'

'It also has a lot of torque and towing power, which they use for the adrenaline junkies and their new sport, wingboarding.'

Joe cut his eyes at Kurt. 'Wingboarding?'

'It's like parasailing, only you have a chute above your head and a wing beneath your feet.'

'We're going to fly onto the island?'

'*Glide* onto it,' Kurt said. 'Akiko will pilot the boat as we get up to altitude and then tow us in. We cut the cord about a mile out and ride the sea breeze toward the island. Instead of crawling out of the water like a couple of amphibians, we'll drop in from the sky like a pair of owls.'

'What if they have radar?'

'Doubtful,' Kurt said. 'That island is supposed to be abandoned and off-limits. They won't have a radar installation, searchlights or anything else large or obvious. Nothing out in the open that would give them away. At best, they'd have a surveillance system of hidden cameras and motion detectors. But they'll be outward-looking, watching the perimeter for intruders approaching from the sea. Not inward and monitoring the deserted center of the island.'

'So fly in over the top of their perimeter and what?'

Pulling out a pair of goggles with large, oddly shaped lenses, Kurt said, 'These have infrared sensors built in. By approaching from the sky, we'll get a full view of the island. Whatever Han's people are doing, they'll need lights, power and equipment. All those things produce heat. Heat that will be easy to see on an otherwise cold and deserted island.'

Joe understood perfectly. 'We'll scan the island as we descend and then follow the heat trail like it's the Yellow Brick Road.'

'I'll scan,' Kurt said. 'You're the pilot. I'm counting on you to do the flying. And the landing. On the roof of one of those buildings.'

Clad in black neoprene, Kurt and Joe took their positions on a twelve-foot wing at the back end of the powerboat. They stood side by side, each of them with one foot forward and the second foot back, behind and canted sideways, a stance that provided balance and control.

Backpacks strapped to their shoulders held the compact oxygen bottles, masks and fins that they would use to swim off the island once they found Superintendent Nagano and any clue suggesting what Han was up to.

With their feet set, they grabbed a pair of guide cables that would allow them to maneuver the wingboard and the parasail that would rise up above them. A short video told them how to control the wing.

'This doesn't seem too hard,' Joe said. 'Lean left, it turns left; lean right and it turns right.'

'How far in do you want me to take you?' Akiko asked.

Kurt had already done the calculations. 'Get us within two miles and then give us a little waggle. We'll pull the cord.'

Her eyebrows went up. 'Two miles? That's a long way out.'

'According to the information I read online, this contraption has a glide ratio of twelve-to-one. With the cable fully extended, we'll be almost fifteen hundred feet above you. High enough to cover three and a half miles. But considering the headwind and our inexperience guiding this thing, I want a safety margin to play with. Two miles will do just fine.'

Akiko nodded, glanced at the GPS receiver and then looked back over her shoulder at the two of them. 'Ready?'

Joe reached up and double-checked a pair of goggles currently perched on his head. His were designed for night vision. While Kurt's looked for heat, Joe's amplified the available light. As they closed in on the island, Joe would pull the goggles down in front of his eyes and look for a landing spot.

With the goggles strapped securely to his head, Joe gave the thumbs-up and set both hands on the guide line.

Kurt did the same. 'Release the cable.'

Keeping one hand on the wheel, Akiko reached over and pulled on a lever to her right.

Clamps released and the parasail billowed out behind Kurt and Joe, filling with air. The lines snapped taut and pulled them back as the wing beneath their feet disconnected from its moorings.

In an instant they were airborne and rising fast, as the cable spooled out from a drum in the back of the boat.

They climbed with surprising speed as the two wings provided ample lift. By the time the cable was maxed out, Kurt could see all of Nagasaki lit up, but all he could see of the boat was the shimmer of the wake it was leaving behind.

Working together, he and Joe practiced a few maneuvers. The wingboard responded easily, working in perfect tandem with the parasail above. The ride through the cool night air was smooth as glass.

'Easy peasy,' Joe shouted over the wind. 'The trick is going to be controlling it once the cable is cut. The wings are staggered like an old biplane. As long as we keep the parasail filled, we'll have control. But if our forward speed drops too much and the sail collapses, we're in trouble.'

Kurt looked up at the graceful curve of the parasail stretched above them like a crescent moon. 'If that happens, we pull the emergency release and dump the wing; we'll lose some distance but we can parachute down. Did you pick a landing site?'

'I studied the satellite image,' Joe said. 'There are forty buildings on that island with a flat roof. Plenty of landing spots. Which one we pick all depends on the angle of our approach. I'll make a final choice when we get closer.'

'You lead, I'll follow,' Kurt said.

Kurt nodded and reached for the radio strapped to his arm. 'Turn toward the island. Keep an eye on the GPS and give us a little shake when we hit two miles. We'll pull the cord and glide the rest of the way in. Once you feel us go, haul in the cable and make your way back to the channel between the island and Nagasaki.'

'Will do,' Akiko said, her voice reaching Kurt through the earbud. 'Good luck.'

The lights below went dark and the wake began marking a curve to the left. A few seconds elapsed before the cable began to haul them around in matching fashion. Leaning to the left in tandem, Kurt and Joe easily maneuvered their flying machine into the turn. As they straightened up, the island appeared. It was nothing more than a dark spot against the shimmer of the sea.

On a direct heading toward it, they began to pick up speed. A few minutes later, the boat began to weave back and forth.

'That's our signal,' Kurt said. 'Here goes nothing.'

He reached forward and grabbed a red handle designed to release the cable in an emergency. One pull brought it back to a safety detent. A second pull finished the job.

The cable snapped free with a metallic whine. The wingboard and the parasail rose unencumbered and began to slow.

Leaning forward like snowboarders ready to move downhill, Kurt and Joe eased the craft into a mild descent. The wake of the powerboat vanished down below as Akiko turned away and in a moment the only sound Kurt or Joe could hear was the wind blowing past them and the rush of blood in their ears.

'Slight crosswind,' Joe said. 'We're drifting to the south.'

They leaned to the left and the board tilted beneath them. For an instant it felt as if it would slip away, but the brilliance of the twin wing system became evident as the parasail above corrected for any overzealous maneuvering done down below.

Having adjusted for the wind drift, they overshot for thirty seconds and then turned back on course. The feeling was incredible. Kurt had made a hundred jumps in various kinds of parachutes. He'd BASE-jumped in a wingsuit and even flown an expendable glider nicknamed the Lunatic Express, but all those descents were either fast and furious or slow and peaceful. The wingboard was somewhere in the middle, controllable with a simple body lean; it responded to the slightest weight shift, but there was a graceful sense to the pace. It moved at forty miles an hour instead of traveling like a bullet the way you did in a wingsuit. 'This is like surfing the sky.'

Joe was grinning as broadly as Kurt. 'If we survive tonight, I'm going to make this my new hobby.'

Kurt glanced at the timer on his wrist and then at the altimeter. 'Eight hundred feet. Been just over a minute. We're more than halfway there.'

As they moved closer, the jagged black shape of the island grew larger and appeared to rise up in front of them. Even in the dark there was something sinister about the place. Kurt could see waves breaking against it in splashes of angry white foam. The abandoned buildings looked like battlements in the low light.

'Time to enhance our vision,' Kurt said.

Kurt reached up and pulled the infrared lenses over his eyes while Joe pulled down the night vision goggles.

Joe suddenly saw the island in green with gray tones. He could see the outlines of the buildings, the narrow overgrown alleyways between them and the rubble strewn in open spaces. The closer they got, the more dilapidated everything appeared.

The island had been abandoned since 1974. Some of the buildings had fallen into disrepair before then. The place had survived several typhoons and hundreds of storms. The concrete shells of the buildings remained standing, but they were crumbling badly, the windows were all gone and foliage growing in the gaps was doing its best to split the structures apart.

'We're right on target,' Joe said, 'but still drifting a little. We should have no problem clearing the first row of buildings and dropping on the second row, closer to the center of the island.'

'Can you tell the condition of the roofs yet?'

'Not really,' Joe said, leaning to the left once again. 'We're still too far away.'

Kurt's view of the island was almost invisible. The cold concrete was actually cooler than the surrounding waters, making the island a dark void in a swath of gray. There were tiny dots of heat here and there, but, based on their size, he knew they were probably rodents and birds that lived on the island.

'Any sign of the Yellow Brick Road?' Joe asked.

'Not even a munchkin or a flying monkey,' Kurt said.

He scanned methodically, but the maze of buildings made it hard to see anything at ground level. 'Can we drift right a little and then come back against the wind? I need a better view of the alleys.'

'We're getting closer,' Joe said. 'We'll have to make it quick.'

They shifted their weight to the right and the wingboard made a graceful turn. Kurt got a view between many of the buildings, spied a dimly glowing area and made a mental note of where it was. 'Can we go a little more?'

'Ten more seconds,' Joe said, 'then we turn back.'

Joe began a mental count as Kurt peered back and forth, looking for any sign of activity.

'That's it,' Joe said. 'Lean hard left.'

Joe leaned into the turn and felt Kurt doing the same. As they threw their weight over and pulled on the control cables, the twin-winged glider pulled up and turned sharply. 'Level off.'

They were now dropping rapidly and picking up speed at the same time. The sea vanished and the outer layer of man-made structures raced by, not far beneath the wing.

'We're going too fast.'

Pulling back on the chute stopped the descent momentarily. The glider ballooned upward as the speed dropped. By the time they leveled off and began descending again Joe could see they were going to miss the landing zone.

'It's no good,' Joe said. 'We're going to overshoot and crash into the mountain. Divert to the left, we'll have to cross over and land in the open area at the front of the island.'

Joe leaned into the turn. Kurt reacted instantly and the wingboard curved toward a gap between the rock wall and the tallest building.

To Joe's amazement, Kurt was still looking through the thermal imaging goggles, following Joe's instructions perfectly, while studying the island for heat sources.

'Straighten up,' Joe said.

They were rushing toward the gap between the central peak and a building to its left. Joe calculated that they'd clear the gap with twenty feet to spare.

Suddenly Kurt pulled on the cables. 'Turn back,' he shouted.

'What? Why?'

'Hard left,' Kurt said, leaning over sharply.

Joe did as Kurt ordered and they turned the wingboard rapidly, whipping it around in a 180. This cost them a lot of speed and momentum and they dropped fast on their new heading.

Trees growing out from one of the buildings scraped the bottom of the wingboard and Joe scanned ahead of them, searching for a landing zone.

There was a wide roof two hundred feet directly ahead of them, but he could see they'd never make it.

'Lean right,' Joe said.

They curved back to the right, dropped farther and thumped onto the roof of another building. The impact was hard enough that they bounced, skidded forward and then spun when the right-hand tip of the wing clipped a vent.

Joe was thrown from the bindings that locked his feet into position. He hit and rolled, tumbling several times and losing the night vision goggles in the process.

He looked up to see the wingboard sliding, stopping and then moving again as the parasail caught the wind off the peak. Kurt was still locked into the bindings and was gathering in the sail as fast as he could.

Joe rushed toward him, caught the other end of the parasail and pulled hard. The parasail collapsed with his effort and the wingboard stopped where it was.

Before Joe could ask why Kurt had called for the dangerous last-minute turn, a helicopter rose up from the far side of the central hill and thundered overhead. It was heard more than seen as all its lights were still out.

'Sorry for messing up our nice approach and landing, but I caught sight of the heat plume from their engines before we crested the hill,' Kurt said. 'Another few seconds and we'd have fouled their rotors in a very painful way.'

'I hope they didn't see us,' Joe said. He glanced into the distance. He could hear the helicopter traveling straight and low. It was still blacked out and moving away from the island. There was nothing to indicate anyone on board had spotted them. 'They must have been using *our* backup landing zone as a helipad. Awfully tight quarters to take off and land in. If I was the pilot, I'd be far more worried about the side clearance than keeping an eye out above me for anything that might be dropping in.'

'They'd be coming back if they'd spotted us,' Kurt said. 'Let's get this chute tucked away.'

Kurt gathered the last of the parasail's material and wrapped it with the guide wires. Joe lifted the edge of the wingboard and helped Kurt shove the sail underneath.

In the distance, the helicopter switched its lights on and banked toward the city. 'They don't seem to be coming back,' Joe said. 'But the real question is, did they take Nagano with them?'

Kurt shook his head. 'It would make no sense to bring him here and then take him away. That was a shuttle run. A drop-off. He's here, all right, probably with your old friend Ushi-Oni. They just can't keep the helicopter here for too long on the chance someone would notice.'

43

Hashima Island

Ushi-Oni stood by a dilapidated building watching the helicopter leave. He would have preferred to be on it, but Han had ordered him to stay behind and had promised to arrive shortly with his payment, assuming the swords were authentic.

They'd better be authentic, Ushi-Oni thought to himself. He'd killed three policemen and half a dozen Shinto priests and monks to obtain them.

He glanced at the sword in his hand. It was the famed Honjo Masamune, if the dying monks were to be believed. Ushi-Oni wasn't sure. He had to admit the weapon was light; in fact, it seemed to weigh almost nothing at all. And how it gleamed.

All around him was rubble, crumbling concrete and tangled vines. The clouds were growing thicker and lower as the threatened storm closed in, but the sword caught what little light was reaching them and amplified it.

Rumor had it that Masamune had worked crushed gemstones into his blades. Oni wasn't sure, he could see nothing of the sort, and such an act would make the weapons brittle and useless for fighting, but the weapon was almost luminescent in his hand.

A rusted metal door opened behind him and Han's lead scientist Gao poked his head out. Gao's face had a feral quality to it. He reminded Ushi-Oni of a rodent emerging from its den.

'You need to come with me,' Gao said. 'Han wants everyone inside.'

Ushi-Oni shook his head. He wasn't fond of closed-in spaces. Time in various prisons had seen to that. Besides, he was sweating. The fever was coming back. He needed more powerful antibiotics. 'You go, I'm staying out here.'

'Suit yourself,' Gao said. 'But I'll need the sword. We have to examine it in the lab.'

Instead of handing Gao the sword, Oni extended it toward the diminutive scientist, bringing the tip within an inch of Gao's chest. 'After I've been paid.'

Gao pulled back, putting some distance between himself and the blade. He took one more glance at Oni and then retreated into the stairwell, shutting the decaying wooden door behind him.

Oni turned to the surroundings. There was not much to see from his vantage point, only abandoned monoliths and a broken hill that had been hollowed out by the miners. Still, the ruined island begged to be explored.

Oni could smell the rain coming, but he didn't care, it might even help quell his fever. Picking a direction at random, he crossed the open expanse where the helicopter had landed and walked out into the dark.

44

Roof of Building 37, Hashima Island

Kurt lay flat at the edge of the building. He studied the terrain through the infrared filter. The central mountain was on his right while a nine-story building lay to the left. A concrete pedestrian bridge several floors below spanned the diagonal gap between the two.

The hillside was dark and cold, nothing resembling a heat source could be seen. The bridge was darker still. And the concrete shell of the building on the far side was like empty caves stacked one on top of the other.

Joe crawled forward beside him.

Kurt looked up. 'Did you find the night vision goggles?'

'No,' Joe said. 'They must have gone over the edge.'

'Better them than us.'

'True,' Joe said. 'See anything?'

'There's an oval swath down there in the clearing,' Kurt said. 'Residual heat left behind where the helicopter sat for the last two hours.'

'Any sign of the passengers?'

'Not yet. No sign of a vent or doorway radiating heat. All these buildings are dark.'

'So much for the Yellow Brick Road,' Joe said.

As Kurt went back to scanning the buildings the rain

began to fall. It came lightly at first, tapping him on the shoulders with a soft patter, trickling through his hair. Soon it was falling steadily, not a tropical downpour but cold, gray rain that would fall all night.

Kurt ignored it for now, concentrating on the task before him. He studied the structures one by one. Across and down, across and down. The tangled complex of buildings impressed him. Built over the decades, some were spaced so tightly there was barely an alleyway large enough for a bicycle to fit between them; others had been built right into each other, with outer walls knocked down and hallways extended.

Han's people could be hidden in any one of them. At least that was Kurt's initial impression.

'These buildings are more dilapidated than I thought,' he said. 'A demolition crew would have a field day here.'

'Might not need them,' Joe said. 'Some of these structures are partially collapsed already.'

With Joe's words, it dawned on Kurt. 'I know where they are.'

'Did you spot something?'

'Not a thing,' Kurt admitted. 'But if you were hiding on this island, would you set up shop in a building that could collapse at any moment, one that couldn't keep the rain out or the wind from howling through?'

Joe grinned. 'Probably not. You think they've gone underground?'

Kurt nodded. 'They dug coal out of this island for decades. The mine has several entrances and large open galleries where it's warm and dry.'

'Sounds inviting,' Joe said. 'Let's go.'

The first stairway they came to was a fire escape connected to the outside of a building. The rusted metal was flaking badly and had pulled away from the building in several places. Definitely unsafe.

Kurt pushed on it with his boot and the entire thing swayed. 'That's not going to support either of us.'

'Let's find another way,' Joe said.

He found a caved-in part of the roof where one side of a concrete slab had dropped. It angled down into the building like an off-ramp. The wet surface was slick and they scaled it carefully, sliding the last few feet.

The interior of the building was a dank, fetid world. Rainwater was dripping through a hundred cracks in the ceiling; plants and vines grew in many places. Several inches of muck covered the floor.

'Housekeeping must be on strike,' Kurt mused.

The infrared goggles were useless inside the dark concrete building, but they soon found an inner stairway, forced the door open and began descending toward a bridge that led between two buildings.

'If we cross here, we can get down to the ground level without having to go outside,' Kurt said.

'Staying inside won't keep us dry,' Joe said, sidestepping some more runoff, 'but at least it'll keep us out of sight.'

They crossed the span with caution, avoiding the gaping holes and burgeoning cracks that suggested the bridge would not remain in place for much longer. And came out on the other side. Kurt dropped down to one knee and signaled for Joe to hold up.

'I was wrong,' Kurt whispered.

'You? No.'

Kurt nodded. 'Not everyone is out of sight. There's a patrol on the hillside. Two men. From up there, they will see us as soon as we hit open ground.'

Patrolling in the rain was miserable duty. So thought every soldier who'd ever been forced to do it.

Han's men were no different. They did as ordered, but they didn't have to like it. They started out hiking up the central hill that dominated the island; climbing through the foliage was even more difficult than navigating the slick and well-worn stairs. The arrived at the top of the hill and took their positions.

'You see anything?' the leader of the two asked.

His partner shook his head. 'Something's wrong with my equipment,' he said, pulling off his night vision goggles. 'All I see are flares.'

The leader pulled the hood back on his rain slicker and stepped over to his subordinate. Each of them had a pair of night vision goggles, but the scopes were less effective in the rain. Raindrops, like all water, bend and refract light. Studying the terrain through the falling drops was like looking through a kaleidoscope.

The leader looked through the goggles and then handed them back. 'Turn down the resolution.'

He did the same with his own. The lightning in the distance was another problem. The goggles had a circuit that prevented it from blinding them, but it still caused flaring on the screen that lasted for several seconds each time it flashed.

'Why are we even out here?' the subordinate said, putting his goggles back on and pulling the rain gear up over his head.

'Because the boss wants you here,' a voice said.

Han's men turned but they were too late. One took a tree branch to the face, the other a gut punch and then a knockout blow to the back of the head when he doubled over.

By the time they woke up, they were bound and gagged, tied to a tree, and had been relieved of their weapons, ponchos and night vision gear.

Dressed in the rain gear they'd taken from Han's men, Kurt and Joe looked more like they belonged. They crossed the hill, found another stairway and made it down to level ground. Using the infrared goggles, Kurt spotted the residual heat from the helicopter once more. It was rapidly fading from the rain.

He turned his attention to the walls beyond the landing area. Several openings had been cut in the mountain and were now barricaded. Through the human eye they all looked the same, but through the heat sensitive goggles one of them shimmered a magenta color.

'Across the field,' Kurt said. 'The shaft on the far left. That's the one.'

'No sign of any guards,' Joe said.

'Let's not wait for any to show up.'

Kurt flipped the goggles up once more and sprinted across the open ground. Arriving beside the tunnel, he pressed himself against the wall. Joe took a position right behind him. A quick look confirmed what Kurt needed to know. 'Tunnel is empty but venting heat.'

Joe glanced up at the rain falling steadily from the heavens. 'Warm and dry,' he said. 'Looks good to me.'

Kurt nodded. Without another word, both of them slipped quietly into the tunnel.

The ground was turning to mud as Ushi-Oni continued his exploration of the island. He'd never been in such a haven of decay and he found himself marveling at the beauty of it. The crumbling buildings, piles of rubble and stark emptiness spoke to him.

This is what the world would be like after men were gone, he mused. *It wouldn't take long for nature to erase the insignificant stain mankind had worked on the planet. Not long at all.*

The wind picked up as he neared the seawall and he decided he'd had enough. He turned around, began the journey back toward the laboratory and stopped.

A faint glow was emanating from the debris ahead of him. He held still for a moment and then moved closer. The light vanished and then reappeared.

Using the samurai sword, Oni slashed at a bush that got in his way. The branches fell, cut clean through. The light was more visible now. Oni was looking at a tiny screen with a low-powered LED attached.

He bent low and pulled it from the rubble. Recognition came instantly. He had in his hands a damaged pair of night vision goggles. The front plate was missing and the screen was cracked, but the goggles were still operating, and they were obviously the type military and police forces used to make assaults under cover of darkness.

Oni looked around, expecting to be shot or attacked at any second, but nothing of the sort happened. Still, the high-tech device didn't just fall from the sky like a . . .

The words died in his mind. He looked up at the vacant monolith beside him. The rain shrouded it in a jacket of mist and white noise. The damage to the goggles was consistent with a high-speed impact or a long drop. One side was dented and scraped, the other unblemished; parts were broken off. And though he'd only made a cursory search, the missing parts were nowhere that Oni could see.

Perhaps they did fall from the sky after all.

He switched the damaged goggles off, clipped them to his belt and went looking for a way into the building.

45

Kurt and Joe moved quietly through the tunnel as it bent back and downward into the mountain. A small berm had been built toward the front to keep water out, but the rainwater pooled quickly and soon found its way around the rudimentary defense, traveling in a narrow channel at the center of the tunnel before vanishing over the edge of a vertical shaft that dropped into the depths. An elevator on the near side looked abandoned.

'This thing looks like it hasn't been used in years,' Joe said.

Kurt took a brief look down the vertical shaft with the infrared scope. 'No heat coming up the shaft either. They're not down there. Must be farther back.'

They moved on and soon found the first signs of recent occupation. The old electrical cables had been replaced and the new wire along the wall was connected to a string of LEDs that glowed dimly.

When they came to a split in the tunnel, Kurt studied the ground using the IR goggles. The residual heat of footprints could be seen. Most of them went left. Kurt followed.

Joe put a hand on his arm. 'Are you sure?'

'Yellow Brick Road,' he whispered. 'We're in a high-traffic area.'

His faith was rewarded when they came to a pair of plastic-coated, triple-sealed doors. The handle glowed from the heat of the last person to touch it.

Kurt flipped up his goggles. 'Han has been doing some remodeling.'

Joe nodded. 'Something tells me these aren't the hospitality suites.'

Kurt tested the door handle. 'Unlocked,' he whispered. 'Let's make an entrance.'

Switching off the safeties on the weapons they'd taken from Han's guards on the hill, they prepared to move into the room.

With slow precision, Kurt pulled the handle down until it clicked and the latch disengaged. He eased the door open and felt a slight wave of air passing over him, as the room inside was kept at positive pressure.

He pushed the door far enough for Joe to aim his weapon inside. But there was no one there to challenge them. 'Empty,' Joe said. 'Let's take a look.'

Joe moved in first and Kurt followed, shutting the door as carefully as he'd opened it. The room was unoccupied, but it was filled with equipment. Complex machinery had been bolted to the floor here and there. Shelves were stocked with prefabricated parts: gyros, servos, robotic arms and legs.

'Your friend Han should talk to someone about this robot obsession,' Joe quipped.

'About a lot of things,' Kurt suggested.

While Joe examined the parts on the shelf, Kurt moved deeper into the room, where he discovered a high-tech

3-D printing machine. It had been left on and was warm to the touch.

He tapped the small screen on a control panel. A series of Chinese characters appeared along with a blank line for a password. He didn't waste his time trying to guess it and moved on.

Beside the 3-D printer was a table, now tilted at a forty-five-degree angle. A sheet covered a figure beneath it. Kurt pulled the sheet back, expecting to find Nagano, tortured and deceased. Instead, he found the half-finished shell of another humanoid robot. No face, no body panels, just a frame with limbs and wires and a power cell. He noticed an air bladder covering the chest and a liquid reservoir.

Joe arrived carrying two robotic arms. 'Can I give you a hand?'

'Very funny.'

'Dr Frankenstein has nothing on this place.'

Kurt nodded, covered the unfinished creation with the sheet and moved to the back of the room. He reached the far wall and realized it was made of smoked glass. He pulled the infrared scope down over his eyes once more but saw only the reflection of his own heat.

Pushing the goggles back up, he pressed his face up against the glass, shielding his eyes from any reflection and trying to discern what was on the other side. He couldn't see much, but he heard something. Or rather he felt it. A vibration coming through the glass. A murmuring sound as if several people were talking in low tones on the other side.

He waved Joe over. 'Do you hear that?'

Joe put his ear up to the glass. 'Conversation?'

'Too repetitive,' Kurt said. 'It's the same words over and over again. More like chanting or praying.'

'If I was Nagano, I'd be praying for help right about now,' Joe said.

They looked around for a door, discovered that one of the panels was held in place by a spring-loaded, magnetic latch. Pressing it once released it and Kurt pulled the door open.

The droning sound grew in volume but not clarity. Kurt stepped deeper into the chamber. There were more unfinished machines under sheets on medical tables around him and, down at the far end, a pair of figures standing in front of high-definition screens. They were watching and then repeating what they saw and heard on the screen, both figures speaking the same phrases over and over.

Kurt gripped his pistol and stepped closer. The figures ahead of him didn't react to him approaching at all. As if they were in a trance.

He found a light switch on the wall, raised the pistol and paused. Strangely, he recognized the phrase they were repeating. They were speaking English. And stranger still, he recognized the voice that was speaking that phrase.

'Japan will never be an ally of China,' the image on the screen said.

'Japan will never be an ally of China,' the standing figures repeated.

Kurt flicked the switch. Neither of the figures reacted. They just kept speaking. Starting and then stopping and then starting over again in an endless loop.

Kurt stepped around in front of them. The two figures were identical, complete with mussed silver hair, deep-blue eyes and three days of stubble. Kurt felt as if he was staring in a mirror – two mirrors, actually. He was looking at robotic versions of himself.

Ushi-Oni paused on the top floor of the dilapidated building. The stairwell to the roof was blocked by debris, but he could see the orange glow from the clouds coming through a gap in the ceiling. He marched toward it, scaled the ramp-like section of the caved-in roof panel and paused at the top. Scanning the entire roof before exposing himself, he saw it was empty.

He climbed out into the rain once again and stood on the rooftop. He saw no soldiers or policemen or any parachutes or equipment, suggesting an assault on the island was beginning, but there was something out of place: a wide, flat object that gleamed in the low light, unlike every other dulled and corroded surface on the roof.

The twelve-foot wing looked like something that had fallen from a plane. But it was obviously in one piece. He found the parasail stuffed hastily beneath it.

'Austin,' he said to himself.

He turned with a start and charged back into the building, racing down the stairwell, as the first echoes from Han's helicopter reached him. Han had to be warned or Austin would destroy everything.

46

Hashima Island

'Japan will never be an ally of China.'

Kurt listened to the words and could hardly believe how like his voice they sounded. Not in the odd way one's voice sounded on a recorded message, but as if the words were emanating from his own body.

The screen flickered. A new video appeared. On it, the Prime Minister of Japan was mentioning the possibility of warmer relations with China.

'We'll see about that,' Kurt's robotic doppelgangers said.

The voices were off this time, especially the second robot's, which slurred the words just a bit. The scene repeated on the monitor.

'We'll see about that,' the robots replied, sounding now more like Kurt and more menacing at the same time.

'They're learning,' Kurt said. 'Practicing.'

'Wouldn't it be easier to program them with a recording and be done with it?' Joe suggested. 'Like the robotic assistant in Nagano's police station.'

'That robot was instantly identifiable as a machine,' Kurt said. 'Its lips moved each time it spoke, but that was just a pretense. These robots are speaking. Forming sounds with exhaled air and shaping that sound with their lips. They're breathing, blinking, even sweating. If I wasn't standing here, you might think one of them was me.'

'They're better-looking than you,' Joe said, then added, 'Strange that there's no one here to monitor their progress.'

Kurt pointed to a bank of computer terminals and server units blinking in the dark. The displays on the screens were constantly evolving. 'The computers are doing the monitoring. Machines training machines. Something tells me this is a very repetitive and redundant process. Until the machines have learned how to act human enough, they probably do this over and over again.'

As Kurt spoke, the robots stepped forward and walked into a different room. Kurt followed. It was a simulator. Similar to the one Han had in his factory but smaller. To compensate for the limited space, there was a curved wall of screens, which lit up all around them.

'That's the joint Trade Pavilion built with Han's money,' Kurt said. 'The Japanese Prime Minister is going to be there tomorrow to sign the new cooperation agreement with China. It's the deal everyone's been talking about.'

'And the Japanese Parliament will vote on rescinding the joint defense treaty with America a few days from now,' Joe said. 'The symmetry is uncanny.'

'And not by accident,' Kurt said. 'But from what I read, the defense treaty isn't in any real danger. The Japanese want more business out of China, but they're not all that interested in going it alone militarily.'

The duplicates began moving forward, walking on treadmills. As they traveled, the scenery around them changed in a virtual sense. They entered through a back door and followed a route that led up to the main hall.

Taking positions in the virtual crowd, they waited as images of the Japanese Prime Minister and the Chinese Ambassador appeared on the stage. A digital representation of Walter Han was there as well, since he'd facilitated the agreement and the rapidly warming ties between the two countries.

Handshakes first and then the signing of a document. The Ambassador signed on the right side before passing a pen to the Prime Minister. The pen was put to paper and instantaneously both mechanical versions of Kurt reacted. They reached into their jackets, pulled out dummy pistols and took dead aim.

'Japan will never be an ally of China!' they shouted, raising their weapons and pulling the triggers.

There were no gunshots, of course, no blanks or even simulated noises, just clicking triggers and a pattern of red dots appearing on the screen as the system recorded multiple hits on the Prime Minister, the Ambassador and another politician. Their deadly task completed, both units took steps toward the right to begin their escape.

The simulation ended there and both machines went inactive and returned their pistols to their shoulder holsters.

The video screens around them changed to a hotel lobby setting and the duplicates walked to one side, where a pair of seats had been arranged. They sat down, crossed their legs, quite naturally, and waited. There was nothing jerky and robotic about their movements. One of the robots even picked up a periodical from a table and licked its fingers before turning the pages.

'Surreal beyond words,' Joe said. 'If Han pulls this off, the whole world will think you killed the Japanese Prime Minister. It'll look like America is desperate to stop the Japanese from pulling out of the treaty. Desperate to stop China and Japan from moving closer.'

Kurt nodded. 'He recorded me in his factory. Gave him enough to build this program.'

'So much for the defense treaty not being in danger,' Joe added. 'If the world sees you shooting the Prime Minister, the vote to pull out of the treaty will be a landslide.'

'Not if we destroy this lab and everything in it.'

'I'm afraid that won't be allowed,' a voice called out from the dark.

The words came from the far end of the room. The voice was Han's.

Kurt turned, but there was no one there, only an intercom speaker attached to the wall. A door swung open behind Joe. Three men rushed in. Two more came in from the other end of the room and Kurt took the only chance left to him: turning on his duplicates and opening fire.

He drilled the first robot with several shots, but the machine responded with incredible speed. It leapt from its chair and charged at him, never wavering despite taking slugs to the chest, leg and face.

The robot tackled Kurt as cleanly as any professional wrestler, slamming him to the floor and knocking the gun from his hand.

Forced into hand-to-hand combat with the mechanical

version of himself, Kurt kneed the machine's solar plexus, but the blow had no effect. He worked one arm free and threw a right cross at the mechanical jaw. It split the artificial skin, but underneath lay only padding, titanium bones and small hydraulic motors.

In response, the robot put a hand around Kurt's neck and began to squeeze, cutting off the blood flow to Kurt's brain. Kurt reached up and dug his nails into the artificial flesh, pulling and ripping, desperately hoping to find wires he might yank out.

It was not to be. There were no vulnerable organs, pressure points or weak spots. No plugs to pull or batteries he could remove.

On the verge of blacking out, Kurt head-butted the machine and broke its prosthetic nose, but the machine only looked back at him with a blank stare and squeezed harder.

As Kurt's world darkened, he heard Joe fighting with Han's human guards. He looked beyond the arms holding him down to see Joe on the ground, struggling with three men. One of them pistol-whipped him.

'Cease this foolish struggle or you both will die painfully,' Han called out.

The struggle was about to end, one way or another. Kurt chose to live and fight another day. He pulled his hands away from the robot and raised them in surrender. Thankfully, the robot stopped crushing his throat, though its mechanical hand remained in place.

With the room now calm, Han strode in. The distinctive click of his shoes on the floor resounded with each step. He crouched beside Kurt and examined the bullet holes that had been drilled into the chest and face of the duplicate.

'Such foolishness,' he began. 'As I told you back at the track, a human is no match for a machine. My creation – my Kurt Austin – is superior to you in every way: greater strength, greater speed, faster reactions. And perhaps most importantly, an inability to feel pain or fear. Something you'll soon wish was a part of your limited human programming.'

47

Shanghai

Gamay found she couldn't sleep. There was too much to worry about, too much she couldn't control.

Paul, on the other hand, was stretched out on the floor of the INN production van and slumbering as if he were in a king-sized bed at the Four Seasons.

Gamay found she had an almost uncontrollable urge to wake him. She left him alone and took a seat at the editing station instead. It was three o'clock in the morning. The air had grown cold and damp in the van. It was still pitch-dark outside except for the security lights in the gated parking area.

Unwilling to risk a hotel, the van had been their accommodations for the evening. But it wasn't a long-term solution. Even if the Chinese didn't figure out where they were, sooner or later someone from the network would attempt to use the van or fuel it or perform some maintenance on it.

And even if none of those possibilities came to fruition, Gamay was certain that both of them would go stir-crazy before too long.

Staring out into the darkness, she noticed movement. This time, she jabbed Paul in the ribs without hesitation.

'What's that for?' Paul said, awaking with a start.

'Someone's coming.'

'Who?'

'I couldn't see.'

'Was it a security guard?'

Gamay shot him a look. 'What part of "I couldn't see" made you ask that second question?'

'Sorry,' he replied. 'Half asleep.'

He rolled up the blanket and pushed it beneath an equipment locker and stood, banging his head against the low ceiling for the umpteenth time. 'Now I'm awake,' he said, stifling any expression of pain or anger.

Peering out through the front window, they scanned the lot for any sign of someone moving around in the darkness. They saw nothing.

A knock on the back door startled them both.

Paul reached for the door.

'Paul,' Gamay whispered in warning.

'What are we going to do?' he said, shrugging. 'Besides, something tells me the secret police don't knock.'

He flicked the lever to the unlocked position and the door swung wide. Instead of policemen or military personnel, the smiling, perfectly made-up face of Melanie Anderson appeared beyond.

She climbed inside and shut the door.

'Why did you knock?'

'You know, Miss Manners and all that.'

'Your mom would be proud,' Paul replied with a smile.

She placed an insulated cup down in front of them. 'I brought coffee. You'll have to share this, but it would have looked odd if I'd brought three cups out to the van for myself.'

'If you knew how much Paul has been dying for a cup, I'd think you were trying to steal him away from me,' Gamay said.

Paul took the first sip and looked as if he'd just sampled waters from the Fountain of Youth. 'Oh, that's good,' he said, handing the cup to Gamay.

The aroma was enough for her, at the moment. She turned back to Melanie. 'You said you were coming at first light. Unless my eyes are going, it's not morning yet.'

'Not my fault,' Melanie said. 'My bureau chief called and told me to come in early. He said we'd been hacked again and that it had something to do with my last report.'

'But you weren't hacked,' Gamay said. 'We made all that up.'

'Which caused no small amount of worry on my part, let me tell you.' She held up a zip drive. 'When I got down here, the chief handed me this and walked away. Said he needed to make some hasty travel arrangements in case he had to leave China early. He suggested I seriously consider doing the same.'

'What's on it?' Paul asked.

'Don't know,' she told them. 'It's encrypted. But the hack was done stateside. Our New York office was breached; our satellite was compromised for two minutes and then returned to our control after transmitting the information on here. It was the same satellite we used to get your signal out. So I'm guessing it's meant for the two of you. Care to take a look?'

Gamay took the zip drive from Melanie's hand, stuck it in the slot on the laptop and powered up. A few moments later, she was looking at a log-in window. She used her NUMA password and was rewarded with a list of files.

'It's from Rudi,' she said, opening the first file. A presentation began on-screen.

Paul was incredulous. 'He sent a PowerPoint presentation? Instead of fake passports, disguises and tickets for the *Orient Express*?'

Gamay laughed. 'You know that train doesn't come this far east, right?'

'I was being facetious.'

Gamay read through the first page of the file. 'Sounds like Priya has been working with the geology team in your absence. They've been studying what we sent them and they believe they've figured out where the water is coming from. Han's mining operation created a deep-earth fissure, releasing water from beneath the transition zone.'

Paul leaned forward. 'That's two hundred miles down.'

'Water under intense pressure,' Gamay said, reading and summarizing. 'Z-waves caused by the water being released from a mineral known as . . . ringwoodite.'

'Ringwoodite?' Paul said.

'Did I say that correctly?'

'Perfectly. It's just . . .' He hesitated. 'Read on.'

Gamay gave Paul a sideways look. He was holding back. But instead of prodding him to spill what he knew, she scanned the next few lines, again summarizing as she went. 'Attached you'll find our evidence and calculations, along with two separate presentations to use. One is highly technical, the other is done in generalities. Due to the vast amount of ringwoodite and the nature of the ongoing fractures, total hydraulic release cannot be calculated at this time. But if left unchecked, it would likely result in a seawater rise of two thousand feet by end of decade.'

'Two thousand feet?' This from Melanie.

Gamay double-checked to make sure she'd read it correctly. 'That's what it says.'

'Read on,' Paul said calmly.

'Other calculations become speculative,' she said, picking up where she'd left off. 'Including a theoretical doomsday scenario, according to which the entire surface of the planet is covered in water within fifty years. Despite the extreme nature of this scenario, the possibility cannot be ruled out. For reasons that remain undetermined, the fractures of ringwoodite seem to be self-perpetuating and accelerating. Branching in all directions and spreading. Each new fracture releases more water. Which, in turn, causes additional fractures.'

The three of them were crowded around the computer now.

'And I thought I was the one who came up with crazy stuff,' Mel said. 'Doomsday scenario? Entire world covered with water?'

'I know it sounds irrational,' Paul said, 'but if the water is coming from that far down, it could be a real possibility. Believe it or not, there's more water trapped in the deep layers of rock than in all the oceans of the Earth. Three or four times as much. It's trapped in the minerals and held under incredible pressure. But if that pressure was released and the water began forcing its way to the surface . . .'

'You know about this?' Gamay said.

'Of course,' Paul said. 'It's deep-earth geology.'

'Why didn't you bring it up when we were first exploring the rise in sea level?'

Paul shrugged. 'I considered it early on but ruled it out as a possibility. The only process known to bring water up from that depth is a large magma plume, followed by volcanic eruptions. And volcanic activity was down for the past year.'

Gamay turned her attention back to the data put together by the science team. A graphic showed the fissures created by the Chinese mining operation. 'The crustal fractures extend downward beyond any existing measurement. They appear to be branching in all directions.'

'That's where that field of geysers came from,' Paul said. 'We couldn't see to the end of the field. Who knows how many there are. Hundreds, maybe thousands. All pumping water up from the depths.'

Gamay had overcome the shock of discovery and was quickly flipping through the other files.

'What are you looking for?' Paul asked.

'Anything that mentions getting us out of here.' She came to a file labeled *Instructions*. 'Rudi has given us an address to proceed to.'

'Safe house?' Paul asked hopefully.

Gamay typed the location into the computer. 'Not sure.'

Melanie leaned over to look at the map. 'That's not a safe house,' she said. 'That's the Shanghai bureau of the Ministry for State Security. Local headquarters of the secret police.'

Paul leaned back. 'And I thought Rudi was on our side.'

'Maybe he thinks it's the last place anyone would look for you.'

'He's not asking us to hide there,' Gamay told them, reading on. 'He wants us to turn ourselves in. But only to a man named Zhang. Make that a general named Zhang.'

Paul sighed. 'Well, that ought to speed up our trial and make it easy to get a firing squad together.'

'We have to trust Rudi on this,' Gamay said. 'He's obviously got something in mind.'

Paul nodded. 'Can we borrow the van?'

Mel shook her head. 'And lose my exclusive on the biggest story ever? Not on your life. You two share the coffee. I'll drive.'

48

Hashima Island

Walter Han watched as the robotic facsimiles of Kurt Austin returned to the workbenches and lay down. The movements were both as smooth and as awkward as any human's. One machine limped where a shot from Austin's gun had damaged its leg. It hopped up on the bench, favoring the injured leg and grasping for balance as it reclined. Reddish liquid oozed from the bullet wounds and soaked the right leg and torso.

The second robot was undamaged.

'Hydraulic fluid?' Han asked.

'No,' Gao said. 'We used a layer of gel between the artificial skin and the inner structural panels. It creates a supple feeling and allows a constant body temperature of ninety-eight-point-six degrees. If you shake the machine's hand, it feels like muscular grip beneath the soft flesh – as it should. The hand also feels warm. One of the technicians decided to color the gel so it looked roughly like blood in case the robot was damaged.'

Han reveled in such details. 'Give that man a bonus,' he said. 'I wouldn't have thought of that myself.'

Studying the robot, Han almost hoped it would be 'wounded' on the mission. He would then put a bullet in

Austin in exactly the same manner. A touch that would erase any doubt as to Austin's guilt, once his body was found.

The robot deftly unbuttoned its own shirt, revealing another wound. 'How many bullet strikes?'

'Four on the primary machine. A superficial wound on the backup,' Gao said. 'I can't believe Austin was able to fire so quickly and accurately. Although the spread of impacts shows them to be quite random. "Lucky shots," as the Americans say.'

'Not lucky for us,' Han said. 'Nor do I think the shots were random. Austin is very astute. He realized what we were planning and was trying to disable the machine, even if it meant his life. By targeting four different areas of the robot, he was more likely to do permanent damage.'

'Let's hope he hasn't done so,' Gao said, then turned to the robot. 'Lie down flat. Transmit diagnostic report to the main computer.'

The machine lay back and went still. Han had insisted on complete realism and for that reason there were no ports or power plugs hidden under the hairline or the body panels. All data and power regeneration was done wirelessly.

'We can always switch to the backup,' Han noted.

'I wouldn't,' Gao said. 'This machine began its training first. It progressed faster. The backup is inferior.'

'They're the same.'

Gao shook his head. 'Despite a common belief that all machines are identical, it's simply not true. Minute differences in the construction of the components create physical differences. A slightly less efficient servo here, a fractional change in hydraulic pressure there. Even different operating temperatures cause different physical responses. Combine that with the way our artificial intelligence system learns how to mimic human actions – by trial and error and without constant outside direction – and one machine slowly proves its superiority over the other.'

Han understood this. He was just surprised it could be so large a difference. 'Austin must have sensed it. That's why he concentrated his fire on this one.'

'You're giving him too much credit.' Gao pointed to the facial wound. 'Austin made a mistake firing at the skull. He must have assumed that a human-looking machine had a human-like physiology, and so he fired at the head because that's where the brain must be. My guess is, he hoped to hit the robot's hard drive or the CPU. But unlike a human's, our robot's brain is not in the skull; it's hidden away, near the right hip, to prevent exactly that. All Austin did was deform the face covering and damage one optical processor.'

Gao took out a scalpel and cut away the skin at the neck, before pulling the face cover, hair and scalp off. He tossed it in the garbage like a used Halloween mask. 'Not salvageable.'

He turned to one of his assistants. 'Get the 3-D printer up and running. Make sure the polymer mix is right. We'll need a new facial covering and a lower skin panel for the right leg. We'll also need an optical processor and a secondary hydraulic assembly.'

'How long is this going to take? We have to be off the ground in an hour.'

'Thirty minutes,' Gao said. 'No longer.'

Han nodded. 'Get to it. And have your other technicians work up a Zavala facsimile. Use the Austin backup as the underlying chassis. Adjust the size and shape.'

'We won't have time to perfect it,' Gao said. 'We don't have video or voiceprints of Zavala.'

'He's available,' Han said. 'Get them for him now. It doesn't have to be perfect. But I want both of them seen at the pavilion.'

Gao nodded. 'I'll get it done.'

'Good,' Han said. 'In the meantime, I'm going to conclude my business with Ushi-Oni.'

49

Han met Ushi-Oni in the tunnel, where the former Yakuza assassin stood with the Honjo Masamune gripped in his palm.

'Austin and Zavala have been chained up,' Oni said. 'But you should kill them immediately.'

'It'll have to wait.'

'Why?'

'Because if you kill them now, *rigor mortis* will set in,' Han explained. 'In addition, their bodies will begin to cool down. They'll be cold and stiff by the time the authorities find them. Two minor details that will make it easy to establish a time of death well before the assassination took place. Which will effectively rule them out as suspects and give instant credibility to every conspiracy theorist who suggests an alternate, perhaps Chinese, cause of the incident. I would expect a man like you to know these things.'

Oni stepped forward, his eyes wild. 'A man like me knows you don't leave loose ends around. That's why I've never been caught. And it isn't about to happen here and now.'

'Lower your voice,' Han said, reestablishing control over the situation.

Oni did as he was told but continued to fume. 'Mark

my words,' he said. 'They've seen you, they've seen me. As long as they're alive, we're all in danger.'

'They'll be dead in less than twelve hours,' Han said. 'You can be the one to kill them, if you want. But you'll do it when and how I say. Otherwise, you'll generate more "loose ends." For now, they live. In the meantime, I need to get that sword out of your hand before you hurt some-one with it. Come with me.'

Han turned deeper into the mine. Oni hesitated. 'Why don't we speak outside?'

'Because it's pouring rain and I need my people to examine that trinket you're carrying.'

'I've become rather fond of it,' Oni said.

'You won't be when you hear the story behind it.'

Han led Oni down the hall to another section of the mine that his people had taken over and modernized. He opened the triple-sealed door and held it wide.

Oni shook his head. 'You first.'

'Very well.'

Han stepped inside another laboratory. This room was smaller and cramped in comparison to the production room where the robots were assembled. It was filled with machines that would have been familiar to any metallurgist.

'What is this place for?' Oni asked.

'My people use these machines to analyze ore samples we've taken from mines and quarries around Japan. Mostly abandoned ones,' Han admitted. 'Centuries old.'

They'd been at it for nearly a year. Retrieving, testing and storing what they found. The fruit of the effort sat in labeled metal canisters stacked on the far side of the room. The number of containers had grown continuously, looking now like thousands of beer cans in an overzealous supermarket display.

'What are you looking for?' Oni asked.

'A rare alloy that we believe to be present here in Japan.'

'And the swords? What do they have to do with it?'

Han figured Oni would have put it together by now. 'These weapons were crafted by the masters of Japanese swordmaking. Based on the legends that describe their strength, flexibility and resistance to corrosion, it's possible they were made with trace amounts of that alloy. If we're right and we detect the alloy in the swords, all we have to do is find out where the ancient swordsmiths mined their ore and we'll be on the right track.'

As he spoke, one of Han's men was using a device known as a plasma mass spectrometer to analyze the blade on one of the swords that Oni had recovered.

The plasma torch flared behind a dark pane of glass, still bright enough to illuminate the room in a garish light. The sample was subjected to several seconds of the high-temperature torture before the beam was extinguished.

When it was removed from the spectrometer, the tip of the weapon was glowing red, melting and deformed. As it cooled, the computers analyzed the particles melted and blasted from the surface of the blade and printed out a report.

'So that's why you wanted Masamune's journal?' Oni said.

Han nodded. 'It was rumored to contain the secrets of

Masamune's craft. His endless quest to create the perfect weapon. We'd hoped it would tell us where he obtained the ore he used to forge the blade.'

'And does it?'

'Unfortunately, no,' Han said. 'Most of his journal is filled with philosophical nonsense about creating a weapon that would punish evil and not harm the innocent.'

Oni laughed. 'A fool's conscience.'

'Perhaps,' Han said. 'But he believed he had achieved just that with the weapon you're holding now.'

Oni narrowed his gaze and then glanced at the shimmering sword.

Han explained. 'By chance, or because you have a fine eye for craftsmanship, you've chosen the most valuable sword of all for your memento. That's no simple antique you possess; it's the Honjo Masamune itself.'

Oni grinned. He knew. Or suspected.

Han picked up another of the swords; it had a darker, thicker blade than the one Oni held. The steel appeared to have a reddish tint to it. Not rust, but closer to the color of dead roses or dried blood. 'This is the weapon for you. It's known as the Crimson Blade. It was created not by Masamune but by another swordsmith, known as Muramasa.'

Oni held his ground for the moment. 'Muramasa?'

Han nodded. 'Muramasa was alleged to be Masamune's protégé, though there is some debate about that. At any rate, it's well accepted that Muramasa spent his life trying to outdo the great Master, to forge a better weapon – a more powerful, more resilient, more deadly weapon. And in that last category, he undoubtedly succeeded. This weapon, this Crimson Blade, was by far his greatest creation. Throughout Japanese history, it has been renowned for its ability to take life and build wealth. It has brought power, fame and fortune to all who possessed it. Even the legend – meant to discredit Muramasa – tells the true story of its superiority.'

'What legend would that be?' Oni asked with a suspicious glint in his eye.

'Muramasa had tired of being considered an apprentice to the Master,' Han said. 'He challenged Masamune in an effort to prove who among them was the finest swordmaker. Masamune agreed and both men consented to be judged by the monks of a local order. They crafted great swords and, under the watchful eye of the monks from the temple, lowered their blades into a fast-running stream, with the sharpened edges facing the onrushing water.

'As the monks watched, the Crimson Blade cut through everything that came its way – crabs, fish, eels – anything the force of the stream brought to it was sliced cleanly in two. Across the stream, the Masamune, perhaps the very sword you hold now, divided the waters without a ripple, but it cut nothing that was living. Only leaves and other inanimate debris that floated past.'

Han continued. 'As the contest wore on, Muramasa laughed at the old man's weapon. In one version of the legend, he calls it an impotent blade. When the monks motioned for the weapons to be raised, the Crimson Blade of Muramasa came from the stream stained with blood. The Masamune dripped only crystal clear water.'

'A clear victory,' Oni said.

'You would think,' Han said. 'Muramasa certainly did. But when the monks pronounced their judgment, they chose the old Master and not the apprentice. Muramasa's Crimson Blade was deemed bloodthirsty and evil for destroying all it touched while the Masamune spared the life of the innocent. Is that really the sword you wish to keep for yourself?'

'"The innocent,"' Oni scoffed. 'There's no such thing.'

'Perhaps,' Han said. 'But you hold the weapon of a saint, not a sinner. Understanding true power the way you and I do, we both know which blade is truly superior.'

Oni studied the blade in his right hand and then stretched out his left. With a flip of his fingers, he beckoned for the other sword.

Han tossed it too high and Oni snatched it out of the air, grasping the hilt in a perfect catch. With a weapon in each hand, he compared them, swinging them this way and that, moving them in circular and then slashing motions.

'There is a heft to this weapon,' he said, looking at the Crimson Blade. 'It feels . . . more substantial.'

'It suits you,' Han said. 'You know it does.'

'Fine,' Oni said. Without warning, he tossed the Honjo Masamune in the air toward Han.

Han grasped for the hilt of the sword, catching it awkwardly with one hand and bringing the other up to stop it from dropping to the floor. In doing so, he accidentally wrapped two fingers around the blade. He drew his hand back instantly, with blood streaming from a pair of razor-like cuts.

He grunted in pain, shook the hand and grabbed a towel to stanch the bleeding.

Oni laughed. 'Too bad you're not a fish or an eel,' he chided. 'The pretty blade would have left you unbloodied.'

Han handed the weapon carefully to his lab technician. 'Analyze it,' he said, 'but it's not to be damaged.'

'A souvenir for yourself?' Oni said.

'A symbol,' Han replied. 'One the Japanese people will respond to with zeal. Much as you did. The Honjo Masamune is the sword of your ancestors. It has always represented Japanese power and independence. Its reappearance at this very moment will galvanize the Japanese public and help them to throw off the American shackles they've worn since this sword disappeared.'

Oni laughed. 'And I suppose they'll never notice the Chinese shackles replacing the American ones.'

So Oni had guessed at least that part of the plan.

'That's the great thing about symbols,' Han said. 'They shine in the sky like a brilliant light. People fixate on them, mesmerized and unable to see what's going on right beside them.'

50

Kurt and Joe had been taken deeper into the mine where they were chained to a cast-iron pipe, thicker than a man's arm. The pipe ran downward into the depths of the pit beside them and upward until it disappeared through a grate in the ceiling.

Facing each other with their hands chained around the pipe and the opening of the pit to the left of them, they were secured in a very effective jail. It was good enough that once Han's men had double-checked the locks, they walked back up the tunnel, leaving Kurt and Joe to themselves.

'Kind of weird to see you wrestling with yourself in more than a metaphorical fashion,' Joe said.

'Even weirder to lose,' Kurt admitted. 'Humans: one. Robots: one.'

'What?'

'Nothing,' Kurt said. 'Just keeping score.'

Joe studied the surroundings. Only the dim glow of the distant LEDs lit the tunnel, but just enough light to see by. 'I'd say we've been in darker spots, but I don't think that's literally true. Nice of them to leave us alone, though. They must think there's no escape from this.'

Kurt placed his feet on the wall and pulled with all his might. The pipe moved a few inches, but it didn't come loose. 'Probably anchored every ten feet or so.'

'In which case, you'll never pull it free,' Joe said.

Kurt could not disagree. 'Brute force isn't the only way to get out.'

He stood up, studying the grate above them. Even though it was clogged with debris, water dripped through it, falling here and there and running down the wall in a sheet.

'Rainwater,' Kurt said. 'This is an air shaft. It goes all the way to the surface.'

He found a foothold and climbed up the side of the wall to test the strength of the grate. Using the pipes for leverage, he leaned across the pit and stretched upward, putting his shoulder into the metal lattice and pushing.

Like the cast-iron pipe had, the grate moved just enough to tease him before jamming against some obstruction. Kurt pushed again, but his footing gave way. He dropped awkwardly, his shackled hands sliding down the pipe. If not for a deft move to the side, he would have dropped into the shaft.

Scuffed and scraped, Kurt sat back down. 'If only General Lasalle were here.'

'I don't remember any Lasalle on our payroll,' Joe said.

'He works for the French,' Kurt said.

'Then we're out of his jurisdiction.'

Kurt laughed. 'He's probably long gone anyway. The last time he showed up was to rescue the narrator in "The Pit and the Pendulum."'

'Ah,' Joe said, suddenly getting it. 'Is that the one where the rats chew through the ropes?'

'That's the one,' Kurt said. 'Don't see any rats around here, though.'

'Wouldn't be much use against these chains,' Joe said. 'But it's a nice thought.'

Kurt gazed downward, but it was so dark in the pit he could see nothing past the first twenty feet. He kicked a stone off the edge and listened to it fall.

Click . . . Clack . . . Clunk . . . Splash . . .

'Flooded,' Joe said.

'I expect the lower levels are all flooded,' Kurt said. 'Without the pumps running all these years, the seawater would seep in. If all else fails, we could risk going down and swimming through the tunnel.'

'You're forgetting the iron pipe we're chained to.'

'It'll be rusted to nothing down there, especially if that's saltwater.'

Joe shifted position and looked down. 'Let me get this straight. You want to drop into a flooded mine shaft, search for a flooded horizontal tunnel, swim through it in pitch-black conditions, with our hands in chains, and no idea where it leads or whether it's caved in or blocked by debris. All on the chance it comes out somewhere advantageous.'

Kurt feigned offense. 'I didn't suggest there was a high probability of success. Just that it was an option.'

'Try zero probability,' Joe said. 'In fact, if there's such a thing as a negative probability, I'd go with that. Even if we made it through and found another vertical shaft, we'd have to scale the walls with our bare hands.'

'I was thinking we could come up in the elevator we saw on the way in,' Kurt said. 'I realize the machinery doesn't operate, but the framework would make for an easy climb. If we can find the air shaft we passed on the way in.'

'Another big if,' Joe said. 'We'd be more likely to swim ourselves into a dead end, drown down there and never be found.'

'At least Han wouldn't be able to dress my body in the clothes those robots are wearing and frame us for the most blatant assassination since the Archduke of Austria in 1914.'

'Hopefully, this one won't start a new war.'

'The war is already on,' Kurt said. 'It's all about influence. And Han is going to pull off a masterstroke if we don't do something about it.'

'Come up with a better plan than suicide and I'm with you.'

Before Kurt could reply, the beam of a flashlight appeared in the tunnel as two people came toward them dragging something along the ground.

Only when the glare of the flashlight was pointed away did Kurt recognize Ushi-Oni's jaundiced face and another of Han's men. Carried between them, held up by the arms but with his legs dragging on the ground, was the lifeless form of Superintendent Nagano.

They tossed Nagano down and chained his hands around the pipe. The jailer with the keys unlocked Joe and pulled him to his feet.

'Am I first for breakfast?' Joe asked. 'Fantastic. Steak and eggs will do just fine.'

Oni backhanded Joe, striking him across the face and sending him to the ground. Before Joe could spring to his feet, something sharp and cold jabbed him in the back. He felt it split the wetsuit right between his shoulder blades. He dropped back flat on the ground, the tip of a sword up against his skin.

'Han ordered me not to kill you yet,' Oni said. 'But if you stand too quickly and impale yourself . . . that's on you.'

Kurt could see the sword plainly; it was a different weapon than the one Oni had been carrying earlier. 'Don't get up,' he warned Joe. 'It'll run you through.'

'Quite content to lie here,' Joe said, as he waited until the sword was pulled back and then slowly got to his hands and knees. When he turned around, he was face-to-face with a figure of malevolence.

'Don't think I've forgotten you,' Oni said. 'Every time I move, I feel agony. Every time I sweat from this endless fever, I blame you. I will pay you back for the pain you've caused me. Count on it.'

'Technically, it was the Komodo dragon's fault,' Joe said. 'I was just an innocent bystander.'

'The plan is for your facsimile to die in a car crash,' Oni said. 'That means I get to burn you alive. You won't be so funny when you're screaming for death.'

Joe was dragged off and Kurt could do nothing but watch him go. He hoped Joe had caught the clue that Ushi-Oni had inadvertently handed him.

When Joe and his captors had vanished down the tunnel, Kurt turned to Nagano. 'Superintendent, are you all right?'

Nagano looked up through a mask of pain. Kurt saw no overt injuries to his face, but his hand was bandaged.

'He killed the monks,' Nagano said. 'He slaughtered them.'

'Ushi-Oni?'

Nagano nodded. 'They had the swords. We thought we'd trapped him, but . . . He killed my men. He took my fingers.'

Nagano seemed almost delirious. He spoke without looking at Kurt.

'They ask many questions,' he continued, 'most of which make no sense. But if you don't answer, they shock you. It comes through the chains. They shock you until you fall and then they start over.'

'What kind of questions?'

'Everything,' Nagano said. 'Then they ask you to read and talk and speak, angrily or quietly. It was like a mind game instead of an interrogation.'

Kurt sat back. 'They wanted to hear your voice and record how you formed your words.'

Finally, Nagano focused on him. 'Why?'

'So they can make a duplicate of you, like they made one of me.'

'A duplicate?'

'A robot that walks and talks and looks exactly like you. Did they take your ID?'

'Everything,' Nagano said, 'even finger and thumb-prints.'

Han did not miss a trick. With Nagano's Federal Police ID and a thumbprint for authentication, he could get into a lot of places that the Austin facsimile alone would not be able to access. 'They're taking Joe for the same treatment.'

Nagano's eyes opened wider. 'They will torture him without remorse until he answers.'

Kurt didn't doubt it. All the more reason he had to act. 'Can you stand?'

Nagano tried to get up but dropped back to his side. 'I don't think so.'

Kurt helped him to a sitting position. 'Your strength will come back. Just relax for now.'

As Nagano took deep breaths and tried to accelerate his recovery, Kurt eased his way out over the pit and started a cautious descent. 'Warn me if someone's coming.'

'Where are you going?' Nagano asked.

'To find a rat with metal teeth.'

51

Joe stood in the center of another modern room. Bright lights came on, sending sharp pains through eyes now accustomed to the dark. He squinted.

'What is your name?' a voice asked via a hidden speaker.

Joe recognized the voice. It belonged to Gao, Han's right-hand man. He studied the room. White plastic walls and reflective one-way mirrors on all sides of him.

'Please state your name or we will have to harm you.'

He was being recorded. From every angle. Cameras behind those one-way mirrors were taking three-dimensional measurements of him. Digitizing him. Enabling a likeness of him to be created to pair with Kurt's. It was obvious. Oni had given him the key when he'd mentioned how Joe's facsimile would die.

Joe didn't feel like playing. Anything he gave them could be twisted and used. All the sounds of his voice could be digitally spliced and remixed to make new sentences. Even arguing with them or cursing them would give them something.

'Name!' Gao demanded.

Joe had to say something. He affected an exaggerated Texas accent for his reply. 'Well, pilgrim, you can call me whatever you want. Just don't call me late for dinner.'

Before the last word had left his mouth, an electrical

shock fired through Joe's body. It was excruciating and he crumpled to the floor.

'The next shock will go for twice as long,' Gao replied calmly. 'Now stand up and tell us your name.'

Joe stayed down longer than he needed to. Han and his people were pressed for time. That's what the guard had told them. This was Joe's chance to make the delay worse.

Another shock was sent forth. Joe winced and twisted as the energy passed through him, causing his muscles to tighten and lock. He bit through part of his tongue in the process and felt a wave of relief when the pulsing stopped.

'Stand up and state your name,' Gao said.

Slowly, Joe got to his feet. He remained stooped over on purpose. *Record this,* he thought. Looking up, he gave them a twisted countenance. His face as screwed up as he could make it. To enhance the effect, he did his best *I, Claudius* imitation, faking a stutter and a facial tic.

He turned from camera to camera, giving them a good look. Gao must not have been watching directly because he simply asked his question one more time.

'State your name.'

'"What's in a name?"' Joe said, sounding as British as he possibly could. '"A rose by any other name would smell as sweet . . ."'

There was a pause and for a second Joe thought he might have gotten away with it, but the surging pain of the electric shock hit him again. This time, it was stronger and lasted longer.

Some part of his mind knew they couldn't kill him

if they hoped to use his replacement. But that meant little as he flopped around on the ground like a fish out of water.

It was a full twenty seconds of agony before the current was shut off. Joe's body shook, his teeth hurt and one particular metal filling felt as if it had melted. His mind was an absolute blank.

'We have calibrated the current to cause maximum pain but no lasting damage,' Gao said. 'We can do this all night. Now stand up, state your name and read the following paragraph.'

The projected image of a statement came on and Joe tried to focus. Pretending to surrender, he got to his hands and knees, thought up a new prank and wearily began to straighten. He wasn't sure how long his body would hold out, but he would die before he would give them anything they could use.

With his hands on the rusted pipe and his feet on the wall, Kurt climbed down into the pit. He was ten feet below the rim when he encountered his first obstacle: one of the anchors that held the old pipe in place.

It was still attached to the wall, but loosely. Sixty years of erosion had seen to that. Working it back and forth with a controlled force, he soon broke it loose from the rock.

He slipped the chains around it and slid down farther. The next anchor was completely corroded and Kurt didn't even have to strain to break it in half.

He continued down. The farther down he went, the

more rusted the pipe became. With each move, flakes and dust fell like red snow. Every few feet, the chain caught in a crevice on the pipe.

Kurt was looking for a connector where two sections of the pipe had been joined. During his years salvaging wrecks (and sinking other ships on purpose), he'd learned that corrosion always set in first at the joints. Those were the weak points in any system. Microscopic gaps allowed water to pool and rust to bloom. Mechanical stress of movement caused metal fatigue and damage. Even on the oldest ships, hull plates rarely gave way, but rivets and hatches failed with regularity.

With the rainwater dripping down from above and the seawater rising and falling with the tide, Kurt would soon find a spot where corrosion had worked enough of its magic. The connection might even look healthy from the outside, but the metal itself would be eaten away internally like a rotten tree.

He was still searching for the weak spot when his feet hit the water. He dropped in, fought against the natural buoyancy of his wetsuit and descended into utter darkness.

The chain scraped along the pipe as he descended. When his thumb pushed through a rusted section, he knew he'd struck gold. Holding his breath and positioning the chain where he felt the corrosion had done the most damage, he pulled with a sudden jerk.

The back half of the pipe crumpled and he pulled again. More progress, but not enough. He began sliding the chain back and forth, using it like a saw. He could feel the jagged metal giving way: a chunk here, a section there.

Suddenly, the chain burst through and he was free and swimming.

He kicked upward, bobbed calmly to the surface and took a deep breath.

A circle of light could be seen up above. He'd come down forty feet. The climb would be a joy.

Han watched the farce in the recording booth without a hint of glee. Zavala was on the floor again, having endured several additional rounds of shock treatment. He'd used three additional accents and recited an Irish limerick before collapsing once more.

He now lay in a heap, breathing heavily but otherwise unmoving. Steam rose from his scalp.

'Enough,' Han said.

'But we don't have a voiceprint yet,' Gao replied. 'In fact, we don't have anything, unless you want the robot to act out *Romeo and Juliet* or spout lines from American TV commercials.'

'He's beaten you,' Han said. 'Can't you see that?'

Gao stared at his boss.

'He knows what you want,' Han explained, 'and he's willing to die rather than give it to you. He might even be goading you into killing him on purpose.'

'Okay,' Gao said. 'So what do you want me to do?'

'Remove him from the equation,' Han said. 'Finish the body panels and program Zavala's robot to be mute unless addressed directly. Austin's facsimile will do all the talking. It will be enough that Zavala is seen with him and caught on camera driving the getaway car.'

Gao looked frustrated, but he didn't protest. 'I can also upload a generic American voice just in case he has to say something.'

'Be quick about it,' Han said. 'And tell my pilot we're ready to leave.'

Joe lay on the floor, exhausted, drenched in sweat and waiting for the next round of torture to begin. Each session of electrical shock had been longer and more painful than the last, each wave of muscle spasms worse than the one before. He felt as if he'd done a triathlon and wrestled a bear afterward for good measure, all without moving from the spot.

This will probably be the next wave in fitness training. Get the body of an Adonis without doing any work. Joe laughed at the thought, but the laughter hurt his chest and he stopped as quickly as he could.

Taking deep breaths to slow his heart rate and trying to still the trembling in his legs, it was a while before he realized the next session was overdue. A minute of silence stretched to several and Joe remained where he was. No demands came over the speakers, no new threats and not so much as a static shock from the metal plates.

A sense of satisfaction crept in. They'd given up. He'd worn them down and survived. He'd won.

The door opened and a pair of Han's men came in to get him. They lifted him by the arms and hauled him up to his feet.

'No fight left in this one,' the first of the men said.

Not at the moment, Joe thought. It was an effort even to stand.

They marched him out of the room and into the tunnel. A strange sound was echoing off the walls. Joe realized it was the helicopter lifting off outside. Han was leaving, putting his plan in motion, while Kurt and Nagano were still chained up and Joe himself could hardly walk. His thoughts of victory felt suddenly premature.

They marched him down the tunnel, rounded a slight curve and closed in on the air shaft. Only now did Joe realize how dimly lit the tunnel really was, especially after the brightness of the room he'd been tortured in. He could barely make out Kurt and Nagano, sitting by the wall. And then he realized there was only one figure present. Kurt was gone.

52

Joe was thrown to the ground as the guard realized he was missing a prisoner. He rushed forward, grabbed Nagano. 'Where's Austin?'

'What can I tell you?' Nagano said. 'He escaped.'

'How? Where did he go?'

'He slipped the chains,' Nagano said. 'You must have given him too much slack.'

'And then he left you here?'

'Yes,' Nagano said, 'the ingrate. After all my help and guidance.'

Kurt heard every word; he was only ten feet away, just below the lip of the air shaft. He knew what would come next. With his feet wedged against one of the wall anchors and his left arm wrapped around the pipe, he worked a stone loose from the wall and held it in his right hand.

'Not possible,' the guard insisted.

Nagano was tossed aside and the guard pointed his flashlight deeper into the passageway. Then he looked down into the shaft.

Kurt threw the stone the instant he saw the man's face, hitting him in the jaw and snapping his head back.

Nagano helped the guard to the ground by chopping his legs out from under him with a sweeping kick.

The guard landed at the edge of the pit and Kurt

reached up, grabbed him by the shoulder and pulled him over. The man tumbled face-first, hitting the wall on the way down and crashing into the water below.

At the same instant, Joe charged the second guard, tackling him and slamming him headfirst into the wall. They fell to the ground together, where Joe landed a kidney punch and then followed up with a head-butt to the jaw.

Kurt pulled himself out of the pit and rushed to help Joe, who was struggling with his opponent. It took only seconds for the two of them to finish the fight.

'You're slipping,' Kurt said. 'You should have had this guy in three moves.'

'I'm not exactly at the top of my game,' Joe said. 'While you were going for a leisurely swim, I was giving the performance of a lifetime.'

Kurt found the keys and unlocked Joe's chains, then his own and then Nagano's. They gagged the guard, took his weapon and chained him up.

'What about the guy who went for a swim?' Joe asked.

Nagano shook his head. 'He didn't resurface.'

With Kurt holding the guard's pistol, they moved quietly down the tunnel, pausing when they heard someone approaching.

Pressing into the shadows, they watched as another of Han's men approached with a pair of long wooden cases in the crook of his arm. The man was dressed in a lab coat. He wore thick glasses. And had his hair long in the front.

He reached one of the plastic doors, brushed the hair

out of his eyes and pressed a button. A green light blinked and a soft push opened the door. He went inside and shut the door behind him.

'Let's go before he comes back out,' Joe said.

'Not so fast,' Kurt replied. 'I want to stop by the gift shop before we leave.'

Kurt crossed the tunnel and made his way to the plastic-coated door. Placing his hand on the same button he'd seen the technician press, he, too, was given a green light. He eased the door open and found the technician on the far side of the room, removing a polished sword from its case.

Kurt coughed lightly and cocked the hammer on the pistol. The technician straightened and then turned, putting his hands up instinctively.

'You speak English?'

The man nodded.

'Good,' Kurt said. 'That will make this easier. On your knees.'

The technician got down awkwardly but kept his hands up. The hair fell in his eyes again and he attempted unsuccessfully to blow it away with a puff of air.

'You might want to consider a haircut,' Kurt said.

The technician nodded and Kurt reached over and snatched the nearest sword from its case. The weapon was beautiful. It shimmered in the fluorescent lighting of the laboratory.

The door opened again and this time Joe and Nagano slipped in.

'Did you find your souvenir?'

Kurt held up the samurai sword.

Nagano took one look and spoke its name. 'Be careful with that. You hold a national treasure in your hands. The Honjo Masamune. Hidden by Shinto monks for seventy years.'

Kurt looked to the technician. 'Why does Walter Han want these swords?'

The technician answered. 'That one is a symbol of Japan.'

'And the others?'

The technician hesitated. Kurt pointed the sword toward him. 'I could give you that haircut now if you'd like.'

The hesitation ended. 'We're studying them.'

'Obviously.' The labful of equipment around them was quite impressive. 'Why? What's Han looking for?'

'An alloy,' the technician said. 'It's called Golden Adamant. It has . . . unique properties. So far, it's only been found deep within volcanic fissures. It's believed Japan has a source. Possibly, under Mount Fuji. One of these swords may have been made with such an alloy. We were told to learn where the swords came from, how they were forged, what their metal contents are and in what manner the alloys were blended. Most importantly, to determine where the ore was mined.'

Joe's eyebrows went up. 'Now we know what Han's people were looking for at the bottom of the East China Sea.'

'It was a first effort,' the technician said. 'But the mine played itself out.'

'How was it done?' Kurt asked.

'Ultrasonic waves and high-intensity vibrations combined

with a carbon-silicon fracking liquid,' the technician told them. 'A unique system allows us to mine deeply without drilling.'

'Sounds logical,' Kurt said. 'Did you intend to bring up vast amounts of subterranean water along with it?'

'Water was always released in the process,' the technician said. 'It's marginal.'

Kurt's eyebrows now went up. 'Marginal? Maybe you're not aware of just how much water you're releasing. Your fractures are bringing up millions of gallons every second of every day. Enough to flood the coastal plains around the world in a year if we don't stop it.'

'Impossible,' the man said.

'You'll see how possible it is very shortly,' Kurt said.

'Not if we don't get out of here,' Joe mentioned. 'Every minute we delay makes it more likely that someone notices we've gone missing.'

That was true. Kurt looked back at the technician. 'We had an equipment bag when we came in here. I've lost the claim check, but if you could point out where it's been stored . . .'

The man glanced toward a locker. Joe pried it open and found their bag, complete with swim fins, masks and the small oxygen bottles. The infrared goggles lay beside the pack. 'It's all here. Including our radio transceiver.'

'Any guns?'

Joe looked through a couple other lockers. 'No.'

'Take this one,' Kurt said, handing it to Joe. 'I'm going to carry the sword. After all this time, it should be returned to its rightful owners.'

Joe took the pistol and Kurt waved the technician to his feet. 'You're coming with us. You've got some explaining to do.'

Nagano gagged the technician and took a radio from his belt, while Kurt opened the door and checked the tunnel both ways. The tunnel was clear. 'Let's go.'

They started for the exit and were soon approaching the assembly room. As they moved past, the door swung open without warning and two of the workers came out, speaking to each other in Chinese.

They stopped in their tracks as they noticed Kurt and Joe and their gagged colleague.

Kurt pushed the technician aside and lunged toward the new arrivals, but they dove back through the doorway and slammed it. Seconds later, an alert was called out over the intercom. 'The prisoners have escaped. They're in the main tunnel. Repeat. Prisoners have escaped.'

Kurt tossed their hostage aside. The man would only slow them down. There was nothing to do now but run for it. 'Go, go, go!' he shouted and the three of them rushed toward the exit of the mine.

53

Gao was still in the recording room when the warning came out over the intercom. He responded instantly. 'Where are they?'

'Main tunnel. Outside the assembly room. They're armed.'

Ushi-Oni was standing next to him. 'Sound the alarm.'

'This isn't a military base,' Gao snapped. 'We don't have alarms.'

The rage in Oni's eyes scared Gao enough to stop talking. He pressed a different button on the intercom panel. This put him in touch with the control room. 'Control, this is Gao. The Americans are on the loose. They just attacked a technician outside the main assembly room. I suggest you send some men to hunt them down.'

There was a brief moment of silence before control reported in again. 'Our men are out checking the perimeter.'

'Call them back.'

'There's no point in that. If the Americans were in the central tunnel, we have to assume they've left the complex by now.'

'I warned Han of this,' Oni said. 'They will be the end of us.'

'I think you are overreacting,' Gao said. 'Even if they

left the mine, there's no way off the island. The helicopter is gone. There are no boats. What do you think they're going to do, swim?'

Oni glared down at him. 'That's exactly what they'll do. Why do you think they came here in wetsuits, carrying fins and masks?'

'Impossible, it's nearly three miles to the mainland,' Gao said. 'The current will sweep them out to sea before they ever get close to the beach.'

'These men work in the ocean,' Oni pointed out. 'They're trained divers. If you think they won't make it, you're a bigger fool than I thought. An hour in the water with fins and they'll be on dry land. It will take no longer. And that's if they don't get picked up by a boat.'

Gao began to sweat. He suddenly realized the danger. There were, in fact, no boats on the island, as per Han's orders. But that meant Austin, Zavala and Nagano would be home free once they reached the surf. He pressed the intercom button. 'Control, how many men do you have?'

'We're down to ten men in the security squad, plus you and the technicians.'

It wouldn't be enough. 'Activate the warbots,' Gao said. 'Put them in search-and-destroy mode.'

'But our men are out there, too.'

'We don't have time to program the discriminator function,' Gao said. 'Station the men on the seawall, with orders to guard the stairways and the easy routes to the water. The warbots will spread out and flush the Americans toward our guards. If they spot anything in the water, human or otherwise, they must shoot on sight. No captures this time.'

'Yes, sir.'

Gao was shaking with adrenaline, but Oni looked on him with a newfound level of respect.

'I didn't think you had it in you.'

'Had what?'

'The instinct to kill so ruthlessly.'

'It's us or them,' Gao said. 'There's no way out of here for us. If the Americans reach the mainland, this island will become our prison.'

The mainland was a long way off, as Kurt, Joe and Nagano ran out into the night. The rain still fell from the dark sky, but the night had cooled and several layers of fog now clung to the hill behind them.

Traveling a hundred yards from the entrance, and well aware that the pursuit had already begun, they took cover inside the first building they found.

Crouching in the dark and listening to the radio they'd taken from the technician, they heard every order.

Kurt looked at Nagano. 'What did they say?'

'My Chinese is a little rusty,' Nagano said. 'Something about men at the seawall. And war machines.'

Gazing through an opening in the dilapidated building, Kurt saw the first 'war machine' emerge from the mine's entrance. It was the size of a lawn mower and it marched on six legs like a giant insect. Glowing LEDs – that looked almost like eyes – were visible as it turned toward them.

'Get down,' Kurt said.

They dropped behind the concrete of the building's structural wall. When Kurt looked up again, he saw the machine marching in the other direction.

'Where's it going?' Nagano asked.

'Toward the dock,' Kurt said. 'Trying to head us off at the pass.'

'What, exactly, was that thing?' Joe asked.

'Han calls it a warbot,' Kurt said. 'I was given a demonstration of them inside his factory.' He pointed to the pistol in Joe's hand and then held up the sword he was carrying. 'From what I witnessed, neither of these weapons are going to be much use against them.'

Kurt dropped back down as two more machines came out of the tunnel. Each of them took a slightly different path. 'They're spreading out,' he said. 'No telling how many they have, but sooner or later one of them is going to come this way.'

'It won't be easy getting to the water if they know we're coming,' Joe said. 'There are only a few spots around the island where it's safe to get in the sea. Three stairwells and the dock.'

'We can be certain that those are already guarded,' Nagano said.

Joe nodded. 'Which means we might have to go over the wall and jump for it.'

Kurt wasn't sure that would work. 'All that gets us is a fifty-foot drop into churning sea, with rocks and concrete pilings below us. Time the waves wrong and we'll be killed on impact; even if we get it right, we risk being thrown back into the wall before we can get past the breakers.'

Nagano looked at the two men. 'I competed in a triathlon down here years ago,' he said. 'The currents are treacherous and my hand is useless. I won't be able to keep up, let alone swim all the way to the mainland. You should go on without me. Perhaps I can distract these war machines while you escape.'

Kurt shook his head. 'We didn't come all the way here to get you just so we could leave you behind. Besides, why swim when we can fly?'

Certain that Austin, Zavala and Nagano were out of the mine, Gao risked leaving the safety of the recording room and making his way to the control center. Ushi-Oni accompanied him, scraping the wall with the sword Han had given him to replace the Masamune. Sparks jumped here and there as the sword ground across tiny specks of flint.

'Do you mind?'

Oni ignored the comment and continued the annoyance all the way to the control room.

The men inside turned with a start as Gao and Oni entered.

'Any sign of them?' Gao asked.

'Nothing yet.'

Gao approached the closest console. Video feeds from sixteen different warbots were spread out on four different screens. A second wave of sixteen additional machines was deploying. An overhead view of the island showed them fanning out and working their way from the mine.

Oni approached and looked over the same map. 'You're leaving the west side of the island unprotected?'

Gao knew that. 'There's nowhere safe to climb down to the water on that side,' he replied. 'And they would hardly dive off the west side of the island when they need to swim east to get to shore.'

'You wouldn't,' Oni said, 'but you're still underestimating these men.'

Gao shook his head. 'I know they're trained divers, but they're not fools. Swimming around the island and fighting the current makes it a far longer and more treacherous swim. It also makes it far more likely that we'd spot them in the water and shoot them dead. They'll go for the nearest entry point and swim away from the island as fast as they can. And that means they'll be on the east side.'

Oni stood back and Gao gave a new order. 'Have some of the robots swing wide and loop around to the perimeter. Order the rest to go block by block and flush them out. Set them in area control mode so they can converge on the targets as soon as they're spotted.'

The controller hesitated. 'The farther we spread the net, the more likely the Americans are to slip through.'

'The warbots use wide-field infrared sensors,' Gao said confidently. 'Ten of them can cover the ground of a hundred men.'

'And if the Americans hide in one of the buildings?'

'Then they'll play right into our hands. In a few hours, the operation in Nagasaki will be complete; the Prime Minister and some of his Cabinet ministers will be dead and Austin, Zavala and Nagano will be wanted men. At that point, they'll have nowhere to escape to. The whole world will be looking for them.'

Kurt went from one corner of the building to the next. Warbots were guarding each intersection in his view; others were marching past, setting up positions beyond.

Joe came back from the far side of the building. 'Another one on the far side.'

'Coming this way?'

Joe shook his head. 'Just sitting at the intersection.'

'They're establishing area control,' Nagano said. 'Cutting off every avenue of escape before they begin the search. We would do the same – we call it a double box.'

Kurt remembered Han saying the warbots could replace the police. 'That means we're surrounded,' he said. 'Probably several blocks deep. Even if we could get past these warbots, we'd run into others.'

He took a breath and sat back trying to visualize exactly where they were on the island. As he recalled photos and the map he'd studied, an idea came to him. 'Find the stairs,' he said finally. 'We have to go up.'

'And then?'

'If this is the building I think it is, there's a structural brace on the roof connecting it to the next building. Not a real bridge. But if we're careful, we can crawl across it.'

'That'll get us past this group, but what about the next layer?' Joe asked.

'I have an idea that should take care of that,' Kurt said.

Joe grimaced. 'If you're thinking what I think you're thinking, I wish you'd stop thinking it.'

'It's all we've got,' Kurt said.

Nagano interrupted politely. 'Would you two mind cluing an old detective in? I have no idea what you're talking about.'

'We have to lure those warbots in here,' Kurt said. 'As many as possible.'

'And then?'

'There's a bridge on the roof. If most of the warbots are converging on this building to search for us and the rest are cordoning off the exits, we should be able to crawl across to the next building and make our escape.'

'Won't the machines follow us?' Nagano asked.

'I don't think so,' Kurt said. 'Han's race car was only capable of following known pathways. It stayed on the track while I cheated and cut across the infield. If these warbots have a similar program, they won't consider the rusted-out structural brace to be a pathway. They won't attempt to cross it.'

Nagano nodded. 'And by the time they get back down to the bottom, we'll be several buildings over and taking flight.'

'Sound plan,' Nagano said. 'All you have to do is get their attention.'

'You two start climbing,' Kurt said. 'I'll let them know we're here.'

As Joe and Nagano found a stairway, Kurt made his way to the main entrance and studied the position of the two robots. The one to the left was the nearest. Knowing they had cameras on board, he decided to make it look good. He eased his way outside and stopped – pretending to freeze in his tracks as the warbot turned toward him.

He dove to the side as a red laser dot locked onto him and the first gunshots rang out. The bullets whistled past, inches from his head.

Kurt crawled into the building and stayed low as the machine began moving his way. It fired again as it approached.

'That's it,' he said. 'You've found us. Now come and get us.'

When the sound of the machine approaching became audible, Kurt left his covered spot and rushed to the stairs. He bounded up the first flight as the warbot entered the building at the front of the structure and began scanning.

He'd noisily climbed four flights of stairs before slowing down. There, he found an opening that had once been a window and glanced out into the dark. He could see other machines heading their way.

The plan was working – except for one thing. The first machine was moving faster than Kurt had expected. Much faster. It was already on the stairs two flights below him.

Kurt took off and raced up the next few flights. There were no doors to shut, no obstacles to create, nothing he could find that would slow the machine down. Then again, it was probably pointless; he'd seen them batter through plenty of doors in the simulation.

Passing the seventh floor, he could hear Joe and Nagano banging against something up above. 'How are we doing?' he shouted.

'First miscalculation,' Joe shouted. 'Roof door is pad-locked. We're trying to break it down. But, hey, there was bound to be at least one problem with the plan.'

'One problem would be fine,' Kurt shouted, 'but we have two. The lead warbot isn't waiting for backup.'

'So slow it down,' Joe shouted.

Easier said than done, Kurt thought. He considered the sword in his hand. 'Too bad Masamune didn't make rocket launchers.'

'Should we look for another way up?' Joe asked.

Looking around, Kurt spotted something that might be of use. 'No,' he shouted. 'Keep working on the door.'

'What are you going to do?'

'My best exterminator routine.'

While Joe and Nagano continued to batter the door two flights above him, Kurt swung the Masamune at the dilapidated railing along the edge of the stairwell. After hacking through the rusted metal at the bottom, he wrenched the obstruction out of his way.

That done, he rushed to a pile of rubble, where part of the wall had collapsed. He found a sizable wedge of concrete lying on the floor. It was too heavy to lift, but getting low and pushing with both legs, he was able to slide it across the floor. He pushed it to the edge of the stairwell and waited.

The robot was two flights down now, moving and scanning and moving again; it had an almost alien style of locomotion. It paused on each landing, scanning the area for any heat signatures.

Just a little farther.

Finally, it made the turn. Appearing out in the open ten feet below Kurt.

With a mighty shove, Kurt pushed the two-hundred-pound chunk of cement over the edge. It dropped straight down, hitting the robot just off center, crushing several of its appendages and literally flattening it.

Its six legs splayed out in all directions and for a second Kurt thought he'd destroyed it. But the robot began to move and the slab of concrete slid off of it and onto the floor. Freed of the weight, the machine sprang back up to its feet.

'And I thought roaches were hard to kill.'

Back in action, the machine tilted upward, locked onto Kurt with the targeting laser and opened fire.

Kurt dove out of the way, but he needn't have bothered. Down below, an explosion rocked the stairwell.

Kurt risked a glance. The barrel of the weapon was sheared off and what remained was splayed out. It had blown itself apart when the warbot opened fire.

'The concrete slab must have bent the barrel,' Kurt said. 'Just as I planned.'

The robot was not destroyed, but at least it was neutered.

Kurt took off, charging back up the stairs. 'Back in the lead,' he shouted. 'Humans: two. Robots: one.'

He reached the top floor and found the door open where Joe and Nagano had finished breaking it down. Stepping through and wedging it shut again, he stepped out into the rain. Joe and Nagano were standing at the edge of the roof, staring at a gap between the building and its neighbor.

Joe gave him the bad news. 'Hate to tell you, amigo. But the bridge is out.'

'The brace should be here,' Kurt said.

Joe pointed to the corroded remnants of a mounting that jutted out from the edge of the building a grand total of eight inches. 'I think it used to be here.'

Kurt shook his head ruefully. 'Old photos,' he muttered. 'Never rely on old photos.'

Glancing over the edge, Kurt could see a dozen of the warbots heading their way. Others had undoubtedly already entered the building. 'Unfortunately, the rest of our plan is working to perfection. The warbots are coming in droves.'

'Now what?' Nagano asked.

Kurt studied the building across from them. The gap was only six feet and the roof of the other building was a half story lower than the one they were standing on. He pointed across the gap with the sword. 'We've only got one choice.'

The three of them exchanged glances, backed up a few feet and then ran for the edge. They jumped at the last instant, propelling themselves up and across the gap, before dropping down through the darkness.

'Warbot number eight is out of action and off-line,' the controller said.

Gao was staring at a blank screen. 'What happened?'

'Isn't it obvious?' Oni said. 'The rifle exploded. The barrel must have been damaged by the impact of the concrete block. A man would have known that and avoided firing. So much for your perfect robots.'

'The others will finish them,' Gao said confidently. 'There's no way off that roof.'

Gao switched the video feed to a different machine and they all watched as it passed the damaged warbot and climbed the stairs all the way to the roof. It burst out through the door and scanned every quadrant.

After a brief delay, the controller spoke. 'No targets in sight.'

'What about the other floors?' Gao asked. 'They may have doubled back.'

The controller flicked through the data screens. 'We have machines on every level of the building now. No thermal signature on any floor. No sign of movement. We've lost them.'

Gao pushed the controller out of the way and looked at the telemetry data himself. 'This is impossible. They have to be in the building somewhere.'

That Oni was looking over his shoulder, breathing down his neck, made it all the worse.

'Show me a map of the island,' the assassin requested.

'Why?'

'Indulge me.'

Gao fumed but did as requested. The screen flicked and a wire outline of the island and all its buildings appeared. 'Red dots show the positions of the warbots,' Gao explained. 'Most of them clustered in the building the Americans and Nagano had been in moments ago.'

It took only a second for Oni to see what he needed. 'Do you have something to stop those machines from killing me by mistake if I go out there?'

'An identifier,' Gao said, pointing to a rack of devices hanging on lanyards by the console. 'As long as you're

401

wearing one of those, the machines will recognize you as a friend and they won't target you.'

Oni looked pleased. He pointed toward Gao with the sword. 'Give me one,' he demanded. 'And put one on yourself.'

'Me? Why?'

'Because I know where the Americans are going,' he said. 'And you're coming with me.'

54

Nagano was limping.

'That jump hurt you,' Joe said, taking as much of Nagano's weight on himself as he could.

Nagano winced and then forced a smile. 'Actually, the jump was fine, but the landing was quite painful.'

'A couple of sake bombers back on the mainland and you'll be good as new,' Joe said.

Nagano laughed, but he needed a rest. Kurt went ahead to scout out the building, so they sat down and waited for him to return.

After a few minutes, Kurt appeared. 'No sign of our robot friends.'

'Thankfully, they don't have wings,' Joe said.

Kurt nodded and broke out the NUMA transceiver. 'Time to call for help,' he said, turning it on and waiting for it to sync up. When a green light told him it was ready, he pressed the transmit button. 'Akiko, are you out there?'

Several seconds went by without a response.

'Let's hope she hasn't tossed the transceiver overboard because it's a piece of modern technology,' Joe said.

'Akiko, this is Kurt. Do you read me? Press the transmit button on the side of the receiver if you do.'

Static, and then: 'I know how to use a radio, thank you.'

'Glad you're still with us,' Kurt said. 'Have you had any problems?'

'Aside from bailing rainwater all night, no.'

'Wish we could say the same,' Kurt replied. 'Good news is, we've got Nagano. Bad news, we're being hounded. We're going to meet you halfway. Can you get the boat in position?'

'Yes,' she said. 'Absolutely.'

'Watch for us,' Kurt said. 'We're going to use the wing and the parasail.'

'I'll collect you as soon as you hit the water.'

Kurt acknowledged the transmission and put the transceiver away. 'The diagonal bridge is three levels below us. Let's go.'

They made their way down the stairs and found the diagonal bridge that they'd crossed on the way in. After scouting for robots, they stole across the bridge and entered the building they'd landed on. They soon located the main stairwell and began climbing until they reached the top floor and the fallen concrete slab they'd used as a ramp on the way in.

Scaling it was slow and difficult; it was slick with rainwater, grime and mold.

Kurt moved upward on his hands and knees, the Honjo Masamune still clutched in one hand, which slowed him down enough that Joe was the first to reach the summit.

As Joe's head rose above ground level, someone started firing at him. Bullets hit around him, kicking up waterspouts and blasting chips of concrete from the rooftop.

Joe dropped back and slid down the wet slab, collecting Nagano and Kurt on the way.

'Wasn't expecting a welcoming party,' Kurt said.

'Let's see who it is,' Joe replied.

He eased his way back to the top, held the 9mm pistol out over the edge and fired several shots in the general direction of the target. Enough to get anyone to duck.

With a second to take a look, Joe glanced over the edge and then dropped back down again.

'Robots?' Kurt asked.

Joe shook his head. 'Yakuza assassin with an ax to grind. Or should I say sword. He's got a pistol in one hand and that *katana* in the other.'

'Is he alone?'

'Han's man Gao is with him.'

'Throw your weapons out and surrender,' Oni's voice boomed across the rooftop.

'So you can frame us for murdering the Japanese Prime Minister?' Joe shouted back. 'No thanks.'

'Then come up and fight,' Oni said. 'Or wait for the robots to come up and tear you apart. It makes no difference to me.'

'He does have us at a disadvantage,' Nagano said.

'And he's not wrong,' Kurt said. 'The situation is only going to get worse when the robots arrive.'

'So we charge him and take our chances,' Joe suggested.

'I thought you were against suicidal plans,' Kurt said.

'In principle,' Joe said. 'But we're running out of options.'

'I have an idea,' Kurt told him. 'Keep him talking. Fire a shot his way every once in a while to keep his attention on you.' As Kurt spoke, he held up the sword. 'I'm going to flank him . . . samurai-style.'

As Kurt moved off, Joe crawled up the slab and triggered off a single round as a conversation starter. 'You don't have much to hide behind up there,' he pointed out. 'Out in the open and all exposed. All I need is one good shot and you're a dead man.'

'You'll never get that lucky,' Oni laughed. 'But if you want to come up and play, I'll allow it. I'll even let you get to your feet and give you a fighting chance.'

'I suspect he's probably lying,' Nagano said.

Joe laughed. 'And I suspect you're right.'

In response to the offer, Joe held the gun over the opening and fired again.

As Joe distracted Ushi-Oni, Kurt rushed to the far side of the building. A brief glimpse outside told him the army of six-legged robots were surrounding the place and crawling inside.

He saw at least a dozen. There would be no slow, methodical search this time. Just a swarming attack.

'Time is not on our side,' Kurt whispered. 'Time for desperate measures.'

Climbing out through a window, Kurt made it to a ledge on the side of the building. Inching along the ledge, he came to the rusted fire escape that he and Joe had declined to use on the way down.

He could hear Joe shouting at Ushi-Oni.

'If the robots fill us full of lead, that will be hard to explain to the coroner,' Joe shouted.

'We'll just dump your bodies in the channel and let the sharks have you,' Oni replied. 'The police can look for you forever. It makes no difference to me.'

Kurt reached out for the fire escape and grabbed the railing. The structure swayed as he hooked one leg over the railing. He waited for Joe to snap off another round.

With the gunshot echoing, Kurt pulled himself onto the fire escape and did his best to steady it. The metal stairs creaked and groaned, but they didn't collapse.

He went up. Moving with deliberate care. One arm, one foot, the next arm and the next foot. He carried only the sword.

As he got near the top, the stairs began to pull away from the wall. The upper anchors were completely loose, just resting in small holes of eroded concrete. Only a length of wire, wound in a figure eight from the railing to the wall, kept the whole stairway from breaking away.

'Definitely not up to code,' he whispered, reaching past the railing and grabbing the wall. Finding a handhold, he eased the fire escape toward the building until it made contact with the wall.

Out on the roof, the taunting continued.

'You might want to save that ammunition. The crawlers will be here soon.'

Joe's reply was to fire off several additional shots, perfectly spaced to give Kurt the time he needed.

Kurt leapt over the wall and onto the roof. He raced forward with the Honjo Masamune in his hands, closing on Oni and Gao as they took cover.

Gao saw him first. 'Look out!'

Oni spun, raising his pistol to fire, but Kurt slashed down with the samurai's weapon and knocked the gun from Oni's hand, taking part of the assassin's thumb with it. Payback, in some sense, for what Oni had done to Nagano.

The pistol clattered to the roof and discharged in a random direction. Oni spat contempt and spun away.

Kurt had to change focus and deal with Gao, who was diving for the gun. He intercepted Gao with a kick to the jaw and then sent the pistol sliding across the roof with a flick of the sword.

Now Oni came back at him, swinging the Crimson Blade in a wide arc. Kurt deflected it and then dodged Oni's second attack, stepping deftly to the side. But even with blood pouring from his wounded thumb, Oni pressed forward, fueled by rage.

Kurt counterattacked, slashing at Oni's head, but the assassin's training kicked in and he pulled back and responded with a riposte, one that almost twisted the sword from Kurt's hand.

Kurt clutched the Honjo Masamune and wrenched it free with brute strength. But before he could do any more, he was attacked once again.

'You're an amateur,' Oni chided. 'I'll slice you limb from limb.'

'You couldn't do it before and all I had was a wrench,' Kurt said.

Oni charged again, slashing and taunting Kurt simultaneously. 'This blade has waited two hundred years to taste blood again. Tonight, it will drink deeply.'

Kurt was too busy defending himself to offer a witty reply. He parried to thrusts and attempted a counter by dropping one hand to the floor and lunging low and fast, a move known as a passata-sotto.

Oni hopped back out of the way and then came forward again. The attack became manic. Sparks flew each time the swords came together. Blood from Oni's missing thumb tip soaked the hilt of his weapon and dripped along the blade.

Kurt was hard-pressed and with each flurry he was forced backward toward the edge of the roof. At the same time, he saw Gao crawling toward the fallen pistol.

'Joe!' he shouted. 'A little help!'

Joe was already out on the roof. He charged toward Gao and tackled him. As they wrestled for the pistol, Oni attacked once again.

First, it was a lunge. Kurt dodged it.

Next came a feint that unbalanced Kurt. He slipped on the wet roof and he fell to one knee.

Now Oni went for his head, gripping the Crimson Blade with both hands and bringing it downward in an executioner's chop that would slice Kurt in two.

Kurt raised the Masamune and blocked the downward strike, but he was left in a defenseless position.

With no chance to stand, Kurt lunged forward and drove his shoulder into Oni's thighs. He wrapped his free arm around the man's legs and with a mighty heave lifted up and arched himself backward, releasing Oni as he fell.

Oni flew helplessly over the wall, landed on the fire escape and clung desperately to the rusted metal steps.

The staircase swayed back and then jerked to a stop as the jerry-rigged wire pulled taut.

Kurt stepped to the wall. Oni stared up at him, a strange expression affixed to his face. The Crimson Blade of Muramasa fell from Oni's hand and dropped down between the rungs. It clanked between the steps, then vanished into the dark.

Ushi-Oni clutched at his midsection. His hands came away, soaked with his own blood. The blade had gouged him when he landed on the stairway. It had cut him deep but not fatally.

Kurt didn't wait for him to recover or pull another weapon. With a downward slash of the Honjo Masamune, he cut the retaining wire in half and then shoved the reeling stairway with his foot.

It peeled away from the building, bending and groaning as it collapsed into the alleyway ten stories below.

55

'My robots will finish you,' Gao muttered. Joe held him down, but that didn't stop him from talking. 'You can hear them coming. Stay here and they'll destroy you. Run and they'll hunt you without mercy.'

Kurt grabbed the identifier that hung around Gao's neck and yanked it free, snapping the lanyard. 'I'd be more concerned with what happens when they find you, Mr Gao.'

'What is that?' Nagano asked.

'A transmitter that tells the robots who to shoot and who to ignore,' Kurt said. 'I saw one of these in Han's factory. Turns out that visit was highly educational.'

Gao squirmed and strained against the hold Joe had put him in. 'That'll only protect one of you.'

'More importantly, it won't protect you,' Kurt said. He turned to Joe. 'Let him up.'

Joe released Gao, who stood and made a desperate grab for the electronic device in Kurt's hand.

Kurt pulled back out of reach and held the point of the sword forward. It kept Gao at bay. 'There's a stairway in the north corner of the building. If you run, you might make it. You might even bypass your own machines and get back to your underground lair. But I wouldn't wait around if I was you. Like you said, they're coming.'

Gao looked at Kurt with hatred, but not for very long.

He took off running, heading for the north corner of the building.

'Nice of you to give him a sporting chance,' Joe said.

'He has no chance,' Kurt replied. 'And we could use a little distraction. Let's get the wing to the front edge of the building. We're going to have to drop in pretty hard to get enough speed.'

Working together, they shoved the wing across the rooftop and set in on the wall at the front of the building. They helped Nagano up onto the wing. He dropped to his knees and wrapped his arms through the nylon straps used to carry the wing.

Kurt and Joe took their positions and raised the chute until it caught the wind and rose up behind them.

The sound of gunfire rang out several floors below. One staccato burst, followed by a shout. Two more bursts echoed and then silence.

'So much for our distraction,' Kurt said. 'Let's get out of here.'

'We have to shimmy this thing forward,' Joe said. 'Like a snowboarder starting his run.'

Kurt hung the identifier on Joe. 'You're the pilot. If the robots see us, it's best you don't get shot.'

With the chute billowing in the breeze, they shifted their weight forward and the wing slid off the edge. They accelerated down and away from the building, dropping and picking up speed like an eagle diving from a cliffside nest.

The wing and parasail generated instant lift while the weight of the three men provided momentum, which translated into forward speed.

They soared down the front side of the island across the open area, where the helicopter had touched down. Flying low and fast, they raced across the boundary of the seawall and out over the waves.

If a single gunshot came their way, none of them heard it.

Flying clear, they turned their speed back into altitude, but like any glider not caught in an updraft, that was eventually a losing proposition. Gaining altitude cost them speed and the next drop took them lower.

'We're sinking fast,' Kurt noted.

'Not much we can do about that,' Joe said.

'Let's hope Akiko sees us.'

Riding with the wind, they were carried across the channel at a rapid clip. But soon they were skimming the waves and pulling back on the chute to gain a few seconds of extra airtime.

'Prepare to ditch,' Joe said.

The wing skimmed one swell and then clipped the next, stopping instantaneously. Kurt, Joe and Nagano were thrown forward into the swells. Kurt went under, tasted the saltwater on his lips and came up in time to see the chute settling into the waves.

Joe popped up from under the chute, clearing the lines and swimming away. Nagano was treading water next to him.

Since the hollow wing floated, the three of them grasped its edges.

'See anything?' Kurt asked.

'No, but I hear something,' Joe said.

A second later, Kurt heard it, too. A motorboat racing their way. It came out of the darkness, detectable only by the white bow wave, until the lights came on at the last second.

Akiko leaned over as she pulled alongside. 'About time you came back,' she said. 'A girl could drown out here, waiting in the rain.'

Kurt helped Nagano into the boat; Joe climbed in behind them. Before they could move, fiberglass began exploding around them as rifle shots from the island came their way.

Dropping flat onto the floor of the boat, Kurt shouted to Akiko, 'Kill the lights! Get us out of here!'

She reached up, gunned the throttle and turned the wheel. The boat spun and leapt forward, but the onslaught continued.

Kurt felt a bullet scrape his arm. He watched the windshield shatter and the marine radio explode as a shell hit it dead center. The transom and the back end of the boat took a dozen hits or more before they finally drove out of range.

Akiko kept the throttle open.

'Everyone okay?' Kurt asked.

Nagano nodded. Joe was bleeding from a flesh wound on his thigh but was otherwise unhurt. Akiko picked fiberglass shards out of her hair.

The boat continued on, putting distance between them, the warbots and the gunmen on the island, but smoke was pouring from the motor housing. They made it a mile or so before flames erupted from beneath the cowling.

'Shut it down,' Joe called out, grabbing a fire extinguisher.

Akiko pulled the throttle back to zero and the boat began coasting. It continued to slow until its momentum was used up.

Joe lifted the engine cowling and doused the flames with a fire extinguisher. One look told him they were stuck. 'That's not fixable.'

'Now what?' Akiko said.

Kurt turned toward the mainland. The sky was beginning to lighten over Nagasaki. Dawn was almost upon them.

'You two stay here,' he said to Akiko and Nagano. 'Wave down any passing ship you see. Joe and I are going to swim for it.'

'It's a full mile to shore,' Akiko said.

'At least,' Kurt said. 'Let's hope the tide is with us.'

56

Shanghai

It was still dark as Paul and Gamay walked across the vacant plaza of the People's Square in central Shanghai.

'This was once a racetrack for horses,' Mel told them. 'But the Communist Party didn't like gambling, so they put an end to that and made it a park.'

'How appropriate,' Paul said, 'considering we're about to bet our freedom on a long shot.'

They continued across the park and approached a government building. It was unofficially known as the Oyster because the lower levels were hidden from view by a graceful curve of concrete and glass, which one had to pass under before approaching the front doors.

There was no hesitation. All the important decisions had been made. All that remained was to see how things played out. They arrived at the door, waiting patiently as Mel used her credentials to placate the guard outside the building.

'Why don't I go in alone?' Paul said. 'If it goes badly, you two still have a chance to escape.'

Gamay shook her head. 'For better or for worse, remember?'

'This is definitely worse.'

'It'll be fine,' she said. 'Besides, prison can't be any worse than sleeping in a van.'

'If only that were true,' Paul said. 'Still, we're overdue for an upswing in fortune, that's for sure.'

They stepped inside and came to a checkpoint that was manned twenty-four hours a day. Several guards came up and began rummaging through their equipment. 'Credentials,' one guard said.

Mel produced her network ID and began to explain, 'These two are part of my new production crew. They're . . .'

The lead guard ignored her, staring intently at Paul and Gamay. After a second of indecision, he shouted something in Chinese and waved his crew forward. The Americans were soon surrounded.

'We're here to see General Zhang,' Paul said. 'We're here to surrender. We have something he needs to see.'

Melanie repeated the phrase in Chinese.

The leader shook his head and picked up a phone. The other guards drew their guns. One of them tried to force Paul to his knees.

'Allow them to enter.'

The voice came from the shadows. All eyes turned in that direction and the frenetic activity ceased.

From the depths of the lobby, a short, stocky figure emerged. He wore a full military uniform in the pea green color of the People's Liberation Army. His chest was bedecked with medals and his hat – his cover – was pulled down tightly, shading his eyes.

The security crew snapped to attention.

'Search them thoroughly and see them to my office,' the new arrival said.

'General,' the lead guard said, 'these two are wanted criminals. They are listed on the sheet as priority one apprehensions: Enemies of the State.'

The General stared laser beams at the security agent. 'I gave you an order.'

'Yes, General.'

Paul and Gamay watched the events unfold with a running translation from Mel. It was easy enough to see they'd found General Zhang.

'I guess Rudi has a friend here after all.'

Searched thoroughly and relieved of all their equipment, they were taken into the building and separated from Mel. Paul and Gamay were led up to a seventh-floor office. They were left inside on their own.

'Now what?' Paul said.

'We wait,' Gamay said. 'Let's hope General Zhang is willing to listen.'

Paul certainly hoped so. He turned and gazed out a large picture window, with its view over the building's shell and out onto the plaza. The gray morning had arrived.

'Those windows don't open,' General Zhang said. 'So if you're thinking of escaping . . .'

He came through the door with the laptop under his arm. Paul turned his way. Gamay stood respectfully.

'We wouldn't have surrendered, if that was the plan,' Paul said. 'Are you General Zhang?'

'I am,' the General replied. 'And the two of you are Paul and Gamay Trout, members of NUMA and American citizens. Some would say you're also spies. Certainly you're both here illegally. And, I must inform you, that is a crime punishable by death.'

Paul doubted there would be any firing squad, but years in a Chinese gulag were not out of the question. 'We're hoping all of that can be avoided,' Paul said. 'We're not here as spies but as messengers. That's why Rudi contacted you. He's trusting you to hear what we have to say.'

'"Trusting me"?' the General said. He laughed lightly, removed his cap and placed it on the desk. 'Only if he's a fool.'

'But you do know him,' Gamay said, standing up, 'don't you?'

'Rudi Gunn sent me a message. He asked me to hear you out. He implored me to listen based on our previous contacts during the *Nighthawk* catastrophe. You two were part of that also, if I'm not mistaken.'

Paul and Gamay both nodded.

The General sat on the edge of his desk. 'I spoke to many people in your government that night. Most of them were arrogant, combative and pigheaded. But Rudi gained my respect. He spoke facts instead of positions. He sought results instead of posturing for leverage. For that reason, I've agreed to hear you out. But I warn you, that's all I've agreed to.'

Understanding the connection between Rudi and Zhang gave Paul more confidence. 'Rudi told you how to defuse the bomb that had been placed aboard the Chinese aircraft. Gamay and I risked our lives to get that information to Rudi in the first place.'

'Admirable,' Zhang said, 'but irrelevant to me. You were trying to save your own cities at the time.'

'There's truth to that as well,' Gamay said.

Zhang waved toward the seats near his desk. 'Down to business,' he said. 'Tell me, what could possibly be worth violating my country's sovereignty and risking your lives over?'

'Better if we show you,' Paul said. He reached for the laptop. 'May I?'

Zhang handed it over and Paul began the presentation. He went through the data methodically, explaining step by step how they'd discovered and measured the accelerating rise in the sea levels; how they'd traced it to the East China Sea and then to the deepwater mining operation. Finally, he explained the science that led them to the fissures cutting through the continental plate and the unfathomable amounts of water held in the layer of ringwoodite down below.

General Zhang watched the presentation calmly, interrupting with an occasional question but otherwise waiting patiently for Paul to finish.

'You make it sound so plausible,' he then said. 'But why would the water still be rising to the surface if the mining operation has been abandoned for a year?'

'We don't know,' Paul admitted. 'But have your geologists look at the data. Have them run any test or experiment they want. They'll come to the same conclusion.'

'And I'm supposed to believe this isn't a desperate ploy to make us reveal the nature of the subsurface operation?'

He spoke with great sarcasm in his voice, but Paul sensed

it was a perfunctory question. While he considered how to respond, Gamay took it upon herself to reply.

'General,' she said politely. 'Do you really think we'd throw our freedom away on a lie? If we're wrong, you'll put us in prison for years until a trade is worked out. We're not spies and we're not pawns. We came here of our own free will, looking for answers. It was only when we were cornered and threatened that we went on the run. You asked what would compel us to risk our lives and violate China's border. The answer is simple: to avert disaster. The same reason Rudi contacted you a year ago when your agents stole the containment unit from the *Nighthawk*.'

Zhang remained quiet. He seemed to be considering everything that was said.

Paul added a few thoughts. 'As a high-ranking member of the Chinese security service, you might already know everything we've told you. In which case, the only decision you have to make is what to do with us. But if this is news, then you're either wondering how it all transpired beneath your nose or if perhaps we're making it up. Assuming that's the case, might I suggest you check on our story? There are plenty of ways to verify what we've told you. The simplest of which is to send an ROV to the canyon and get the truth for yourself. You might also pull a file on Walter Han and see what he's been up to.'

The General narrowed his gaze. 'Walter Han? The industrialist?'

'Yes,' Paul said. 'We have reason to believe the half-buried robot on the video is one of his. And we know for a fact that he's been running around Japan attempting to

421

prevent us and our colleagues from investigating since we arrived there.'

The General looked down and tugged at the crease in his slacks. This news seemed to bother him more than anything else he'd been told. He turned to the windows that didn't open and stared out through them, much as Paul had earlier.

'I'm afraid you've come to the wrong man,' he said finally. 'If Walter Han is involved, then these events are being directed from a position far above mine.'

'And whose position might that be?' Gamay asked.

General Zhang didn't answer.

Paul stepped forward. A reluctant ally was better than a smiling enemy and he sensed that's what they'd found. 'It's your job to protect China, is it not?'

'Of course,' Zhang said.

'Then consider this,' Paul said. 'What we've shown you will become obvious to the rest of the world before too long. The sea level is rising and the pace of that rise is accelerating. The cause is almost certainly the mining operation at the bottom of the East China Sea. That truth is going to come out whether you want it to or not. At this moment, and not for very much longer, you and you alone have the ability to control how that truth is revealed.'

Zhang was listening. 'Go on.'

'There are two possibilities,' Paul said. 'This event can be a massive ecological disaster caused by the Chinese government. Or it can be the result of a rogue industrialist putting the world in danger through his own arrogance and lust for wealth.'

'Blame it on Han,' the General said. 'Find a scapegoat. That's what you're suggesting.'

'*Save face for China,*' Paul corrected. 'If you play the hero by exposing the corruption and singling out Walter Han, you can protect China's reputation. Even if he's backed by your government in some form or another, those links can be erased. Considering the situation, our government will agree to keep it a secret. But you have to act soon. You have to get out in front of this.'

'And Han is thrown to the wolves,' Zhang said.

'Someone has to be. Why not him?'

Zhang folded both arms across his chest, contemplating silently. He did not move for a full minute and then walked back to the desk.

'You two will remain here,' he said. 'I've sent the guards who saw you enter on an early vacation. Don't worry, no harm will come to them. Nor to your friend the reporter. No one else knows of your presence in this building, but, ironically enough, the very people who are hunting you reside several floors above us.'

Without another word, Zhang plucked his hat from the desktop, put it firmly in place and walked out the door.

General Zhang got off the elevator on the ninth floor of the building. He strode down the hall, arriving outside an office at the far end. A second layer of security stood at attention as he approached.

'Is the Lao-shi present?' he asked a two stripe corporal.

'Yes, sir,' the corporal said. 'He's not to be disturbed.'

'I will see him,' Zhang said.

'But sir, he . . .'

'I will see him . . . now.'

The corporal fell silent. Nothing could be worse for a low-ranking enlisted man than to face conflicting orders from higher-ups. In the end, Zhang was a general and Wen was a politician. The uniform made the difference. He snapped a salute, opened the door and stood aside.

Zhang wandered in and discovered Wen sitting on a couch, watching the morning news . . . from Japan.

Wen did not look up. 'I left orders not to be disturbed.'

'So you did,' Zhang said. 'I countermanded them.'

Wen was not a reactionary man – few who held such power were, as they didn't need to be – but his frame tensed at the insubordination.

'Leave me, General,' he said dismissively. 'I did not call for you. And unless your forces have finally proven competent and captured the Americans, I have no desire to speak with you.'

Wen had forced every military and police organization in the government to share in the search for the Americans. Such was his power. It was Zhang's reason for being in Shanghai when he would have preferred to remain in Beijing, but Wen had refused him that luxury.

He stepped forward. The cap was removed once again. 'The Americans have indeed been found,' he said. 'And they tell a most interesting story.'

Only now did Wen give Zhang his full attention. 'Where are they? I will see them at once.'

'That will have to wait.'

Wen stood up and the benign old face looked suddenly

menacing and evil. 'You dare defy me? I thought you were smarter than that.'

Zhang wondered if he was making a mistake. Wen was the second-most-powerful man in the country and the main architect of so much mischief. While the Chinese Premier ran the country and dealt with the day-to-day operations of the Communist Party, Wen remained behind the scenes, manipulating levers most did not even know about. He could make or break anyone, even a man as important as General Zhang.

Then again, China was no place for the timid. It was more like ancient Rome than Western governments. Power was collected and wielded. It was taken, not given. And Zhang now had a chip to play. 'What is Walter Han doing for you in Japan? We know he's a proxy of yours.'

'That question will cost you dearly, General.'

'Nevertheless, I will have an answer.'

The standoff continued. Wen stared, unused to being challenged in any real fashion.

Zhang stood rigid, holding his ground.

Finally, Wen turned away. He walked to a small table and sat down. Another half-finished game of Go was arranged on the table. Wen reached into the pot and pulled out a black stone.

'Hands where I can see them, Lao-shi.'

'Are you arresting me?' Wen asked.

'That depends on what Walter Han is up to in Japan,' Zhang said. 'And on his connection with the mining disaster at the Serpent's Jaw.'

'Ah . . .' Wen said. 'So you know a thing or two.' He

turned his full attention to the game board and refused to honor Zhang with another glance. He pointed a bony finger toward the television screen. 'Watch the news,' he said. 'Soon you will see.'

57

Nagasaki Prefecture

Kurt and Joe emerged from the water on a stony beach. Tossing their fins aside, they raced across the beach like competitors in a triathlon. The similarity ended when they smashed the window of a car, silenced the alarm and hot-wired it in record time.

Speeding down the coastal road, Kurt stated the obvious. 'We need to get to the Friendship Pavilion before the signing ceremony.'

'We could go to the police,' Joe suggested.

'And tell them what?' Kurt asked. 'Robots that look exactly like us are going to shoot the Prime Minister? The truth will get us sedated and put in a hospital for the delusional.'

'At least it would give us an alibi,' Joe suggested. 'We can hardly have assassinated the Prime Minister if we were being medicated in a psych ward at the time.'

'That won't save the Prime Minister or implicate Han,' Kurt said. 'And I intend to do both.'

'How?'

'Catching him in the act. Ripping the masks off those robots in front of the TV cameras.'

'Great idea,' Joe said. 'But if we're one minute late . . .'

'I know,' Kurt said, changing gears and charging through the traffic. 'We'll have played right into his hands one more time.'

A mile down the road, Kurt pulled over in front of a store that had yet to open for the day. He and Joe broke in and rummaged through the clothes on the rack. Grabbing some items, they raced out and drove off.

'We're a regular two-man crime wave,' Joe said. 'We've stolen a boat, a car and clothes all in the last twenty-four hours. If this keeps up, Nagano will be right to claim it's the foreigners doing all the lawbreaking in Japan.'

'Let's hope he gets the chance.'

Kurt drove on until the traffic became impassable. The area near the pavilion was packed with visitors, members of the media and security teams. Every road Kurt turned down was either mired in gridlock or cordoned off.

'Ditch the car,' Joe suggested. 'We'll go on foot.'

Kurt parked and the two of them got out and ran. Soon they were queuing up with the crowd and then passing through a metal detector before entering the pavilion.

'Wonder how the robots managed that?' Joe whispered.

'Probably came in the back door,' Kurt said. 'Betting Nagano's ID came in handy for that.'

'Where do you think we'll find them?'

'Not sure about the others,' Kurt said, 'but my duplicate will be front and center at the signing, so the whole world will have a perfect view of the action. The others will probably be arranged along an escape route. The real question is, how do we stop them? They're a lot stronger than us and basically bulletproof.'

Joe gave him a brief smile. 'I've been wrestling with that question ever since I saw you wrestling with yourself, and losing.'

'And?'

'Remember the pat-down at Kenzo's castle?' Joe said. 'They used a big electromagnet to wipe out the programming from any devices we might have concealed. We can do the same to our robotic twins.'

Kurt grinned, as he always did at Joe's brilliance. 'Can you rig one up?'

'All I need is a large metal nail, an extension cord and an outlet to plug it into.'

The ceremony was a formal one. But like so many things in politics, it was primarily driven by the needs of the press. TV cameras were arranged. Photographers with their tripods and bags of equipment were given floor space up front. Reporters with recording devices stood shoulder to shoulder behind them.

Han watched the throng assemble. It would all be over in a few minutes. He would be on his way back to China and glory. He found his heart racing in anticipation.

Finally, the Japanese Prime Minister and the Chinese Ambassador arrived.

Their handshake lasted a full thirty seconds so everyone could capture the image in just the right way. Flashes went off in a dizzying, almost hypnotic display.

The Ambassador stepped to the podium and offered a short statement. He gave way to the Prime Minister, who spoke at some length. Han stood proudly behind them, along with a few others who'd helped make this moment a reality.

While everyone else watched the politicians, Han squinted against the glare of the lights, looking for the facsimile of Austin. The three robots were on autonomous mode now, with Austin's machine programmed to make its angry declaration and shoot as the last copy of the agreement was being signed.

The Nagano facsimile would be waiting down a back hallway, guarding the way out. While the Zavala facsimile had made only a brief appearance – to assure it was seen by the cameras – and then returned to the getaway vehicle. Which, in a delicious twist, was Nagano's unmarked police car, taken by Ushi-Oni when he abducted Nagano from the Shinto temple in the mountains.

Everything was in place. The plan was perfect.

58

Friendship Pavilion

The Nagano facsimile stood in a vacant hall near the back of the building. It had no true thoughts, as such; its processors had simply determined that this door was the most likely to be blocked by security once the event occurred.

It would remain here until the next phase of the operation began, ensuring access to the outside parking lot. When the Austin facsimile unit appeared, both units would leave the building together. Pacing to be determined by threat activity.

Until then, it would continue to run its human mimicry program and ensure that the door remain unlocked.

Its optical processors detected the approach of two maintenance workers, identifying them by uniform. A secondary routine built into its programming determined they were not a threat, while a third routine caused it to smile and offer a slight bow.

At the same time, a different algorithm designed to scan faces and make a recognition, if possible, failed to operate. This occurred not because the function was off-line but because the men approaching had their caps pulled down far enough to block most of their features.

Still, absent a threat determination, the machine remained in a passive state and the human mimicry program continued as the priority function.

A subroutine of that program limited the amount of time the unit could stand still and stare – two obvious giveaways in robotic performance. After three seconds of watching the subjects' approach, the Nagano facsimile looked away, raised its left arm in a crook and used its right hand to pull the cuff of its sleeve back.

At the same time, it directed its optical sensors toward the watch on its left wrist. It did not record the time – time was kept perfectly within its CPU – nor did it have any understanding of what it was doing. The act was merely part of its program.

Behavior mimicked successfully, its next directive was to fold its arms, exhale and look out the small window in the door.

Damage detected.

Its internal sensors reacted to sharp impact in its lower back. The outer padding had been punctured. Self-protection routine kicked in and the machine spun, reaching for its weapon. But before it completed its turn, all processing ceased.

Kurt removed the sharpened metal rod from the replica's back and held it cautiously in rubber-gloved hands. A bare copper wire was visible wrapped around the length of the rod in tight coils. It led back to the rubber sheathing of a hundred-foot extension cord. That cord led to Joe, who crouched beside the wall socket he'd plugged it into.

Kurt had plunged the metal spike through the artificial flesh and padding of the replica. The hundred-volt current of the Japanese electrical system did the rest, creating a cycling electromagnetic field and a power surge in the robot at the same time. In the blink of an eye, it disrupted the robot's CPU and erased its programming.

The Nagano facsimile didn't cry out in pain or react in any outward way. No sparks flew. No mechanical seizures. It just turned slightly to the right and shut down. Now it stood as still as any mannequin.

Kurt waved a hand in front of its eyes.

Nothing.

Joe came running up, gathering the extension cord in loops as he approached. 'What did I tell you?'

'You're a genius,' Kurt said. 'Are you sure this thing isn't going to wake back up?'

'Not after that shock,' Joe said. 'Even if it did come back online, it won't have any programming files. It won't know what to do. It'll just stand there.'

'One down, two to go,' Kurt said. 'Let's lock this thing in that broom closet where we found these uniforms and get moving.'

Han waited as the Prime Minister finished his lengthy speech. *Finally,* he thought.

The ceremonial pens were handed out. Six copies of the agreement placed on the desk. The first copy was signed and the pens placed aside. New pens appeared for the second copy. And so on.

As the fifth copy was being autographed, the Ambassador

accidentally dropped his pen. It fell off the table and rolled onto the floor. Both men picked it up together.

'Cooperation,' the Prime Minister said.

Everyone laughed. The final copy was placed on the table. Han could barely handle the adrenaline.

He looked out into the crowd once more to reassure himself. The Austin facsimile was creeping closer, pushing confidently through the crowd, toward the front of the photographer's row. It looked ready to draw its weapon and open fire. But something was wrong.

'No,' Han whispered. 'No.'

Pen was put to paper. The facsimile burst forward, throwing a photographer aside. 'Japan will never be an ally of China!'

The machine raised a pistol and was tackled as it opened fire – not by members of the security detail but by the real Kurt Austin. Four shots rang out. The bullets flew low, drilling the platform and little else. The crowd shrieked in unison and began to scatter.

Han could hardly believe his eyes. He stood motionless for a second, stunned. And then he fled.

Kurt tackled the machine and plunged the metal rod into its back, but aside from a moment of stiffness, the machine hadn't been affected. It functioned without restraint and threw Kurt off with a violent jerk of its arm.

Kurt flew several feet and knocked over a group of vacant chairs as the machine stood and opened fire again. The shots hit members of the Prime Minister's security detail, who'd formed up around him and were trying to

434

get him out of the room. Three men went down in rapid succession. A fourth fired back before he, too, was gunned down by the robot.

Kurt looked at the rod in his hands as if it had betrayed him, but the truth was simpler than that. Someone in the fleeing crowd had tripped over the cord and pulled it from the socket.

Kurt grabbed a chair and smashed it over the back of the machine.

The robot was knocked off balance, but it didn't fall. It turned and belted Kurt, knocking him over a camera dolly.

With Kurt knocked aside, the facsimile took one more shot. This time, the Prime Minister was protected by a civilian, who tackled him from the side, taking a bullet in the process.

Kurt knew he couldn't overpower the robot. He grabbed the power cord, whipped it toward him and plugged it into an outlet beside the TV camera.

As the replica moved forward, looking for a kill shot, Kurt rushed the stage and plunged the metal spike into the spine of his mechanical twin.

The facsimile froze in an awkward position and toppled forward. Kurt held the machine down, pulled the spike out and plunged it in once more just to be sure.

By now, police and paramilitary units were rushing into the room. They surrounded Kurt and pulled him off the robot. Turning the machine over, they froze at the odd discovery. Their collective gaze going from the attacker to the Good Samaritan who'd stopped it and back again.

Kurt didn't have time to explain. He used the sharpened spike to cut into the skin on the replica's neck. Peeling it back, he revealed the automated mask of the machine's face.

The hydraulics twitched as spare signals came and went. The glass eyes stared blankly into the distance.

It was the last Kurt saw of the machine. With an abundance of caution, the police dragged him away.

'Leave him,' a voice ordered.

Kurt looked up. To his surprise, he saw Nagano limping into the room. The superintendent looked like death warmed over, but he wore an official police jacket.

'If you didn't look so beaten up, I might think you were a machine,' Kurt said.

'I'd be in a lot less pain if I was,' Nagano said.

Kurt laughed. 'When did you get here?'

'A moment too late, it seems.'

Nagano helped Kurt up and they climbed onto the stage. The Prime Minister was being ushered out of the room while paramedics tended to his security team and the civilian who'd intervened on his behalf.

'Akiko,' Kurt said, crouching beside her. She'd taken a bullet in the back, diving in front of the Prime Minister.

'I told you I'm good in a fight,' she whispered.

'She has a punctured lung,' the paramedic explained. 'She should be okay. But we need to get her to the hospital.'

'Go,' Nagano said.

Kurt squeezed Akiko's hand as she was lifted onto a stretcher and whisked away.

'I'm guessing you didn't swim,' Kurt said.

'We flagged down a fishing boat shortly after dawn,' Nagano explained. 'We got here as soon as we could. But as you can imagine, without ID, and looking like we did, it was hard to explain who we really were. By the time I found someone to listen, the shooting had already begun. So we ran up here. Akiko ran faster than any of us.'

'She's a hero.' Kurt said. 'She pledged to defend Kenzo. Promised to do the same for me and wound up saving the Prime Minister.'

'Sounds like a promotion.'

'My thoughts exactly,' Kurt said.

Nagano smiled. 'I'm afraid we still have Han to deal with. He seems to have gotten away. If he gets back to China, we'll never extradite him.'

'Don't worry,' Kurt said. 'He won't make it that far.'

59

Han ran when the shooting started, just like everyone else. But he ran for other reasons. And he ran in a different direction. He charged through the back of the pavilion and raced down the access stairs. Several policemen passed him, rushing in the opposite direction and not giving him a second glance.

He reached the bottom floor and the door that Nagano's facsimile was supposed to be guarding. The machine was nowhere in sight and Han didn't bother looking for it. He pushed the door open and raced outside.

His limousine was parked in the VIP lot, around the side. He marched toward it and then stopped cold. The police had the limo surrounded. As Han watched, they pulled the door open, dragged his chauffeur out and forced him to lie on the ground.

Han turned and walked the other way. He was caught. Trapped. With no way out. Then it came to him. The Nagano and Zavala robots would be waiting for Austin's facsimile.

Han could override their orders with a voice command. He looked for the getaway car. It was there, waiting near the exit. It even sported a temporary blue police light, blinking on top. A brilliant touch.

He walked calmly now. No need to draw attention to

himself. He opened the door and glanced inside. The Zavala replica was at the wheel just as he was supposed to be, but Nagano's facsimile was nowhere to be found. *Too bad.*

Han climbed in and shut the door. 'Drive us out of the parking lot and directly to the factory.'

If he could get to the helicopter, he would be out of Japanese airspace in less than an hour.

The Zavala robot put the car in gear, drove a few feet and then stopped. 'Will this be cash or credit?'

'What?'

'Transportation program requires the use of currency.'

Han thought he was hearing things. The voice sounded more robotic than anything he would have approved. *What the hell kind of accent had Gao downloaded anyway?* 'Override all programs and drive me to the CNR factory,' he ordered. 'Immediately.'

The answer sounded like an old machine from sixties television. 'Instruction error . . . Does not compute . . . Instruction error . . . Does not compute . . .'

'I'm Walter Han,' he bellowed. 'And I'm giving you a direct command!'

At this, the figure in the front seat turned toward him. It held a pistol and grinned at him with a wicked smile. 'And I'm Joe Zavala,' it said, the voice suddenly normal. 'And you are not the boss of me.'

The childish joke was enough for Han to see the truth. He grabbed for the door, but it swung open before he could touch the handle.

Austin, Nagano and a squad of policemen stood there.

Austin reached in, grabbed him by the lapels and dragged him out. Holding him up against the car, Austin grinned smugly. 'Humans: three,' he said. 'Robots: one. Game over.'

60

Shanghai

At the office in Shanghai, Wen Li and General Zhang watched the incident unfold live. Replays and descriptions ran in an endless loop. Commentators spoke in breathless tones. But nothing compared to the filmed unmasking of Han's mechanical assassin.

General Zhang had seen enough. 'It appears your play for dominance has been cut off.'

On the screen, aerial shots from a helicopter showed hundreds of police and military units swarming the prefecture building, surrounding it in layers three and four deep. Han could never hope to escape it.

'No room for liberty,' Wen said cryptically. 'Side one cannot live.'

'But China will,' Zhang replied. 'This is not the fault of our nation or our system. These are the acts of a madman. He will be sacrificed, of course.'

Wen looked over at Zhang. 'You've found a way to save face.'

'I have,' Zhang said. 'I will need everything you possess on the seafloor mining operation. And on Walter Han.'

'It will be delivered,' Wen said. He turned back to the

screen and chose not to rise from his seat. 'Please leave me now.'

Zhang turned and opened the door. Standing in the doorway, he spoke to the guards. 'The Lao-shi is not to be disturbed. Consider him under house arrest. No one is to see him and he is not to leave the room.'

The soldiers answered in unison and stood at rigid attention. Zhang looked back into the office before closing the door. Wen appeared strangely peaceful and content. The weight of the burden was gone from his shoulders. The long struggle was over.

61

East China Sea
Three Weeks Later

Kurt Austin stood on the deck of the Chinese fleet tender *Giashu* as a hook was lowered from a deck crane and guided toward the last of four NUMA submersibles that had been brought aboard the ship.

NUMA, the Chinese government and the JMSDF (Japanese Maritime Self-Defense Force) were cooperating in the investigation of the anomalies at the bottom of the East China Sea.

A Chinese sailor guided the hook into position and ensured a solid coupling. He gave Kurt a thumbs-up. Kurt returned the gesture.

'Much has changed in just a few weeks,' a voice said from behind him.

Kurt turned to see a man in uniform standing behind him. 'I thought generals spent their time on land.'

'We prefer to,' General Zhang said, 'but I wanted to meet you in person. To see if you're real. You've made quite an impression on us over these last two years. Now, here you are, standing on the deck of a Chinese ship as an invited guest. Something tells me the next time you're aboard one, it will either be without permission or as a prisoner.'

443

The General offered a wry smile. Kurt returned it. 'You're probably right,' he said. 'Then again, like you said, things can change.'

'Unfortunately, the rise in sea levels hasn't slowed.'

'We'll get to the bottom of it,' Kurt said, tongue firmly in cheek. 'The worst of the debris has been cleared away and a new docking collar has been fitted to the surviving part of the station. Ingenious, building most of it into the rock. Our sonar scans indicate the interior environment was not compromised.'

'Walter Han's idea,' Zhang said. 'He should have plenty of time to think up new ideas in prison.'

Kurt figured a deal would be cut sooner or later, but the fact that Han was not clamoring to get back to China suggested he was better off in a Japanese prison.

Another sailor approached, carrying a satellite phone. 'You have a call, Mr Austin.'

Kurt took the phone and extended a hand toward General Zhang. 'Until we meet again . . .'

Zhang shook Kurt's hand firmly. 'May the circumstances be as pleasant as they are today.'

As Zhang walked off, Kurt put the phone to his ear. 'This is Austin.'

'I'm glad I caught you,' Superintendent Nagano said. 'You were missed at the ceremony today.'

'Sorry,' Kurt said. 'I prefer to avoid the limelight. How did it go?'

'Perfectly,' Nagano said. 'Akiko was given the honor of presenting the Honjo Masamune to the Prime Minister and the people of Japan. In return, she was given a medal

444

and officially accepted into the Federal Police training program.'

'Looks like she'll have a family now.'

'We take care of our own,' Nagano said. 'I must tell you, she looked resplendent.'

'I bet she did,' Kurt said. 'Was Joe with her?'

'He's hardly left her side since the surgery,' Nagano said. 'They seem to talk endlessly. But from what I've overheard, it's mostly about cars.'

'Figures.'

A whistle got Kurt's attention. Gamay was waving at him from the hatch of the submersible.

'I have to go,' Kurt said. 'All the best.'

'*Arigato*, my friend,' Superintendent Nagano replied.

Kurt handed the phone back, climbed up the ladder on the side of the submersible and dropped down into the hatch. Paul and Gamay were waiting. 'Next stop, the Serpent's Jaw.'

A ten-minute descent took them to the bottom of the canyon. Three other submersibles waited for them. Their lights illuminating the walls on either side of the chasm.

Kurt eased the submarine into position and connected with the new docking collar. With the seal confirmed, he opened the submarine's hatch and climbed out. Paul came with him, while Gamay switched to the pilot's seat.

'I'll pick you boys up when you're ready,' she said.

Kurt closed the hatch and moved to the inner door of the docking unit.

'Not sure why I have to be here,' Paul said, crouching in the tight quarters.

'I thought you'd want to see this,' Kurt said. 'After all, you got us into this with your "Crow and Pitcher" idea. Seems appropriate that you're here for the final answer.'

They reached the inner door. Two Chinese technicians were already there. Deposited by one of their own submersibles. One of them had thick glasses and hair that hung in his eyes.

Kurt cocked his head. 'Didn't I see you on Hashima Island?'

The man nodded. 'I was in the metallurgy lab.'

Kurt nodded. 'Still haven't found a barbershop, I see. What are you doing here?'

'They released me to help with this investigation,' the technician said. 'I know more about this place than most. I helped design the systems.'

'Many of which are still functioning,' Kurt said. 'You obviously do good work.'

'The power is nuclear. The reactor was untouched. When the avalanche occurred, the watertight doors sealed the interior. That's the only reason.'

Kurt had a feeling there were other reasons. He kept it to himself. 'Ready?'

'Yes.'

Opening a side panel, the engineer accessed a manual release for the inner door. Using a large wrench, he turned a spindle and released the latch.

Kurt and Paul pulled the heavy door open. They discovered a tunnel, bored out of the rock and sheathed in steel. Lights running along the top remained lit.

'We need to see the main section,' Kurt said.

'This way,' the technician said, leading them into the tunnel.

The first passageway led to a second and then to a staging area, where stacks of equipment sat undisturbed.

They crossed the staging area and arrived at a huge freight elevator – two cars could have fit in it side by side. 'Do you hear something?' Paul asked. 'A low hum?'

Kurt nodded. *Clue number two.* He climbed onto the elevator and waved for the others to join him. 'Going down.'

They took the elevator down nearly a thousand feet and arrived at a different section of the mine. On the schematic, it was listed as 'Lower Control Room.' It was only supposed to be four hundred square feet, a twenty-by-twenty space. But it proved to be a vast, open cavern. Dark tunnels could be seen all around them.

'It's like Grand Central Station,' Paul said.

Kurt nodded, looking around. Power cables ran everywhere. Fresh tank tracks marked the ground like a construction site. The humming was louder.

The two engineers crossed the room to a control console. Paul and Kurt wandered in the other direction. The steel walls they'd found earlier had given way to an amber-hued mix of rock and Golden Adamant.

'None of this should be here,' the engineer said. 'This is only supposed to be a drop-off connecting the control room to the deep boreholes. This entire room . . .'

His voice trailed off as a rumbling sound became audible. All of them turned to see a bank of lights approaching from one of the tunnels. A crawling machine lumbered

447

into the cavern and then maneuvered to a spot by the wall. Its front end appeared to be damaged. It parked and then used a robotic arm to grab a power cable from the wall that it plugged into its battery pack.

Clue number three. 'All of this is here, because the machines built it for themselves,' Kurt said.

'What?'

'They're still digging,' Kurt said. 'Following their orders. Using their artificial intelligence program to determine the best way to accomplish their goal.'

As Kurt spoke, the engineer from Hashima Island brought up a schematic of the mine on the console. It displayed hundreds of tunnels and rooms that had been drilled and excavated in the last year. They'd pushed the harmonic resonators deeper into the Earth than anyone believed possible, overcoming problems and setbacks. Using the minerals and alloys they recovered to buttress the mine in many places.

'How did you know all this?' Paul asked.

'I didn't,' Kurt said. 'But Hiram Yaeger and Priya reviewed all the data that Han's people had recorded. They came up with this as the most likely explanation. There was no other way to explain the continued and accelerating fracturing of the transition zone down below. The machines had to be digging. Expanding the operation as fast as they could.'

As Kurt spoke, two other machines appeared. One of them went to work on the damaged hauler and began repairing its front end. The second machine crossed the cavern and entered a different tunnel, off to some new task.

'They've constructed other machines,' the engineer said. 'Four hundred and thirty-two of them.'

'But why?' Paul asked.

'Because they needed them for new tasks,' Kurt said.

The engineer was still reading off the console. '"Continue mining until otherwise directed,"' he said. '"Make all efforts to maximize recovery." According to the database, those were the last commands given before the avalanche.'

'And followed to perfection,' Kurt said.

'They've created their own civilization down here,' Paul said. 'It's incredible.'

'Almost feels wrong to shut them down,' Kurt replied. 'But we have no choice.'

He looked at the engineer, who nodded his agreement. The man powered up the interface. Entered a new code and gave the robots a new authorization.

'Hopefully, they'll do as ordered,' Paul said. 'Otherwise, this could be the beginning of the robot rebellion.'

'Authorization code alpha,' the engineer said.

'Authorization code accepted,' a human-sounding voice replied.

'TL-1,' the engineer said. 'Cease all mining operations. All units return to staging areas.'

A brief silence followed. And Paul exchanged glances with Kurt.

'Directive confirmed,' TL-1 said. 'Shutting down resonators.'

The pervasive humming waned and then ceased altogether. The cavern grew deathly quiet until rumbling

449

noises began emanating from the tunnels. Before long, a seemingly endless line of machines began flowing back into the cavern and parking in perfect order.

'Time for us to go,' Kurt said. 'Our job here is done.'

Over the next two weeks, the water blasting from the field of geysers – which numbered over a thousand – slowed and then ceased. The sea levels stopped rising at the same time, leveling off with a total increase of just over eleven inches.

Eight hundred and fifty tons of Golden Adamant was eventually recovered from the mine and remained the property of the People's Republic of China.

Western nations gained their own source of the alloy after deciphering the notes in Masamune's journal, which led them to a mine in a dormant volcanic region of Japan, where he'd obtained the material for his remarkable sword.

He just wanted a decent book to read ...

Not too much to ask, is it? It was in 1935 when Allen Lane, Managing Director of Bodley Head Publishers, stood on a platform at Exeter railway station looking for something good to read on his journey back to London. His choice was limited to popular magazines and poor-quality paperbacks – the same choice faced every day by the vast majority of readers, few of whom could afford hardbacks. Lane's disappointment and subsequent anger at the range of books generally available led him to found a company – and change the world.

'We believed in the existence in this country of a vast reading public for intelligent books at a low price, and staked everything on it'
Sir Allen Lane, 1902–1970, founder of Penguin Books

The quality paperback had arrived – and not just in bookshops. Lane was adamant that his Penguins should appear in chain stores and tobacconists, and should cost no more than a packet of cigarettes.

Reading habits (and cigarette prices) have changed since 1935, but Penguin still believes in publishing the best books for everybody to enjoy. We still believe that good design costs no more than bad design, and we still believe that quality books published passionately and responsibly make the world a better place.

So wherever you see the little bird – whether it's on a piece of prize-winning literary fiction or a celebrity autobiography, political tour de force or historical masterpiece, a serial-killer thriller, reference book, world classic or a piece of pure escapism – you can bet that it represents the very best that the genre has to offer.

Whatever you like to read – trust Penguin.

read more
www.penguin.co.uk